# OLLIE & ALLI

# OLLIE & ALLI

KEVIN ROBERT ALDRICH

# ALSO BY KEVIN ROBERT ALDRICH

Flames of Freedom

Bare Trap

Spellbound

Racing Hearts

*For Holly, Jayda, and Taegon*

# CONTENTS

**1**

THERE ARE things that matter in life, and there are things that don't.

Here is a short and incomplete list of what mattered to Alli Thomas:

- Creating and visualizing ideas
- Understanding and computing numbers (and formulas, etc.)
- Tools that help visualize ideas and compute numbers
- In order to support the visualization of ideas and computation of numbers:
- Sufficient food to provide your body with fuel
- Sufficient clothing to protect your body from the elements, where applicable
- Sufficient shelter to protect your body from the elements and allow for sleep, where applicable

Here is a short and incomplete list of what didn't matter to Alli Thomas:

- Hair

- Makeup
- Fancy clothes
- A nice house
- A fast car
- Nouveau cuisine
- Cleanliness
- Godliness
- The opinions of other people
- Other people, in general

In Alli's experience, most people confused these two lists. And their lives suffered for it.

Which normally wouldn't have concerned Alli at all. If people suffer because their understanding of the world is incomplete or incorrect, then their suffering is a clue for them to change. They should examine their lives, establish an experiment that changes one element of their life at a time, observe the results, maintain any changes that reduce suffering and revert any that don't.

The fact that most people wouldn't even think to do this, might even scoff at the notion, is the first thing that they should change.

No, the suffering of others wouldn't have concerned Alli at all, except that those people somehow felt it necessary to make Alli's life more difficult. Probably in an attempt to bring her suffering up to their level of suffering.

In other words, to make Alli's life as miserable as theirs clearly were.

As the saying goes, misery loves company.

A miserable person said that.

Like Alli's mother, for example.

Here is a short and incomplete list of Alli's mother's most common words of wisdom:

- Comb your hair.
- Stop dressing like a street person.
- It wouldn't kill you to put on lipstick once in a while.
- How can you eat that junk all the time and still stay so skinny?
- Your apartment looks like a garbage truck crashed and tipped over inside.

Here is a short and incomplete list of the wisdom Alli's mother had not and likely never would convey:

- Your code is clean, spare, and amazingly efficient.
- I appreciate the attention to detail in your computations.
- The way you visualize your many fine ideas is intuitive and clear.
- Your latest model describing the rotation of the earth, in particular, is quite elegant.
- I love the fact that you really have a firm grasp on what's truly important in life, as evidenced by your incisive ideas, your use of cutting-edge technology, and your dedication to spending as little energy as possible on the things that just don't matter in life.

As any reasonable, intelligent creature would do, and as recommended above, Alli took steps to mitigate her own suffering. After much experimentation and observation, she now avoided other people, including her mother—especially her mother—except when it was absolutely necessary to interact with them.

Fortunately, modern technology made this easier. Most required tasks, like food delivery, research, and the like, could be done on the internet with little or no interpersonal interaction. Similarly, the internet made it easy to find like-minded people,

people who possessed a correct understanding of what truly mattered in life, and share ideas and computations with them from anywhere in the world.

Unfortunately, modern society being what it was, biased toward extroverts and social interaction, Alli was unable to completely isolate herself from people who did not share her priorities.

Case in point: employment.

In order to reduce her suffering and escape from her childhood home, her mother's house, Alli had to obtain and maintain employment. The first job she found was as a small business accountant. The work suited her, as it focused on numbers and ideas, albeit within the mundane context of capitalism and profit-seeking.

The owner of the firm, Mort Samuelson, had quickly recognized Alli's numerical talent during the initial job interview. After a brief period of training and attempted indoctrination, during which Alli demonstrated that she knew more about the business in thirty minutes than her trainer had gleaned in over fifteen years as a valued employee, Mort assigned her a host of small businesses and left her to her own devices.

When the business owners complained about Alli, as most of them eventually did, Mort would talk to Alli about her "people skills" and assign her to a new client.

After the first year, during which Alli vastly improved the accounting systems and practices of every grateful client within the first week, then typically received increasingly caustic complaints within the subsequent two weeks, Mort learned how to manage his accounting savant (as he called her).

He sent her to each new client for one week, then replaced her with one of his other accountants. Alli would fix whatever problems the business had and set up an efficient system that was simple to maintain. Then, the other accountants would manage that system and schmooze the client (Mort's words) for the duration of their relationship with Mort's firm. The clients received a simple and accurate accounting system that minimized their tax burden. Mort received a recurring revenue stream to add to his bottom line.

Alli was his fixer, he said. In his words, Alli was his Ali. The greatest of all time.

A reference, Alli later learned on the internet, to the boxer, Cassius Clay, who changed his name to Muhammad Ali as a rejection of the slavery he felt was inherent in his birth name.

Given that fact and her situation, Alli felt that Mort should call her Clay, not Ali.

But, really, Alli didn't care about any of that. She only cared that Mort's paychecks were sufficient to cover rent and utilities at a small studio apartment on the west side of the city, as far as she could be from her mother without losing convenient access to the city's mass transit system.

After five years, though, as the job became routine to Alli and even the most convoluted businesses proved little challenge for her to overhaul, her performance suffered.

At least, that's what Mort told her.

For Alli, she was simply focusing on what mattered most: her ideas.

Climate change. Sub-atomic particular structure and movement. Shifts in the production patterns of agriculture in developed nations and their impact on access to food around the world. Analysis of the shifts in the genre tastes and buying habits of readers in English-speaking countries. Prediction of the future of mankind based on observable trends over the course of its history.

The subject matter was varied. Alli's interests were wide-ranging. But, at their core, all of these disparate subjects shared one thing in common.

They could be observed.

Anything that could be observed could be measured.

Anything that could be measured could be analyzed, and anything that could be analyzed could be expressed as a mathematical equation, a computational algorithm that, once found, had predictive power for the future.

These were the things that absorbed Alli's attention. These were the things that captured her imagination.

And these were the things that distracted her from the job that paid her rent, that kept her heat on in the winter and her lights on at night.

These were the things that she researched, on the internet and in books purchased on the internet, every spare moment of every day.

These were the things that her mind focused on, that became the ideas she worked to visualize, first in her mind, then on paper or on her computer screen, so others could understand her point of view.

These were the things that necessitated the stack of servers in the corner of her apartment, between the battered second-hand futon on her floor and the dusty counter in her unused kitchen. Servers that were running her code, performing complex computations twenty-four hours a day, every day.

These were the things that she was thinking about on a chill, grey Monday in early November when she pushed through the front door of Mort's ground-floor office space in lower downtown, south of Fulton Street.

"Alli," called Mort from the door of his glass-walled office. "Could you come in here please? Right away?"

Alli hadn't even made it as far as her desk, hadn't set down her shoulder bag or removed her parka. She changed course, closed Mort's glass office door behind her, and sat heavily on the faux-leather chair in front of Mort's desk, its world-weary cushions sighing beneath her, her parka bunched around her like an inflated airbag, her shoulder bag riding on top in her lap.

Mort sat folded into his swivel chair, the soft leather seat long ago molded to his parabolic form. His dark-framed glasses were perpetually threatening to slide down his nose to freedom, held back only by the stubbornness of the bulbous, rosaceous tip.

Mort normally swept the few surviving strands of hair from the top across his bald pate, smoothing them down for safekeeping. But today they stood straight up, echoing the apparent disquiet of the mind beneath them, swaying in the breeze from the heating duct above his desk like those fifteen-foot-tall inflatable pencil people Alli saw flailing outside of car dealerships and furniture stores.

"You're killing me here, Alli." Mort's voice was like sandpaper, if the sandpaper had smoked for thirty years, then quit for the healthier habit of gargling razor blades.

"Am I?"

Alli furrowed her brow. It was tough to shift so quickly from a deep consideration of the impact of striking lithium miners in Bolivia on the pace of climate change to the triviality of Mort's imaginary demise. Like deep sea divers who have to rise slowly from the dark depths so as to avoid decompression sickness, Alli always felt slightly queasy when jolted from entertaining her own thoughts to entertaining Mort's.

"How can I let you keep slacking off? Huh? Tell me, what am I supposed to say to all of those people?" Mort gestured through the glass walls at the rows of desks filled with employees casting furtive, sidelong glances at the office, trying to spy on their meeting.

"Why would you say anything at all?" said Alli, confused by the question and only half listening.

"You're three hours late, Alli," said Mort, his shoulders by his ears, his hands held wide, palms up toward the ceiling like he was praying for guidance from a higher power. "It's almost lunch time."

"I'm not hungry," said Alli, still distracted. "I just ate."

Mort stared at her for a long moment. He sighed and flopped backward in his chair, sending it into a slow spin.

"Alli, you're the smartest person I've ever met."

He paused, looking at her.

Alli assumed he was waiting for her to thank him, but she didn't feel the need. He was merely expressing his opinion, first of all, and while it was nice of him to think so highly of Alli, his opinion was irrelevant. He could just as easily have thought her a dolt. Like most people, he could still easily think so if Alli pissed him off or he got a stomach ache from eating a piece of bad seafood at lunch. The opinions of most people were capricious and emotional, with very little basis in fact or reason.

Secondly, the need of most people to rank themselves in relation to one another annoyed Alli. Who was the prettiest, the richest, the funniest, the smartest? People were constantly creating relative measures of importance using criteria that were utterly trivial, at best, and completely subjective, at worst. A relative ranking of intelligence was useless. What mattered was not the intelligence of the thinker but the quality of the idea. How could it be tested? How could it be improved? Anyone, at any time, could have a great idea, or make a good idea better, regardless of some arbitrary measure of their intelligence. Alli would do nothing to encourage this inane tendency toward meaningless comparison. It just increased the general suffering in the world.

And so she just sat quietly and looked back at Mort, knowing what was coming.

He sighed again, then chuckled. "I mean, you passed the CPA exam without even studying."

Mort had the tendency to rehash her performance on this exam whenever he was irritated with her, whenever he called her into his office for a dressing down. Alli could only endure the forced march down Memory Lane. She supposed a listing of her achievements made Mort feel better about ultimately not punishing her for whatever infraction had necessitated the meeting.

First he mentioned her passing the exam. Next he would mention the speed with which she completed it.

Mort shook his head and chuckled again. "And in two hours? It's a sixteen-hour exam. Insane."

Then he would mention the way that the other certification requirements—a certain number of relevant college credits and hours of experience—were waived upon further questioning from the licensing board, which was understandably curious about her performance on the exam.

"And the way you answered the board's questions. Threw it all right back in their faces. Made them look like they didn't know their own business. Like they'd never really thought about it before. Like they were the students and you were the teacher."

Alli had merely explained her ideas about the subject. She had had no thought of making the members of the licensing board look bad or feel bad about themselves. If they felt that way, it was their own doing, not hers.

"They had to certify you. You gave them no choice. They would have looked like fools if they hadn't." Mort grinned at her. "Even bigger fools."

They had granted her the certification, which had earned her a raise at work. It was that raise, and the subsequent annual increases, including one promotion to what Mort called "Senior Accountant", that had funded the modest server farm currently cranking away in her apartment, performing her latest calculations for when the human race would extinct itself.

Estimates ranged from a few years (mostly from religious fanatics, with little real reasoning behind it) to a few hundred thousand years, but Alli expected it would return an estimate in the thousands or tens of thousands of years. Human nature was simply not evolving fast enough to prevent the overconsumption of natural resources, the human-driven climate changes that would limit the habitable—let alone arable—surface area, and the greed-driven wars for control of that surface area that would combine first to curtail the species, then, eventually, to end it.

The promotion had also extended the range of her job assignments, which now required her to occasionally travel outside the city's perimeter. No concern to Alli, except that the city's mass transit system did not extend to these far-flung places. With as small a portion of her raise as she could manage, she was forced to purchase a car.

She bought a 1974 VW Super Beetle for eight hundred dollars from an eighty-seven-year-old man down the street from her apartment. His macular degeneration had gotten bad enough five years earlier to make him stop driving. He didn't admit that fact until two months ago when he ran into a telephone pole when he thought he was pulling into his own driveway.

He'd fixed the damage to the front end, but the chassis was still rusted in spots, the dull grey primer paint unlikely to fully prevent further damage from corrosion over the winter months. But the engine was sound, the brake hydraulics worked and the brake pads were fairly new, the heater was functional, and the tires had plenty of tread.

It now sat in the parking lot behind Alli's building in a space assigned to her apartment. It sat there for as long and as often as Alli could manage. She only brought it out when absolutely necessary to travel to and from a work assignment.

Alli didn't mind driving, but it tended to distract her from whatever idea she was working on at the time. She preferred mass transit, where others could worry about traffic and the random, idiotic movements of other people cutting in front of them or driving too fast or darting across the tracks. She could spend that time working through the delicious investigative tangle of her latest idea.

Like the Bolivian miners. Lithium was a key component in

the batteries of electric cars. Would the Bolivian strike curtail EV battery production enough to reduce supply and raise prices to a prohibitive level, thus extending the demand for cars with internal combustion engines long enough to push climate change onto a species extinction path?

That would have to be one hell of a strike.

Mort cleared his throat. Alli put her thoughts to one side and returned her attention back to him.

"I should fire you," Mort said.

Another common threat. Where such a threat would stoke fear in most people, in Alli it just stoked a feeling of annoyance. She didn't want to waste time looking for another job.

And she didn't want to slow her computations. Loss of this job would require her to cut back her expenses, which would mean shutting down the server farm until she had a new stream of income that would fund the electricity to run it.

But it didn't matter. Mort often threatened, but so far had never followed through.

"And this time, I might," he continued. "But I've got one job for you." He raised one finger in the air, held Alli's gaze, a twinkle in his eye. "One chance for you to redeem yourself."

Alli kept her face as neutral as possible. Mort packaged every new assignment as if it were the greatest mental challenge Alli would ever face. He might have had success as an impresario if his life had taken him down a different path.

Mort's animated expression crumbled.

"It's my wife's brother's kid," he said. "My stupid nephew, Oliver."

Alli waited patiently as Mort's eyes blurred in memory, presumably of Oliver and his sister.

"He's got a deli out in Darby."

Darby was twenty miles west of the city. No mass transit. Alli would have to drive to reach it.

"Jen started looking out for him when his parents died in a

crash a few years back. Says he's got plenty of customers, but his books are a mess. Place is about to go under."

Alli resigned herself to the inconvenience. A fifteen minute drive every day for a week was a lot more convenient than searching for a new job, especially with both winter and a recession approaching.

"His grandmother started that place a thousand years ago. If it goes under, my wife will never forgive me."

Mort leaned forward, one elbow resting among the mess of papers on his desk, and pointed at Alli.

"You fix that business," he said. "You clean up those books and you make that business show a profit." After a moment's thought, he added, "And you do it all before Thanksgiving. I don't wanna listen to Jen bitch and moan during the football game."

He leaned back, his chair squeaking, and stared at Alli. His eyes showed none of the indecision, none of the mental anguish they usually had during these talks. None of the battle between what Mort felt he should do and what he wanted to do.

Alli felt a shiver down her back.

"If you don't," said Mort, his voice quiet and even, his eyes dull, "you're fired."

This time, Alli knew that he meant it.

Three weeks.

Three weeks to turn another small business around.

Alli had done that a million times before, and in far less time. Why should this time be any different?

**2**

OLLIE WOOD PUSHED through the metal back door of his deli into a narrow back alley, letting the door stand open. He hadn't bothered to put on a coat, so he shivered in the early morning November chill in his white t-shirt, slate grey chef's pants, and his apron, turned down to his waist. The automatic lights were still on above him, painting the dumpsters, the trash bags, and the dirty runoff water with a silver edge. The sun was just starting to tint the horizon between the tall buildings. Ollie stamped his feet and blew into his hands while he waited for his meat guy, Terry, to arrive.

"Hey, Olliewood!" called Terry out the window of the Drayger's Meats delivery truck as he threaded through the narrow alley behind Ollie's building. Terry held his hand out the window and Ollie slapped it as he walked toward the back of the truck.

The door slid up from the inside. Terry had parked and walked into the refrigerator unit in the back of the truck through a door in the front cabin. Ollie looked up at Terry towering over him from the bed of the truck.

"How's business, my friend?" said Terry, his breath puffing into a thin cloud in the refrigerated air.

"It is what it is, Terry."

"Must be good. This is your third shipment this week."

"Can't run a deli without fresh beef."

"Well, I'm sure Mr. Drayger thanks you."

"You ever met Mr. Drayger?"

Terry scoffed. "They don't let me into the country club these days. Unless it's through the employee entrance."

He gestured to boxes of cold meat in the refrigerated rear compartment of the delivery truck. "Whatcha need today, boss? Got pastrami, corned beef, beef brisket. Hey, I got some tongue, huh? Some beef tongue? You want some of that?"

Ollie shook his head, smiling slightly. Terry was always trying to upsell him on both the exotic and the traditional foods, but Ollie's deli wasn't that kind of place.

"Whaddya mean? People love tongue." Terry leered. "The ladies love it, anyway."

Ollie kept his head down and didn't react to that comment. Terry had a good heart, but he had a tendency to get a bit graphic with his banter sometimes, and Ollie didn't want to encourage him. Let him save that kind of talk for someone else.

"How about some turkey breast? You got any of that?"

"Oh, good one." Terry leered again.

Ollie had walked right into it that time. Nothing could be done about it now. He just slid his eyes away and kept his face neutral, hoping Terry wouldn't riff off of Ollie's question.

Terry brought up a huge oblong mass of turkey, dropped it down on the metal floor of the truck with a thump, squatted down beside it.

"That's a big one." He slapped his hand on the frozen turkey. "Twenty pounds. Got—" He leaned back, looking over his shoulder, counting. "—six more just like it."

"Okay, great. I'll take two of the breasts—"

Terry chuckled. "Yeah, you will."

"—and a hundred pounds of whole brisket." Ollie craned his

neck to look further past Terry toward the back of the truck. "That salami back there?"

"Of course," said Terry. "You want it, I got it."

"You got any soprasetta?"

"Unless you want soprasetta. Sold outta that yesterday." Terry rummaged around in the back. "We got hard salami, genoa, some mortadella, bit of finocchiona…"

"Salsiccia? Got any salsiccia?"

Terry stood up, held his hands out to the side, a large stick of salami in each. "Do I got salsiccia. What'd I say? You want it, I got it."

"Yeah, okay," grinned Ollie. "I'll take four of the salsiccia."

Terry weighed and measured Ollie's order right there on a desk and scale in the back of the truck, piling the meat on the deck of the truck, level with Ollie's face.

"Okay, boss," said Terry. "You wanna pay this like usual?" He tallied the cost on a calculator and held it out to Ollie.

"Yep," said Ollie, not bothering to look at the amount. His voice strained as he balanced two briskets and a turkey breast in his arms and headed toward the door. "Just take it out of the account and send me the receipt."

"You got it, boss man."

Ollie made two trips for the brisket and the turkey, setting the meat on a metal table just inside the back door. After the second trip, he swiped up a plastic bag he'd left on the table earlier, then headed back out.

Terry squatted down and handed the remainder of the order, the four sticks of salsiccia, into Ollie's arms.

"Anything else I can do for you, boss?"

"No, that's it." Ollie held out the bag to Terry. "A little something for lunch. You can't live on Funyuns."

"I challenge you on that, my friend. I lived through high school on Funyuns."

"Yeah, well," Ollie lightly punched Terry's rounding gut with a grin, "you're not in high school anymore. There's a brisket sandwich in there."

"With the mustard and the onions?"

Ollie held his arms out wide. "You want it, I got it."

"Oh, baby," said Terry, looking inside the bag.

"There's a little something extra in there for little Max, too. But don't tell Sheila. She'll have my ass for giving him sugar."

Terry chuckled. "You know that's true." He leaned down to give Ollie a pound hug from the truck. "Thank you, my friend. I'll see you in a few days."

"Have a good weekend, Terry."

"That's up to the Browns, boss," said Terry, standing. "They win, good weekend. They lose?" He grinned, one hand above him on the handle of the door to the back of the truck. "Still a good weekend. But a bad hangover." He rolled the door down with a metallic rumble and slammed it shut.

As Ollie carried the salamis inside, the truck growled to life and pulled away down the alley.

He loaded one turkey breast and two of the briskets into the walk-in freezer in the hallway, then put the other breast and the salsiccia in the walk-in cooler beside it. He brought the remaining two briskets into the kitchen.

Ollie's deli was small, but efficient. Everything had its place, and everything was kept neat, tidy, and clean. Ollie couldn't think otherwise. His brain just wouldn't function if the world around him wasn't in order.

Freezer, refrigerator, and dry storage in the back on the left as you faced the front of house. Office and dishwashing room to the right.

Three steps down the short hallway and the room opened up to the kitchen. Square, red tile sloping down to drains in the center. Butcher and prep station in the back on the left. Ovens and grills along the wall the right. In the middle of the room, two sets of cooking stations, facing each other across three racks of storage shelves and hanging storage for the pots and pans. Each cooking station had a four-burner gas stove, a salamander, a warming rack, and a prep counter.

Every surface, from floor to ceiling, was squeaky clean. Including the floor. Especially the floor. It was extra work, but Ollie insisted on it. And if you kept it up as you went along, wiping down in the few seconds between orders or during the few minutes when there was a lull in the action, it wasn't too hard.

The center stations formed the room into two narrow aisles, just wide enough for two chefs to stand back-to-back at their stations. Tight. Not ideal, but the best Ollie could do. Real estate leases were expensive, and his deli somehow seemed to gain more customers and lose more money every year.

Past the cooking stations was the front of house, a wide service window beyond which was another counter with a cash register on it. Customers came in the front door, lined up in a four foot by ten foot space in front of the register, placed their order, and waited, working it out with the jumble of other customers to make room for new orders and for waiting orders alike.

Ollie knew all of his regulars by name. If you came in more than once, he was gonna ask your name. It's just what he did. He was giving people food. Giving them life. Like a mother. Ollie liked to know the names of his children.

Ollie dropped the two briskets in the butcher station and immediately set to work prepping the meat. Some delis bought their meat already cooked and seasoned and ready to slice. That's why Terry stocked the pastrami and the corned beef in his truck, why he was always trying to sell Ollie on it. They charged a little more for the meat if they'd done the prep work for you.

But Ollie preferred to prep his meat himself. It took hours to do it that way. Sometimes days. But it made for a healthier and more delicious sandwich in the end. And it made it Ollie's sandwich, not just some ingredients that anyone could have slapped together between two slices of bread. It was personal. An expression of Ollie himself.

And it made his customers happier.

That was the ultimate goal, after all.

Happy customers, happy Ollie.

Ollie's deli served basically five sandwiches: pastrami, corned beef, beef brisket, turkey, and a muffaletta. Everything was locally sourced and made from scratch by Ollie.

Everything, that is, except the bread. He had been wanting to bake his own bread for years, but couldn't afford the renovations needed to install a proper bread oven. He'd need to expand into the space next door and couldn't afford the extra rent, let alone the cost of the build-out.

Today's bread delivery would be along in about half an hour, long enough for Ollie to get the brisket ready. He'd purchased a hundred pounds of beef, but it had come in four freshly-butchered twenty-five pound pieces. With two of them in the freezer for tomorrow, Ollie set to work on the others.

First, he trimmed the excess fat and set it to one side. He had a smoker out back, as far away from the dumpsters as possible without upsetting any of the other businesses on the block. He kept the brisket trimmings to use on the top rack of the smoker, putting them in a hotel pan he'd poked holes into, like a rectangular colander. As the fat rendered in the heat, it would drip slowly through the holes onto the brisket below, keeping the meat perfectly moist while it smoked.

Ollie pulled out two hotel pans and lay the trimmed briskets inside.

Today, felt like a wet/dry day.

One wet marinade, one dry rub.

Ollie pulled out a stainless steel bowl set it on the counter in front of him, resting his hands on either side. He took a deep breath and felt his mind settle down into his body.

Ollie made the rub different every time, depending on how he felt that day. There were a thousand variations on a dry rub recipe for beef brisket, all of them claiming to be the best. All of them claiming to have some secret ingredient.

But there were no real secrets. Just flavors. A whole world full of an endless choice of flavors.

Brown sugar, black pepper, salt. A few cloves of fresh garlic. Some people liked to use dried onion or onion powder, but Ollie preferred it fresh, either chopped or, occasionally, caramelized.

That was the base, more or less, of any brisket rub. Sometimes Ollie would throw in paprika or cumin or coriander or oregano or a blend of several. Sometimes dry mustard or chopped parsley or dried citrus. Sometimes he'd use dark brown sugar, sometimes light brown sugar. Sometimes he'd add cayenne pepper or chilis or even ghost pepper, when he was feeling devilish. Sometimes he'd add cocoa powder to temper the spice.

A whole world full of an endless choice of flavors.

What made a rub unique wasn't the choice of ingredients. It was the heart of the chef, the feelings and emotions as the chef conceived and created the dish. Ollie chose his ingredients like some people chose their clothing. They were an expression of himself, of his thoughts and emotions on that day, in that moment of creation.

And always, always, he kept his customers in his mind while he cooked. That was his ultimate goal: to make his customers happy.

When he sold a brisket sandwich, tucked neatly in foil sandwich wrap in a brown paper bag, and he watched his customers pull it out of the bag and rip the foil wrap open before they'd even taken two steps from the cash register, then saw their eyes close, their shoulders relax and their head roll back, heard soft moans come from them as they chewed, oblivious to the dozens of other people around them, listening and watching, the customer lost in a world of flavor, flavor that Ollie had created, that was the ultimate high. That was heaven for Ollie.

Today, he added paprika, coriander, and oregano to the bowl. Dark brown sugar for the bittersweet molasses taste. Cayenne pepper for some heat. He minced eight cloves of garlic, diced six onions. Salt and pepper. Mixed it all in the bowl, coated one of the briskets with olive oil, then smothered it with the rub, working it in like he was massaging a woman's back after she'd had a long day at work. Slowly, tenderly, carefully, consciously. Working the rub into the muscle with his fingers, working it in deep and slow, covering every inch of the brisket, top and bottom.

Once done, he covered the hotel pan with two layers of plastic wrap, set it to one side, and turned to the other brisket.

A wet marinade can use just about anything for flavoring. Many of them use the same ingredients as a good dry rub: garlic, onion, paprika, oregano, cumin, coriander, salt, pepper, and so on. To those ingredients they may add brown mustard, horse-radish, or peppers for some bite. Worcestershire sauce. Maybe soy sauce or honey or ginger, if you wanted an Asian twist. Citrus for some brightness. Even ketchup or tomato paste. The possibilities were endless.

But every wet marinade needs some kind of acid. Acid breaks down the tough muscle fibers and carries the other flavors deep into the meat. Wine, beer, liquor, vinegar, citrus juice, Coca-Cola, Dr. Pepper. They were all acidic. They all did the job, and Ollie had tried all of them at least once.

Today he reached for a bottle of artisanal gin he'd purchased from a local distillery. Owned by Darren and Fatima Wilson, a beautiful young couple who had moved there from Silicon Valley five years ago to try their hand at doing something they loved:

making small-batch spirits. And they were good at it. Ollie wasn't a big drinker, but he used alcohol in his marinades all the time, so he had developed a sipping palate for it. Darren and Fatima's copper-pot rye whiskey was amazing, but their small-batch gin was incredible. They used cardamom and citrus with the juniper, and the result was earthy and floral and complex on the tongue.

Ollie pulled a bottle from dry storage and poured it into an 8-quart square plastic Cambro container. Next, he cut a dozen limes and squeezed the juice in with the gin, swirling it around to mix it up.

A twist on a gin and tonic. Pun intended.

He added cardamom and clove and cumin to complement the cardamom in the gin.

With those spices, the marinade was taking on an Indian vibe, like a cup of chai tea. Ollie added ginger, cinnamon, and dark brown sugar, leaning into that inspiration, letting his heart and his creativity lead the way.

He finished with olive oil, salt, and pepper, mixed it well, then poured it over the brisket in the deep hotel pan, letting the marinade rise up and cover the brisket completely. He covered the pan with two sheets of plastic wrap and brought both pans into the walk-in refrigerator to chill overnight.

"Morning, Ollie," called a woman's voice from the front of house.

He heard Sarah, Ollie's sous chef, lock the front door behind her.

"Sandwich on the counter, Sar," called Ollie from the walk-in. "Scramble with fontina and bleu cheese today."

"Damn, Ollie," she said. "You're making me feel bad."

"You bring the coffee?"

"Yeah, of course."

"Then don't feel bad." Ollie came back out of the walk-in carrying two hotel pans with dry rub briskets inside that he'd prepped the day before. "A breakfast sandwich is nice to have. Coffee is a necessity."

Sarah unwrapped the sandwich that Ollie had set on the counter. Steam rose up from the thick slices of toast.

"Texas toast and bacon, too?" Sarah clucked her tongue. "Making me feel bad and making me fat." She took a bite, closed her eyes, savored the flavors on her tongue. She moaned and shook her head. "Damn, chef."

Ollie swung the walk-in door shut with his heel and smiled as he set the pans on the counter of the prep station.

"Paprika," said Sarah. "And..." She worked her mouth slowly. "Garam masala?"

"Garam masala," nodded Ollie, grinning. "Nice one."

Every day, when Ollie made Sarah's breakfast, he would hide some unusual flavoring or ingredient in the dish. Sarah would then try to identify it. It was a little game they played, one that pushed Ollie's creativity and trained Sarah's palate.

"You come up with some crazy shit sometimes, chef." She took another bite. "Crazy good." She nodded her head toward the counter. "Coffee's over there."

Ollie pulled off the plastic lid and took a deep pull from the coffee, feeling the too-hot liquid burn in the best way as it slid down his throat. Ollie used to drink coffee all day, every day, drinking it by the bucket. Then he got a little older and realized he was killing his adrenals, overstimulating his system, and generally riding a caffeine roller-coaster twenty-four-seven. He didn't sleep well at night, was tired every morning, and drank more coffee to counter the fatigue. Then he'd crash, drink more coffee, and so on.

Now, he allowed himself only one cup of coffee per day. Twenty ounces each morning. The wild roller-coaster was mostly gone, but he still woke up thinking about coffee, looking forward to it every morning.

Ollie had asked Sarah if she would bring coffee in each day

so that he would never develop a routine of going to the coffee shop. He knew that if it became second nature to him, there was too much risk of him caving and just going there all the time.

Plus, Sarah had incredible taste in coffee and always brought in the best. Ollie had no idea where she got it from, but he drank it greedily every morning. He allowed himself one big mouthful on the first gulp, then used every ounce of his willpower to force himself to sip slowly throughout the rest of the morning.

It was working, albeit slowly and painfully. His caffeine cravings were still strong, but the headaches were less frequent and less severe. It had only been a month since this new regime began. There were still days when his head felt like it was full of giant steel coffee beans banging against the inside of his skull. But, in general, things were getting better.

In exchange for her coffee deliveries, Ollie made Sarah breakfast every morning. She'd told him it wasn't necessary, but Ollie did it anyway. Sarah was five years younger than Ollie, and she felt like his little sister.

A culinary sister.

She was a brilliant chef. Could work in any of the finest restaurants in the world. Ollie had no doubt about that.

But, for whatever reason, for the last eighteen months she had chosen to work in his little backwater deli. Ollie wanted to make sure it was worth her while. There wasn't much money in it, so he did what he could to continue her culinary education, exposing her to new ways of thinking about food and flavor and service. Things he'd learned in his travels over the years.

And Sarah kept Ollie moving forward, too. Kept him on his game. Kept his imagination stimulated, kept his creativity from stagnating.

"Who's the chick in the beater out front?" said Sarah around a mouthful of scrambled egg and Texas toast.

"What chick?" Ollie winced. He didn't like using terms like that to refer to women. It was demeaning and dehumanizing.

He'd grown up around guys who used terms like that all the time, who probably didn't even know there was another way to refer to a woman. Guys like Terry. Good people, but misogynistic and prejudiced in as innocent a way as someone can be while still being a prejudiced misogynist.

When he left home to go to culinary school, Ollie had gotten perspective on that issue right away from a classmate with a big mouth and an even bigger personality. She'd called him on his shit every time she saw it. Didn't take Ollie long to see where he was going wrong.

In that moment, he had made a conscious decision not to be that way anymore. Women already got enough of that shit just from society in general, doing what it did these days with advertising and pay inequality and gender norms and stuff like that. Ollie didn't want to make it any worse than it already was.

But, Sarah had said it, and the word had just slipped into Ollie's ears and out of his mouth.

"She's just sitting in her car across the street," said Sarah, taking another bite of her sandwich.

They both bent down to peer through the service window and out the plate glass shopfront. Through the lettering that read DOOW EILLO ILED in large, blue block lettering, Ollie saw an old VW bug that had seen much better days. It was painted in grey primer, decorated with rust spots. The front end looked like it had been bashed in and hastily repaired. The windows were half-fogged against the chill morning air, but Ollie could see the silhouette of someone sitting in the front seat, someone with long hair.

"She a customer?" asked Sarah.

Ollie shook his head.

He knew all of his customers by sight. It was a freakish gift he had. If you asked him to pick from a lineup the checkout clerk at the grocery store he'd visited every week for the last three years, he would have no clue. But he could recognize the face of every single person he'd ever handed one of his sandwiches in the nine years since he took over his parents' deli. He wouldn't necessarily know their name, but he could recognize their face.

Even though he couldn't see this person's face, something about her told Ollie she was unfamiliar. Maybe it was the shape of her head or the car she drove, which he would have noticed before. Something told him this person was new.

"Never seen her before," he said.

"Well, if she's a newbie, she's hella early. Lunch service doesn't start for four more hours."

Ollie went back to the prep area and sliced the briskets for today's service.

He finished slicing the first brisket, set the slices back in the pan, and glanced out the window.

The car was still there.

He finished slicing the second brisket, set the slices back into the pan, and carried them both toward the walk-in.

The car was still there.

He set the pans on a shelf just inside the door of the refrigerator. He'd bring them out an hour or two before lunch service so the meat could slowly warm to room temperature. That brought out the flavor more.

He grabbed a turkey breast that he'd pulled from the smoker the previous day, carried it to the prep station.

The car was still there.

He sliced the turkey, brought it back to the cooler.

Car still there.

He lingered in the chill of the walk-in, letting the door shut behind him. He was obsessing about the car, about the woman. And Ollie knew himself. He didn't like to admit it out loud, but he knew he had an obsessive personality. He knew he'd keep checking out the window every five seconds, checking to see if the car was still there.

If he was in the walk-in, where there were no windows, maybe he could distract himself long enough for the obsessive thought to flit away on the wind like every other thought.

Ollie straightened the shelves, organizing the lettuce and the tomatoes, the dressings and sauces. He shuffled the tubs of pickles, organizing them by size and flavor, dills in front, bread-and-butter in back. He checked on the corned beef and pastrami supplies. Still plenty left from yesterday. Good to go on those.

Those were more traditional deli meats, and Ollie had plenty of customers who preferred them. Usually older folks from the neighborhood, customers who had known Ollie's parents, had grown up in the area, married and had children and grown old in the five square blocks that Ollie had called home for eighteen years.

The same area he now called home again.

But the area was turning over. Gentrification. First the artists had come. They'd joined the crowd in front of the register in their paint-splattered jeans or their colorful second-hand outfits and hats. The sculptors had stone dust still in their rough fingers. The fingernail beds of the painters were rimmed in Cadmium Red or Cerulean Blue.

Then came the artisans. Small-batch coffee or cheese or liquor, like the Wilsons' distillery. They came to the deli, too, tall and lean, dressed in plaid shirts tucked into spotless jeans with cuffs rolled up over equally-spotless sneakers made of eucalyptus fibers or something equally eco-friendly and overpriced. They had thick, carefully coiffed hair, colorful three-quarter-sleeve tattoos, and tortoise-shell glasses. Though they tried to look like they didn't, like they were just regular, hyper-educated folks like you and me, they had money. Lots of money.

From there, the hipsters followed. Dressed like the artisanal entrepreneurs, but without the imagination, without the drive, without the spark of idealism. The hipsters rode the artisanal vibe like they rode an Uber, not for what they could contribute, but for what they could get out of it. A certain feeling of panache, of being on the forefront of something. Or maybe they felt like they had sophistication and good taste because they were the first of their hipster friends to discover the delights of paying fifteen dollars for an eight-ounce cup of orange juice made from artisanal oranges hand-squeezed on an artisanal juice press and grown in the artisanal backyard of the artisan who owned the artisanal juice shop.

Still, the neighborhood was waking up again. Customers were coming in, word was spreading. For all their many mockable qualities, hipsters were mostly decent people, even if they tended to think they were the center of the universe. And for all their faults, they were good at bragging. When they found something good, like Ollie Wood's Deli, they told the whole world what they'd found. Facebook, Twitter, Snapchat, Insta, TikTok. Whatever the social media service du jour, they wanted to be the first to bring the news to the world. Modern-day Magellans.

And that was good for Ollie.

Satisfied with the organization of the walk-in cooler, Ollie pushed the long metal stalk to open the door from the inside.

And immediately ducked his head to look out the front window.

Damn.

The car was still there.

**3**

ALLI SAT in the front seat of her car, the heater warming the tiny space to a comfortable temperature, fogging the windows against the cold air outside.

Science at work.

It was still early, not even nine o'clock yet, so Alli was killing time until she felt it was a reasonable hour to knock on the door and get to work.

Okay, that was a lie. She didn't want to get to work because she was too engrossed in the book she was reading, Michio Kaku's newest, an exploration of ten-dimensional space.

Most popular science was watered-down bullshit, simplified to the point of banality to make it understandable to the general public, hyped to the heavens to make a tagline that would capture the attention of the Star Wars generation.

But Kaku's work was different. He had a knack for presenting complex subjects in a way that appealed to the masses and the masters at the same time. And this particular topic, ten-dimensional space—or hyperspace, as Kaku called it in a rare lapse of judgement—had the potential to revolutionize physics and, therefore, the world. Kaku claimed it was the Theory of Everything that Einstein could never quite find, and from what Alli had read so far, he just might be right.

She stuffed a bacon, egg, and cheese biscuit from the McDonald's down the street into her mouth, the wrapper crinkling in her hand as she bit down. The biscuit was dry and soft. The bacon was oily and flaccid. The egg was spongy and square in exactly the way that real eggs aren't.

Alli noticed this like one would notice a dilapidated house passing by outside the window of a moving train. Silent, distant, momentary. She didn't even taste the sandwich. Didn't care to. It was just food, just nutrients to fuel her body.

Most people didn't think too hard about the gas they put in their car. Most modern gas was adequate for combustion, and so they bought the cheapest gas they could find.

That's how Alli felt about food. Find the cheapest fuel that was adequate for cellular respiration.

McDonald's fit that description just fine.

Alli nearly choked on her cheap fuel when she heard a sharp rap on the window right beside her ear. She froze, time stopped, bacon, egg, and cheese biscuit in her open mouth, eyes staring at her book, not breathing.

Had she imagined the sound? Was she still asleep, dreaming about the day ahead? Was she caught in a hyperspace loop, stuck in time?

She heard the sharp rap once more.

Time resumed its normal pace. Alli resumed chewing her biscuit, set her bookmark in place and closed her book, then rolled down the window two inches. Cold air immediately rushed in, diluting the heat inside.

A man stood beside her car. He was in a t-shirt, visibly shivering, hands stuffed deep in his pockets, arms held close by his side. Why he hadn't thought to wear warmer clothes on such an obviously chill morning, Alli didn't know.

She never knew why people did what they did. She suspected they didn't, either. Their actions so rarely made sense.

"Yes?" she said through the opening.

The man bent at the waist, peered in through the crack in the window. His eyes were clear and brown, with flecks of orange.

Interesting eye color. Was that a recessive trait or a genetic co-dominance?

"Can I help you?" said the man.

"No, thank you," said Alli. She rolled the window up again and opened her book once more, relieved that the disruption was so short-lived. Just another good Samaritan nosing in where he wasn't needed.

She slid back into Kaku's mind like slipping back into a warm bath.

Alli jumped at another rap on the window. She rolled it back down, only an inch-and-a-half this time. The man needed to be penalized for wasting her time.

"Yes?"

"Sorry, it's just you're sitting out here in front of my deli," said the man, his face showing what Alli assumed he thought was a disarming smile.

She had to admit, there was something vaguely calming about it.

"We don't open for another four hours," he said. "If you come back at—" He checked his watch. Why, Alli didn't know, since he'd already told her they opened in four hours. With that much information, he should know what time it was without looking at his watch. "—11:30, there shouldn't be much of a line yet."

Again, did he need to consult his watch to know that information? It seems like that information would be independent of the current time.

"Thank you," said Alli. "I'm not hungry."

She started to roll up the window again, but the man—who, if he had meant "my deli" literally, instead of the odd sense of ownership some employees felt for their place of work, must have been Alli's new client, Oliver Wood—set his hand on it. Alli considered rolling the window up anyway, squeezing Mr. Wood's fingers in the window as punishment for both his interruption and his presumption, but decided against it for now.

"Sorry," he said, "sorry." He took his fingers from the window and held up both hands apologetically. "It's just odd that you've been parked here for so long, so early in the morning."

Alli wiped the fog off the windows on the inside of the windshield and the right side of the car, peering at the street signs.

"I don't see any parking restrictions noted for this area," she said. "Am I parked illegally?"

"No..." he said uncomfortably, "no, you're not. It's just—"

"Then why are we having this conversation?"

"I just... You're out here..." He was shrugging his shoulders and moving his hands back and forth on a flat plane in some gesture that had no real meaning that Alli could discern. "You're making me..."

Alli waited patiently for him to organize his thoughts. She had not always been so patient, but had been forced to develop the ability over the last few years, waiting endlessly for her clients to wrap their scattered minds around the simple elegance of whatever system Alli had created for their accounting.

"I just wanted to make sure you were okay," he said at last.

Finally, Alli understood. Mr. Wood had a savior complex. Common for men of a certain age and upbringing.

"Thank you for your concern, Mr. Wood," said Alli, "but I'm perfectly fine."

She started to roll up the window again.

"How did you know my name?" he asked, shaking his head with a perplexed smile.

Alli released a deep breath. Her patience was wearing thin.

"You said this was your deli," Alli said. She pointed toward the deli through the opening in the window. "Your name is on the window."

The man looked behind him at his own shopfront, as if to confirm that what Alli said was really true. As if he wouldn't know that without looking.

People were so stupid.

But it gave Alli the opportunity to roll the window up all the way.

"Right, right." She heard the man's muffled voice on the other side of the foggy glass. "Oh. Well... okay." His voice trailed off into a mumble. "Have a... good day, then."

Thankfully, mercifully, he walked away, leaving Alli alone again with Mr. Kaku.

When Alli looked up again, the windows of her car were clear. The sun was bright. The car was uncomfortably warm and stuffy. Cars were parked along the curb in front of and behind her.

Alli checked her watch.

It was 11am.

She had finished Mr. Kaku's book. As always, he had given her a great deal to consider.

She would be grateful for the distraction while she plodded through her assigned work for the day.

Alli set the book carefully into her shoulder bag beside her laptop and got out of the car. The front door of the deli was locked. Alli rapped sharply on the glass, waited until a young woman came to the window, turned the lock, and cracked the door open.

The irony of the juxtaposition was not lost on Alli. She was now the intruder, the young woman no doubt desperate to return to whatever work Alli had interrupted.

"We don't open for another hour," said the woman, "but you're welcome to line up along here." She gestured along the length of the shopfront window. "You'll be first in line."

That much was obvious. There was no one else on the sidewalk.

"I'm not here for food," said Alli. "I'm here to fix your accounting systems."

"I didn't know we had any," said the woman drily.

"Then I'm here to build one for you."

The woman leaned back over one shoulder, pulling the door closed as she did.

"Ollie," she called. "Someone here for you."

Mr. Wood came out from the back of the deli, wiping his hands on a towel, his apron pulled up around his neck, stained with yellow and brown splotches.

"Oh," he said as he approached the door, "hello again."

He unlocked the door and held it open, but did not turn to allow Alli to pass.

"Hello, Mr. Wood," said Alli, holding out her hand with her business card in it.

Mr. Wood didn't look down, just kept those orange-flecked eyes on hers as he reached for her hand. Because of this, he misunderstood her intention and attempted to shake her hand instead of taking her business card. As a result, he shook her fist and crumpled her card.

"Oh, shit," he said, taking the crumpled card from her hand. "Sorry about that."

He attempted to smooth out the card by pulling it tight between his fingers, then by smoothing it against his palm.

Alli didn't bother to tell him those tactics wouldn't work. And she didn't bother to give him a new card. It was his own carelessness that crushed the card. He could live with the consequences.

"Alli... " He held the card between his fingers and frowned at it. "Alli Thomas? Is that, like, Israeli?"

How humans had managed to survive as long as they had was one dilemma that science would never resolve.

Alli plucked the card from his grasp and pulled it taut.

"Alli Thomas," he said, his voice rising and falling like a roller coaster on her last name. "That makes more sense." He grinned.

Again, Alli felt oddly calmed by his smile.

"I'm from Samuelson Accounting," she said.

Mr. Wood nodded at her, his broad smile now just a pleasant curve of his lips.

When Mr. Wood did not respond, Alli added, "I'm here to fix your accounting systems. Or," she gestured vaguely toward the back of the deli where the other woman had gone, "to build them, as the case may be."

Mr. Wood's pleasant smile flipped into a pleasant frown, his brow as creased and crumpled as Alli's business card.

He shook his head slowly. "I'm sorry, I don't think I called anyone about an accountant."

"I'm not privy to the details of your business arrangement with my employer," said Alli, practicing her patience. She did her best impression of Mr. Wood's calming smile.

Judging by the look of mild alarm that appeared in those curious eyes of his, her impression was not a good one.

"I'm sorry, I think you must have the wrong place," said Mr. Wood, handing Alli's damaged business card back to her and closing the door.

Alli stepped forward, blocking the door with her body, preventing it from closing fully. She had no desire to waste money, gas, or time driving back and forth to the main office to clear this issue up. She knew she was in the right place. She knew it was Mr. Wood who was confused.

"I assure you, I do not have the wrong place, Mr. Wood," she said, taking out her cell phone and dialing Mort's number, her shoulders wedged between the door and the jamb to keep the door from closing. "I'm sure my employer can help clear this up for you." She handed the phone to Mr. Wood as she heard Mort's voice answer.

On the phone, Mort had a voice like a cannon being amplified through a stadium PA. Alli had no idea how Mort's slouched and flabby body generated so much resonance, but if she had put him on speaker, the front window of the deli would likely have shattered at his first utterance.

"Hello?" said Mr. Wood tentatively. He held the phone a few inches away from his ear as his confused frown deepened. "Uncle Mort?"

He held the door open for Alli. She waited just inside by the front window while he wandered away with her phone. She could hear Mort yammering through the handset, heard Mr. Wood spluttering objections.

The waiting area was rectangular and small and completely empty. There was nothing between the window and the register. No tables or chairs. No counters along the walls. Nowhere for a patron to sit or even stand while they ate their food.

The floor was a clean, if clearly ancient linoleum, with a checkerboard pattern of two-inch squares alternating black and white at an angle to the front counter. The counter itself was white laminate, chipped and cracked in many places, but, again, reasonably clean and tidy. It ran the full width of the room, but was empty except for a cash register at one end and a cluster of condiments and napkins at the other.

Mr. Wood handed Alli's phone back to her.

His calming smile was gone. His orange-flecked eyes were dark.

"We're opening soon," he said. "Unless you want to help with the service, you can wait in the office."

"Fine," said Alli. "I can get started on my work."

Mr. Wood grunted. He led her through a hinged drawbridge-style flap in the counter between the register and the wall. The cash register was ancient, at least thirty years old, if not older. Like everything else in the room, it was battered and visibly worn, but clean. Scratches made its tiny blue-on-blue LCD display nearly unreadable, and several of the physical buttons were broken or missing entirely, though it seemed that the most important ones were still intact. Alli could tell at a glance that it wasn't network-capable, without even an Ethernet connection, let alone secure Wi-Fi capability. But she wasn't sure it even had an SD card slot or a data port of any kind at all. If that were true, it meant there was no way to get the data from the register onto a computer for storage or analysis.

On the other side of the front counter, they walked through a doorway into the kitchen and down a narrow aisle, edging past the woman who had opened the door earlier. Another person, a man who looked like the kind of pole used to clean light fixtures in high ceilings, was working in a second aisle on the opposite side of the gas burners in the center.

Finally, Mr. Wood led them through a doorway in the back, down a short hallway into the office.

Or what may once have been an office.

Alli was not at all sure it could ever regain such an exalted status.

The room was a tiny, windowless box no more than eight feet long by eight feet wide, with ceilings low enough for Alli to touch without reaching. And Alli was of average height, not a tall person. The ceilings could not have been more than seven feet high.

Boxes were stacked into precarious towers that covered the entire face of the wall to Alli's right. On her left was a plastic chair and a folding table that had been pushed against the wall as a makeshift desk. Underneath were more boxes, with barely enough room for someone's knees to fit between them.

The top of the desk was an improvement only because there was only one box there, its top open. Unfortunately, instead of piles of boxes, there were piles of papers scattered seemingly at random across the desk. Alli could see that they were invoices and business letters and other Paperwork of Some Importance. Many of them were still in their envelopes, unopened. The box, too, was half-filled with such paperwork.

Alli groaned internally. She, no doubt, would be the one to sift through the mess, trying to make sense of all of those papers.

Above the desk was a corkboard covered with even more papers, some of them yellowed and torn, along with an endless array of small handwritten notes with such memorable urgings as "Order more lettuce" or "Turn down thermostat when closing" or, Alli's instant favorite, "Lock the front door".

Honestly, if a note pinned to a corkboard in an uninhabitable back room was meant to remind someone to do something as simple and obvious as lock the front door, there were far bigger problems at work than an accounting system could remedy.

With a sinking feeling, Alli noticed the one thing that was conspicuous for its absence: a computer.

She wasn't expecting a rack of servers, blinking away in an air-conditioned room in the back of the shop. She wasn't expecting a 27-inch iMac or a high-end PC tower. She wasn't expecting a MacBook Air, or a modern PC laptop, or even a Chromebook like they gave to school children for free these days.

No, Alli was expecting an old relic of a PC, running Windows 2000 or even Windows NT. Some dusty, beat-up enclosure with a corded click mouse that was hidden under reams of paper.

At this point, a setup like that would have thrilled her to no end.

This deli had nothing.

It was completely manual.

"You don't have a computer," Alli said flatly.

"We're a deli."

"A deli without a computer."

"People don't eat computers."

"People do everything else on computers."

Mr. Wood stared at her, all hint of friendliness gone from his face.

"Not here, we don't."

Alli held his gaze, trying hard to control the irritation surging through her body. She normally wouldn't get this upset—would get upset at all—about a client's situation. Setting up a new accounting system was a trivial task for her, even in the most dire of cases. In a matter of minutes, Alli could assess a business's ailing accounting system and envision the remedy in her mind, seeing clearly the steps she would need to implement to build a robust and sustainable replacement.

But only if she could access their records.

On a computer.

And this place, this man, with his sudden flip from warm, calming smile to cold gaze, was starting to grate on her nerves.

She held her tongue in check, took a mental deep breath.

Practice patience.

"Are these..." Alli gestured to all the boxes.

"Records," nodded Mr. Wood. "Going back..." He shrugged. "...a while. To when my parents were running the place."

"When was that?"

Mr. Wood shoved his hands into his pockets. "I took over nine years ago."

Alli nodded. "And what is your system?"

"Excuse me?"

Alli turned her head sharply toward Mr. Wood, her patience slipping. Was he hard of hearing?

"Your system."

He seemed confused.

Not hard of hearing, then. Just hard of thinking.

"Your system for keeping track of your records. What is it?"

He pointed to the open box on the desk. "I put this year's records in the box."

Alli's heart fell. She knew what was coming.

"On January 1," Mr. Wood continued, "I start a new box."

There it was.

"That's your system?"

Mr. Wood nodded.

"So you don't have a system." She stared hard at him.

All Alli's patience was gone.

Any desire to practice patience, gone.

"No computer," she said through gritted teeth. "No system."

Mr. Wood shrugged. "I didn't ask you to be here." He walked away. "If you need anything," he called over his shoulder, "I'm busy."

Alli stared daggers at his back, then looked around the room at the piles of boxes filled with papers. Papers she would have to sift through.

One by one.

And enter—manually—into a computer.

One.

By.

One.

She clenched her fists.

This job was going to be the end of her.

**4**

OLLIE COULD BARELY CONTAIN his fury as he stomped away from the office, leaving the accountant standing there in disbelief.

Good. Fuck her. And fuck Uncle Mort and Aunt Jenny for sticking their noses into his business. He didn't need their help. This was *his* business, *his* family's business. Not theirs. And he had run it just fine for almost a decade.

He didn't ask for their help and he didn't want it.

Sarah caught his eye and arched one eyebrow at him as he walked back to his station.

"Don't say it," he growled.

"Don't need to."

And that was enough.

That was all the reality check Ollie needed.

His business was in trouble. Real trouble.

He was in trouble.

He knew it, in the back of his mind. But he hadn't wanted to think about it, hoping that if he just kept going, just kept working and making great food, everything else would just take care of itself.

And it had. The business had more customers than ever.

But, somehow, the bank account was still dwindling. Ollie

had mortgaged his parents' house and shifted all of his personal savings into the business account and now had nothing left to give. Once the business account ran out, Ollie would be broke.

The business would go under. He'd have to sell the house, unable to pay back the mortgage.

And Ollie would be out on the street.

That pile of papers in the back room just reminded him of it all.

Which is why he never went back there, opening the door just long enough to toss papers in the box.

He knew it was a mess. He knew it was careless.

And he felt bad about it. Ollie was a meticulous man, meticulous with his recipes, with his dishes. Meticulous with his station and his prep and his food storage. He was meticulous with cleaning and maintenance. The deli was old, but everything in it worked as well as it possibly could because he was meticulous about taking care of it. Every surface was a clean as it could possibly be. Ollie's heart simply wouldn't settle until that was the case every night.

But that office, that office was a nightmare.

Literally.

Ollie would dream of being trapped in there at night, pounding on the door, no one around to hear him, to set him free. The boxes would fill with more and more paperwork, towering higher and higher above him like a tsunami wave, with Ollie unable to escape that tiny room, until the wave broke over him, the boxes tumbled down on him, the paper drowned him, swept him under, unable to breathe beneath their crushing weight. Until darkness came over him, his chest tight from screaming and lack of air, and he blacked out and died.

Then he would sit up straight in bed, chest sucking in greedy breaths, his t-shirt stuck to his body, his sheets cold and damp with sweat.

That happened at least three or four nights per week.

For the last few years.

As he stood at his station, prepping sandwiches for the lunch rush, he knew that his aunt and uncle were right.

He needed help.

He just didn't want it.

~

"Opening," called Sarah as she walked toward the front of the deli.

Ollie looked at the clock. It was already noon. The last half-hour had flown by in the tangle of his thoughts, the tightness of his chest, and the calming, familiar motion of his hands building brisket sandwiches.

He heard the click of the deadbolt and the squeak of the door hinge, and then the warm chatter of customers filled the deli, mingling with the rich smell of brisket and bread and mustard, and swept all of the uneasy thoughts from Ollie's mind. He rinsed his hands in a sink and dried them on the back of his apron as he walked out front.

He waved hello to the customers, reached across the counter to hug a few of his regulars. He asked about their kids and their grandkids, about aches and pains or jobs and businesses. Mrs. Crandall's knitting. John Alain's bass lessons.

This was what it was all about. Family. Friendship. A sense of community.

And great food.

There was nothing like great food to bring people together.

The front of house crowded with people and a line continued through the door, snaking back along the length of the front window and down the sidewalk.

Ollie lost himself in the rhythm and joy of greeting customers, taking their orders, delivering their sandwiches, and watching them savor their first bites before they even stepped outside. After selling all of the sandwiches they'd prepped in advance, with a line of customers still covering the front window, Sarah slipped into the back to help Tom make more.

Ollie stayed out front with the customers.

When the last customer had gotten their sandwich and left with a smile and a "thank you", Ollie looked up at the clock. Two hours had passed in a heartbeat. Despite the early morning, despite the poor sleep the night before, despite the crush of customers for the last two hours straight, Ollie felt energized, alive.

He walked into the back, where Tom and Sarah were packing several orders into large white paper bags.

"Did you add the pickles into Mrs. Shaw's bag?" asked Ollie.

"You bet, boss," said Tom. "And I put some sugar cookies into Mr. Hargeson's order, too."

"Oh, good. How many?"

"Three," said Tom. "That okay?"

Ollie twisted his mouth. "Better make it two. Tina will kill me, otherwise. She's trying to get her dad's blood sugars down."

"You got it, boss."

Tom was a fairly new hire. Ollie had brought him on two years ago when it became too difficult for him and Sarah to handle the lunch rush by themselves. He was young, only twenty. Only eighteen when Ollie had hired him. Tall, lanky, covered in piercings and tattoos, most of which he or his friends had done themselves. His hair was trimmed short, almost bald, and dyed white blonde.

He looked a little scary, probably, to many people. But he was a good kid.

Two years ago, he'd just come out of high school and had no prospects, no direction. He'd come in around three o'clock one day, hungry, but didn't have enough cash for a sandwich. He and Ollie had got to talking and Ollie had taken a liking to him almost immediately. He offered Tom a sandwich in exchange for his help in delivering meals to some folks in the neighborhood who no longer had the mobility to come in to the deli themselves.

He'd watched Tom interact with Mrs. Dunbarton, a sweet woman in her nineties, a retired scientist who'd lost her husband a decade earlier and now suffered from advanced macular degeneration. Standing in her entryway, her lace-covered buffet on one side, a coatrack in the corner, on the floor against the wall a tray filled with carefully aligned boots and shoes that hadn't been worn in a decade, she held Tom's face in her hands, pulled it down to an inch from her own, turning her head from side to side to get a good look at him with her peripheral vision. Tom didn't say a word, didn't even flinch when she did it. Just waited patiently, bent in a bow while Mrs. Dunbarton examined him, patted his cheeks tenderly, and pronounced him "a good boy".

How many eighteen-year-olds fresh out of high school would have been that patient, that kind? Tom even thanked her when she said it and gave her a hug when they left a few minutes later.

With Mr. Hargeson, Tom had gotten to talking about the Indians and whether or not the new pitcher they'd signed in the off-season would amount to anything. They'd stayed there for half an hour while Mr. Hargeson ate, Mr. Hargeson in his recliner, Tom on the couch, the two of them chatting like they were grandfather and grandson.

Ollie had known right then that he'd offer Tom a job. But then they delivered to Ms. Stonnard, a woman in her seventies who'd had a tougher life than anyone should have to endure. And that was just what Ollie had gleaned from rumor, gossip, snatches of overheard conversation, and allusions from the older customers who'd grown up around Ms. Stonnard.

As a result, Ms. Stonnard was mean.

Cantankerous.

Ms. Stonnard didn't like anyone. Didn't really even like Ollie.

But she took an immediate shine to Tom when Ollie introduced him.

An "immediate shine" for Ms. Stonnard meant that she let Tom come into her house, all the way in through the entryway, through the living room, and into the kitchen to set her lunch on the table.

She'd never even let Ollie in the door before, always snatching the lunch bag from Ollie's hands while he stood on the doorstep and shoving her payment at him before closing the door in his face.

When Ms. Stonnard let Tom come inside like that, Ollie knew he was a keeper.

And he'd been right. Tom didn't know a thing about food or cooking when Ollie had hired him, but he was eager to learn, willing to work, and a quick study. If Ollie had handed him a textbook on cooking, Tom would probably still be struggling to boil water. But Ollie took a hands-on approach, showed Tom what to do with each recipe, each cooking technique, and let him practice in the kitchen. Now he was as reliable a line cook as any coming out of the Culinary Institute. And both Ollie and Sarah trusted him completely.

They made the rounds together, delivering nine meals to eight customers. Mr. Maxwell took two meals himself, both lunch and dinner, just about every day. Ollie tried his best to mix things up to make sure he was eating a full diet, giving one brisket sandwich and one turkey with sides, sometimes including a salad or a bit of cut fruit.

Even though the sun was shining, the air was getting colder. When Ollie stood on the customers' doorsteps waiting for them to open their doors, the air had the smell of snow, a cold sting that snaps at the back of your nose. Winter would come early this year.

When they got back to the deli, Sarah was halfway through

the dinner prep. At lunch, they just served sandwiches. But at dinner, they added sides like cornbread, salad, coleslaw, baked beans, roasted corn on the cob, or hot mac and cheese. The offering varied with the seasons and the availability of fresh ingredients, and every dish had Ollie's unique twist. But Ollie knew that some of his customers depended on him for their meals each day, and like with Mr. Maxwell, he wanted to be sure to offer them food that was delicious, but also healthy and nutritious.

The three of them worked quietly, prepping dinner. Tom plugged his phone into a speaker and played some old blues tunes off a streaming playlist. The music mingled with the food, mingled with Ollie's mind and heart as he prepped the meal. He added more smoke, more spice, more pain and beauty to the beans, the cornbread. He sautéed some collard greens with bacon to go with the cornbread, mixing the pot liquor into some mashed potatoes, channeling the vibe of the Son House, Robert Johnson, and Mississippi John Hurt tunes swirling in the air around them.

Food, for Ollie, was more than just sustenance. Food was an expression of love, a gift to another human being, a way to say, "I care about you. I want you to live, to love, to thrive." It was a mother's gift to her children, the gift of continued life on top of her original gift of life itself.

Ollie didn't think of his customers like they were his children and he their mother. But he did think of his work as a weighty responsibility. When a customer came into the deli and bought a sandwich or a dinner plate, whether they knew it or not, they were asking Ollie to care for them, to sustain them for that one meal. The food that they ate, the food that Ollie prepared, would become a part of them for at least a little while. It would mingle with the muscles and the cells of their body and fuel them for a time.

And Ollie believed that the emotions of the chef infused

with the food when it was prepared, and that those emotions passed on into the customer, as well. That's why home-cooked food tasted different from store-bought. Sure, the ingredients might be slightly different, the kitchen equipment and the preparation techniques might vary, but butter was butter and heat was heat. What really made the difference, what really made home-cooking so good was the love that was poured into it by the chef.

Some people chose their clothes each morning based on their mood for the day. If they were depressed, they wore black and grey. If they were feeling bouncy and energetic, they wore bright yellows and oranges. If they were feeling sexy, they wore tight clothes and short skirts. If they were feeling bloated and fat, they wore long, flowing clothes.

Ollie did the same thing with his cooking. He tried to channel his moods into his food, even when he was feeling angry or sad.

He never wanted negative emotions to seep into his cooking, but they were a part of the human experience. He didn't want to block them in any way. He wanted his food to be real.

When he was upset, he used his cooking as a way to transform the feeling. By letting go and pouring that feeling into his cooking, it transformed from the toxic spice of anger or the gauzy, metallic taste of sadness into something more, something wonderful, something redemptive and hopeful.

Food was love for Ollie. And adding love to anything can only make it better. So it was with negative emotions. When mixed with love in a dish, they became rounder, deeper, wholly human. The process somehow encapsulated the exquisite and beautiful pain of being human.

Cooking in this way didn't always make Ollie feel better when he was down, but it usually did. And he believed that his customers could feel it, too. A brisket sandwich, made with the exact same recipe and the exact same techniques in the exact same kitchen on two different days would taste completely different because the chef would be different each time. The same person, but different emotions, different thoughts, different feelings.

Music was the same way, filled with the transformative power of love. And Ollie let the exquisite and beautiful pain of the Mississippi blues pour into him, through him, into the food. He let it transform his mind and his heart and his cooking.

His anxiety was still there, his fear of what that woman was doing locked in the office, of what she might find, of what she may tell him he had to do.

The deli was started by Ollie's grandparents, then run by his parents. Now it was under Ollie's stewardship.

And he didn't want close it.

He didn't want to say goodbye.

He wasn't ready for that.

That would bring a pain that no dish could transform.

5

When Mr. Wood left her amid the catastrophe that was his office, Alli closed the door, leaned back against it, and took a long, deep breath to calm herself.

It didn't work.

When she opened her eyes again, the chaos was still there, still speared her heart like white-hot barbecue skewers.

It wasn't the external mess that bothered her. The back seat of her car was probably just as messy. She hadn't looked back there in quite some time, but wouldn't be surprised if that were the case.

What bothered her was the mental mess that the office represented.

The back seat of Alli's car—or, more specifically, the floor in front of the back seat—was just a repository for old fast food wrappers or boxes or other non-organic detritus. It was a garbage can, an administrative duty. She would empty it once a year and never think about it, otherwise.

But the mess in Mr. Wood's office was data. Information.

Worse, it was useful, necessary information.

For it to be in such a chaotic state signified that Mr. Wood was abdicating his responsibility to find, understand, and maintain the truth about his business. The truth as represented by his accounting system.

A business was many things: customer base, marketing, word-of-mouth, products, shipping, supply chain, and so on. But all of those functions were represented in one way or another in the accounting of the business. It was all present on the general ledger, on the income statement and the cash flow statement and the balance sheet.

Alli could forgive a business for keeping terrible records. Most people were idiots who didn't understand their core business, let alone how to keep track of it. Even many trained accountants were barely competent, at best.

But to not even try at all, as Mr. Wood was doing here, that was an affront to the truth. That was an insult to human curiosity, to the human need for understanding, for research and thought and scientific inquiry.

And now it was up to Alli to make it right.

It was up to her to sift through this morass of information and piece together the story of Ollie Wood Deli.

Finding the story in the data was fun.

Sifting through mounds of paper and entering their contents into a database, not so fun.

First things first. Alli needed a to-do list. In the face of so much chaos, it was simply easier to use a list to keep her thoughts organized. Plus, it freed her brain to think of more interesting things. She pulled out her phone and tapped in her list.


**To-do list:**

- Get access to bank accounts
- Get computer
- Clean office

- Scan files
- Get new POS system
- Analyze data

Alli called Mort for authorization to access the bank accounts for the business, then called the bank to set up her profile on her personal laptop.

She checked the account balance and sifted through the transaction history. She could immediately see some potential red flags, but suspended her judgement until all of the information was taken into account.

The balance of the account was insufficient to purchase a computer and still handle the average monthly expenses over the last twelve months.

Ollie Wood Deli really was a hair's breadth from insolvency.

Alli called Mort once more and secured approval and a budget to purchase a computer system for the company. It was essentially an interest-free loan, to be paid back in installments over the next twelve months.

That was definitely not something they would normally do for a client, but Mr. Wood was Mort's nephew, so he was willing to bend the rules. And it gave Alli enough budget to purchase a decent system, with appropriate software, and to set her mind more at ease about the Herculean task ahead of her.

She had to drive all the way to the other side of the city to find the computer she needed, fighting through traffic the entire way. While she was out, Alli stopped at her own work to borrow a Xerox XTS-D, a handheld optical character recognition scanner that would immensely streamline the data entry process.

Alli had long ago figured out how to rig up a paper hopper to feed stacks of paper into the scanner one by one, and she'd built a custom script to extract the data from the scanned image. Instead of Alli looking over each piece of paper and typing in the numbers on it, the scanner would recognize the contents of the page and convert them into digital form. Then, her script would detect the data and automatically enter it into the appropriate fields in Mort's proprietary accounting software.

Thankfully, aside from a few hand-scrawled notes here and there, the paperwork in the boxes had seemed to be mostly typed, which would aid the OCR process immensely.

The sun was setting when Alli hauled all the equipment in the back door of the deli. She cleared off the desk, checking the dates on the paperwork scattered there and setting them into the open box, then putting the box on the floor to clear the desktop.

She wiped the desk down with some cleaner she found in a tall cabinet in the room next door, scrubbing hard with a rag to remove the grime and gunk and some black streaks that may once have been alive. The streaks were pointed toward the door, so Alli figured whatever microscopic fungus had been unfortunate enough to take root on the desk had been desperately clawing for the door and had ultimately failed to escape. Eyeing the stacks of boxes around her, Alli idly wondered if she would wind up with the same fate.

It took another hour for her to get the computer set up, installing Mort's accounting software, along with the customizations she had made to it, and getting the OCR scanner connected and running. Satisfied that her tools were working properly, Alli now set her mind to the paperwork itself.

She needed an inventory. She couldn't proceed in a logical way, couldn't even devise a logical path forward, until she knew what she was dealing with. She had to first pull out all the boxes and organize them by year, then go through each one to first confirm that there were no misfiled papers, then to classify the paperwork within each box.

That would be a very long and very tedious process.

Alli felt the weight of the task squat heavy on her shoulders, crushing her. This kind of mundane, mindless work destroyed her soul. It took so much time and returned so little value. All Alli could think about during tasks like that was how much better spent the time would be if she were working on a problem or tweaking some code or designing an experiment. Something interesting. Something important.

But the mundane tasks still needed to be done, and there was no one else to do them. And Alli didn't want to get ahead of herself, to let the enormity of the situation stop her from moving forward.

The only way to tackle a huge problem was to take it one step at a time.

Start with the boxes.

She pulled out every single box and stacked them on, under, and around a metal table she found in the hallway outside the office, being careful to allow room for the employees to move in and out of their refrigerators and access the back door.

It was not easy.

There were a lot of boxes.

Alli counted forty-nine by the time she was done.

If each box really represented one year of entries, then there were forty-nine years of paperwork for this deli slouching against the wall. That meant records dating all the way back to the early seventies.

That was a lot of paperwork to be sitting around in boxes.

Time to fix that problem.

Alli went back to the cabinet in the neighboring room and pulled out a broom, a mop, a bucket and some soap. She swept out the office, then filled the bucket from a hot water spigot beside the cabinet and mopped the office floor.

The handle of the mop was incredibly heavy, made of some old wood that was harder than concrete. By the time she was finished mopping, Alli's hands and arms were like rubber noodles.

Or maybe she just wasn't used to that kind of work and didn't have the muscles for it.

Still, as tired as her arms were, Alli still went so far as to wipe down the walls. She didn't normally focus so much on her physical environment, didn't care much about it at all, really. But with all the data just sitting out in that room, Alli felt like the office itself were her computer. Like the boxes were the hard drive.

A ridiculous notion, but Alli couldn't resist the urge to straighten the office, to put it in order.

To make it right.

That task finally done, Alli wiped her brow with her arm. It came back as slick and shiny as the office floor. The office was as clean as she was willing to make it, the streaks on the floor from the mop water slowly evaporating, the acrid smell of the ammonia-based cleaner stinging her nose. The floor was clear, the desk held nothing but the monitor, keyboard, and mouse Alli had just purchased, the computer tower resting on the floor below. Alli had taken all the papers off of the corkboard and set them into their own box to be organized later.

She was ready.

With a heavy sigh, she took the first box off the stack in the hallway.

Thankfully, though there was some misfiling, the first twenty-five boxes that Alli examined each contained paperwork from only a single year, as Mr. Wood had stated. If the boxes had been a haphazard mishmash of documents from any year, all randomly scattered throughout the stacks of boxes, Alli would have lost her shit completely. Thankfully, that was not the case.

She sat on the plastic chair beside the desk, setting the boxes on the floor. For each box, Alli removed every single piece of paper and set them into stacks on the desk. She had one stack for accounts payable, others for accounts receivable, inventory, and accrued expenses. What cash receipts she found, she set into one more stack, but those were spotty. It was clear she would need to reconcile the paperwork with the bank statements to get a clearer picture of the true cash flow of the business. And if Mr. Wood's cash transactions were as well-recorded as the rest of his paperwork, there could be significant gaps in the records that would never be filled.

Once the sorting and stacking was done, Alli carefully set each stack into one of five empty boxes she'd set aside, one for each type of stack. She wrote the year in black marker on the side of the now-empty box she'd just gone through, and stacked it against the far wall. Once she'd scanned in all the paperwork, she would organize the originals back into their boxes by year for Mr. Wood's record-keeping, if he wanted it.

The twenty-sixth box Alli opened had more paperwork than the others, most of it yellowed and dry. The pages were handwritten, the ink faded in spots. The script was ornate and precise, almost calligraphic. On the sheets, lines and boxes had been drawn across the page like a spreadsheet. It looked like the lines were drawn by hand using a ruler, as they were very straight, and Alli could see slight overruns at some of the edges, where the person drawing them had stopped the pen just a millimeter too late. Still, despite these slight imperfections, if these were really drawn by hand, the attention to detail, the precision, the meticulous care given to that simple, mundane act was remarkable.

And necessary.

Alli examined the script more closely and saw that the first entry on the page was dated from 1952. Long before computers and spreadsheet programs were in common use by small businesses. Alli was sure there were pre-printed general ledger books back then, but whoever had kept this record had made their own, drawn it by hand. Alli appreciated the will to do things yourself, and to do them right.

She clawed through the box and found page after page in similar format, all hand-drawn, all filled with that same precise, calligraphic handwriting.

Because the pages were hand-drawn and carefully organized, they held a lot more records than the more modern boxes, which were just piles of invoices and receipts and notes. In that first box, Alli found records spanning from 1952 through 1961. In another she picked up later, the records dated from 1965 to 1969.

Other boxes filled in the gaps and added even more years, dating all the way back to 1943, the very first entry being the purchase of the building itself for three hundred fifty-six dollars from someone called Mr. Fredrick Martin.

By the time she was finished, Alli had found and organized nearly eighty years' worth of accounting records.

But it had been no mere accounting task. It was a research project, an archival of primary documents from the history of this location. In those records, especially the older, hand-written ones, were details about life in this town in the forties and fifties and sixties, details that local historians might find interesting, even thought-provoking. Possibly even paradigm-shifting, depending on the state of local historical theory and research. It wasn't Alli's area of interest, but she was excited to pass copies of these documents on to someone who might be inspired to use them to their fullest potential. If Mr. Wood was amenable to the idea.

Alli stretched, arching her back, and heard her spine pop. She groaned as her muscles protested the movement, the ache radiating from her atlas to her coccyx.

"You should eat something."

Alli started at the noise, a sudden intrusion on the silence that for hours had been filled only by the quiet rustle of paper, the soft scrape of cardboard, and the sound of her own thoughts.

She turned to see Mr. Wood leaning against the doorjamb. He looked as tired as Alli felt, dark circles set deep beneath those fascinating eyes.

"I'm not hungry," Alli said.

"I find that hard to believe." Mr. Wood checked his watch. "It's one AM. You've been in here for more than twelve hours."

Alli checked her own watch and confirmed the time. It had taken her roughly eight straight hours to sort through the boxes, and she hadn't even started scanning in the paperwork yet.

She stood from the chair, her knees stiff from so many hours spent sitting. Again, she stretched her back, closed her eyes and arched backward, felt the stretch across her abdomen, her chest. She rolled her arms up, cat-like, toward the ceiling, the muscles of her arms and sides elongating, blood returning to muscle fibers that had been starved for oxygen.

She opened her eyes and saw Mr. Wood watching her from the doorway, his arms folded across his chest. The man was thin, of average height, maybe five-foot-ten-inches tall, three or four inches taller than Alli herself. But though he was thin and lean, he had a muscularity to him, a sense of physicality belied by his corporeal form. It was almost as if he projected his will onto his form, superimposed it on his bones like a hologram. For the people around him, even though their eyes took in this rangy, sleep-deprived form, their other senses absorbed the gravitas of that other presence.

It was like a scent. You can look at a sparkling clean kitchen and see nothing but appliances and tools. But when the scent of freshly-baked chocolate-chip cookies reaches your nose, your impression of the scene changes completely from one of a sterile, professional workspace to one of comfort and home.

That was what Mr. Wood was like to Alli. A dichotomy for the senses. A paradox of perception.

Alli's perception in that moment faded, the edges of her vision clouding like the vignette of an old photograph. Like one that might have been taken back when Mr. Wood's grandparents purchased the building from Mr. Fredrick Martin.

Could that be Fredrick Martin of Martin and Hough Bank?

The thought was like a distant whisper shuffling through the back of her mind.

"Woah," said Mr. Wood, stepping into the room as Alli's body tilted toward the wall. "Careful."

He held his hands out toward her, ready to help, but Alli steadied herself first with a hand against the wall.

She'd nearly fainted. Lack of blood to the brain from the sudden change in blood pressure as she stood up? Or lack of glucose due to not having eaten in so long?

"Still think you're not hungry?"

Could be either reason. Or both.

Alli nodded to Mr. Wood. No harm in eating, just in case that was the cause.

"Come on," he said. "I'll fix you something."

Alli followed him out of the office. The kitchen was dark, lit only by a few soft emergency lights distributed at intervals along the wall. Mr. Wood led her into the front of house where he pulled a stool around to the counter.

"The stoves and ovens are off, but I'll fix you something cold."

Alli set her elbows on the counter, rested her head in her hands. Fatigue stole over her, like the darkness was wrapping a warm blanket around her shoulders. She wanted to sleep for a few hours, but she wanted to finish all of the data entry first. She still needed to scan in all the documents she'd just sorted, then validate the database to be sure it had all come in without error.

Only then could she start doing her real job, which was finding the right system for this business. Finding the right way to tell its story through numbers.

She heard the cooler door open and close. Lights came on in the prep area. She watched the curve of Mr. Wood's back as he bent over the counter, listened to the rhythmic tapping of his knife against the cutting board, a rapid tap-tap-tap, followed by a scrape, then repeating, like the rhythm of a jazz drummer.

As much to prevent herself from falling asleep as from any curiosity about what he was doing, Alli stood from her stool and walked to the prep area. On the counter, she saw an assortment of vegetables sitting beside a pan full of sliced turkey. She leaned against the counter to one side of Mr. Wood.

"What are you making?"

Mr. Wood didn't look up.

"Bit late for brisket," he said, "but turkey salad sits well enough at this hour."

"I don't like mayonnaise," said Alli, shivering at the memory of the mayonnaise and ketchup sandwiches her mother would feed her when she was a small child. Some people liked that flavor combination. Alli had even heard that people in Utah would intentionally mix them together and dip their French fries into the resulting abomination. And she'd once enjoyed the sandwiches as a little girl. But she couldn't stomach them anymore.

"Not that kind of turkey salad," said Mr. Wood.

She watched him chop the meat and the vegetables and mix them in a metal bowl.

"I don't like radishes, either."

He ignored her, slicing the radishes cleanly and efficiently and adding them to the bowl without even a defiant glance in her direction.

In another, smaller metal bowl, he poured oil, lemon, chopped onion, and a small pile of chopped up greens, then whisked them together with a fork and poured it over the meat and vegetables, tossing the whole combination and seasoning it with salt and pepper.

While that bowl sat, Mr. Wood went to the dry storage and returned with a half-loaf of bread. He sliced it into cubes, the bread crunching and flaking as he cut through it.

"Day old," he said without looking up. "Good for croutons."

He added the croutons to the bowl and mixed them with the fork in a motion that looked so natural it seemed that it was an extension of his very thoughts.

He then dumped the contents into a shallow, white ceramic bowl.

Alli followed him back to the front of house, where Mr. Wood set the bowl on the counter and handed her a fork. She sat heavily on the stool and ate.

Food was fuel, and her body needed fuel.

But this fuel was more than just an energy source.

This fuel did more than just provide nutrients to her body.

Alli was no epicurean. Far, far from it. But this simple salad lit up her taste buds in a way she'd never experienced before.

The vegetables were fresh and crisp, and had more flavor than Alli had known they could have. The lettuce didn't taste like cold tissue paper. Instead, it crunched between her teeth. The taste was cool and refreshing, like cold running water from a fresh mountain stream in late winter. The cucumbers were similar, cool and crisp and clean.

Alli hesitated over the radishes, but she was tired and hungry, and there were too many radishes to pick them all out of the salad. To her surprise, instead of the piercing bitterness that normally turned Alli away, the thin-sliced radish instead contributed a spicy pepperiness to the salad.

The tomatoes were sweet and burst in her mouth like a firework when she bit into them. The turkey was tender and light, adding just enough substance to make the dish feel like a meal.

The dressing was tangy and bold, but there wasn't so much of it that it dominated the dish. It tapped like that jazz drummer, didn't bang like a construction worker swinging a sledgehammer. The croutons had already absorbed some of the dressing and added a crunch and a comfort, like taking a bite of bread while eating a bowl of soup.

The dish, in short, was incredible. A simple salad, made before Alli's eyes in a matter of minutes. Yet it may have been the best thing Alli had ever eaten in her entire life.

Why would she think that? Was her fatigue pushing her toward exaggeration in her thinking?

No. She had been oblivious to the sensory experience of food for most of her life because the experience was not worth her attention. The food she had eaten to that date had been utilitarian, at best. Wonder bread, mayonnaise, and ketchup. Processed pseudo-meats and even more heavily processed pseudo-cheese. Fast food sandwiches and burgers, more corn than meat or bread.

Food had always been a means to an end, simple fuel to sustain the life that mattered to her, the life of her mind. Her body was just a transport and feeding mechanism for her mind.

But this food, this salad, was a new thing, a new sensation, one that gave rise to a whole avenue of exploration for her. What percentage of humanity had access to fresh food? Of those, what percentage had the expertise to cook the food not just safely, but well? Was it important to the human condition to experience food in the way she was experiencing it, forkful by delicious forkful, in the darkness in the deli with Mr. Wood standing quietly on the other side of the counter? Or was it sufficient for humanity to continue to think of food as Alli had always done, as mere fuel?

It was a similar line of thinking to the age-old questions about art. Was art, both its expression and its enjoyment, an integral part of human nature? Or was it a superfluous outgrowth of humanity's success as an apex predator, a purposeless sideshow that stemmed from the indolence of ease?

The scrape of her fork against the bowl shook Alli from her

thoughts. She looked down and was surprised to find the bowl completely empty.

"That was delicious," she said, hearing the incredulousness in her own voice.

Mr. Wood smiled. "I'm glad you liked it." He took the bowl from her, turned, and rinsed it in the sink behind him, then carried it into a room the back. Alli heard him set it onto a metal surface, a sink or a counter.

He came forward again, materializing from the dim lit gloom cast by the emergency lights. "It's very late. How far away do you live?"

Alli shook her head. Her body was already digesting the food, pulling the nutrients into her bloodstream. She could feel her energy returning.

"I still have work to do," she said.

Mr. Wood frowned.

"I can't leave you here alone all night."

"I assure you, Mr. Wood, I can be trusted. I have no intention of stealing from you."

Mr. Wood stared at Alli and rocked his head back as if she had just struck him.

"I'm not worried about you stealing anything," he said. "I'm worried about someone breaking in or something going wrong. Some equipment breaking or you needing something."

Alli hadn't considered that point of view. She waved him off.

"I'll be fine," she said, "thank you. I'll just be in the office scanning papers and validating data. There's nothing I'll need beyond what I already have."

Mr. Wood looked at her thoughtfully for a long moment. Alli returned his gaze, trying with her eyes to instill confidence in him, to implant in his brain the understanding that Alli was not some helpless fair maiden in distress from a fairy tale. He was the heroic type, but she didn't need a rescuer or a protector. She was fully capable of managing her own affairs.

Which, from the state of his paperwork, was more than she could say for Mr. Wood.

And yet, as she stared back, trying to project these understandings into his head, she found herself instead mesmerized by his eyes. The glow from a nearby emergency light caught them in just the right way to highlight their clarity, their depth. It was like staring into deep pools of clear, faintly tea-stained water. The orange flecks seemed to glow. In her reverie, Alli imagined those orange flecks like koi fish in a tea-stained pond. They seemed to swim back and forth in Mr. Wood's irises.

Alli jerked herself upright, shook the daydream from her mind.

Maybe it wasn't a daydream. It was nearly two in the morning, after all.

Maybe she was more tired than she thought.

"Are you sure you don't want to go home and sleep for a few hours?" Mr. Wood said. "If you're too tired to drive, I'm happy to drive you myself. I'll even come back and pick you up in the morning, if you like."

"No, thank you," Alli said. "I'd rather keep working."

She rose from her stool and carried it back around the other side of the counter. As she hesitated with it, unsure where it belonged, Mr. Wood kindly and quietly took it from her and set it in the corner.

He was an unusually observant man, Alli decided.

And a talented chef.

But now it was time for her to do her job.

"Thank you for the meal," she said, nodding her head toward him.

Mr. Wood nodded back, and Alli walked through the gloom to the office. In her mind, orange koi were swimming through tea-stained water.

Odd thoughts on a late night. She would be glad to focus on her work once again.

**6**

Ollie thought he was a workaholic.

No, he didn't think it. He knew it.

But next to this woman, Ollie looked like a pot-smoking slacker.

For a moment there, as he'd stared at her while she sat on the stool in the dim light from the emergency lamps, while he'd wondered what on earth made her tick, he'd gotten lost.

He'd lost track of himself for a moment. His head floated away from his body, from the deli, from all of the worries and the work and just drifted away.

It was something about her eyes that had done it. There was nothing remarkable about their appearance. They were brown eyes, not too wide, not too narrow. Neither exceptionally clear nor exceptionally dark. But they had a kind of edge to them, a kind of depth that wasn't visible, but somehow came through with force whenever she looked at him.

And in the darkness that night, they seemed to glow like a beacon, a lighthouse in the fog. It was the strangest feeling, but Ollie felt like her eyes were pulling him forward, leading him somewhere. To safety, maybe.

Or, more likely, he was just exhausted and his brain had finally turned to mush.

He couldn't understand how Alli wasn't feeling the same way.

Or maybe she was, and was just too stubborn to admit it, to him or to herself.

Either way, there was no way Ollie was going to leave her in the deli alone all night. For one thing, he'd only just met the woman that morning. She had the bona fides as an accountant, and Uncle Mort had vouched for her on the phone, but Ollie didn't know her from a stranger on the street.

Plus, even though it was improving, the neighborhood still wasn't the safest, especially late at night. It was mostly bored teenagers breaking into unlocked cars and stealing stupid shit, or walking into open garages in the middle of the night for the same purpose, but there were more unsavory characters out there, too, and Ollie would feel terrible if anything happened to the woman while he was at home in his bed trying unsuccessfully to sleep.

Fortunately—or unfortunately, as the case may be—Ollie had spent the night at the deli on more than one occasion in the past. He went out back and banked the heat in the smoker, letting the brisket and turkey breast he'd put in there before dinner continue to smoke all night—another way things could go wrong in the night—then grabbed a blanket and pillow from a box in the back of the storeroom.

The office door was open and the woman was setting a stack of paper into some kind of plastic hopper that was connected to a thin rectangular box. It looked like a weird meat slicer, but instead of slices of meat, the box buzzed and clacked and spit out pieces of paper it had taken from the stack.

She was sitting at the desk staring intently at a computer screen—a screen that hadn't been there that morning—and typing away at a keyboard—which also hadn't been there that morning.

Ollie knocked softly on the office door. The woman turned her head without turning her eyes, still typing on the keyboard, before finally flicking her eyes toward him.

He held up the blanket and pillow, then set them down on top of a stack of boxes beside the door.

"Just in case," he said.

The woman just turned back to her screen and her keyboard. No "thank you", no "that's very kind of you", not even an "I thought I already told you I was fine." No acknowledgement of any kind beyond that brief flick of her eyes.

This woman was a real piece of work.

"Where did that computer come from?" Ollie asked, his voice sounding shrill and thin and loud in his ears. He didn't know the exact balance of his bank account, but only because he didn't enjoy the feeling he got when he looked at it after barely making payroll every month. But he was pretty sure there wasn't enough in there for a new computer.

Not that he wanted one, anyway.

"I bought it for you," Alli said without looking up.

"With your own money?" Ollie frowned. He barely knew this woman, and he definitely didn't want to be indebted to her.

"Don't be ridiculous," she said, again without looking at him.

Ollie waited for more explanation. When it seemed none was coming, he said, "Then how—"

"Your uncle extended a short-term, no-interest loan for the purchase."

Her words struck him like a ten-pound Steelhead across the face.

"Wait, what?" The fatigue that had been creeping over Ollie fled in an instant, replaced by a flare of anger. "I didn't ask for that. And I didn't say that was okay."

Alli finished typing with a staccato stab of her fingers on the keyboard, then turned in her chair toward him, her face open and frank and seeming not the least bit tired.

The woman was a machine.

"You didn't need to. Your uncle—or, perhaps more accurately, your aunt—has full fiduciary authority over this business. Shared with you, of course, but equal in decision-making authority." She turned back to her screen. "I've been granted full access to your accounts and license to make necessary purchases on behalf of the business. That includes the securing of loans, where appropriate."

Ollie felt his mouth fall open, felt the air sweep over his teeth and his tongue as he sucked in a sharp breath. He simply could not believe what he had just heard.

First, his aunt had as much control over the business—*his* business, *his parents'* business—as he did.

Second, she'd granted that authority to this woman, this stranger.

Third, this woman was making promises that Ollie would have to keep. Buying computers that he didn't want. Incurring debts that he didn't want to have to repay.

"But... that's..."

His spluttering inability to form a coherent sentence only made Ollie even more angry.

No, not angry.

Well, yes, angry. But there was more.

He'd left a promising culinary career behind to come back here and keep his family legacy alive. Granted, he was no Thomas Keller or Alain Ducasse, but he was no backyard barbecue dad, either. And he was learning. Growing in his abilities. And his prospects.

He'd left all that behind after his parents' accident.

He could have just sold the deli, but he felt like he owed it to their memory to keep it going. They'd always talked about Ollie taking over someday—someday far into the future—becoming the third generation of Woods to own the deli. He didn't want to destroy their dream.

And yet, after all that sacrifice, after nine years of hard work, now he came to discover that his aunt had been pulling the strings the whole time? That she had as much say in the business as he did?

And now some total stranger off the street was telling him how to run the business he'd grown up with.

"No," he said, shaking his head. "No, that's fucking bullshit."

The woman didn't even turn her head, just kept typing on her keyboard.

"That's bullshit. I won't allow it."

This was all Uncle Mort's doing, and Ollie was going to give him an earful. He patted his pockets.

"Where's my phone? I'm calling Uncle Mort."

"You might want to wait a few hours," the woman said drily, again without looking up.

Ollie started to ask why, then realized.

Fuck.

It was after two in the morning.

Aside from it being totally rude and completely unnecessary, if Ollie called his uncle right then, he'd just wake him up, piss him off, and have no shot at a reasonable conversation about how his own relatives were fucking him over.

The situation would still be the same in a few hours as it was right now. Ollie could wait.

As much as he wanted to unleash on his uncle right then and there, he could wait.

The woman glanced sideways at him, then sighed at her computer screen.

"If you're just going to stay here," she said, "you might as well help." She handed him the stack of papers that had formed in front of the little meat slicer along with a small box of large paper clips. "Separate these by year, bind each one with a paper clip, and put it into the appropriate box." She pointed to the boxes stacked against the wall, each of which had a year, or a range of years, written on the side.

Ollie wanted nothing more than to just throw the papers in her face, to toss the computer on the ground and stomp it to pieces, smash it with a baseball bat and do the same to the wall of boxes. He hated this room and everything in it.

He hated it because it held all of the things he didn't understand, didn't want to think about.

He was a chef. That's all he had ever wanted to be. All he had ever cared about.

When he was six years old, he would stand on an overturned milk crate in the prep station, his father's smell of sweat and Old Spice on one side, his mother's warmth and the scent of flowers that followed her everywhere on the other side, and make sandwiches with them.

When he was ten, he and his father would experiment with new marinade recipes late on a school night when he was supposed to be asleep.

When he was twelve, his mother had taught him how to use the smoker, how the heat was different in different parts of the smoke chamber and how it affected the texture of the meat, how different types of wood in the firebox impacted the flavor, and how that interacted with the marinades and the rubs. They would spend hours testing different combinations, then leaning over the counter and pulling apart the tender meat with their fingers, stuffing the long strands into their mouths and discussing what they tasted, what they smelled, how they felt. His mother would write careful notes in a small notebook she used for only that purpose. She always wrote down Ollie's comments as carefully and thoughtfully as her own.

By the time he was fourteen, he was inventing his own recipes for marinades, rubs, and sandwiches, doing his own experiments on various combinations in the smoker. He would bring the results to his parents for taste tests, tweaking the recipes until all three of them were either laughing from how bad it was or moaning from how good it tasted.

At seventeen, he'd left home to go to the Culinary Institute of America in New York and hadn't come back for more than a few days at a time since, too busy with the hectic, workaholic lifestyle of a young professional chef, too busy exploring new flavors and culinary techniques and ideas, ideas he could share with his parents at the times when he was able to come home for a brief break.

Until the car accident that took them both.

Until he'd come home for the funeral, quit his job in New York, and taken over the deli.

Since then, he'd never gone more than ten miles from where he stood in that moment, staring at a handful of paperwork and a room full of boxes. He went nine years ago from a life where the whole world of food and flavor lay before him to a life confined to a tiny box in a tiny neighborhood in a tiny town outside a tiny city.

Ollie wasn't a businessman. He'd never wanted to be one.

He'd tried for nine years to pretend he didn't have to be one.

But now it was obvious he was wrong.

Like it or not, he owned a deli.

That made him a businessman.

Along with his aunt and uncle, apparently.

He sighed and set to work doing what he'd been told.

At six AM, the last stack of papers came off the little meat slicer thing, what the woman—Alli. Her name was Alli—had called an optimal charcoal recognition scanner, or something like that.

No, that wasn't right.

That didn't even make sense.

It was late.

Or early.

Ollie hadn't slept in a long time, and his brain wasn't working right.

The slicer thing was called OCR something. It scanned the papers into the computer and put them into whatever app she was using. That's all Ollie knew.

And, to be honest, that was a lot more than he even wanted to know.

But, once he'd put the last stacks of scanned papers into their boxes and piled them neatly back against the wall, Ollie set his hands on his hips and looked around the office.

The floor was clean and clear. The boxes were organized and labeled. The desk was tidy, with only the monitor, keyboard, and mouse sitting atop it.

The corkboard was empty, without the chaos of pinned letters and papers and notes that his parents had left for each other a decade earlier. What papers from the corkboard that were relevant to the business had been scanned and filed. The rest—empty envelopes with notes scrawled on them, old post-it notes, napkins used as notepads—were tucked into a manila folder for Ollie to review at his leisure.

With all of these changes, Ollie felt a little bit better about the room. It seemed a little more organized, and it gave him a tiny scrap of hope that he might be able to climb on top of the mound of trouble that his business had fallen into.

And he'd learned a few things, too.

Ollie knew his grandparents had started the deli, and that it had been in his family for a long time, but he had no idea it dated all the way back to 1943.

Seeing that first entry on that paper brought back a lot of memories. He recognized his grandmother's beautiful hand-writing from letters and birthday card she had given him when he was young, before she died.

Gams must have been the bookkeeper when the business first opened. It made sense with her personality. She was warm and loving, always there for a big hug or an Oreo cookie—her favorite, despite the diabetes she developed in her later years—to sneak to Ollie before dinner. But she was quieter than his effusive, gregarious grandfather.

PapPap was a people person, through and through. He liked nothing more than to be at the center of a crowd, to be the center of everyone's attention. He could turn a mob of angry strangers into best friends, laughing and slapping each other's backs, within minutes, just by telling a few jokes, teasing a few people who seemed game, setting everyone at ease and helping them to feel camaraderie with each other. He brought people together. It was his superpower. And it was the reason why the deli had once been a fixture in the neighborhood, a place where people gathered together.

But, while Gams was just as kind and welcoming to other people, she was quieter, more serious, more level-headed. She would have had the better temperament for bookkeeping, no doubt.

The first entry, recording the purchase of the building, also reminded Ollie of an old black-and-white photo he'd seen a hundred times in a photo album, probably still stuffed in a box or a drawer back at the house. It showed Gams and PapPap standing in front of the deli with a tall, thin man in a dark three-piece suit. The man wore round wire-framed glasses, and he was balding, thin wisps of light hair carefully swept across the broad dome of his head. His expression in the photo was flat, serious.

His expression and his hair both stood in stark contrast with PapPap, whose thick dark hair piled in luxurious mounds atop his head, and whose smile was broad and bright. He had his left arm around the tall man's shoulders and held the man's right hand in a hearty handshake. Gams stood on the other side of

PapPap, her hands folded in front of her, an amused expression on her face.

PapPap had that thick hair until he died. From the progression of pictures in the albums, Ollie knew it turned from jet black to salt-and-pepper. But for as long as Ollie had been alive, PapPap's hair had been white as a cloud, and just as fluffy and billowy. He used to joke that Gams had always accused him of having his head in the clouds, so he just started carrying the cloud along with him wherever he went.

Now, Ollie could place that old black-and-white picture. He wasn't completely certain, of course, but he was pretty sure that the tall, thin man was Mr. Fredrick Martin, who went on to build one of the largest banks in the region and die one of the wealthiest men in the country. Before all of that, apparently, he had sold Ollie's grandparents the very building Ollie stood in.

"Do we still own the building?" he asked.

"No," said the woman, Alli. "Looks like your parents sold it to a commercial real-estate firm in 2009 for five hundred thousand dollars." She frowned. "Seems low for the market."

He was twenty-one years old in 2009, already living in New York. But he didn't remember his parents saying anything about selling the building.

He wondered what have caused his mother to sell a building her parents had bought, one that they still owned outright, one that their entire livelihood depended on.

As if she'd heard his thoughts, the woman continued, "Looks like they used the proceeds to make improvements on the property. There are entries here over the next year for architect's fees, construction costs, materials, permits, and so on. They either improved this property or worked on another one." She turned to Ollie. "Does your family own another location?"

Ollie frowned and shook his head.

"What about your home. Do you live in your parents' house?"

"Yes," Ollie nodded, "but it's the same house my grandparents owned way back when."

"Did your parents do any significant construction on it recently? An addition, maybe, or an extensive remodel?"

Ollie shook his head. "I don't think so. They never talked about it."

"Would they tell you if they had?"

"I'd be surprised if they didn't." He frowned. "But even if they hadn't, I would know. I'm living in that house now, and it's exactly the same as when I grew up. Same with this place." He gestured around them at the deli. "Nothing has changed here since before I left home."

Alli frowned.

"Does it matter?" asked Ollie. "I mean, it was more than ten years ago. Does it matter what they did with the money?"

"No, not really," said Alli. "But if you still owned the building, you'd have a lot more cash flow than you do now. You'd be collecting rent from the other businesses in the building."

Ollie snorted. Ollie's deli was in one corner of the building. There were only two other businesses in the space, a tattoo parlor two doors down and, on the opposite corner, a barber shop owned by a guy named Max Hessle, a regular who was old enough to have known Ollie's grandparents when they still ran the deli. There was one more space, directly beside Ollie, that had been vacant for years.

"I doubt there's much money coming from those businesses," he said. "One of them is vacant. Another gets two customers a week. The only one doing any business is the tattoo parlor."

The woman shrugged and turned back to her computer screen.

Ollie checked his watch. Six-fifteen. Ollie's bread delivery would be there soon, and it was time to start prepping for the day.

The woman—Alli. He had to start remembering her name—asked to shadow Ollie that day. She said she wanted to observe their normal business practices to look for what she called "optimizations".

Sounded like hell to Ollie. He didn't want some bean counter breathing down his neck all day writing something on a clipboard every time he threw away a spare cut of fat from the brisket or used too much mustard on a sandwich or something. He didn't want her weighing every piece of turkey he put on his sandwiches. He would not reduce his food, his creativity, to numbers on a spreadsheet.

He told the woman as much in no uncertain terms.

She followed him anyway.

To her credit, she kept to herself. No clipboards, no notes, no weighing of any kind. She just watched him from a spot near the hallway where she could see the prep area. He caught her nosing around in the coolers at one point, but other than that, Ollie forgot she was even there. He just fell into his work, as usual.

She showed the most interest when the bread delivery came, grilling Jackie, the delivery person, about delivery frequency and cost per unit and terms of payment and all kinds of stuff Jackie barely knew anything about. When she wasn't satisfied with Jackie's answers, the woman took down the number of the bread company so she could call them directly herself.

Jackie looked like she'd been ambushed by the feds on a drug raid or something. Totally stricken, caught completely off guard. She was worried that she'd done something wrong, that the woman was going to call her boss and get her fired. Ollie spent ten minutes calming her down, apologizing to her and promising she wouldn't get fired, not because of him, at least. He even threw in an extra sandwich for the trouble, on top of the one he gave her every day as a thank you for the delivery.

At seven-thirty, Ollie cooked up Sarah's breakfast. He offered to make some for the woman, but she declined, polite but cold, choosing instead to just watch as Ollie made an omelette with a bit of Spanish rice, saffron, chicken, and seafood. A cross between a Western omelette and a Spanish paella. Sarah came in around eight with Ollie's coffee, apologizing that she hadn't brought any for the woman. Sarah got all the ingredients in the omelette except the bay leaf, but Ollie could hardly blame her for that one. He'd only used it when he'd sautéed the chicken and rice.

Tom came in around nine and Ollie forgot all about the woman, losing himself in the routine of the day. It was Saturday, and the lunch rush would be twice the size of the weekday traffic. The three of them threw themselves into their prep work, as usual, and fielded the lunch rush when it came, heavy and noisy and chaotic, just the way Ollie liked his customers to be.

At one point, in the thick of the lunch crowd, with the front of house crammed with happy customers chattering away at each other and at Ollie, Sarah, and Tom, Ollie caught a glimpse of the woman standing in the corner by the cash wrap, just watching.

Silently watching.

She seemed to see everything, say nothing. She didn't even seem to eat anything. She had to be starving, but when Ollie offered her a brisket sandwich, she turned him down. The stray thought crossed his mind that maybe she hadn't liked the salad he'd made for her the night before, but she'd seemed to enjoy it just fine at the time. She'd cleared her entire plate.

She was just an odd duck.

Soon, the sweep of the crowd carried his mind to other things. Then there were deliveries and dinner prep and Ollie didn't think about the woman again until late that evening, around nine, when the dinner rush had ended, the food had been put away, the smoking meats had been swapped out, the meat had been prepped for tomorrow, the dishes had all been washed, and the whole place had been wiped down and mopped. Ollie said goodbye to Tom and Sarah, locking the front door behind them, and noticed a light on in the office.

"Still here?" he said to the woman.

She was typing away on her keyboard again, staring at her screen. Ollie nearly vomited when he saw a Big Mac wrapper on the floor behind her.

"What the fuck is this shit?" he asked picking it up like he'd found a used condom in a public park.

The woman turned long enough to glance at what Ollie was holding, then turned back to her screen.

"Food."

Ollie was so shocked by the sentiment that, at first, he couldn't think of a single word to say in response.

Then he couldn't decide which of the thousand words rushing through his mind he wanted to say first.

"This is not food."

She shrugged. "Food is just fuel. Those nutrients work as well as any others."

Ollie couldn't believe his ears. That sentiment ran so contrary to everything he believed, everything he'd ever been taught, everything he'd built his life around, that he thought for a second that he was being punked, that maybe there were hidden cameras in the corners of the office or something.

Then he realized that the woman actually meant what she'd said.

And maybe she really hadn't liked his salad.

The woman turned off her computer, gathered her bag, and stood to leave.

"I'll be here at eight AM," she said. She stopped and stared at him for a moment, tilting her head like a dog who'd heard an odd and interesting noise. Then, she said, "I've got some ideas that will keep your business from falling apart."

No smile, no hint of teasing or humor in her use of the phrase "falling apart". She just pulled that trigger all nonchalant-like, watched the bullet slide right through Ollie's heart, and walked away, letting herself out the front door.

It was true.

The expert had come in, climbed through all of his mess, organized and analyzed everything, and came to the conclusion Ollie had feared all along.

His business was falling apart.

His worst fears realized.

His limbs heavy as heavy as a side of beef, Ollie dragged himself to the front to lock the door again. Through the window, he saw the woman get into her beat-up old VW bug and drive off into the night.

No apologies. No condolences. Not even a softening of her tone when she said it to Ollie. When she sniper-shot him through the chest.

Just cold facts.

Food is fuel.

What a charming woman.

**7**

ALLI WAS THERE EARLY the next morning, sitting in her VW bug on the curb across from the deli at seven AM. The heater had warmed up during the drive from her apartment, The inside of the car was toasty, the tiny engine puttering in the thin morning light, the windows fogged against the chill November air outside.

She was re-reading the Michio Kaku book. She found that in a second reading immediately after the first, she often picked up on nuances she'd missed on the first pass. And the ideas swirling in her mind from the first read-through often coalesced around passages she read the second time, precipitating from her mind like a seed crystal dropped into a supersaturated solution.

But this morning, uncharacteristically, she was having trouble focusing on the text. Her mind kept wandering to her work.

That was very unusual. She never voluntarily thought about her work. She didn't hate it, really. She just didn't care about it. It was merely a way to pay for the requirements of life: rent, utilities, food, books, computing equipment. She did her job when it needed to be done and normally didn't waste a moment of thought on it otherwise.

But here she was, outside of expected working hours, sitting with a wonderful text full of mind-expanding ideas, and all she could think about was the deli.

Why were Mr. Wood's suppliers paying themselves from his accounts? How was that even possible, let alone legal? And why would Mr. Wood allow that practice to continue? Was he unaware that it was happening?

And what had been done with the five hundred thousand dollars from the proceeds of the sale of the building? It seemed a rash decision to sell such a valuable asset while still maintaining the business, but stranger things had happened in business before. It may not have been a decision Alli would have made, but it's possible there were good reasons for it.

The two sets of questions were very different, of course. One was occurring in the present-day and had an immediate and alarming impact on the operation of the business. The other was a mystery from the distant past, nearly fifty years earlier.

But something in Alli's mind linked them together, inexplicably.

Probably just because of the intensity of the work the prior day.

No, two days ago. She hadn't slept at all for more than thirty-six hours. The two days had melded together. She'd crashed last night as soon as she got back to her apartment, falling asleep in her jacket and her shoes, the strap of her bag still slung around her neck.

Now she was rested again, but there were so many things wrong with this business, so many things to fix. And so many of them were so obvious, even to a normal accountant. It didn't take a genius to know that your cash register should have been built this century, that it should be able to communicate with a computer in some way. It didn't take a master accountant to know that a business should own at least one computer, and that the records should be stored in that computer, not shoved into boxes stacked in a back room.

And it didn't take a gifted businessperson to know that you shouldn't grant your suppliers direct access to your accounts and allow them to withdraw payments at their own behest.

That arrangement was just ridiculous, and the unbelievable senselessness of it, the sheer recklessness of it, nagged at Alli's mind. She had grown accustomed to the unfathomable depths of human stupidity over the years, but this was a whole new realm of idiocy that even she hadn't thought could be possible.

And Mr. Wood, while clearly clueless when it came to his business, was just as clearly gifted and intelligent when it came to other things, like his food and his customers.

He wasn't an idiot.

Not a total idiot, anyway.

Alli jumped when she heard a sharp rap on her window next to her ear. She rolled it all the way down in an angry huff and saw Mr. Wood standing outside. Today, at least he'd had the sense to throw a puffy winter jacket over his white t-shirt and apron.

"Good morning, um... Alli," he said. "Have you eaten breakfast yet?"

Mr. Wood's presence confused Alli. It made sense that someone who thought of himself as a heroic protector, a savior of the world, would have come out the other day to investigate the strange vehicle parked outside his place of business. Defending the neighborhood from threats and potential threats and people who were no threat at all. But for him to come out today, when he knew who Alli was and what she was doing there, made little sense.

And why would he care if she'd eaten breakfast?

Alli had to admit that her heart was racing, her mind was unsettled. The inability to concentrate on her book, the disquiet in her mind about the shocking ineptitude in Mr. Wood's business practices, and then the sudden noise on the window so close beside her all must have combined to trigger a cortisol cascade, a fight or flight response in her body, a primal defense mechanism that wound back through her DNA for millennia.

But she hadn't noticed her heart racing like this until she'd rolled down the window and seen Mr. Wood standing there.

The sudden noise, then. That was the cause of it.

That, plus the shock of the cold air against the warmth of the car.

That must be it.

Mr. Wood still stood there, bent over at the waist so his head was even with hers in the window.

Breakfast. He'd asked if she'd eaten breakfast.

Alli shook her head and glanced at the passenger seat, where a fast-food bag sat unopened.

Mr. Wood followed her glance to the bag. His face contorted into a grimace. Alli watched his eyes, those unusual, beautiful eyes, as they slid from the bag to the back seat of her car. They widened in shock.

Alli was not the cleanest person in the world. She would be the first to admit that.

Actually, her mother would be the first to admit that.

But, Alli couldn't argue the point.

What she could argue was its importance. Her external environment simply needed to be clean enough to avoid disease and for her to travel through it unimpeded. So long as there was no toxic mold or distracting smells in the air, and provided she wasn't tripping over things or having to constantly move things to find a place to sit, she was fine with whatever mess accumulated around her. She didn't really even notice it.

And Alli didn't see the point in wasting time and energy constantly trying to push back the inexorable tide of entropy in the universe. It was a Sisyphean task. The character of the universe favored entropy, and all the tidying up of humanity was merely a spit in the wind. If the character of the universe was messy, who was Alli to argue with it?

That included the back seat of her car. It was really too small for anyone to sit in, though even if it weren't, Alli rarely, if ever, traveled with a passenger, let alone enough passengers to require someone to sit in the back.

So, she used it as a garbage can.

No perishable items. Nothing that could leak or decay. Nothing with an overly strong smell.

Mostly just fast food bags and napkins and cups.

"Good lord," said Mr. Wood, staring in the back seat.

Okay, a lot of fast food bags and napkins and cups.

"Did all of that come from you, or do you drive a high school football team around when you're not at work?"

Alli looked over her shoulder, which was more than she'd done probably since she'd bought the car.

In the foot wells in the back seat, there was a layer of fast food bags and napkins and cups that was at least ankle-deep.

Maybe calf-deep.

Fine. A whole lot of fast food bags and napkins and cups. Perhaps an excessive amount.

Alli turned her head back, marked her place in her book, and closed it on her lap.

"Is there something I can do for you, Mr. Wood?"

Mr. Wood was still gawking at the back of Alli's car, but he managed to drag his focus back to her.

"No," he said, "but there's something I can do for you."

He reached through the open window, pulled up the door lock, and opened the door. Cold air flooded in, freezing against Alli's still-warm pant legs.

Alli was shocked by Mr. Wood's presumption. To just open her car door like that without asking seemed a violation of Alli's personal agency, her right to dictate her own actions and choices.

Another unmistakable sign of a man with a savior complex. They always think they're right.

Then again, most men think they're right, regardless of whether or not they have a savior complex.

Just as she was about to chew Mr. Wood's head off, he held out his hand to her and smiled that calming smile of his. It was crooked on his face, his teeth only visible on the left side, like a cartoon grin. But on his face, it looked boyish and charming.

And it gave Alli that odd calming feeling again.

It was his eyes, she decided in that moment. The smile reached into his eyes, warmed them, made them almost glow, the clear brown color becoming limpid, the orange flecks practically glowing. Alli remembered her vision of koi fish swimming in tea-stained water from the other night, and felt a flush in her cheeks, hot against the cold air.

She bit her tongue and spared Mr. Wood the reprimand he deserved for his presumption. She looked out the windshield and sighed. She wasn't getting any reading done, anyway. Not with the irritating inability to focus that was plaguing her that morning. She might as well go inside and get to work.

She put her book in her bag and slung it over her shoulder, then climbed out of the car, ignoring Mr. Wood's outstretched hand. Though she knew he thought he was being gallant and gentlemanly, Alli was perfectly capable of getting out of her own car without assistance.

She had no use for a knight in shining armor. There were no dragons here.

"Okay, Mr. Wood," she said. "What is it you want to show me?"

"Not show you," said Mr. Wood. "Do for you."

He held his arm out toward the deli, inviting Alli to walk with him, then grinned, an expression that was somehow even more disarming than the crooked smile.

"I'm going to make you breakfast," he said.

Alli felt herself, inexplicably and irritatingly, smiling back at him.

❧

❧

After the salad the other night, Alli knew Mr. Wood could cook. But she wasn't expecting the riot of flavors that exploded on her tongue when she bit into the breakfast he had made for her.

She closed her eyes, practically involuntarily, as she chewed.

She saw colors behind her eyelids, blues and pinks and pale reds.

She felt things, emotions, as the food caressed her tongue. Vague memories of warmth and joy, like curling up under a blanket by a fire with a good book on a cold, snowy night. She even had a faint memory of a smell, leather and pipe smoke, a memory Alli hadn't had since she was a teenager.

"Damn, chef," said Sarah, her voice muffled by a mouthful of food. She was sitting beside Alli at the front counter, chewing slowly, moaning softly, and shaking her head, eyes closed.

The dish looked like a pizza, but without the sauce or the cheese. Just the crust. For toppings, it had eggs, cut in half and cooked so that the yolk was viscous, but not hard. Green herbs were sprinkled on top, along with a bit of red spice that gave the dish just a bit of heat and a slightly smoky flavor. When Alli bit into it, the crust crunched in her mouth and the yolk of the egg split and slid warm and thick and creamy over her tongue. A hint of salt sprinkled over the dish added some bite.

"Flatbread, paprika, cayenne, tarragon, chive, basil, salt, and seven-minute eggs," said Sarah, rattling off the list in one breath between bites and moans.

"Sometimes simple is better," said Mr. Wood with that disarming, crooked smile again.

The dish didn't seem that simple to Alli. She didn't even know how to cook an egg, let alone cook one that would wind up looking, tasting, and feeling exactly how she wanted it.

She could chop vegetables and sprinkle spices, though getting the proportions right would require a scale. But she didn't have the slightest clue how to make a pizza crust.

"Did you make the crust yourself?" she asked.

Mr. Wood winced. "No. I wish I could, but I don't have the equipment to bake bread here." He gestured toward Alli. "That's why Jackie delivers the bread every morning."

Right. The bread company. One of the suppliers taking freely from the business accounts.

"If I had a bread oven, I'd make everything myself."

"Why don't you get one?"

"You should know the answer to that. You're the money wizard."

Alli took another bite and chewed while she looked at Mr. Wood. He didn't seem to even be aware of his ability to borrow money, let alone be willing to do it. If all he needed was the capital to acquire a bread oven, he could easily have it. Alli didn't know what they cost, but it couldn't be more than ten or fifteen thousand dollars.

When she mentioned this, he said, "Even if I could find the money, where would I put the oven?"

Alli looked behind him, through the service window, at the small working area.

"We use everything in here every single day," Mr. Wood said, gesturing around the space behind him. "We can't rip anything out. And, even if it would fit, a deck oven can't replace the convection ovens over there." He pointed toward the back corner, where two ovens stood atop each other against the wall. "They work in different ways and cook different kinds of food. You can't roast a brisket in a bread oven."

Alli put the last bite of her breakfast in her mouth. She still didn't care much about food, but she had to admit that there was a significant difference between the fast food she normally ate and the delicious breakfast Mr. Wood had served her.

A difference on her tongue and in her mind, that is. She doubted there was any difference to her body. As far as her digestive tract was concerned, a carbohydrate was a carbohydrate, whether it came from a gourmet dish or a three-day-old Big Mac.

"Surely you must have thought about this in the past," said Alli, dusting crumbs from her hands over her plate. "Do you have a plan for what you would do, if you could?"

Mr. Wood took Alli's empty plate, held it in both hands, waiting while Sarah took her last bite. He stared down at the plate, furrowed his brow, and pursed his lips, as if debating whether or not to speak.

"If I could," he said, slowly and carefully, then quickly added, "and I know I can't." He looked up at Alli, then glanced at Sarah, who raised her eyebrows as she chewed. "So I'm not getting my hopes up or anything here. But if I could, I'd rent the empty space next door, knock down this wall," he waved toward the wall on Alli's right, "and expand the whole space. Bring in a deck oven, widen the galley, add another grill, maybe even some seating for the customers."

"Have you calculated the cost of that project?" asked Alli.

Mr. Wood scoffed.

"Way more than I can afford."

"Have you calculated the cost?"

Mr. Wood sighed.

"I don't need to calculate the cost." He said the last few words in a mocking tone, imitating Alli. "It's too much." He picked up Sarah's empty plate and carried both back toward the dish-washing room. "Even if it's a dollar," he called over his shoulder, "it's still too much."

"He's afraid of debt," said Sarah to Alli.

"So it seems."

"And he's afraid of losing this place." Sarah glanced all around at the space. "It means a lot to him."

Alli nodded. She could understand the weight of history that resided in these walls. It shouldn't impact business decisions, and it was totally emotional and had nothing to do with reality, but she could understand it. She wasn't completely unsentimental. While she would prefer to eradicate all memory of her own mother, let alone physical reminders of her existence, she could see how someone like Mr. Wood would want to preserve something his grandparents had started and his parents had continued. Something that had probably given him a lot of fond memories over the years.

"And I'm pretty sure he's afraid of numbers," said Sarah. "I don't think I've ever seen him use so much as a calculator, let alone keep a budget."

"Or use a computer."

Sarah laughed, a short, sharp rueful laugh that made Alli smile. "It's a miracle he even has a cell phone," she said. "The word 'technophobe' isn't strong enough to describe our Ollie over there."

Fear was one of the most dangerous emotions in the human experience. Fear could oppress an entire population or incite them to commit unimaginable atrocities against other humans. It could be bent toward anger or inaction with equal ease in the hands of a skilled manipulator.

And in an individual, it could keep them from taking even the smallest step toward a better business, a better job, a better life. Even when all the numbers added up, when the rewards far outweighed the risks, when there was no logical reason to hesitate, still fear could incapacitate someone and prevent them from making a decision, from taking action and moving in a positive direction.

Fear was a killer. A killer of dreams. A killer of men. A killer of progress.

The only other human emotion that even came close in terms of its dangerous impact was love. Just like fear, people would do unimaginable things for love.

And fear for someone or something you loved?

That was the most dangerous combination of all.

**8**

Ollie set the dishes in the sink with a clatter, the sound filling the tiny dishwashing room. The room was deep and narrow. It held little more than a deep metal sink at the end, a series of racks for drying pots and pans and dishes on one side, and shelves full of cleaning supplies on the other.

And beyond the cleaning supplies, on the other side of the wall, was the office.

The epicenter of all of his troubles.

Ollie knew what the woman had said was reasonable. If he wanted to expand, he should run the numbers. Find out the rent next door, estimate the build-out costs, look up the equipment costs. Then make some guesses about how much money they'd spend in supplies for making bread and the additional utilities costs. Figure out how much they'd save from that versus what they were paying now for deliveries. Then make some more guesses about how much more food they could make, how many more customers the could accommodate. How long it would take to pay back the loans.

Ollie shivered.

He didn't like thinking about money. And he liked thinking about debt even less.

But he wasn't an idiot. He knew he was being silly. His grand-mother had kept the books meticulously. His mother had kept them, too. There was no reason for him to be so afraid of the numbers behind his business. They were the lifeblood of the business, after all. If his food was the beating heart of the deli, money was the blood it pumped.

Ollie knew that, and he knew he was being a fool for not paying closer attention to it.

Or any attention at all.

But this was how his dad had handled things since at least when Ollie was old enough to notice. If it was good enough for his dad, and if it worked for his parents, who was Ollie to mess with it?

And who was this woman, Alli, to mess with it? Anger flared up in him again, but he took a deep breath to settle himself.

His anger should not be directed toward Alli. She was just doing her job.

Ollie's anger was really for his aunt and uncle. They'd lied to him for nine years, nine years when he'd visited their home, spent Thanksgivings and Christmases with them. Cooked for them. Talked with them, talked about the deli, about his parents, about his life. He'd even talking in very vague and general terms about his struggles with the business side of things.

And they'd never mentioned their ownership in the deli. Not once.

His uncle had offered to help out several times. That much was true. And Ollie had turned him down every time, thinking he was just being polite. Not wanting to take advantage of his uncle or force him to work when he didn't want to, out of obliga-tion toward his nephew.

And Ollie didn't want to dig into the details with his aunt and uncle, either, embarrassed by what they might find.

But even then, his aunt and uncle had kept their involve-ment a secret. Even with all of Ollie's excuses and deflections about the health of the business, they never let on that they knew the truth, that they could see everything for themselves.

Why? Why the hell would they have done that? It would have been better if Ollie had known, if he could have talked to them about it, gotten their advice on the best way to run the business.

But what would he have done if they had told him?

Honestly? He probably would have walked away, left the business in their hands so he could move on with his life.

He would have used them as an excuse to just let it all go, leave it in their hands. That way, if the business went down, it would be on them.

Would Ollie have been better off that way?

Ollie shook his head and flipped the handle on the faucet with a stab of his hand, rinsed down the plates.

He didn't know.

Or didn't want to know.

As usual, the Sunday rush was just as heavy as Saturday, and Ollie lost himself in the routine of preparation, service, and cleanup. First lunch, then dinner.

He was vaguely aware of the woman, Alli, coming in and out of the kitchen, fiddling with some of the wires and the ancient wi-fi router by the prep station. The thing had to have been ten years old if it was a day. His parents had gotten it just before the accident. Ollie remembered his dad being so excited to be able to walk around with his phone and not have to pay for the data usage. When Ollie's mom reminded him that they were still paying for the internet, Ollie's dad just waved her off, ignoring the comment.

Kind of like Ollie tried to ignore things.

At least he knew where the tendency came from.

The dinner rush had ended. Ollie and Sarah cleaned up in back while Tom emptied the cash register, counted the take, and put all the cash in a thin, scuffed, rectangular leather bank deposit bag, zipping it shut and leaving it on the front counter by the register for Ollie to deposit on the way home. Tom came back to help finish the cleanup, and Ollie saw Alli walk past him from the back with something shiny and white in her hand.

She walked to the front of house, where the cash register sat, but she was blocked by the wall. Ollie couldn't see what she was doing. She went back and forth between the office and the front counter several times, until Ollie's curiosity got the better of him.

"What are you doing, Alli?" he asked.

"Bringing your commerce system into the twenty-first century." She stopped halfway down the galley, between Ollie and Sarah, her head tilted in thought. "Actually, I had to bring it through the twentieth century to get there. I think Napoleon might have been the last person to use your old cash register."

Sarah snorted in laughter. Ollie shot her a look.

"What?" Sarah shrugged. "It was funny." She turned back to the counter and scrubbed at a stubborn spot of grease. "And true," she shot over her shoulder.

Ollie shook his head in frustration. This Alli woman had been there for three days and already she was changing everything, messing everything up.

"What do you mean my 'old cash register'?" said Ollie to Alli's back as she slipped behind the wall into the front of house again.

He heard a grunt and a clatter, and then he had his answer.

"I mean your old cash register," said Alli, her voice strained as she hauled the old register around the corner.

Her back was bent backwards, and the cash register rode on her chest. She looked like one of those Olympic dead-lifters if the weight were too much and their balance had gone too far backwards. Her knees were bent like she were sinking into the floor. They pointed forward while the rest of her sank behind. If she kept going that way, she'd fold up like a scissors jack.

But she was a stubborn one. And determined. She staggered forward, crab-walking under the awkward bulk of the machine, still trying to get to wherever she was going with it.

Ollie darted forward to help. Tom came around from the other side of the center station at the same time. Ollie got there first and lifted the register off of Alli's chest.

She was right. That old register was a relic. It may even have been one that Ollie's grandparents had bought before they died.

And it really did weigh a fucking ton. Ollie could barely hold it himself. He had no idea how Alli had even gone three steps with it. Tom gave Ollie a hand and together they hauled the register into the back hallway and set it on the table by the back door.

"Okay," said Ollie as they came back into the kitchen, "please tell me why we just took out a perfectly good cash register?"

Alli and Sarah were behind the wall, standing at the front counter. Alli called back over her shoulder, "There was nothing good about that register, let alone perfect."

Tom and Ollie rounded the corner and stood on the other side of the counter, as if they were customers.

"It worked just fine today," said Ollie, "and yesterday and every other day for the last nine years, and every day for..." He threw up his hands, guessing at a number. "...thirty years before that." How old was that register, anyway?

He looked down at the counter and saw what looked like a white tablet computer with a smaller tablet in front of it. Both were sitting on a white metal box. The whole unit was a third of the size of the cash register, if that.

The front tablet, facing Ollie, had a slit along the bottom, a slot just above that, and an icon at the top, above the wide, crystal clear touchscreen. A solid green light at the top stared up at him. It was a friendly green color, probably carefully chosen by some Silicon Valley wonk to engender feelings of happiness and accomplishment in Ollie when he spent his money. A little dopamine hit that would encourage him to spend, spend, spend all the time.

He'd seen these rigs in shops all over the place. Wireless payment terminals that made it so easy to spend money that you didn't even know you were doing it. They were slick and beautiful and made life so easy for everyone.

He hated them.

He'd rather have one of those old-fashioned registers any day. Forget the plastic-coated thing sitting by the back door. If Ollie had his way, he'd use one of those towering, ornate nickel-and-bronze machines from the early nineteen hundreds, the kind you see in movies where the man behind the counter pushes hard on the metal levers with the little round tabs at the end, selling chocolate bars for two pennies to some little kid way down below him on the other side of the counter. The register dings and a little flag comes up in the window and the drawer rattles open, then makes that rush-and-snap sound when the man pushes it shut again with a thrust of his hips.

You could trust those registers. If something went wrong, you could open it up and fix it, most of the time with just your fingers. Otherwise, a simple screwdriver and a pair of pliers would get it done. With these high-tech things, you had to sit on the phone for two hours waiting for some low-wage tech support rep in India or Cambodia to read a script to you while your customers sat there waiting to pay for their food.

"Your old register, a," Alli held up one finger toward Ollie, "didn't interface with your accounting system, so all transactions had to be manually recorded, which is prone to error. Granted," she added drily, "you didn't have an accounting system, so you had much bigger problems, but I digress." She held up another finger. "And b, it forced your customers to pay with cash, which required appropriate signage out front, a certain amount of either customer dissatisfaction, when they didn't have cash and couldn't get their food, or product shrinkage, if you gave it to them for free because you felt bad." She held up a third finger. "And c, discouraged customers who might have been hungry, might have wanted to try this great deli they'd been hearing about, but didn't have any cash on them. *Never* had any cash on them, because, really Mr. Wood, who carries cash anymore?"

"And the buttons would stick," said Sarah.

"And that one button was broken," added Tom.

"Oh yeah, the double zero one?"

Tom nodded.

"That's right. I had to push the single zero twice every time." Sarah shook her head. "What a pain in the ass."

"And d," Alli held up a fourth finger, "there was no way for you to easily change your menu or your prices and still be able to keep track in an automated way."

She paused.

"I could keep going, if you like," she said, "but at some point I'll need to remove my shoes and socks to keep counting."

Sarah snorted.

Ollie glared at her.

She shrugged. "It was funny," she said, and gave Ollie a wicked grin.

Ollie pulled in a deep breath, as if reeling back in all of his anger, all of his resistance, all of his yearning for simpler times, simpler methods of living, then sighed, a quick, heavy exhale.

"How does this fucking thing work?" he said.

**9**

ALLI WAS PLEASED with the new setup. The point-of-sale register was working seamlessly, recording transactions in real time in her accounting software, including total amount, merchant fees, and even customer information, when it was available. All flowing over the Wi-Fi to Alli's computer in the back office.

Mr. Wood had cleared out the shelf beneath the front counter and set the cash box there. The resulting setup was clean, modern, and convenient.

That day, when customers had first come in for lunch service, Alli had hung around in the corner for a while, watching how Sarah and Mr. Wood used the new terminal and listening for feedback from the customers. Mr. Wood struggled with the terminal at first, but Sarah had immediately understood how it worked and she helped him get up to speed.

And the customers, every single one of them that Alli saw, loved it. Each of the first twenty customers commented on the new system and said something to the effect of "thank goodness I don't have to carry cash around anymore. This was the only place I ever had to use it."

Alli was sure there would be some customers who still used

cash, still preferred it. Older customers, especially, or customers whose work was mostly cash-based. Service providers, restaurant servers, anyone who worked in a gratuity-based line of work.

But as she ran a quick report in the back office to aggregate the data after the lunch service had ended, she could see on her screen that, despite the Ollie Wood Deli having been a cash-only business for eighty years, ninety-nine percent of the customers that day had paid in a non-cash way.

And now, Alli could finally get a clean read on the cash flow for the business.

She leaned back in her chair and went through her mental checklist.

Digitize the historical records. That was done.

Automate the bookkeeping system. Also done.

Modernize the POS system. Done.

Normally, she didn't have to do any of these things. With all of the other businesses she'd worked with in the past, all of those systems had been in place. She'd swapped the software or tweaked some of the hardware here and there. But most of her job in the past had been to untangle the mess of tracking and reporting that these businesses fell into. They were often under-staffed and usually didn't understand their own technology well enough to plan a system that would work on its own without their intervention. Their systems always required some manual input.

Alli would simply build a more efficient system for them. She'd update their inventory management and show the business owners how to maintain it in the future. She'd build out their reporting suite so it automatically output reports the business owners had been building manually. This made tax season simpler for them, but it also allowed the business owners to keep better tabs on the health of their business, since there wasn't so much effort required to see the data.

Alli would teach them how to use the reports. She would teach them what to look for, what metrics and ratios to watch. Quick ratio for liquidity. Receivable days for asset management. Return on sales for profitability. She'd show them the connections between their income statement, their balance sheet, and their cash flow statement. These were all very basic business tools and concepts, but hardly any of the business owners Alli worked with knew what they were or how to use them.

Alli was not surprised, of course. Analysis required thought, and most people avoided thought like they avoided their dentist. They would do it once or twice a year, if they were told to, but otherwise they tried to forget all about it.

So, Alli would try to make things even simpler for them. She would set up automated alerts for various criteria. Unusually large deposits or withdrawals. Transactions from unusual sources or at unusual intervals. Triggers when certain ratios or metrics went above or fell below certain levels.

Most businesses, once established, didn't really change much. The amount of money coming in and going out might fluctuate, especially if the business was seasonal or demand-based. But the players usually stayed the same. The same suppliers month to month. The same types of customers. Alli could program alerts that would monitor all of these parameters and alert the business managers whenever something unusual occurred. She would include links in the alert itself that brought the manager back to the correct report that would explain the reason for the alert and show them all the data they needed to correct it.

All of this work was trivially easy for Alli. She had already written most of the code she used and just needed tweak it slightly to suit the specific business. And she automated everything as much as possible, knowing that most business owners couldn't be bothered to learn the technical aspects of the system, even if it was critical to their own business.

It usually took Alli one or two days to set everything up and a third day for testing. Then she would show the business owners what she'd done and start teaching them how to use the system.

After two or three days of teaching, most of those business owners just wanted Alli to hang around and do the work for them. They stopped listening to her explanations of the system and started asking for the analysis, for the output.

In other words, they didn't want to learn anything. They just wanted Alli to tell them what to do.

Once that happened, it was usually only a day or two before Alli got switched to another job. Customers didn't seem to like the way Alli responded to their infantile need to be cared for, to be coddled.

She never lost her temper. She'd never yelled at a client, never insulted them anywhere but in her own mind.

But she refused to spoon-feed them. These were adults running a business. They should grow up and learn how to do their jobs well. If they refused to do that, Alli couldn't help them.

No. She could help them.

She just wouldn't help them.

But the Ollie Wood Deli had been in unusually bad shape. It hadn't even had the basics in place. No POS system, no database, not even a computer.

Alli had changed all of that. It had taken six days just to get everything set up and working properly and tested to Alli's satisfaction. Sarah and Tom loved the new system, since they didn't have to handle grubby cash all day or battle the irascible old cash register any more. Even Mr. Wood was grudgingly acknowledging that the customers seemed to love it. He finally admitted that it was a lot easier to use than the old system, even if it did take a while for him to figure it out.

Alli had shown him how to use the backend systems, but she

was sure to show Sarah and Tom, as well. She didn't know what Mr. Wood's level of technical proficiency actually was, but Sarah's use of the word 'technophobe' didn't bode well for his ability to maintain the system once Alli was gone.

To his credit, though, Mr. Wood showed a keen interest in learning everything Alli was doing. He never asked her about the numbers or what she was seeing with the business, but he was very curious about all of the hardware. He wanted to make sure he understood as much as he could about how things were set up, physically.

In fact, he was a very physical-minded man, in general, Alli had decided. He spent more time considering the world around him, things he could see and touch and feel, than he did on the world inside him, thoughts and ideas and concepts.

Alli would normally dismiss him as simply a typical person, content to sleepwalk through life, taking orders from other sleepwalkers, who took orders from still other sleepwalkers. Ultimately, at the very top of the chain, there were original thinkers, people with ideas and energy and deep curiosity about the world. But they were very few and very far between.

Mr. Wood was not one of those rare individuals, but he didn't strike Alli as a sleepwalker, either. His genius with food was incontestable, as least as far as Alli could tell from her own taste buds—not a reliable source—and Sarah's deference—a far more reliable source. And he had plenty of ideas and curiosity about things related to his food.

And his customers. He really seemed to love his customers.

Alli was impressed by his patience. She couldn't stand individual people, let alone a crowd of them, let alone a crowd that appeared twice a day, every day of the week. Sarah and Tom had staggered schedules that gave them each some time off every week on the slower days.

But Mr. Wood was there every single day.

And Alli figured it was that burden that was holding him back. He seemed to take his responsibility to the deli very seriously. Far more seriously than it warranted, in Alli's opinion. She only had a few days' worth of accurate numbers, but she could already tell the business was bleeding cash. In the absence of investment capital, the prudent thing to do would be to shut the deli down before Mr. Wood wound up so deep in debt he would need to sell his personal assets to escape.

But she didn't even have to raise the question to know what his answer would be. She'd only known him for a few days, but she already knew he would never close the deli voluntarily.

And so it was Alli's job to see to it that he wouldn't have to.

That sentiment was new to Alli. She'd never taken her own job so seriously before. Once the systems were set up and running, Alli had never cared if the business owners learned it, used it, or just fell back into their old sleepwalker habits of pretending the world should conform to their wishes just because they visualized success while lying in bed each morning and each night.

But there was something about the Ollie Wood Deli that made her care. Not a lot, but enough for her to want to see things through, to find a path to profitability.

Mr. Wood had the talent, and his business had the potential. If Alli could just pinpoint some of the problems and correct them, she felt confident she could turn the business around.

And, now that she had her systems in place, the first place to start looking was on the supply side.

Alli needed to figure out why the hell Mr. Wood's suppliers had access to his business accounts and correct that issue immediately.

∼

She was still in the office when Mr. Wood came in with a sandwich for her after the dinner rush had gone and Sarah and Tom had left, calling out their goodbyes to Alli as they headed out the front door. Alli accepted the sandwich gratefully, and her stomach said the same.

She hadn't eaten since Mr. Wood had made her breakfast. Without asking, she'd been added to the morning ritual. When she came in each morning, there were two portions of breakfast ready, one for Sarah, one for her.

At first, she'd objected, but received only a stony stare from Mr. Wood in response.

"He's going to feed you whether you want it or not," chuckled Sarah, seated beside Alli, as Mr. Wood walked into the cooler in the back to get something in preparation for that day's lunch service. "It's his thing. And if you're eating what he considers to be sub-par food, he'll feed you for that, too."

"Why? What's wrong with eating fast food? The nutrients are the same, no matter where they come from."

"Is that what you eat?" Sarah scanned Alli from head to toe. "You stay that skinny on a fast food diet?" She shook her head. "Shit, if I ate fast food all day, I'd be the size of a truck and I'd have a face that looked like a yard full of gophers. Not thin like you, with your shiny cover model skin." She turned back to her breakfast. "You must have some good genes in your family."

Alli snorted. "You've obviously never met my mother."

She'd worked out a deal with Sarah to alternate coffee pick-ups. The coffee shop was out of Alli's way, but she didn't like the idea of taking something from Mr. Wood without giving anything in return. She didn't want to be beholden to anyone for anything.

But she was starving that night, so she didn't even think twice about taking the brisket and coleslaw and cornbread Mr. Wood held out to her.

"How goes the battle?" he asked, leaning against the doorjamb. "You solved all the world's problems yet?"

Alli had immediately stuffed her face with large forkfuls of brisket and coleslaw, and a bite of cornbread. She held up one finger to Mr. Wood while she finished chewing, her cheeks rounded out like a squirrel in autumn.

Her mother would be aghast.

"Mr. Wood," she said, then swallowed the last bit of her mouthful, "do you realize that several of your suppliers have direct access to your business accounts and are making withdrawals on a regular basis?"

"Mr. Wood?" he said.

He smiled that comforting smile again, and Alli's shoulders relaxed. She hadn't realized how tense she'd become while sitting at the computer reviewing the numbers.

"We've been working side by side for a week now. I think we know each other well enough for you to call me Ollie."

Alli looked at him. His arms were folded across his chest, accentuating the curve of his sizable biceps. They pushed the edges of his t-shirt sleeves far up to his shoulder joint.

For such a lean man, he did seem to have strong arms. Both his biceps and his forearms were noticeably muscular, with large veins standing out in long ropes along their length. He did not seem the type to frequent a gym, nor did he have the time, so Alli assumed his bicep strength came from lifting meat and boxes of vegetables and such, and his forearm strength undoubtedly came from constantly chopping things.

Alli had never really noticed his arms before, but here, late at night, when she was tired and hungry and he was standing there in the doorway, staring at her with that crooked smile on his face, suddenly both calming and maddening all at once, and curiosity in those orange-flecked eyes, she noticed them.

She noticed his muscular arms, his muscular chest, his flat stomach. She noticed his hair, long and tousled, like he had been too distracted all day to worry about how it looked. She noticed the stubble shading his sharp cheekbones and covering his full chin. She noticed his wide mouth, his full, pink lips.

Lips that were twisting upward into a smile at the corners.

"You okay, Alli?"

Alli shook her head, pulling herself back to her senses.

"You spaced out on me for a second there."

Alli closed her eyes and took a deep breath. She checked her watch. Nine PM.

"Sorry," she said. "It's getting late and I haven't eaten."

She took another bite of food, as much to buy silence as to gain nutrients. She was not the type to space out. Not in that kind of scenario, at least. When she was bored, dealing with a prattling client or listening to yet another lecture from Mort, sure. She would space out then and let her mind wander back to whatever theoretical problem she was considering at the moment.

But that was not the case here. Her mind was fully focused on the problem at hand, on the supply problem at Ollie Wood Deli. There was no reason for her to lose focus.

And her mind hadn't wandered to considerations of ten-dimensional space. She had been thinking about how Ollie looked in his t-shirt. For the love of God, those were the pointless musings of the uneducated and uninspired. It was the stuff of sleepwalkers.

It was not like her.

She swallowed her mouthful of food. "You didn't answer my question."

He stared at her for a long moment, then furrowed his brow and shook his head.

"Sorry, what was the question again?"

Not for the first time, Alli wondered if his avoidance of all things analytical was merely a typical aversion to math or something more pathological.

"Your suppliers," she said. "Several of them are making regular withdrawals directly from your account, as if they have direct access." She clicked a few buttons on her screen. "Daisy Bread Company and Drayger's Meats make multiple withdrawals each week." She clicked a few more buttons. "Then there's Maxwell Restaurant Supply, which seems to be making monthly withdrawals."

"Right, sure. That's for napkins and forks, that kind of thing. And the others are our meat and bread vendors. They make deliveries all the time."

"And that's understandable for a business of this nature, Mr. Wood."

"Ollie."

Alli smiled curtly.

"Ollie."

The name sounded odd, almost musical, in her ears. And the roundness of her lips, the flick of her tongue as she said it out loud felt odd, too. Almost like she'd been saying it for years, even though Mr. Wood was the first person named Ollie that she'd ever met.

"But it's highly unusual," she continued, "for a supplier—or anyone, for that matter—to have direct access to the accounts of a business they don't own or control."

Ollie shifted his weight to his other foot. "I mean, it's just autopay, right? People use it all the time."

Alli shook her head. "Autopay is one thing. It's prior consent to issue a charge against your account on a set schedule in a specified amount or percentage of funds outstanding. It's not the same as direct access. Autopay arrangements don't give your creditors direct access to your account."

Ollie shifted his weight back again and rubbed his hands along his muscular biceps. "How do you know they have direct access?"

"I can see from your bank statements." She clicked to a new

screen on her monitor and pointed toward it. Ollie came closer and leaned over her shoulder to see.

A tingle ran along Alli's neck as he stood behind her. She could feel him, could feel his warmth.

And she could smell him. She expected him to smell like food, like meat or onions or something. But instead he smelled like cedar and moss, mixed with black cherry.

She swallowed hard and continued. "You can see from these codes here," she pointed at the screen, "that these are withdrawals, as opposed to charges billed against the account. That means someone at these suppliers has permission to make direct withdrawals from your account."

Ollie stood straight again, and the warmth Alli had felt was replaced by a flush of cold air and an odd feeling of disappointment.

Alli took another bite of brisket. Clearly, her brain needed more glucose. It wasn't functioning properly.

"I do have a running tab with each of those companies," said Ollie. "When they make a delivery, they always ask if I want to just add it to the account." He shrugged. "That's how it's always been since I took over the place. That's how my parents did it, so I just kept it going."

Alli nodded slowly.

Despite decades of research, the human brain was a mystery that had not yet yielded its secrets to modern science. But it was a familiar playground for Alli, and she'd become accustomed to the vagaries and mysterious machinations of her own mind. When she was studying a new subject or pursuing a new hypothesis, she often felt like she was searching in the fog at night with a weak flashlight, sensing things still unseen in the murky darkness around her, waiting for them to connect and flood the darkness with understanding.

She felt that way now. There was some kind of connection here, some relationship between the bits of information Alli had taken in over the last week. She didn't know quite what it was yet, but she would find it. She knew her own mind, and she knew that she would make that connection, eventually.

What that connection would be, and what it would mean for Ollie Wood Deli, was a mystery yet to be solved.

108

**10**

Leaning against the door jamb, Ollie's mind drifted as he looked at Alli.

Her hair pooled at the base of her neck as she sat at the computer. It gathered and spilled over, like a waterfall cascading into a pool at her shoulder, then running down an outlet over her back and the swell of her chest.

He swallowed hard and stopped his mind before it got too far in thinking about the swell of her chest. He shook his head to clear it.

"Sorry, what was the question again?" he asked, feeling like a fool.

Of course, that was a common feeling when he was around Alli.

Alli.

He'd had trouble remembering her name in the beginning. And he hadn't wanted to use it, too angry at her presence to even bother.

But over the last week, she'd shown that she wasn't just some heartless bean counter looking to pinch pennies wherever she could. She seemed to honestly care about Ollie's business. She was even pushing Ollie to think harder about his dreams for expanding it.

She sounded just like Sarah when she did that.

In fact, she and Sarah were a lot alike. Both sharp as a knife. Neither one took any bullshit from anyone. And both were always interested in something, always thinking about something interesting.

"Your suppliers," said Alli.

She showed him something on the computer, but Ollie had trouble focusing. He'd leaned over the back of her to see the monitor better, but it also let him see that swell of her chest better, too.

He pulled his eyes back to the screen. He was not going to be that guy who would leer at a woman and find any excuse to look down her shirt.

But, it had just happened. When he'd leaned over her shoulder, his eyes had flicked downward, involuntarily, only for a moment.

But it was enough.

It was a very good moment.

Alli had worn a black business jacket over the top of a blue button-down shirt that day, tucked into a pair of jeans that hugged her body in all the ways that Ollie wished he could hug her himself. And she'd left the top two or three buttons open, leaving her neck and the top of her chest bare for Ollie's imagination to run wild on.

Honestly, he needed to get laid. It had been a long, long time. Years and years. Almost as long as he'd been running the deli. So long that Sarah had stopped saying, "You need to get laid, Ollie."

He just didn't have time to date women. The deli was his lover, his girlfriend, his wife.

That was so sad.

He hadn't thought about it much, but ever since Alli showed

up, he'd been feeling horny as hell. I guess spending all of your time with a dude and a lesbian didn't really get your mind thinking about sex too much. But now that Alli was coming around every day, that's where Ollie found his head going more often than he would have liked.

He had no idea if she was interested in him.

Probably not.

Almost definitely not.

She was too smart, too focused to waste time with a fucking deli owner.

And for all Ollie knew, she was more Sarah's type than his.

But that didn't stop his mind from wandering where it shouldn't.

Like it had in that moment, when he leaned over Alli's shoulder in front of the computer.

And like every other moment, Ollie just clenched his jaw, ground his teeth, and pulled his mind back out of the gutter.

But he didn't like the sound of where his mind had wound up once he hauled it out of there.

Alli had been talking about bank accounts and direct access. Like he'd told her, Ollie had inherited his suppliers and their financial arrangements. At the time, he'd been so overwhelmed with his parents' accident, the funeral arrangements, and taking over the deli that he'd grasped at any lifelines he could find. Not having to source his meat and bread and kitchen supplies was a blessing.

But now Alli was telling him there was something wrong with the way he was paying for that blessing.

Ollie had no idea why it was a problem. All the people he'd dealt with at those suppliers were good people, honest people. The owners of the companies had even come to his parents' funeral and paid their respects, shook Ollie's hand in the receiving line at the wake and looked him in the eye, told him how sorry they were. And he believed them. They seemed to really mean it.

So what if they were drawing directly from his bank account? Ollie would just be auto-paying them, anyway. And he trusted them to only take what they were owed, so what did it matter?

But, Alli seemed really bothered by it. And Ollie trusted her to do what was right for the deli.

Maybe that was the real problem.

Ollie trusted Alli completely after knowing her for only a week.

That was not unusual for him. His default was to trust people until they proved they couldn't be trusted. Maybe Ollie was just a naive idiot, an easy mark for people to take advantage.

Maybe he needed to pull his head out of his ass and finally start acting like an adult.

Like a business owner.

He had a good teacher now.

He had a feeling Alli would be a hard-ass as a teacher, though.

Hardass.

And that was all it took to send his mind back into the gutter.

**11**

THE NEXT MORNING, after eating some kind of fish Ollie had cooked for breakfast—something Alli definitely would not have chosen to eat that early in the morning, but which turned out to be delicious and light and not at all fishy—Alli checked off the completed items from her to-do list and added the next batch of tasks.

**To-do list:**

- Daisy Bread Company
- Drayger's Meats
- Maxwell Restaurant Supply

"You keep a list of things you need to do?" asked Ollie as he cleared Alli's dishes from the counter.

"Of course," Alli replied. "You don't?"

"I don't need a to-do list."

"That explains the state of your office when I arrived."

Alli set off from the deli toward the first address in her phone.

The bread company was her first stop, the closest of the three suspect accounts she had found in the ledger.

The Daisy Bread Company was located only a few miles west of the deli, a short ten-minute ride through the cold morning air. The sun was barely peeking over the horizon, and Alli's wiper blades scraped and stuttered over the frost still stuck to her windshield. She should have scraped it off before she left, but had chosen instead to let her antifreeze washer fluid work its chemical magic. That, plus the friction of the blades and the slowly increasing warmth from the rising sun would clear her windshield soon enough.

Until then, though, she was forced to drive while leaning forward in her seat, peering through a small hole in the frost layer. Fortunately, it was still early enough that traffic was light. And she was headed away from the city, toward an industrial part of town, so most of what traffic existed was headed into town in the opposite direction.

Squatting on the corner at an intersection of two sleepy streets, the Daisy Bread Company building was a one-story rectangle with cinder block walls painted a bland beige color. The color of bread dough, Alli realized. The Daisy Bread Company name and logo were painted in blue on the two walls that bordered the streets.

The building itself was surprisingly small. For some reason, Alli had expected an operation that would fill an entire block, maybe an entire square block. But the building itself was a fraction of that size, bordered on one side by a manufacturer of telephone headsets and on the other by a building subdivided into warehouses for lease. One contained a bicycle repair operation, another some kind of custom machining shop. Two other spaces were empty.

The parking lot out front was small, but it was full. Bakeries are early-morning ventures, Alli remembered. At eight AM, she was practically catching the swing shift.

She parked on the street and knocked on what appeared to be the front door of the building. The main entrance, if it had one, was not clearly marked, and the only door she could find facing the street was made from windowless metal and painted the same bland bread-dough color as the rest of the building.

Not unusual for an industrial operation with no customer-facing component, Alli supposed. From what she had gleaned from their ancient website, the Daisy Bread Company was a B2B operation, dealing solely with businesses like Ollie Wood Deli that used their product to create other products for sale. The Daisy Bread Company did not sell directly to consumers, so they had little use for a sales floor or a lobby. That space was better utilized for bread-making equipment or management offices.

Alli waited in the cold air, holding her arms close over her chest for warmth. When her knock was not answered after a few minutes, she knocked again, louder. After a few more minutes, she pounded on the door with the side of her fist.

B2B or not, it was unprofessional for the Daisy Bread Company to have no way to accommodate visitors to their head-quarters. Alli was beginning to wonder if she would be spending all day dealing with idiots.

She snorted, her breath steaming in the morning air.

Of course she would. She spent all day every day dealing with idiots.

Although not at Ollie Wood Deli. None of them were idiots. Not geniuses, perhaps. There were no Ada Lovelaces or Richard Feynmans preparing brisket sandwiches every day. But definitely not idiots.

In just a week, Alli had become spoiled by association with a higher grade of human.

Finally, she heard the staccato beat of hard bootsteps against cement growing louder on the other side of the door. Alli stepped back as the door swung outward. A man leaned out toward her, his hand still holding the door handle.

He was tall and thin and wore a white apron. His long hair was tied back and covered with a paper bonnet, and his face was obscured by clear plastic protective eyewear and a paper face mask. Noise-dampening headphones curled around his neck.

"Can I help you?" he asked in a tired tone that suggested that he had little interest in helping Alli at all.

"I'm looking for your finance department, please. Accounts receivable."

"A count of what?"

Definitely going to be an idiot day.

"Accounts recei—" Alli took a deep breath and did her best to smile. "Is your manager available?"

The man closed the door in Alli's face. She heard him yell for someone on the other side of the door.

And then she waited. More interminable minutes. The sun finally rose high enough to share some of its warmth with Alli, a ray or two falling on her back. She immediately relaxed into it, not realizing how much her muscles had been tensing against the cold.

Alli was about to pound on the door again when it opened. This time, a much older man answered, a short, round man with salt-and-pepper hair and thick-framed glasses. Though his receded hair was cut short against the sides of his head, he also wore a paper bonnet, but no face mask. Alli could see his bushy mustache and his friendly smile.

He threw the door wide, letting it clatter against the outside of the building, and filled the doorway with his prodigious girth.

"I didn't ask for delivery of a beautiful woman this morning, but who am I to complain?"

He bellowed a loud guffaw that rattled the metal door and seemed to reverberate through the cinder block walls and concrete floor.

"What can I do for you, dear?" he said, once his unrequited laughter had finished.

Alli smiled weakly. She didn't think the man realized what a misogynistic buffoon that comment made him sound like. He probably thought he was being charming.

"My name is Alli Thomas."

"Nice to meet you, Alli," he said, holding out his hand. "I'm Bill Barker."

Alli considered the outstretched hand for a brief moment before shaking it. It was as ample as the man himself, the skin dry and rough.

"Hello, Mr. Barker," Alli said curtly. "Are you the manager here?"

"Worse than that," Mr. Barker said, leaning toward Alli and winking conspiratorially. "I own the place."

His bellowing laughter again shook the walls, and Alli waited with as much patience as she could muster for him to stop.

"May I speak with someone in your finance department?" asked Alli in the sweetest voice she could muster. Probably just a shade sweeter than hydrochloric acid, but she was trying to learn from Mr. Wood.

Ollie.

A faint smile curled her mouth at the thought of his name.

"Accounts receivable, specifically," she said.

"You're looking at them," said the man with another guffaw.

The man used laughter in his speech like most people used periods in their writing. In the back of her mind, Alli wondered if anyone actually found the man funny. She supposed that, somewhere, there was a Mrs. Guffaw, probably equally rotund and jolly and clueless, baking cookies and pies all day, waiting in their kitsch-stuffed home for grandchildren to visit or Jehovah's Witnesses to knock on the door so she could invite them in for a sweet treat and a glass of warm milk.

Alli explained her situation as succinctly as she could,

repeating herself several times and enduring countless belly laughs until the man finally shook his head.

"I'm sorry, dear. I wish I could help, but we don't handle billing here anymore. We got bought out by a larger company, oh about fifteen years ago now."

He leaned in toward Alli. "Got a nice chunk of change for that one," he said.

If she'd been closer, Alli suspected he would have elbowed her in the side like old crew members from a gang of bank robbers. She was fairly sure he would have been the getaway driver. Or, more likely, Thug #3, standing in the back wearing a full ski mask, holding a shotgun with no bullets.

"Took the missus to Disney World that year." He leaned back and chortled softly, as if lost in a reverie of their time cavorting with Mickey and Minnie. "The big bosses handle all the money stuff now."

"Do you know where I can find them?" asked Alli. "The big bosses?"

"Sure, let me get you their address."

The man invited her inside, closed the door, and led her into a wide-open factory floor filled with enormous mixing machines, conveyor belts, ovens, pallets of flour and yeast in paper sacks, and a small army of people watching and checking and bagging and packing a variety of baked goods, from breads to rolls to sweet treats. The room smelled of fresh-baked bread, and it was warm and humid from the ovens, a sharp contrast to the cold air outside. The sound from the machines was deafening. Alli understood why the first person who'd opened the door had carried ear protection, and why no one had heard her knock.

They walked along the edge of the room to a short hallway that was home to several offices. The man brought her into one of them and shut the door, sealing out the noise remarkably well. He rummaged through the drawers of a desk that was surprisingly tidy.

She noticed a stack of papers on one corner.

"Is this a price sheet?"

The man glanced at the stack and nodded.

"Do you mind if I take one?"

"Knock yourself out," he said, then handed her a business card. The name on the card was Thomas Murkin, Controller at a company called Petterson Holdings, LLC.

"This is the entity that purchased your company?"

"Them's the ones. The big bosses now."

Alli thanked him and made her way as quickly as she could back through the deafening work floor and through a sea of guffaws that followed her all the way into the outside air. For a moment, she was afraid the man would walk her to her car, but he just waved goodbye. The metal door swung shut behind her and she was left alone in the warming air and the blissful silence.

First stop done. On to the next.

**12**

OLLIE'S DAY was as busy as ever. Maybe even busier than usual, for a weekday.

Ollie did what he always did, what he'd done every day for nine years: prep the food, make the food, serve the food, clean up after the food.

He had always enjoyed the process. Sure, it wasn't cutting edge cuisine, but it was satisfying work. Ollie enjoyed making his customers happy.

And yet, somehow, the work seemed a little bit empty that day.

Even though there were more customers than usual, and they all seemed happy.

Even though the whole operation ran easier and smoother than it ever had, thanks to the new cash register. Or "POS system", it was called. Ollie had no idea the old register had been holding things back so much.

In fact, they were so busy that day that Ollie feared they might sell through the brisket he'd prepped for lunch service. Ollie, Sarah, and Tom were running around like crazy trying to keep up with the unexpected rush.

There was no reason at all for the day to feel so empty.

Ollie should have been ecstatic with the increased business. He should have been completely absorbed with the work.

And yet, he kept eyeing the door. Kept eyeing the clock. Watching and waiting.

He finally realized what he was watching and waiting for.

But he didn't realize it until she walked in the door just before the dinner service began.

"Hungry?" he asked Alli as she passed him in the kitchen and nodding a greeting to him.

"No, thank you," she said over her shoulder. She sounded distracted, maybe even bothered. Ollie wiped up his station and carried the pan with the brisket he'd been marinating into the cooler, then leaned against the doorway to the office.

"What's up?" he said. "You okay?"

Alli didn't answer him, just typed away at her computer.

Ollie had noticed her tendency to do that. She wasn't big on small talk. Wasn't big on pleasantries. At first, he'd been offended, thought she was rude. But as he'd gotten to know her better, he realized that she just didn't seem to notice any question or comment that didn't have any clear reason, that didn't relate to any real problem she was working to solve.

All those things people say just to fill the silence, just to hear something, anything. Someone talking. Someone making a noise. Something to reassure them that they were not alone.

Alli didn't need any of that.

Ollie was pretty sure Alli would be totally fine if she were completely alone.

She might even prefer it.

Even though she was personable enough when you talked to her, Ollie didn't get the feeling that Alli was what you would call a "people person". Ollie was a people person. Ollie's dad had been a people person.

His mom, not so much.

Alli, not at all.

"How'd it go with the suppliers?" he asked, stepping into the room and standing behind her chair to see what she was bringing up on the monitor. More bank statements or ledger entries or something. Numbers, numbers, numbers.

Ollie was getting used to the accounting stuff. Slowly. It still freaked him out completely, but he felt safer with Alli there. He trusted her to explain things to him and to figure out anything that was truly awful.

He trusted her. With his business.

Ollie had only known the woman for a week, and already he was trusting her with the most important thing in his life.

Alli tapped a few more keys on her keyboard, pulled up a few more screens, then sat back in her chair, nodding to herself.

She turned in the chair to face Ollie. The way she looked up at him, the way her brow dipped down toward her nose, the way her deep brown eyes flashed with intensity and passion, took Ollie's breath away. His heart raced, pulsing in his neck, his chest tightening just for a moment before he remembered to breathe again.

Alli didn't seem to notice.

"We may have a problem," she said.

Ollie listened to what Alli said, nodded as she explained all that she'd done and all that she'd learned that day.

But he didn't see what the problem was.

"So, all of our suppliers are owned by the same company?"

"That's correct."

"This Petterson place?"

"Petterson Holdings, LLC," Alli nodded.

Ollie folded his arms over his chest and pinched his chin

between his thumb and forefinger. He turned these facts over in his mind, looking for whatever it was that Alli had seen.

He didn't want her to think he was stupid. He didn't want to slow her down or hold her back. He wanted to help her, but he just couldn't think as fast as she did. He didn't know as much about business or numbers.

"Okay," he said, finally, giving up. "But what's the problem with that? I see headlines about companies buying smaller companies. Seems like it happens all the time."

"Corporate acquisitions are very common," said Alli. "But in this case, what worries me is that the companies owned by Petterson Holdings are the companies with direct access to your business accounts. No other suppliers have that access, despite the fact that they pre-date your involvement in the business."

"So?"

Alli sighed with what seemed to Ollie like barely restrained exasperation. A tingling feeling swept back from his nose into his eyes and across his cheeks. He felt sweaty and hot.

"So," Alli said, her voice smooth and quiet as if she weren't annoyed at all, even though Ollie felt sure she was, "if your parents were using direct access as a way to simplify their accounts payable process—which would have been incredibly foolish, but certainly simpler—I assume they would have used that approach with all of their suppliers. Or most of them, at least."

"Right." That made sense. If the process made their lives easier, why not set it up with everyone? "So, the fact that they only did it with these three means they weren't doing it for convenience."

Alli nodded.

"Then why were they doing it?"

Alli stared hard at him, the intensity in those brown eyes pulling him in. He felt like he was falling forward, like if he wasn't careful, if he didn't break that gaze, he'd fall flat on his nose on the office floor.

Or fall into Alli's arms.

"That," said Alli, her eyes flashing with determination, "is what I intend to find out."

# 13

ALLI HAD no idea why Ollie was acting so weird that evening. He kept staring at her in a way that made Alli feel very uncomfortable. Not in a bad way, but in a way she'd never felt before, a way she didn't understand and, therefore, didn't enjoy.

She focused on the question at hand, both to distract herself from those strange feelings and because the conundrum was really starting to irritate her.

Alli had no idea why those three suppliers had direct access to the accounts of Ollie Wood Deli. Maybe it was a demand from the holding company. Maybe Petterson was a private equity firm that had seen an opportunity in the local restaurant supply market, had purchased several smaller supply businesses as a way to quickly enter the space, and had imposed this payment requirement on all existing clients of those businesses.

If that were true, it would have been a completely bone-headed move by Petterson. No small business owner in their right mind would grant a supplier direct access to their accounts, no matter how critical those supplies may have been to their business.

Alli wasn't even sure that kind of payment arrangement was

legal. It seemed like it would violate some kind of statutory definition of separate entities, would create some kind of legal or tax complications. It made it seem like the holding company owned their own customers. That was the kind of thing an amateur money launderer would try, not something a legitimate investor would do.

She needed to learn more about Petterson Holdings.

She figured she might as well start with the business cards on her desk. She had three copies now, one taken from each of the three businesses she'd visited that day. The Daisy Bread Company, Drayger's Meats, and Maxwell Restaurant Supply had each given her the same story. Each had been purchased by Petterson Holdings about fifteen years ago. And they had each given her the same business card.

Thomas Murkin, Controller.

Alli glanced at the time on her computer monitor. Too late to call Mr. Murkin today, but that would be the first order of business in the morning.

In the meantime, she searched the internet for Petterson Holdings and found an innocuous website extolling the virtues of "a private equity firm interested in preserving the character of the local community by supporting its homegrown businesses and improving the quality of life for all of its residents". The firm was mission-driven, the website claimed, founded and funded by local businessmen looking to give back to the community they'd lived in their whole lives.

Angels, they were, according to their own website. Motivated purely by altruism and generosity of spirit.

Which, to Alli, meant they were definitely up to no good.

The only question was, were they up to the typical no-good that most capitalistic private equity firms pursued? That is, buying businesses, stripping their cost structures ruthlessly, then reselling them for a profit? Or were they up to something else altogether?

If they'd bought Ollie's suppliers more than a decade ago and still owned them, they were stripping and selling.

So what were they doing?

Alli scrolled through their list of investments. They were widely varied. Not just the three businesses she'd visited, but also local companies dealing with metal manufacturing, machining, auto repair, even a small credit union and a local internet company. Their investments showed no pattern beyond the fact that all of them were local.

Alli sat back in her chair. She stared at her screen, but her eyes were unfocused. They were looking inside, at her mind.

Petterson Holdings and the direct access issue.

Something here nagged at her.

The other thing that nagged at her was the sale of the building years ago.

If Ollie's parents had needed money for a remodel, there were so many other ways they could have gotten it without giving up such a valuable asset. They could have increased rents on their tenants or borrowed against the equity in the building.

Selling the building outright was drastic, the kind of last-ditch thing you would only do if you were desperate and had no other choice.

Alli couldn't see any connection between these two nagging mysteries, beyond the fact that they were both mysteries. But she trusted her mind, and her mind kept bringing them both up. Kept bubbling them both into her consciousness.

So Alli would do what she always did: follow the path her mind laid out for her and see where it led.

She turned in her chair at a knock on the door.

Ollie leaned against the doorjamb again, two plates in his hands. His lean, muscular frame. His tousled hair. A brilliance in his unusual eyes that seemed to glow in the dim office light.

"It's late," he said.

Alli glanced at the time. Hours had passed since she'd last looked at it. Seemed like just minutes.

Ollie held up the two plates.

"Can I take you out for dinner?"

**14**

OLLIE SAT across the front counter from Alli and watched her from the corner of his eye while she ate.

He didn't want to seem creepy by staring at her, but he couldn't seem to take his eyes off of her.

The only light came from a pendulum lamp overhead. It gave a shine to Alli's brown hair that looked like she wore a crown. She took a bite of the spaghetti and meatballs Ollie had prepared using beef brisket and pork he'd picked up at the market that morning. She sliced off a piece of meatball, then twirled some spaghetti on her fork, stabbed the piece of meatball like a cap over the twirled pasta, then swabbed it all through a pool of sauce before putting it in her mouth. Ollie smiled at the precision and logic of her process.

Ollie watched Alli's lips close over the spoon. Her soft, supple pink lips. He watched her shut her eyes as, slowly, she pulled the fork, gleaming and clean, out from between those lush lips. She moaned softly, and something deep within Ollie stirred.

"Good?" he asked, his voice a husky whisper.

"Oh my God," said Alli, her eyes flickering open, staring at Ollie.

There was pleasure in those eyes, and a kind of longing. Just for an instant.

Ollie held them, those boundless brown eyes, for as long as he could before his embarrassment overcame him and he looked away, down at his own plate.

"So good," she said. "Where did you learn to cook like this?"

Ollie shrugged.

"My parents taught me most of what I know," he said. "Right here." He gestured with his fork toward the deli around him. "I grew up in this deli."

He took a bite of his own pasta and chewed it thoughtfully. Alli just watched and waited.

She wasn't one to shy away from silence in a conversation.

"I went to culinary school in New York once I got out of high school, then worked in the city for a few years before taking this place over."

"Did they teach you in school how to experiment with flavors, or is that something you brought to it yourself?"

Ollie smiled, remembering the times he'd been chewed out by more than one instructor at culinary school for tampering with the recipes. Even the dean had had words with him at one point. She didn't discourage his experimentations, just impressed upon him the importance of mastering the stated curriculum if he wanted to graduate.

"I had one or two teachers who helped me understand how flavors work together. But I suppose I brought most of it myself." He shrugged again. "My parents and I liked to experiment a lot. Came up with a lot of terrible dishes," he grinned, "but came up with some delicious ones, too."

He took another bite. Alli just watched him in silence for a long moment, seeming to be lost in her own thoughts.

"What about you, Alli? Did you always want to be an accountant?"

Her eyebrows shot up.

"I still don't want to be an accountant," she said. "It's just a means to an end."

"Oh, really?"

"Why do you seem so surprised?"

"It's just that you're so good at it, that's all."

"Don't confuse ability with enjoyment."

Her eyes had dulled, her voice grew flat. Ollie felt an odd pang of loss and a sense of shame at having said or done something wrong.

"You're strong," Alli continued, nodding toward his arms. "You'd probably be good at digging ditches or moving furniture. But, would you enjoy it?"

Ollie laughed. "Fair point."

Alli had a way of cutting through bullshit that Ollie had never seen in anyone before.

And the thought that Alli might not like her work had never occurred to Ollie. It made sense now, though. Someone as smart and talented as Alli could probably do a million jobs well.

In truth, Ollie had only ever been good at one thing, cooking. He didn't really have the option to make a living at anything he hated. He just wasn't good enough at anything else for someone to pay him to do it.

But if she could do so many different things, why was she settling for something she hated?

He let that question sit, though, and went in a more positive direction instead.

"If you don't want to be an accountant," he asked, "then what do you want to be?"

Alli pushed her food around her plate with her fork for a long moment. Ollie had never seen her act uncomfortable before, but she seemed so now. Almost shy, like she was hesitant to talk about it with him.

"You don't have to tell me if you don't want to," he said softly. "I know how delicate dreams can be."

She looked at him then, her eyes wide and searching. The more she stared, the more her eyes bored into him, the more nervous he felt. Scared, almost. Like a rabbit frightened into immobility by a sudden noise. He felt like her eyes were like spotlights searching the depths of his soul.

And he was afraid of how she might judge what she found there.

Finally, Alli's gaze softened, her face relaxed. Relief washed over Ollie, like he'd passed an important test. Relief so strong he thought for a second that he might start crying right there in front of her.

"At home," said Alli, "in my apartment, I have a bank of servers."

Ollie lifted his eyebrows. He didn't know what that meant. A bank was a place to keep your money, and servers worked in restaurants. What the hell was a bank of servers, and why would it be at Alli's apartment?

"Computers," she explained, probably seeing the confusion on his face. "A bunch of computers stored in a metal rack. I have six of them running right now back at home."

"Why do you need so many computers?"

Alli pushed her food around her plate again for a moment.

"Because I'm trying to solve the mysteries of the universe," she said quietly.

Ollie started to smile, thinking she was making an offhand joke, then realized there was no humor in her face, no smile in her eyes.

She was serious.

After a moment, she looked up at him, her eyes hard and wary.

Challenging him to mock her.

Ollie kept his face straight, curious. Interested. Not a hint of disbelief or mockery.

But that didn't mean he didn't have questions.

"What kind of universal mysteries can be solved with six computers in an apartment?"

Alli's eyebrows drew downward, her brow furrowed.

Ollie thought he'd lost her. His question had offended her and now she'd never open up to him again.

Then she laughed, a sound like a quick scale played on a trumpet, bright and joyful. It flashed through the dark room, turning night to day for a moment.

Ollie couldn't help but laugh with her.

"That's a good question," she said, smiling at him from under a few strands of hair that had fallen in front of her eyes.

She shrugged.

Ollie smiled at that, too.

"It would be easier if I had more processing power," she said, "but we can't all have access to endless CPUs. We can't all be Ray Kurzweil, with literally all of Google to power our simulations."

Ollie had no idea who Ray Kurzweil was or how he could use a search engine to run simulations. He wasn't even entirely sure what simulations were when it came to computers. But it was clear enough that this guy was in a position Alli would like to be in.

"What kind of questions are you trying to answer?"

Alli shrugged again.

So many shrugs. So much hesitation and uncertainty.

Ollie had never seen this side of Alli. Granted, he'd only known her a week, but she had always come across as completely confident, one-hundred percent absolutely sure of everything she did, without question. This side of her, this shy, uncertain side of her, was a shock.

And it was nice to see.

"I suppose part of my problem is that I want to answer so many different kinds of questions."

She took another bite of pasta, chewed it slowly, and swallowed it before continuing.

"I'm interested in ten-dimensional space. Hyperspace," she said with a gesture toward Ollie, as if that word would make things clearer for him. "The kinds of questions Michio Kaku thinks about."

She loaded another forkful of food, but let it rest on her plate.

"But I'm also interested in nanotechnology and its potential in the medical field." She lifted her fork, but stopped it halfway to her mouth. "Among other applications, of course."

Ollie nodded quickly, his lower lip protruding in an expression that was meant to convey that he knew what she meant, that of course she would consider the applications of nanotechnology beyond just the medical field.

What he was really thinking was that this gorgeous woman across from him was far and away the smartest person he had ever met in person, and was the smartest person he had ever even heard of in real life.

There were smart people on TV and in books and in the news and stuff like that. They were all probably close to as smart as Alli. But they were just characters in stories or far-away people in the news. They weren't real people, people that Ollie knew or knew of.

This was a living, breathing genius sitting right in front of him, on the stool in his deli, eating the spaghetti and meatballs he had made for her.

He gave up all hope of ever impressing her with his smarts or of keeping up with her intelligence in any way. Forget all this Star Wars stuff about hyperdrives and nannybots. He would be lucky to keep up with her just on the accounting stuff.

But no wonder she didn't care about accounting. If she was capable of understanding all of these space-age ideas, the accounting for Ollie Wood Deli must bore her to tears.

"And then there are the logistical questions," Alli continued, "like income inequality and world hunger. The problems of distribution and equity. Those seem like low-hanging fruit that would be good to solve."

"You could solve world hunger?"

Alli spread her hands out to her sides. "Some people in this county alone throw away more food each day than other people get to eat." She shook her head. "It's not a problem of not having enough food in the world. It's a distribution problem. We're not getting the food to the people who need it."

Ollie nodded. This was a problem that he did understand. Maybe not on a country level or a global scale, but he understood food and getting it to people who couldn't get it themselves.

"But some people can't afford it," he said, "even if you could get it to them."

Alli scoffed.

"Money has become a millstone around our necks. It was once a useful abstraction to avoid the exchange and transportation issues that hindered the barter system, but now it's used as a scorecard, a way for people to make themselves feel better and to make other people feel worse. If I have money and you don't, I'm better than you. That's how we use it now. It's a crutch for our insecurities. And our advertising paradigms perpetuate it. If people would just stop comparing themselves to each other and look for ways to make the world more like it could be, make it more efficient and equitable, then everyone would feel better about themselves."

"I didn't peg you for a politician."

"Politician?" Alli recoiled in horror. "I'm not. I would never work in politics. Not in a million years. That is the worst system humans ever invented."

"What? Government?"

"Yes," she said, heat in her voice. Her eyes flashed. She leaned forward on her stool, her elbows on the counter. She was into it, into the discussion. Ollie had found something she really cared about.

And he loved it.

He loved seeing her like this. Passionate. Full of anger and indignation and hope and curiosity and wonder.

This was the real Alli Thomas.

She was alive in that moment.

And Ollie felt lucky to be allowed to see it.

Ollie listened, rapt, as Alli railed against the concentration of power in the hands of a few people, elected or not. She went on to give brief overviews of nanotechnology, microbiology, quantum physics, and multi-dimensional space.

Ollie understood very little of what she was saying, though he did his best to work out the broad strokes of each topic.

What he did understand was Alli's passion. Ollie had found the thing that made Alli feel alive.

For Ollie, it was cooking and watching customers enjoy his food.

For Alli, it was thinking about these massive, galactic-scale problems.

Neither one was better than the other. Everyone had their passion, and every passion had its place. That's what Ollie believed, anyway. If everyone could find and follow their unique passion, the world would be perfect.

Sadly, most people didn't find their passion.

Most never believed it was worth looking for.

Of those who did, most gave up the search early on, getting too confused or distracted by all the haters and the well-meaning parents who never found their own courage, their own passion. They fell prey to the admonitions to "get a real job", or to "always have a fallback, better safe than sorry".

Even for those lucky few who did find their passion, most of them lacked the self-belief to really pursue it. All those well-meaning admonitions and countless advertisements telling us we were incomplete and unworthy (unless we bought Product X or Widget Y) had a tendency to sink in deep over time and undermine our confidence.

It was a rare individual who found and followed their passion with enough conviction to make a difference in the world.

Ollie knew he was one of those people.

And he knew how fortunate he was.

It seemed to him that Alli could be one of those people, too.

And her passions were big. Large-scale. While Ollie's passions could feed a neighborhood, Alli's passions could feed the world, could potentially alter the course of human history.

But she wasn't acting on them. Not yet, anyway.

"What do you do when you solve these mysteries?" he asked her.

Alli shrugged yet again. She was shrugging so much, Ollie was starting to fear that her arms would fall out of her shoulder sockets.

"I don't know," she said. "I haven't solved one yet."

"Has anyone else solved one?"

Alli shook her head. "Not that I know of. Great progress has been made, but these are big problems."

Ollie nodded slowly. "You're kind of on the cutting edge of this stuff, aren't you?"

"I try to keep up on the research," she said, chewing a bite of meatball.

A tiny speck of sauce rested on the corner of her mouth. Ollie resisted the urge to reach across the counter and wipe it clean with his thumb.

He wanted to hold her chin in his hand, to run his thumb

across her cheek, feel her skin, feel her lips. They looked so soft, so red from the dim overhead light.

And from the pasta sauce, probably.

And the light in her eyes, the passion in her voice when she spoke made that urge even stronger.

But Ollie resisted that urge.

He didn't have time for those kinds of thoughts. He had too much else to worry about with the deli and its finances. He didn't want to complicate things by getting involved with a girlfriend.

Even if Alli would have him.

She had shown no interest whatsoever, and probably never would. She would no doubt be more interested in a college professor or a high-powered nuclear scientist or something, not some small-town deli chef.

"Is there some place you go to keep up on that stuff? I mean, aside from the library and books and that kind of thing. Is there, like, a website or a YouTube channel or some kind of forum where people talk about this stuff?"

Alli scoffed, stabbing food onto her fork. "There are a million sites where idiots spout a bunch of nonsense. Conspiracy theories and space opera bullshit with no scientific underpinnings, no proofs of any kind."

"Are there any that aren't filled with idiots?" Ollie said with a subtle smile.

Alli looked up at him and her face immediately softened.

The sight of it quickened Ollie's heart.

"Yeah," she said, her voice barely a whisper. "Yeah, there are a few."

The air between them suddenly felt charged.

Hot and dry and buzzing, as if the electricity from the lone light above them had dipped down and formed a magnetic current running back and forth between Ollie and Alli.

Ollie's palms grew clammy. His mouth and lips went dry.

He couldn't tear his eyes from hers.

And he didn't want to.

Not for a moment.

"Okay, cool," he said, his own voice rasping through his parched throat.

They stared at each other for the eternity of two seconds before Alli tore her gaze from his.

It felt like she were tearing a piece of Ollie's soul, yanking it up from his gut and out through his eyes.

She dropped her gaze back to her plate.

The moment shattered, Ollie gathered himself, wiped his hands on his apron.

"What, um..." He cleared his throat. "What do they say when you post your ideas there?"

"Where?"

"On those websites? The ones without the idiots?"

"Oh." Alli pushed her food around her plate, then set her fork down with a loud rattle against the side of the porcelain. "Um, they don't say anything." She looked away, to her side, into the darkness, rubbing her hands along her thighs as she sat. "I've never posted anything."

The electricity was still there between them, but where before it was powerful, pulling them together like two magnets, now it was scattered and messy. And it was pushing them apart, like magnets flipped around, sliding past each other whenever they got close together.

"Oh," said Ollie, his face suddenly feeling hot. Had he crossed a line? Touched on a sore subject for Alli? "Maybe you should," he muttered.

Alli didn't respond, just kept looking into the darkness.

Away from Ollie.

Ollie's cheeks burned so hot he felt like his whole face would melt off and drip onto the counter.

He'd definitely hit a sore spot. And he'd just made it worse.

Not knowing what else to do, he gathered both plates in his hand, even though there was still food on them.

He stopped, briefly. His mouth opened of its own accord and he heard his voice say, "If you want to."

He turned back toward the kitchen and walked into the darkness.

He'd hit a sore spot, then poked it hard.

Then he went and squeezed it, hard, just for good measure.

Like a fucking idiot.

# 15

ALLI SAT in her car outside the deli the next morning. The windows were fogged against the exceptionally cold air outside.

Temperatures had been dropping recently as autumn slid softly into winter, with morning temperatures averaging roughly forty degrees Fahrenheit.

But now that slide had become a plunge. The air that morning was barely thirty degrees.

Below freezing.

Cold enough to snow.

Alli had the car running, the windows clouded with the blast from the heat registers on her dashboard, but she could still see her breath inside the car. She had pulled her wool hat down low to cover her ears, but the wool gloves she wore were too porous to retain much of her body heat. She blew into her cupped hands and reminded herself to get a pair of windproof gloves.

She'd reminded herself the same thing every day last winter.

But her thoughts that morning weren't focused on her winter gear.

She couldn't stop thinking about last night, about dinner with Ollie.

About what he'd said to her.

"You should post your ideas on those websites," he'd said.

The sound of his voice uttering those words had rattled in Alli's mind all night. It had haunted her dreams. Just as she would drift from N1 sleep into the deeper N2 stage, she would hear Ollie's voice and startle awake, her blood thick in her ears, hissing like the jeers of a Roman coliseum full of esteemed scientists.

When she did manage to dream, that coliseum came to life.

She stood in the dirt in the center of the ring. All of her heroes sat in the stone seats that surrounded the arena. Curie, Lovelace, Feynman, Kaku, Einstein, Lisa Randall, Niels Bohr.

They didn't shout encouragement to her.

They hurled insults.

With a sword in one hand and a shield in the other, Alli stood helpless while snarling lions devoured her flesh, bite by bite, and her idols tore her to mind to shreds with their words.

The words hurt far worse than the lions.

At four in the morning, when she couldn't take any more abuse, she'd gotten out of bed, dressed in the dark, and driven to the deli. She'd been sitting there in her car for hours. Her fogged and frozen windshield had gone from frosty darkness to opaque light as the sun rose behind it. She'd shivered and blown plumes of steam and tried to warm her hands against the air put forth by her struggling car heater.

But mostly she'd endured that same nightmare again and again.

It plagued her while she was awake.

"You should post your ideas on those websites," he'd said, then had added at the end, "if you want to."

As if it were as simple as wanting it.

Alli wanted it. She wanted her ideas to be heard, to be debated.

But every time she thought of it, she heard her mother's voice in her head.

*Why do you waste your time on all that science crap? No man wants a woman who is smarter than him.*

Alli had no illusions about the idiotic opinions of her mother, but she could not shake the feeling that welled up in her. The feeling she'd had whenever her mother had criticized her.

The feeling she still had whenever her mother criticized her.

It was a gnawing emptiness in the bottom of her stomach, a dull ache that wormed through her body like a cancer.

That was what she felt when she imagined posting her ideas. First the excitement of finally joining the conversation.

Then the gnawing ache in her stomach.

The only consolation, the only balm to the pain of this waking nightmare, to the recurring lash of this whip, was the memory of Ollie's voice.

And the look in his eyes.

Hope.

He had hope in his eyes last night.

No. Not hope.

Belief.

He believed in her.

She could see it in his eyes.

Those unusual eyes.

"You should post your ideas. If you want to."

She took out her notepad and started a new list.


**Ideas to post:**


- ...


Alli waggled her pen above the paper, tapped it against her lips.

Ollie didn't know her.

He didn't know her ideas.

He believed in her based on one week of watching her work through his accounts.

Given the state of that office when she arrived, any sort of organization, however rudimentary, must have seemed miraculous to Ollie. A man dying of thirst does not critique the liquid offered to him. He drinks it gratefully and praises the giver, even if the liquid is dirty dishwater.

And Alli was grateful for Ollie's encouragement, for his belief in her.

But he didn't know what he was saying.

He didn't know Alli. Not really. And he didn't have any basis for his belief.

Alli knew better.

As much as she loved to think about these subjects, to learn about them and to run her simulations, her experiments on her servers, she knew her thinking wasn't at the level of her heroes.

She was no idiot, mind you. She was better off than ninety-nine percent of humanity when it came to these subjects. But she was at the very bottom of the remaining one percent. And she was reading the thoughts and speculations of those at the very top.

What could she possibly contribute to them? How could she possibly influence their thinking? At best, she would state ideas they had already considered. At worst, she would waste their precious time with misguided, uneducated, unsophisticated hypotheses.

Alli wasn't sure if she could survive either outcome.

Better to wait.

To work harder.

To keep studying, keep thinking, keep refining her ideas until she came up with something she knew was groundbreaking. A truly revolutionary idea that would make her heroes take notice and accept her into their hallowed circles.

Yes. That was the best way forward.

Alli jumped in her seat at a sharp rap on the window beside her left ear. She rolled down the window. A gush of frigid air locked all of her muscles and froze the hairs in her nose.

She was expecting Ollie to be standing there.

Instead, it was Sarah, bundled in a heavy overcoat, a hat, and a long, colorful scarf. Her bare hands held a cardboard carrier with three paper coffee cups stuck into it.

"What are you waiting for?" she said.

Alli tilted her head, confused.

Sarah turned to one side and waved her hand toward the deli.

"Come on, get moving." She stamped her feet and waited for Alli. "Can't sit out here forever."

Ollie was setting out two plates of breakfast when Alli and Sarah walked in the front door. A blast of warm air greeted them, and Alli's clenched muscles immediately relaxed.

The warm air was redolent with the rich, sweet smell of maple and cinnamon and warm bread. Alli sat on a stool in front of one of the plates and found the source of the delicious scent.

"Challah French toast," said Sarah.

Golden brown French toast, piled high with strawberries and blueberries, dripping with maple syrup and dusted with powdered sugar.

"Nothing fancy today," Ollie replied. "On the first cold day of the winter, you just want comfort food, like your grandma would make for you."

"Your grandma made her French toast with challah?"

Ollie shrugged. "So I elevated it. I'm a chef. Sue me."

Alli was already digging into the food while Ollie and Sarah bantered back and forth. She'd been up for hours, freezing in the car outside, and didn't realize how cold and hungry she was.

The French toast was thick and fluffy and piping hot. The outside was crisp, softened just a touch by the warm maple syrup dripping over it.

"Cinnamon in the egg wash," said Sarah, chewing on her first bite. "And nutmeg." She took another bite. "Clove?"

Ollie nodded. "Very good, chef," he said.

"Same to you," she replied. "This is incredible."

"I guess you like it, too," Ollie said.

It took Alli a moment to realize he was talking to her, so lost was she in her enjoyment of the dish. It not only delighted her tongue, but it soothed her stomach, as well. The heat from the food warmed her from the inside out, filling her empty belly and suffusing her whole body with its rich flavor. It was a feast for all of her senses.

Between the food and the warmth of the deli, Alli had slipped into a half-catatonic state. She felt comfortable and safe, and her sleepless night was catching up to her. She wanted nothing more than to curl up on a pile of cushions in the back near the warm ovens and sleep for a few hours.

She settled for a long drag on the coffee Sarah had bought for her.

"It's delicious, Ollie," she said. "Thank you."

His smile was slight, but his eyes lit up at her words.

That light in his eyes warmed her body even more.

"Tom's car wouldn't start this morning," Ollie said to Sarah. "Too cold for it, he thinks. So he'll be in a bit later than usual."

Sarah nodded.

"What's your day looking like, Alli?" he asked.

Alli swallowed her mouthful. "More legwork. Gonna try to track down Thomas Murkin, see what he can tell us."

"The guy from that company?"

"Petterson Holdings, yes. He's their controller."

"Controller? That sounds corporate and overlordy," said Sarah around a mouthful of food.

"It's like a chief accountant," said Alli.

"You think he'll know what's going on?"

She shook her head. "No idea," she said, digging in her fork for another bite of French toast, "but it's the best lead we've got."

**To-do list:**

- Visit Petterson holdings

Based on the slick professionalism of the website and all the stock photos of corporate prosperity it displayed, Alli expected Petterson Holdings to be housed in a tall, glittering office building in the center of town. Or at least the corner unit of an upscale office park on the outskirts.

Instead, the address on the business cards took her to the old factory district on the far side of the city. She followed her GPS off the main road into a complex of large buildings, hulking rectangles of patched and stained brick, with rusted metal doors and bricked up windows. A hundred years ago, this area would have been the industrial heart of the city, employing hundreds of metal workers, brick workers, textile workers, and the like. Now, the place was a shadow, a faded photograph.

The road was pocked with potholes, and Alli's car bumped and scraped over rough-laid train tracks before she found the building she wanted.

Far from a glittering skyscraper, Petterson Holdings was located in the back corner of an old foundry that had been converted into several warehouse-like units. She drove past a sign-making shop, a welding business, and someplace calling itself JD Motorsports. Their tall warehouse door was rolled open. Inside were a handful of huge men with long chin beards and muttonchops, wearing bandannas, leather vests, and t-shirts, despite the frigid temperature. As Alli parked and got out of her car, the sound of grinding metal and pneumatic drills punched the air.

At least Petterson Holdings had a front door. And a functional window, through which Alli could clearly see a reception area with a desk and a receptionist.

Definitely a step up from the other places she'd visited recently.

The receptionist was young, but polite and professional. She told Alli that Mr. Murkin would be in meetings all morning, but could meet with her for thirty minutes at two o'clock that afternoon, if she was willing to come back.

Alli took the appointment, gave the young woman her name and phone number, and sat in her car, wondering what she could do for the next five hours. She pulled up the Petterson website on her phone and found herself scrolling again through the list of companies they'd invested in.

One of them was JD Motorsports, Inc.

Alli got out of her car and walked toward the sound of grinding metal and pneumatic drills. Seeing her approach, a squat, bearded man with overly muscular arms that hung out from his sides like penguin flippers got the attention of the others.

Alli braced herself for a flurry of misogynistic comments. Catcalls, perhaps, like she sometimes received when walking down the sidewalk past construction sites. Maybe wolf whistles or other signs of misdirected masculinity.

Instead, the noises in the shop ceased entirely. All of the workers came to the front door, a huge roll-up metal door that occupied the entire front of the unit, at least fifteen feet tall. The workers formed an ominous receiving line, standing with their arms folded or their hands clasped in front of them. Some of them still held a wrench or a hammer or some other kind of tool.

All of them wore neutral looks and hostile body language.

An interesting reaction to a woman walking across a parking lot. Hardly what Alli would have thought these kinds of men would consider a threat.

Alli counted seven standing in the line, waiting and watching as she walked. As she drew near, one of them stepped forward. He was taller than the others, save for one giant standing on one end of the lineup, and slimmer.

Though to call this man slim was akin to calling a planet small.

Everything is relative.

The man was twice as wide as Alli, half again as tall, and infinitely more muscular. He wore shaggy mutton chops and a mustache that curved past the sides of his mouth and extended down his chin, somehow continuing past the bottom of his jawline.

It was an impressive feat of directional pruning.

His chops and mustache were of dark hair shot through with generous amounts of grey, giving the man from a distance, with his black boots under dark jeans, leather vest over a grey t-shirt, and copious arm tattoos, the appearance of a walrus who had gone through a midlife crisis and joined a biker gang.

He stepped forward and held his hand out to Alli. She shook it with a perfunctory snap.

"Welcome to JD Motorsports," the man said, his voice a deep rumble that Alli felt in her chest. His words and his delivery were welcoming, but his tone held no warmth. "I'm JD." He gestured toward the lineup behind him. "That's the crew." He turned back to Alli and folded his hands together. "What can we do for you so early on a frosty morning, miss?"

Such formality. Alli wondered if they lined up like this for every visitor or if she was somehow special.

"Do you greet every new customer with such pageantry?"

The man's eyes narrowed slightly, his head tilted to one side for a moment before he decided to give her a polite smile.

"When they come from Petterson, we spare no expense," he said.

His lips were smiling, but the narrow eyes, the hard stare, and the way the man leaned slightly toward Alli did not convey friendliness. Nor did the way the giant in the back slowly smacked his massive monkey wrench against one palm.

"That's very kind," Alli said, "but I'm not from Petterson. I'm just killing time before I can meet with Mr. Murkin."

At those words, the mood shifted completely. The men in the lineup relaxed visibly. Their folded arms and their tensed shoulders dropped. Their tools fell by their sides. They all turned and went back to their work inside.

The man in front with Alli lost his menacing stare and unclenched his hands. He glanced behind him at his crew, then returned his attention to Alli. He still wore a polite half-smile, but now his eyes were duller, less interested.

Now Alli was just some random woman coming to interrupt his work.

"Killing time?" The man laughed tunelessly. "Well, when you see him, tell Murkin," he spat on the ground beside them, a glutinous blob of bubbly white mucous, "JD says hello."

He turned away from Alli and strode back into the warehouse.

Alli hurried to follow him.

"Are you the owner of this business?" Alli called to his back.

"Uh huh."

"Do you mind if I speak to you for a few minutes?"

The man didn't stop walking, didn't turn to look at Alli, and didn't respond.

"Just a few minutes, I promise, Mr... JD."

"Mr. JD?" The man shared a look and a smile with one of his crew that he was passing, the giant. "I like that. Call me Mr. JD from now on, Mug, okay?" The giant lifted his chin in acknowledgement, then dragged his gaze slowly across Alli's face and back to his work.

Alli followed JD deeper into the warehouse, past several vehicles propped on jacks or hoisted on hydraulic lifts, past a row of machines that looked like drills or presses or grinding tools. There was even something that looked like a CNC machine or 3D printer of some kind.

Alli was surprised and impressed that this burly crew would have something as technologically advanced as a 3D printer at their disposal. They seemed more like the forge-and-anvil type to her.

"We're not meatheads, despite the way we look," JD said. He had stopped walking and was watching Alli as she looked at the machines. Her surprise must have shown on her face. "Carl over there," he nodded toward one of his workers, "has a computer science and software engineering degree from Cal Poly. He was pre-IPO at Google. Came back here for something to do in his retirement."

Alli looked back at the man he had indicated. Carl was a squat man who looked to be in his late-forties or early-fifties. Hardly retirement age. He was rotund in a solid way, like a hippopotamus, with Hell's Angels attire and a chops-and-stache pattern of facial hair that would have been all the rage during the Civil War. He fit the mold of the rest of them. Alli wondered idly what he might have looked like during his computer programmer days.

It took Alli a long moment to process what JD had just told her, to rearrange the mental model she had constructed of this place and the people in it. She looked back at the giant, Mug, and wondered if he might have had a doctorate in Elizabethan romance novels or something. Mug just stared back and raised one eyebrow.

With a start, Alli realized that JD had started walking again. She hustled to catch up.

There were no walls in the warehouse, just a deep, cavernous space that ran for several hundred feet straight back from the front door, ceilings lost to darkness high overhead. The side walls were not part of the original structure. They must have been added when the foundry building had been partitioned. They were made from some kind of plaster or stucco. At the back of the space was a fifteen-foot wall of exposed brick that formed the other side of the original foundry building.

In the far back, near the brick wall, it was darker and warmer and quieter than up front. Three desks were arranged in a column, their surfaces covered in neat piles of paper, a computer atop each one. Daylight still filtered back from the massive warehouse door, but most of the light came from small lamps set on the desks. Between the white daylight and the soft yellow light from the desk lamps, the darkness that otherwise might have felt gloomy took on a comforting fireside feeling.

JD sat in a swivel chair behind one of the desks and gestured for Alli to sit in a chair beside it.

"You want us to convert that little bug of yours?" he said, leaning back in the chair and putting one foot on the opposite knee.

Alli frowned. "Excuse me?"

JD gestured toward the men working up front.

"That's mainly what we do here these days. We convert ICE vehicles to electric."

"ICE?"

"Internal combustion engines." He uncrossed his legs and leaned forward, his elbows resting on the desk. "We're saving the world here, miss. One gas-guzzler at a time."

"But you call this place JD Motorsports. And yet, you're getting rid of all the motors?"

JD chuckled, a surprisingly rich sound that made Alli want to chuckle along with him.

"We made the pivot from high-performance engine mods to electric conversion maybe ten years ago," he said. "Wasn't worth changing the name. People already know us as JD Motorsports."

Alli nodded. "No, I'm not here so you can convert my car to electric."

JD aimed that hard stare at her again.

"Then why are you here, miss?"

"I'm here because Petterson Holdings, LLC lists you as one of their investments on their website."

"Those assholes have a website?"

Alli couldn't tell what took her aback more, the fact that JD had called Petterson "assholes" or the fact that he would be surprised that any business had a website in this day and age.

Though, now that she thought of it, she wasn't sure if Ollie Wood Deli had a website.

"I'd like to ask you some questions about your business," Alli said, choosing to ignore JD's question. "About your accounting, in particular."

"You a cop?"

"No."

"Reporter?"

"No."

He thought for a moment.

"FBI?"

"No."

"Then why do you care about my books?"

A niggling thought popped up in the back of Alli's mind, like a warning light on a car's dashboard.

"I'm currently working for Ollie Wood Deli, serving as their accountant on a consultative basis."

"A consultative basis?"

"And I've found some peculiarities in the payment arrangements with several suppliers."

JD tapped the desk lightly with one hand, then leaned back in the chair again and folded his arms over the hulk of his chest.

"What kind of... peculiarities?"

"Direct withdrawal."

"You mean autopay?"

Why didn't people ever hear what was said? They only heard what they wanted to hear, what fit into their existing mental models.

"Not direct payment," Alli said sharply. "Direct withdrawal. The suppliers have direct access to the accounts of Ollie Wood Deli and are able to withdraw payment at their discretion."

JD lowered his head and whistled softly. He chuckled and shook his head.

"Man, they got that place over a goddamn barrel. Poor Ollie Wood must have done something stupid."

Alli leaned forward.

"What do you mean by that?"

JD scoffed at Alli. Then his eyes narrowed. He leaned toward her.

"If you're not working for Petterson and you're working for this deli, why did you go into Petterson earlier?"

"I told you," said Alli. "I've set up a meeting with their controller, Mr. Murkin, for two o'clock this afternoon."

JD stared at Alli through those narrowed eyes for a long moment. His stare started out hard and evaluating, then softened.

"I hate to tell you, but he's going to cancel that meeting."

"Then I'll reschedule."

"He'll cancel that one, too. And the next one and the next one until you just stop trying."

Alli pressed her lips into a thin smile. "I can be very persistent."

"Oh, I believe you." JD grinned. "But no matter how persistent you are, you're never going to meet with Thomas Murkin."

"Why not?"

JD sat back in his chair again. "Because Thomas Murkin doesn't exist."

**16**

WITH A DAMP RAG in his hand, Ollie wiped the last of the scraps from the lunch service off the metal counter of his workstation. He was about to head out to the smoker to rotate the meats when Alli burst through the front door, her face dark as a thundercloud. She stomped—actually stomped—through the kitchen, nearly body-checking Sarah, and into the office, slamming the door behind her.

"Someone needs a hug," said Sarah. She looked at Ollie. "I'll flip you for it."

Ollie rolled his eyes and threw his rag onto the counter.

He knocked softly on the office door, then opened it slowly.

Alli was standing in front of the computer, staring toward the monitor. But she didn't seem to be looking at it. Just standing in front of it, hands pulling her hair back off her forehead like she wanted to rip it out altogether.

"Everything okay in here?" said Ollie.

Alli didn't respond.

"You know, if you're trying to trim your hair, scissors usually work better than just yanking it out."

Alli didn't respond.

Okay, not Ollie's best joke, but, come on. It was worth at least a patronizing smile.

Ollie stepped into the office and shut the door behind him.

"What's wrong?" he said.

Alli turned to him and folded her arms across her chest. Her eyes were blazing with anger, and Ollie immediately felt ashamed and afraid, like when the teacher asks you to stay after class. He had no idea what he'd done wrong, but he didn't want to find out.

"Have you ever heard of Petterson Holdings, LLC?" asked Alli.

"Petterson Hol... no," Ollie shook his head. "I mean, I met a guy named Petterson once. Jack Petterson. Is that the same guy?"

Her arms fell to her side and she stepped toward him. So palpable was her anger, so strong the menace coming off of her, Ollie took an involuntary step backward.

Alli was like a force of nature.

And right now, nature was pissed.

"What do you know about Jack Petterson?" she said, her words clipped.

Ollie shrugged, trying to shake off the tight ball forming in the center of his chest. "Nothing, really. He was at my parents' wake. Came up to me and introduced himself, said how sorry he was. Said he was an old friend of my parents."

"Had you ever met him before?"

Ollie shook his head.

"Ever seen him before?"

"Why are you grilling me like this? What's going on?"

Alli's face hardened and she took another step toward him. "Had you ever seen him before?"

Ollie felt a heat climbing up his neck. He didn't know what Alli was trying to find out or what she thought was going on, but Ollie's initial shame and fear was turning into an anger of his own.

He hadn't done anything wrong. Not knowingly, at least. And he was getting pissed off at Alli's accusatory tone.

"No," he said, his voice sharp. "I hadn't."

"Ever seen him since?"

"No."

"You sure?"

Ollie took a deep breath, trying to quell his anger.

Trying and failing.

"Yes, I'm sure," he said, his tone as hard and forceful as Alli's. "Now what the hell is going on?"

They stared at each other for a long moment, like heavy-weight boxers at the start of a title fight.

Heat crept further up Ollie's neck, spread throughout his chest. He forced himself to take long, deep breaths, but he could feel his heart beating against his chest like a hammer.

Alli stepped closer, eyes still blazing.

If Ollie had reached out, he could have touched her, could have slid one hand around her waist and pulled her close to him.

Ollie felt himself sweating under his shirt. His mind swam again, this time confused, caught between thoughts of anger and thoughts of Alli being close to him.

He really needed to get a grip.

The anger evaporated from Alli's eyes. She sighed and sat down heavily. All the tension drained from the air.

Ollie released a long slow breath, letting his anger flow out with it. Relief flowed in to replace it.

The other thoughts, the thoughts of Alli being close, they didn't go anywhere.

Ollie grit his teeth and forced those thoughts aside.

He slid over a box from the stack of accounting records against the wall and sat on the corner, across from Alli.

She looked hard at him again, with those deep brown eyes.

The other thoughts tried to push back to the front of his

brain, but again Ollie forced them back, forced himself to look at Alli's eyes, to actually see them. Not just to see what they sparked in him.

He saw that there was no anger in her eyes anymore. No accusation.

Just frustration.

And concern.

And maybe a bit of pity.

Something was troubling Alli.

And now, more than anything, Ollie wanted to know what it was.

He wanted to help.

"How much do you know about your parents?" Alli asked.

"Not possible," said Ollie, shaking his head from side to side.

All thoughts of making Alli feel better had vanished.

His head was filled with his own troubles.

Ollie's mind whirled and tilted, like he'd had too much to drink. Gorge rose in the back of his throat. He choked it down and leaned forward, elbows on his knees, hanging his head down low.

"No way," he said. "I would have known. I would have seen something."

"You were young," said Alli, her voice soft and compassionate.

Ollie wanted to punch the wall, to scream at her to save that compassion for someone who needed it.

Because she was wrong about his parents.

As smart as Alli was, she was dead wrong this time.

"What proof do you have?"

Alli's mouth tightened.

"None, really," she admitted. "Not yet, anyway."

"Then this is just a bullshit theory with no proof."

Alli started to say something, then rolled her eyes and sighed.

"I knew my parents," Ollie said, standing. The spinning in his head had been replaced by rock-solid anger, the sick in his stomach by stubborn indignation. "They would never have gotten involved in something like this."

"It's not uncommon, Ollie."

"It's stupid. And it's wrong. My parents were too smart and too... *good* to get involved in something like this. They were good people."

He paced back and forth in the tiny office space, pulling his fingers through his own hair now, like Alli had been doing just a few minutes earlier.

"Good people make mistakes."

"Yeah, well, not my parents. Not like this."

There was no way his parents would be involved with a loan shark. That was like the mafia or something. Movie stuff. They weren't in fucking Sicily.

Alli kept her mouth shut while Ollie paced. She was wrong about his parents, but she was right to do that. Ollie wasn't going to stand there while anyone talked shit about his parents.

His dead parents.

Nine years they'd been dead, but it still felt like yesterday.

Especially here at the deli. Everywhere he looked, Ollie saw them. Not a day went by when he didn't turn a corner and catch himself expecting to see his dad at the grill or his mom at the register.

Ollie's thoughts were racing. His chest was fluttering. He could feel his heartbeat in the veins of his neck, racing even faster than his thoughts.

He kept pacing, shaking out his hands like he was trying to shake his feelings out, shake out the upset and the uncertainty.

Uncertainty.

There was a thought, a nagging thought in the back of his mind.

In the flurry of thoughts racing through his mind, that one, nagging thought persisted. Like someone standing on the far side of a subway platform while an express train rattled through, their image unmoving, intermittent through the flashing windows of the train cars.

Ollie shook his head then, trying to shake that thought loose.

It didn't budge.

He pulled at his hair, trying to rip the thought out from the roots.

It wouldn't come.

He stopped pacing. He was facing the closed door, his back to Alli. Staring at the blank white door, an inch from his face, like a crazy person.

He didn't care.

Ollie wasn't seeing the door.

He saw his father's face.

Ollie was maybe fourteen years old. It was early in the morning. Ollie's mother hadn't arrived at the deli yet.

Ollie and his father were making an omelette, throwing in all kinds of crazy ingredients. Diced chilis and wild mushrooms they'd found at the farmer's market that morning. Oregano and powdered cocoa. Laughing and experimenting and having fun like always.

A bell rang overhead, a harsh buzzing sound.

Someone was at the back door.

A delivery.

Ollie saw his father's face in his memory like he was standing in front of him right then and there.

One second he was laughing at Ollie's reaction to the terrible taste of their concoction. The next second, his eyes were filled with worry, his face lined, his smile fading.

At the time, Ollie hadn't known what to make of it.

But he was older now. He could interpret the memory differently.

In his mind, in that moment, his dad's face changed from that of a fun-loving man full of life to someone completely different.

Fearful. Aged.

He had stopped laughing. He touched Ollie's cheek tenderly. "Stay here," he'd whispered, then went to answer the door.

Ollie's younger self must have sensed something off, because he had followed his dad. Disobeyed him. He stayed hidden in the hallway, watching through the open back door.

There was a delivery truck in the alley.

Ollie's dad was standing behind it, talking with someone in the back of the truck.

The talk grew more heated, became an argument.

Ollie heard the slam of one door, then another. Two men appeared on either side of his father.

Two very large men.

His dad looked at them both, then spotted Ollie in the hallway through the open back door.

He stopped arguing immediately and held up his hands toward whoever was in the back of the truck.

But one of the large men had followed his dad's eyes and seen Ollie in the hallway, too. He stepped over, staring at Ollie, and pulled the back door shut.

Ollie had shivered at the man's stare. Cold and dispassionate.

He shivered now at the memory.

He hadn't thought anything of it at the time. Just a weird incident that had never been repeated.

But now, thinking back on that memory, things started to click into place.

Before the man closed the door, Ollie had managed to catch a glimpse of the logo on the side of the delivery truck.

He recognized the logo.

He'd seen it four times a week for the last nine years.

Drayger's Meats.

One of the suppliers that Alli had flagged for doing weird stuff with the deli's accounts.

He sighed, a heavy sigh that was nothing compared to the weight that came over his whole body. It was as if the weight had pressed the sigh out of him, squeezed the air from him.

Dad. What did you do?

He turned around to face Alli.

She just watched him, quiet and observant, those beautiful brown eyes taking in everything.

"Tell me what you're thinking," he whispered.

**17**

It hurt Alli to tell Ollie what she had learned, what she suspected. She could see that the news pained him, and that fact pained Alli.

And she was surprised that she felt that way.

Truth was truth, and any pain about learning the truth was usually the result of misconceptions being shattered.

But that was a good thing.

Any false paradigms that we carry in our heads about the world around us will only cause us grief until they were corrected. If you thought your car keys went in the tailpipe, you'd spend a lot of time being very, very frustrated when your car didn't start. That frustration would only go away once you corrected your false understanding and used the car keys properly.

Alli welcomed those kinds of corrections to her own understanding.

But she could see that this particular correction was a shock to Ollie. It hurt him.

And in that moment, Alli discovered that she didn't like to see Ollie hurt.

To be fair, she didn't like to see anyone hurt. She wasn't a sadist.

But most people caused their own pain, and they did so because they were idiots. Their mental models were so obviously delusional and self-centered that they lived lives of constant anguish when the world around them didn't behave the way they thought it should.

But their expectations were mere wishes, not predictions. They were based on fantasy, not empirical evidence and logical hypothesis.

And so Alli had become accustomed to hurting people in this way. She wasn't going to lie to them just so they could perpetuate their false reality. People called such coddling compassionate, but really it was just cruel.

The kinder thing, by far, was to help those people see how utterly ridiculous their thinking was, so they could correct it, bring it more in line with reality, and thus become happier.

Happiness resulted when one's expectations fit with one's reality.

And unhappiness resulted when one's expectations were unrealistic.

When Alli told people—clients, acquaintances, her mother—the truth, she was doing them a favor.

They cursed her for it. They criticized her, ostracized her, even demonized her for it.

But she'd never been tempted to couch that truth, to soften the blow.

Until now.

When she saw the pain in Ollie's face, saw the turmoil and anguish filling those improbable eyes, twisting his handsome features—yes, Alli had admitted to herself that she found them handsome, and believed it to be an objective conclusion caused by an asymmetry in Ollie's face that was pleasing at an instinctive level, probably encoded deep within the DNA of the human species—she found herself wishing she could take back her words, could convey them differently.

Why had she been so angry? That had been unfair, and had probably made Ollie's pain even worse by aggravating him, putting his mind into an overly emotional state even before she told him about his parents.

But, Alli had been angry.

She trusted Ollie. Perhaps that trust was irrational, in and of itself, since she'd only known him for ten days. And Alli's history with humanity would suggest people should not be trusted.

Nonetheless, she did trust Ollie.

But all the way home, she had been stewing in her mind, growing angrier and angrier.

Thinking he'd violated that trust.

Thinking he'd lied to her, hidden important information from her.

Thinking he'd tricked her.

As JD had predicted, Mr. Murkin's receptionist had phoned Alli around noon to reschedule their meeting.

Alli had visited two other "investment" companies listed on the Petterson website, two businesses run by friends of JD's. JD had called them to let them know Alli was coming, to let them know they could speak freely to her.

And speak freely they had.

And what Alli had learned had formed a clear pattern.

Petterson Holdings, LLC was a front for a man named Jack Petterson. Mr. Petterson was a loan shark, at best. A money launderer, at worst.

Actually, it could be worse than that. If he was laundering money, there was the question of where that money came from, and why it needed to be laundered.

But that was beyond the scope of Alli's investigation. She was not a member of law enforcement, and she didn't necessarily have concerns about breaking the law. There were far more illogical and idiotic laws on the books than there were useful ones. It was irrational and, in some cases, impossible to follow every single law to the letter.

Alli didn't condone violent crime or crimes against children. Even crimes against defenseless animals were reprehensible in Alli's mind, though one could argue that the modern system of food production amounted to one giant, state-sanctioned crime against defenseless animals.

It was for that reason, and others like it, that Alli's belief in the law was fluid, at best. If the government could defend the law in some circumstances and prop up systems that broke it in others, then the law itself became meaningless.

And some laws, while they may have been well-intentioned, were just foolish. The sale of currently illicit drugs, provided there was no coercion or peddling to children, was reasonable in Alli's mind. If an adult of sound mind chose to partake of a drug, that was their choice. They could make the choice of their own free will, and they could suffer the consequences.

Laundering of drug money was a way to circumvent laws that existed to protect humans from their own stupidity. And those laws, however noble, were futile and stupid.

Only a conscious effort by every human to lift their own minds from the mud could protect the species from its own stupidity.

And most humans didn't want to work that hard. They'd rather watch Instagram reels or TikTok videos for hours on end and wait for someone to tell them what to do.

Alli's stance on the legal system was still an imperfect moral framework. She knew that. It was still a work-in-progress in her mind.

As a result of this stance, though, Alli wasn't against Petterson's activities, per se. If he was a loan shark, that was fine with her. Consenting adults entered into agreements, however foolish, with other consenting results and suffered the consequences.

What angered Alli were Petterson's tactics, especially as they related to the Ollie Wood Deli.

And what angered her even more had been Ollie's failure to inform Alli of the reasons for those tactics.

But now that she saw the pain on his face, the confusion and anger followed by the shock of realization, of some memory falling into place, Alli realized that she had fallen victim to the same mistake she saw so often in others.

She had assumed that Ollie was hiding information from her, that he was knowingly and deliberately breaking the trust that Alli had extended to him.

But now she could see that he had no idea. His parents had never told him anything, and he had never noticed.

Things were finally falling into place for Alli, though. The mystery of the direct withdrawal situation was solved. And Alli hadn't chased it down yet, but she suspected the sale of the building was somehow wrapped up with Jack Petterson, as well.

Alli figured that Ollie's parents had run up a debt of some kind and had sold the building to Mr. Petterson in exchange for five hundred thousand dollars to pay toward those debts. Either that hadn't been enough to cover the debt or they had gone on to rack up even more debt. Either way, the direct withdrawal arrangement had been made as a way to funnel more money to Mr. Petterson.

She didn't know how much the debts were or where they came from. But they could not have been above-board or Ollie's parents would have gone through the legitimate banking system. Or, perhaps, they had tried the banking system and had failed to secure credit. They had been forced into the shadows, forced to a loan shark like Petterson.

And they had never emerged.

The reasons didn't matter so much as the current status. Was there still a debt outstanding? What were the terms of the arrangement with Petterson? How could Ollie bring those terms to an end so he could release himself from the onerous arrangement that existed between Ollie Wood Deli and Petterson Holdings, LLC?

In order to answer those questions, Alli would need to go to someone who knew about them. Preferably, someone who was there when the arrangements were made.

Alli would need to find Jack Petterson.

**To-do list:**

- Meet Jack Petterson
- Determine terms of arrangement between Petterson Holdings and Ollie Wood Deli
- End arrangement

"I don't care what your list says. You're not going alone."

Alli had grown fond of Ollie over the last two weeks. In fact, she'd grown fonder of him than of anyone else she knew, and in much faster time than she would have thought possible.

And she was fond of Sarah and Tom, as well.

It was a very strange experience for her, to actually look forward to interacting with people. To be happy to see them each time she did.

But, as fond as she was of Ollie, she still grew tired of his savior complex.

Just because Alli was a woman didn't mean she needed a man to protect her everywhere she went. This was the early twenty-first century, not the early eighteenth century. Women no longer required chaperones and male approval for everything they did.

"This guy could be dangerous," Ollie pleaded.

Down the hall from the office, Alli could hear Sarah and Tom chattering and clattering in the kitchen, prepping for the lunch service. She could hear the sizzle and smell the onions caramelizing on the grill, the meat roasting in the oven. It was still weird, but Alli was getting used to thinking about lunch at nine in the morning.

She checked her shoulder bag to be sure she had everything she needed. Her laptop, pen and paper, car keys and cellphone.

Her courage.

It was all there.

Ollie stood in the doorway, his hands on the outside of the doorjambs, leaning his body inward. His biceps were bulging with the stance, his t-shirt pulled tight against his chest, his face set into a very determined expression.

His orange-flecked eyes were blazing as Alli looked at him, and she noticed her heart beating quickly in her chest. She felt slightly short of breath.

Odd.

She didn't usually feel that way unless she was exerting herself. Perhaps Ollie's misplaced anxiety was affecting her.

"I've met him," Ollie continued. "I didn't think anything of it at the time, but now that I know who he is, he's..." He struggled to find a word. "...sketchy."

"He's sketchy?" A smile curled one side of Alli's mouth. "What does it mean to be sketchy, exactly?"

"You know what sketchy means."

Alli could guess, but she really didn't know what Ollie meant by that word. It was one of those imprecise slang terms that Alli had never bothered to work out.

"It means there's something weird about him. Something dark. Ominous."

"Ominous," Alli repeated. "Did he threaten you?"

"No, of course not," said Ollie. "We were at a wake. My parents' wake."

"And yet he still seemed ominous?"

"He just seemed like the ominous type, you know? Big guy. Beady eyes. Forehead like a... great white shark or something."

Alli laughed. "What is a great white shark's forehead like?"

"You know what I mean."

"Do they even have foreheads?"

Ollie rolled his eyes, but smiled faintly.

Alli's heart beat a little faster at the sight of his smile.

Odd.

"Solid," he said. "Like a block of concrete."

"Must be hard for a shark to swim with a block of concrete in its head."

Ollie stepped into the room, stood in front of Allie, took one of her shoulders in each hand and turned her to look squarely at him.

Her heart beat even faster, her breathing shallow and rapid.

She couldn't blame her physical response on Ollie's anxiety anymore. There was a stronger correlation at work.

His physical proximity.

"Alli, please just let me come with you. I won't say anything. I won't do anything."

"Then why would I bring you?"

He closed his eyes and shook his head slowly, smiling again.

"I just want to be there, just in case."

"In case wha—"

"Just to observe," he said. "Besides, I'm the owner of this deli. I have a right to be there with you."

Alli looked up at him, looked into those remarkable eyes of his, at the handsome asymmetry of his face.

Encoded in her DNA or not, she had to admit, she enjoyed looking at Ollie's face.

Alli pulled in a deep breath and sighed.

She smelled his scent again, like she had the first time they'd met. Cedar and moss and black cherry. Again, Alli thought of her father in his well-worn, wing-backed leather chair, reading with her in front of the fire, his lit pipe resting in an ashtray on the table beside him, a lazy tendril of smoke curling up from it.

Alli pulled in another deep breath, slowly this time, savoring the scent. Faintly layered on top, she smelled spices, too, from whatever rub or marinade Ollie had been using before he came into the office that morning.

Whether it was the intoxicating scents, the memories of her father, the two deep breaths in a row, or, she had to allow, the proximity of Ollie himself, Alli felt dizzy for a moment, felt herself rock backward on her feet, her world tilting around her. She closed her eyes and reached out, reached for anything against which to steady herself.

And found her hand on Ollie's chest.

She could feel his heartbeat through his t-shirt.

Could feel it pulse through the thin fabric under her fingertips.

She could have imagined it, but she thought his heartbeat sped up when she touched him.

She knew hers did.

And definitely not because of Ollie's anxiety.

She kept her eyes closed and sucked in as much sensory data as she could get from her fingertips.

His soft t-shirt.

The warmth of his skin.

His pulsing heartbeat.

The firmness of his pectoral muscles, their smooth arch beneath her palm.

She could even feel the peak of his nipple on the edge of her hand. It grew firmer as her hand rested on it.

Something firmed within Alli in response.

She felt Ollie's hands on her shoulders open and re-close, open and re-close, working further across her back toward her shoulder blades.

Pulling her slowly, subtly closer to him.

She felt his nose against the top of her head, buried in her hair. Heard him pull in a long, slow breath.

Alli leaned into him, pressed her forehead against his soft lips. Felt their warmth, their moisture against her skin.

She brought her other hand to his chest, feeling the ripple of muscle along his sides, along his abdomen, up over the firm swell of his chest.

She could hear his breathing, rapid, ragged, could feel it against her hair, her ear, her neck.

A clomping sound.

Alli wasn't sure if she was actually hearing it, or if it was the sound of her own heart in her ears.

"You wanna use the rest of this brisket today, chef, or just dice it for stew at dinner?"

Alli and Ollie burst apart at Sarah's words, As she clomped down the hallway toward the office in her Doc Martin boots, they burst apart as if a bomb had exploded at their feet.

Sarah stood in the doorway, her expression frozen, her eyes moving back and forth between Alli and Ollie.

A slow smile crept over her lips.

"What're you two doing?" she drawled.

"Nothing—" said Ollie.

"Just discussing—" said Alli.

"Talking about—"

"—our plans—"

"—business stuff—"

"—for the day."

"—nothing important."

Alli wasn't one of those unfortunate pale-complexioned

people whose cheeks showed their every emotion or exertion. She'd never cared about that fact before.

But right then, she was grateful for it.

Yet still she felt her cheeks burn like twin suns.

She avoided eye contact with Sarah and Ollie.

Then realized how silly that was.

How ridiculously emotional.

Nothing had happened. She and Ollie had found themselves in an accidental half-embrace in the midst of a business discussion.

Awkward, perhaps, but hardly scandalous.

And certainly nothing to be ashamed of.

Alli pulled her head up, forced herself to do it. She forced the timid, shaming, irrational thoughts to the back of her mind and fixed Sarah with what she hoped was a cool gaze.

Sarah had been studying Ollie's face. For his part, he was currently studying with great concentration the fine details of a cardboard box of accounting records stacked against the wall.

Sarah pulled her gaze to Alli's, and her smile widened. Alli noticed a mischievous flash in her eyes.

Alli lifted her chin in defiance.

Sarah could mock, if she so chose. She could poke fun.

But Alli would not be made to feel shame.

She had sworn never to allow herself to feel that way again. And she wouldn't start now.

"Discussing unimportant business plans for the day," said Sarah, nodding. "Got it." She turned to Ollie. "If you're done inspecting that box, could you answer my question?"

"Huh?" said Ollie, finally looking at her.

"The last of the brisket from yesterday."

"Right," said Ollie. He wrinkled his brow for a moment. "What about it?"

Sarah grinned again and shot a quick glance at Alli.

Alli's cheeks went supernova, but she did not look away.

"Use it for lunch or dice it for stew?"

"Yeah, sure, sure," said Ollie. "That sounds fine."

"Uh huh," said Sarah, her mouth twisted in a wry smile. "Okay, then." She turned to leave. "You two have fun with your, uh... planning."

She shot a wide grin over her shoulder.

Ollie diverted his gaze back to the floor.

From the hallway, Alli heard Sarah call, "Hey, Tom. Looks like it's just you and me today, buddy. And I'm in charge." She laughed with mock menace.

Ollie peeked up at Alli through the fringe of his thick, tousled hair and chuckled shyly.

Alli again fought the urge to look away, fought the embarrassment rising within her, fought the irrational feeling of wrongdoing.

Nothing had happened. Circumstance. Coincidence. A twist of fate that put them in close proximity and initiated accidental contact.

Alli held her eyes on Ollie's.

And her mind was spinning in this rut, this idiotic emotional rut, worrying again and again about how Sarah had perceived the event, how Ollie had perceived the event.

What Ollie thought about it now.

Was he ashamed?

Did he regret it?

With the way he was avoiding eye contact, it seemed that way. But interpretation was subject to confirmation bias, with our own feelings clouding our perception and our judgment.

And what was there to regret?

Nothing.

Nothing had happened.

Alli clenched her jaw. She wanted to walk away, to be alone to clear her mind and get it back onto an even keel.

To return it to a rational state.

But she didn't want Ollie to think she was angry or ashamed.

So she grit her teeth, clenched her hands into fists, and forcibly ripped her thoughts away from the endless cycle of worry and interpretation and rehashing of the events that had just transpired. She forced them back to the problems at hand.

Petterson.

The deli accounts.

They had serious work to do.

And despite what she had thought earlier, Alli could use Ollie's help.

"Okay, fine," she said.

Ollie looked at her, finally making full eye contact, a quizzical look on his face.

"You can come," said Alli, "but I do all the talking."

**18**

Ollie's heart was still pumping a million times a second when Alli finally looked at him.

And then his heart rate doubled.

She looked pissed.

Her hands were scrunched up into fists so tight the skin over her knuckles had turned white.

Ollie could see the muscles in her jaw flexing as she ground her teeth together.

And that look in her eyes.

That look could burn a hole through steel.

He shouldn't have put his hands on her shoulders.

He shouldn't have pulled her close.

He shouldn't have smelled her hair.

And he definitely shouldn't have kissed her forehead.

But he couldn't help himself.

When he'd touched her, he'd lost his mind. In just that second, just by putting his hands on her shoulders, his mind went completely off the rails.

The curve of her shoulders fit into his palms like they were made for that purpose. Even through the jacket she was wearing, Ollie could feel her skin, her muscles, her bones, her heat.

And then she'd touched him back.

Well, maybe she hadn't touched him *back*. But, she'd touched him.

She'd put her hand on his chest.

Why had she done that?

He didn't know, couldn't remember.

And he didn't care.

That touch had lit him up, made him glow all over, bright and hot like an oven.

One little touch and the mind he'd just lost was gone forever.

He couldn't help himself. The scent of her washed over him. He was swimming in it, swimming in a glorious sea of...

Of what? How could he describe Alli's scent?

It was like... paper. Like old books in a library, but in a good way. Not musty or stale, but rich and real and natural and deep.

And flowers.

Ollie didn't know his flowers, but there was a floral scent behind the paper, sweet and subtle and tantalizingly feminine, but far in the background. Like a promise or a reward for whoever was lucky enough to be allowed into Alli's heart.

That didn't do it justice at all, but her scent was like a drug for him. He'd caught it once before, faintly, when he'd leaned over her to look at her computer screen. His mind had reeled then.

But this time, with Alli just inches in front of him, it overcame him completely, and he dove into it.

And then when she touched him, he drowned himself in it.

Gladly.

Willingly.

The best possible way to die.

And then it was gone.

Sarah came and the moment was broken and then it all felt weird and wrong, like they'd done something wrong.

His feelings were still there.

His body and his heart were still reaching for Alli.

His mind was still reeling, her scent still in his nose.

But something was screaming at him, from some other part of his brain. Telling him no. Saying this was bad, that they'd just been caught doing something wrong.

But how could something that felt so good—and not just good as in, like, *good*, but good as in right—how could something that felt so good be wrong?

So Ollie had just stared at the wall, stared at a box or something, stared at anything that wasn't another human being who might judge him, might shame him. Sarah had said something and Ollie had said something and Sarah had finally left and Ollie mustered the courage to look at the one person whose opinion actually mattered.

The one person he'd look at forever, if she let him.

And she looked pissed.

"Okay, fine," she said.

What the hell did that mean? What was fine? Was she fine? Was she fine with what had happened?

She sure didn't look like she was fine with it.

"You can come, but I do all the talking."

Ollie's anxiety flooded out of him then, replaced by a hollow feeling that was a hundred times worse.

Alli didn't care at all. While Ollie's head and heart were exploding, what had happened had been, for her, just another day, literally, at the office.

"Right," he nodded, trying not to crumple to the floor or throw up at Alli's feet. "Right. Okay."

Alli gave him one last, long, hard look, as if to say, *Don't ever pull that bullshit on me again or I'll cut your balls off and feed them to my cat.*

Ollie didn't even know if Alli had a cat.

But that look told him that, if she didn't, she'd buy one just so she could feed Ollie's balls to it.

Ollie barely fit into the front seat of Alli's old VW bug. His right shoulder pressed against the freezing-cold window, and his left shoulder bumped against Alli's arm whenever she shifted gears.

Each contact send a buzz of heat through Ollie's body, quickly followed by a hammer of shame as he remembered the look on Alli's face before they'd left the office.

They'd been silent with each other ever since, as they left the deli, got in the car, drove into the center of town, and parked on the side of a French restaurant called Les Arômes.

Ollie wondered why they were parking there, but kept his mouth shut. He didn't want to piss Alli off any more than he already had.

Les Arômes was very familiar to Ollie. Or it used to be, anyway. It had first opened about thirty years ago. As the story went, Ollie's father had introduced himself to the new chef in town, an older gentleman, Chef Jean Babineaux, and his wife, both transplants from Paris.

Ollie's dad had been the unofficial welcome wagon for Chef Babineaux. They had hit it off and become fast friends. Madame Babineaux had become equally close with Ollie's mother, and the couples had spent as much time together as two busy restauranteurs could manage. The Babineaux would frequent the deli at lunchtime and Ollie's family would often sit for dinner at Les Arômes. Both families spent as much time in each other's kitchens as at each other's tables.

Ollie was born into that friendship, referring to them his whole life as *tanta* and *oncle*, aunt and uncle. As a kid, he could never pronounce Madame Babineaux's actual name, which was Marianne. He couldn't wrap his young tongue around the guttural French "r". And so they'd settled on Baba, his way of saying their last name. For his whole life, Ollie knew the

Babineaux not as the premier French chefs west of New York City, but simply as Oncle Jean and Tante Baba.

Oncle Jean and Tante Baba had died when Ollie was about ten or eleven years old. Tante Baba, aging and overweight by then, had fallen down some stairs in the restaurant after dinner service one night and broken her hip. She died shortly after. Oncle Jean lost all of his characteristic *joie de vivre* after that, and died only a few months later.

Died of a broken heart, according to Ollie's father.

The Babineaux had no children, no next of kin, and no will. The restaurant went up for auction and was purchased by some kind of investment group who kept the French theme and ditched everything that made the restaurant good. They hired cooks, not chefs. They skimped on food quality to save money. They drove away all of the Babineaux's loyal customers and made Les Arômes a mockery of its former self.

The building itself fared no better. A rare free-standing building in the center of town, Les Arômes had once been some kind of government building back when the town was first founded. A wooden structure with a wide footprint and tall, peaked roofs. When Oncle Jean had owned it, it was beautiful. The walkways were immaculate. The exterior walls shone with new paint. Every lightbulb glowed, with none missing or burnt out.

Now, it was a ramshackle afterimage. Warped boards poked from the siding. There was more flaked paint than actual paint. And the walkways were lined with empty styrofoam cups and discarded wrappers, plastic bags, and other trash.

And as they approached the building, Ollie realized this would be the first time he'd set foot inside since Oncle Jean had died.

Then he realized he wouldn't be setting foot inside at all.

Not just then, anyway.

Alli took one hand from the pocket of her thigh-length

parka, knocked on the front door, and shoved the hand back, deep inside her pockets.

The morning was freezing cold. Even though it was nearly ten in the morning and the sun had been up for hours, Ollie could still see his breath in great clouds in front of him. The temperature in the last day or two had taken a nosedive from the unseasonably warm fifties down to the high thirties.

Kind of like Ollie's relationship with Alli.

He shivered in his pea coat and beanie, but not from the cold air.

Alli pulled her hand out and knocked again.

"They're not going to answer," said Ollie.

Unless someone lived at the restaurant or they'd started a lunch service since the last time Ollie checked, it was unlikely anyone would be working at ten o'clock in the morning.

At a top restaurant, they would. Ollie had started at seven AM when he worked as the sous chef at a Michelin-starred restaurant in New York. And Chef Babineaux had been a famously light sleeper. He used to start even earlier, before the sun rose.

But Les Arômes was not what it used to be. A place like it had become would definitely not be arriving seven hours before dinner service to start prep. Ollie would be surprised if they showed up before noon.

"Why not?" asked Alli, her knock becoming a pound with the side of her fist. The glass pane in the door rattled in its frame.

"It's too early. They won't start prepping for another couple of hours."

"Why not? You start early."

"We serve lunch," Ollie said, then mumbled, "And we care about our food."

He didn't like talking shit about a place when they were standing in front of it. It was bad karma.

"They don't care about their food here?"

Ollie pressed his lips together.

"They'll probably be here in a couple of hours," he said.

Alli checked her watch and sighed. "Not worth going all the way back to the deli. We'll have to find something to do around here while we wait."

The prospect of spending a couple of idle hours with Alli both excited Ollie and unnerved him. As pissed off as she was, she'd probably give him the silent treatment the whole time.

"There's a good coffee shop next block over," said Ollie, gesturing down the street. He usually didn't have a second cup of coffee in a day, but he'd make an exception if it meant he could sit across the table from Alli for a while and try to untangle her anger.

Alli nodded, pulled her fur-lined hood over her head, and stuffed her hands deeper into her jacket pockets.

As they turned to walk away, Ollie heard the rattle and scrape of locks sliding open.

"Yes?" said a woman, poking her head into the narrow space she'd opened in the front door to the restaurant.

Ollie had to look up to see her face. When he did, what he saw looked more like a ghost than a living human being.

The woman was very tall and very gaunt. Her cheeks were sunken, hanging from her cheekbones like the bowls of two spoons. Her eyes were sunken even more, ringed with dark circles.

It could just have been the shadows, but Ollie thought he could see a bit of fading green and yellow tingeing those dark circles, too.

Her eyes were dark as cinders, a stark contrast to her nearly pure white skin. The effect was of a child's stuffed doll, as if the woman's eyes were buttons sewn into the fabric of her face.

"I'm sorry to bother you, ma'am," said Alli. "We're looking for Jack Petterson. May we speak with him?"

The woman's eyes widened for a fraction of a second at the sound of Petterson's name, and fear seemed to spark those dark cinders into flame. She pulled back from the doorway slightly, pulling her face even further into shadow.

"He is..." She darted a glance over her shoulder. "He is not here right now."

The woman spoke with some kind of accent that Ollie didn't recognize. Russian, maybe, or Eastern European.

She started to close the door, but Alli stuck her foot in the way.

Persistent, that one.

"When do you expect him back?" she said.

The woman looked down at Alli's foot in the door and her already slumped shoulders slumped even more.

She seemed utterly defeated. Ollie's heart broke for her.

"We can come back, Miss..." he said, letting his voice trail off, hoping she might fill in the space he'd left.

The woman darted another glance behind her.

"Teresa," she said, her voice nearly a whisper.

"We can come back, Teresa," said Ollie as gently as he could.

Alli turned her head sharply toward him, her eyes glaring.

She was going to be even more pissed at him now.

Teresa looked up at Ollie, gratitude and relief in her eyes.

"Thank you, yes. Please come back later."

Ollie tugged on Alli's arm.

"We'll be back later, then," said Ollie, doing his best to keep his voice calm and friendly, and ignore the daggers Alli's eyes were shooting into him as he pulled her away from the door.

"Come back for dinner," called Teresa from behind them.

Ollie and Alli both stopped and turned back to her. Her face protruded from the slot she'd opened in the doorway, like a mouse poking its head through an opening to see if it were safe to come through.

"He always sits at the table in the corner by the kitchen at dinner," Teresa said.

Her eyes were wide and wild, darting from side to side like she was risking her life just to speak to them.

Ollie got the feeling that maybe she was.

She pulled her head back with a sudden jerk and slammed the door shut tight. The sound of the bolts and locks snapping shut rang in the cold morning air.

Ollie shared a confused glance with Alli.

What on earth were they getting themselves into?

**19**

THE SERVER BROUGHT TWO COFFEES, setting them down on a smooth wood table with a porcelain clatter. Ollie had ordered some long-winded concoction, specifying the type of milk, the type of sweetener, even the ratio of milk to foam and the type of coffee bean. His order felt more like a contract negotiation than a simple purchase.

Alli had just asked for a cup of coffee, whatever they had at hand.

They'd sat in silence until the coffee arrived. Really, there was no longer a need to be at the coffee shop. Whereas before they needed to kill two hours before returning to Les Arômes, now they didn't need to be back until dinner time. They could easily go back to the deli until it was time to return.

But once the strange, timid woman at the restaurant had slid back into her hole, Ollie had kept walking and led them here for coffee.

It was one of those trendy hipster shops that Alli tended to avoid whenever possible. The shop Sarah recommended was similar, and Alli had gotten used to stopping there every other morning to pick up coffee for Sarah, Ollie, and herself. But there, she would place and pay for the order on a cellphone app and just pick it up from a shelf beside the register. In and out in seconds, with no need to speak to anyone.

Here, Ollie had negotiated his beverage and led them to a table to wait. When the drinks arrived in ceramic coffee mugs, Alli knew Ollie wanted to stay for a while.

Normally, Alli would be fine with that. She enjoyed spending time with Ollie, and having an opportunity to do so outside of the confines of their work environment would give them an opportunity to speak about other things.

But today, the mood between them was different.

Soured, it seemed, by the events of this morning.

Ollie was embarrassed. That must be why he hadn't said a word to her since they left Les Arômes. He was embarrassed by Alli's unprofessional actions and was going to let her go, to ask his Uncle Saul for a new accountant.

Honestly, this was the longest Alli had spent with any client, ever. Normally, she would have finished all of the setup more than a week ago and been dismissed days later when the client realized she wouldn't toady to their insipid demands to do all of their thinking for them.

Alli was surprised every morning when Ollie and Sarah and Tom greeted her with smiles and warmth. Each day, she expected that welcome to wear thin, expected their mood to shift and the inevitable dismissal to come.

With all of her prior clients, Alli had looked forward to it.

With Ollie, she dreaded it.

But, she'd finally overstepped her bounds, it seemed. With one simple loss of self-control, one moment of disorientation, one fleeting moment when she'd let her emotions get the better of her intellect, she'd ruined the one working arrangement she'd ever had that she actually enjoyed.

She looked forward to coming to the deli each morning. She woke up each day excited to get out of bed and do her job.

That was definitely a first for Alli.

And now, as he twirled his half-size coffee mug in its saucer, Ollie was undoubtedly searching for the words he would use to break the news to Alli.

"Alli—" Ollie began.

Alli didn't want to hear it. She didn't want him to say those words. Not yet. She wasn't ready to leave yet.

She still had work to do.

"Why did you tell that woman we'd come back later?" she interrupted, saying something, anything, to prevent Ollie from saying what he'd been about to say.

Ollie's eyebrows raised, startled.

"What do you mean?"

"It was obvious that Petterson was in the building somewhere. The woman kept looking back like he was standing right behind her. We could have talked her into letting us in to see him."

Ollie took a deep breath and let it out slowly, staring down into his coffee.

Finally, he shrugged and said, simply, "She was in pain."

He just looked at Alli then, the first time since before everything had happened this morning that he had looked at her openly, with nothing clouding those beautiful eyes of his.

But Alli didn't understand how the woman's pain was relevant to their purpose. Most people were in pain of one sort or another. All the time. And most of the time, the pain was of their own devising, the consequence of their own poor choices.

Even Alli had to admit that her own pain was the result of her choices.

The difference was that Alli was aware of that fact. Most people tried to blame their pain on something or someone else.

Alli furrowed her brow and shook her head at Ollie. "So what if she is? We can't stop what we're doing just because we see someone who's hurting. We'd never get anything done."

Ollie snorted a rueful laugh and nodded at his coffee, then sighed again.

"Maybe that's why my business is failing and you're the one who's rescuing it."

Alli shook her head at him again. She didn't know what he meant by that.

"I can't see someone in pain," he said, "in real pain, and not do what I can to help them."

Ah. His savior complex again.

"It just doesn't feel right."

"But everyone is in pain. You can't help everyone all the time."

"True," he nodded. His face held a profound and hollow sadness that speared Alli's heart.

She didn't like to see Ollie hurting.

"I know you're right." He looked up at her, his eyes clear and bright. The sight stopped Alli's heart. "But I can help someone. Sometime."

And maybe that was the fundamental difference between Alli and Ollie. Alli saw the pain in the world, saw that it was caused by the idiocy of individuals everywhere, saw that she could never cure that idiocy, that people didn't want to help themselves, and so she didn't bother trying. Why waste energy solving a problem that resisted its own solution?

Ollie, on the other hand, didn't look at the system as a whole. Or, perhaps he did, but he didn't care about fixing the entire thing all at once. He was content to help one person at a time. Even if the system fell apart around them, it seemed that Ollie would still be happy that he'd helped who he could.

He'd see that as a success.

Alli would see it as a failure because the system crumbled.

Who was right, Alli or Ollie?

Alli didn't know.

A few weeks ago, she had been certain she was right, certain that finding solutions to intractable systemic problems was the only scalable way to help humanity.

Now, she had spent time with Ollie. She had seen the way he worked with his customers, the way he spoke to his vendors, to his employees. She had seen the way he spoke with her.

Perhaps more importantly, she'd felt the way he spoke with her.

And she could see the impact of those small-scale actions.

It was inefficient. From a systemic point of view, you would need a million, a hundred million similar actions on that small scale in order to effect enough change to correct the system as a whole. Given the intrenched power of the system and the general state of brainwashing and self-hatred that most people carried inside of them, you might need a billion actions to overcome that inertia.

It was impractical to approach the problem in that way.

But maybe practicality wasn't the point.

Maybe the point was simply to do what you could, when you could, for the people you saw around you.

Ollie sipped his overly complicated beverage and looked at her over the rim of the cup, those entrancing eyes filled with compassion for others.

People had told Alli her whole life that she was smart. Some called her a genius, some called her a freak. But, if nothing else, she had lived her whole life believing in her own intelligence.

And now, looking at Ollie, she felt that maybe, for her whole life, she'd been wrong.

They finished their coffee and made it back to the deli in time to help with lunch service. The rush was much heavier than usual, and Alli had been pressed into service at the register, taking orders and helping to bag the sandwiches when they came over the pass-through.

She'd never performed that kind of work before, the kind that involved constant contact with a large number of people. She normally avoided it like she avoided her mother, but today she forced herself to do it.

What's more, she forced herself to push aside the stream of negative chatter in her mind, the chatter that looked for—and easily found—errors, problems in the people who stepped up to the counter.

Some spent endless minutes trying to decide what to order, despite the fact that there were only three options on the menu for lunch and they'd been waiting in line for at least five minutes already, plenty of time to decide before holding up the entire line while they dallied at the register.

Others gave detailed, overly complicated orders that merely wasted time in another way. Sauce on the side or hold the pickles or whatever minute detail they wanted to control. Food was food, and this need to give themselves the illusion of control over their lives was a waste of everyone's time and energy.

And then there were the people who were arrogant or overly boisterous or infuriatingly shy or simply rude. There were the women who treated Alli with contempt, and there were the men who leered at her. It was the usual range of human misbehavior that generally made Alli avoid other people whenever possible.

But Alli forced herself to look past those foibles. That pattern of judgment and subsequent avoidance was a pattern of thinking that she'd used her entire adult life. Now, with Ollie, she'd begun to understand a different pattern, and she was curious to explore it further.

She channeled Ollie as she worked the register, doing what she had seen him do on many occasions.

She used a cheerful voice and asked the customers how they were doing today or what she could get them.

She made inane comments about the weather and complimented people on aspects of their appearance, a colorful hat or a fuzzy scarf, a careful curl of hair or an unusual eye color. The sort of superficial commentary that seemed to placate and subdue the masses by reassuring them that they were still an accepted member of the tribe.

She smiled when they smiled.

She smiled when they didn't smile.

If they launched into some story about some problem they were having, Alli would nod along with them and focus on their words, pushing aside the cascade of thoughts in her head that were solutions to their problem and hypotheses for its origins. When she inevitably found their words to be filled with logical fallacies and unjustified conclusions, she focused on the people themselves, standing right in front of her. The sound of their voices, their postures, the message of their body language.

She tried to see past the idiocy and focus on their humanity, the one thing everyone had and no one could fake.

Alli did this for the entire lunch service. For more than two hours and dozens of customers, she threw herself into the experiment, doing everything she could to remove any bias, to remove her past patterns of thought, so she could simply be present with these customers—these people—while she had them in front of her.

In the end, the conclusion was clear: there was little hope for humanity.

People were absolutely, irreconcilably insipid.

So many people, all of them flawed.

Some were too angry. Others too arrogant.

Some were pitifully cheerful, deluding themselves and annoying Alli.

Others were pitifully melancholy, clearly begging for a kind word from someone, anyone. When Alli would give it to them, she would watch them feed it to their melancholy, watch it be absorbed into their darkness and twisted, the positivity cast aside as an aberrant event. Their melancholy was self-fulfilling and self-perpetuating. They simply refused to acknowledge anything that would prove their negativity false.

It was all the usual madness of humanity, in microcosm in front of Alli's register during those two hours of lunch service in Ollie Wood Deli.

Any random sampling of humanity anywhere in the world—certainly anywhere in America—would yield exactly the same results.

People were irrational. Stubbornly, willfully so.

And they showed no inclination to improve their condition.

Alli sighed deeply when the last customer took their order out the door and walked past the large front window down the sidewalk.

She had tried.

Individual by individual, she had poured as much kindness and compassion as she could muster into each interaction, as Ollie did when he was working the front counter.

And, individual by individual, Alli saw no change. No change in their behavior or their demeanor.

But Alli felt better knowing that at least she had tried. She'd found a new hypothesis and tested it.

Now she could move on.

**20**

LES ARÔMES OPENED for dinner at 5pm. Ollie figured they might as well be there at that time. If Mr. Petterson was not yet available, they would have several hours before closing to wait for his time to free up. But hopefully, he wouldn't have gotten stuck into anything specific quite so early in the evening.

Ollie felt bad leaving Sarah and Tom alone for the dinner service at the deli, especially after the rush they'd had for lunch. More customers than Ollie had ever seen. So many that Ollie had been forced to ask Alli to work the register so he could jump back into the kitchen to help prep the orders.

He'd watched her over the pass as she worked with the customers up front. He and Sarah shared more than a few laughs watching her deal with some of the regulars. They got an interesting mix of characters at Ollie Wood Deli. That was one of the reasons Ollie loved it there. From a few golden-hearted folks to a few very salty ones, Ollie's customer base ran the gamut. Rich, poor, old, young, happy, depressed, angry, sad. Ollie's customers had it all.

And watching Alli deal with it all was a trip.

Ollie had the feeling that in Alli's whole life she hadn't talked to that many people in the space of two hours. She may not have talked to that many people in the space of a whole year, for all he knew. It wouldn't surprise him. Alli didn't seem like a social butterfly, to put it mildly.

But he could see her trying. He could hear her attempting to make small talk. For the first half-hour or so, to each customer that stepped up, she'd say, "Getting cold out there, isn't it?" Every single customer. She didn't even say hello, just led with the weather report every time.

Some of the customers smiled and played along. Others stared at her like she had three heads. Others just ignored the comment and gave Alli their order.

After a while, she tried compliments. She told Mrs. Harrington that she liked her scarf. "That's a beautiful scarf," she'd said. "Is it new?"

Mrs. Harrington had worn that same scarf into the deli every single day for the last eight years. Rain or shine, freezing cold or blistering heat, she wore that crocheted, rainbow-colored scarf.

Eight years earlier, after years of trying, she had finally talked her husband into learning to crochet, so they had something they could do together in the evenings. He'd grudgingly agreed, then found he actually liked it. A lot. The scarf was the first thing he made.

And the last.

He died of a massive heart attack shortly after finishing it. Mrs. Harrington had worn that scarf every day since, in memory of him.

But she was a kind old woman, and she just thanked Alli for the compliment and said no, it wasn't new. It had been a gift from her husband.

Other customers weren't as kind, but Alli kept trying. Ollie had no idea why she was working so hard to reach out to people like that. It didn't come naturally to her at all. But it was fun to watch, all the same.

The lunch rush had been so heavy that they had little time

to prep for dinner. Ollie pulled Alli in to help him get the deliveries ready while Sarah and Tom focused on dinner prep. He figured they could make the deliveries and then head straight to Les Arômes.

Alli drove them both in her little VW bug. Slowly, the blasting heater warmed the air inside the car.

"How'd you like working the register?" Ollie asked her, pointing out the turns for Alli to take as they came.

"Very informative," said Alli.

"Oh yeah? What information did you get from it?"

Alli tilted her head in thought for a moment. "It confirmed my hypothesis. People don't change. They're too stuck in their own irrational attitudes to observe the world around them and alter their conceptions."

"You learned all of that from two hours working the till at a deli?"

"Human behavior is fundamentally consistent. The setting is irrelevant." She looked out the window. "Thought it would be worthwhile to repeat the test in other environments, just to confirm."

Ollie nodded to himself as they wound through the side streets. He'd never met anyone so scientific in his life. So dedicated to logic and doing things step-by-step. Most of the people he knew were a lot more emotional than that.

"You know," he said, "sometimes it takes people a little longer to open up."

Alli turned toward him. Her eyes were blazing again, that flame of intelligence that set Ollie's heart racing every time. "What do you mean?"

Ollie looked out the windshield for a moment, just to collect his scrambled thoughts and let his heart rate settle.

"I mean, it took a long time for the customers to warm up to me when I first got here," he said.

"How long?"

Ollie shrugged. "Months. They're a tough bunch. Old. Set in their ways. Suspicious of new things."

"Irrational and inflexible."

Ollie laughed. "Sometimes. But sometimes, you just need to put yourself in their shoes and try to imagine what they're feeling, what it's like to be them all day, every day. Ask them about themselves. A little at a time, take it slow." He pointed to Mrs. Dunbarton's house and Alli pulled up to the curb in front. "Sometimes it doesn't work, but sometimes you learn stuff that can surprise you." Alli shifted into neutral and pulled up the parking brake, leaving the engine running and the heater on. "And you make a friend in the process."

He invited Alli to help him bring the packages up to the doors and meet the customers themselves. Some of the most interesting people you'll ever meet, he told her.

She wasn't interested. She was happy to just wait in the car, she said.

So Alli drove and Ollie hopped out to make the deliveries. They wound up back at Les Arômes shortly after five PM.

The sun had already sunk below the horizon when they arrived. The streetlights were still warming up and the growing darkness had taken on a dusky pallor.

As soon as Alli turned off the car's engine and the heater stopped blowing, the cold from outside crept in, seeping up through Ollie's legs and into his core. Within minutes, he could see his breath inside the car.

"Let's get inside before we freeze to death out here," he said, blowing on his hands to warm them.

The front door of the restaurant was unlocked. Inside, it was much like Ollie remembered from the times when his Oncle Jean had owned the place.

But now it was worn with age and neglect.

Booths lined one wall. They had once been supple, polished leather, but now were dry and cracked and torn in places. An array of tables dotted the interior of the space. The chairs that surrounded them were the same ones Tante Baba had picked out during their last remodel, a simple and elegant wood-and-metal design that provided comfort and support without distracting a customer from their food or their dinner companions. Now, that elegance was masked by disrepair. The chairs looked worn and rickety, like they were barely able to hold the weight of even the slimmest customer.

Nonetheless, there were two or three parties seated at several tables, and two of the booths were full. But most of the twenty-odd tables were still empty. Ollie remembered the days when the entire room was full of laughing, chattering guests, even at the first seating, with the waiting area overflowing and sometimes a line spilling out the door onto the sidewalk.

He doubted the dining room was ever at capacity anymore.

"Welcome to Les Arômes," said a slender young man in a white shirt and black pants. His voice was smooth, pleasant, and professional, his pronunciation surprisingly accurate.

But his smile did not reach his eyes. Ollie could see at a glance that he was bored with his job.

He led them toward a table near the window, a dark, secluded, romantic spot.

"I'd prefer to sit over there," said Alli, pointing to a table near the back.

The maître d' swerved to the left without breaking stride and seated them where Alli had requested.

At first, Ollie had felt a pang of disappointment when Alli had led them away from the romantic table. The one she requested was on the pathway to and from the kitchen. When the saloon-style kitchen doors swung open, Ollie could hear the clank and clang and chatter of the staff through the open door.

Not romantic at all.

But then he pulled himself back to his senses.

They were not on a date.

They were there to speak with Petterson.

And Petterson, according to Teresa, the woman they had met at the door earlier, always sat at a table in the corner by the kitchen.

There was only one such table.

And Alli and Ollie had just been seated beside it.

Petterson didn't show for a long time, long enough that Alli and Ollie were forced to order coffee, which was weak and watery, then appetizers, which did not live up to their name, to say the least. Ollie had steered clear of the escargot and settled on Tortellini Les Arômes, a tortellini dish made with sautéed Porcini mushrooms in a roasted garlic cream sauce. The tortellini were clearly not homemade, probably frozen or from a box, and the garlic cream sauce tasted more like elementary school paste than anything that should be served in a fine dining establishment.

When Petterson still didn't show, they were forced to order entrées. Alli ordered a Romaine Salad while Ollie chose Prawns Meuniere, thinking no one could screw up a brown butter sauce.

He was wrong.

The prawns were rubbery, as Ollie expected, but the sauce was burnt. They'd cooked the butter far too long, then added extra lemon to try to mask the bitterness. The result was a pungent, acrid taste that Ollie couldn't help but spit out with his first bite.

Alli's salad wasn't much better. The Hearts of Romaine were not good quality and probably came from a plastic bag. The Caesar dressing was definitely from a jar, as were the croutons.

But the lettuce wasn't wilted or brown, and the dressing and croutons seemed edible. Alli ate it, anyway.

Ollie was beginning to fear that they would have to order

dessert. He was trying to decide exactly how they would screw up the Soufflé Grand Marnier when Petterson finally banged through the kitchen doors and sat down at the table beside them.

He did not seem happy.

Petterson wore a dark suit coat and matching slacks over a white, collared, button-down shirt. He looked professional, but not wealthy. His suit was cut in an older style, the fabric clean and well-kept, but clearly not brand new.

He was bald on top save for three wispy strands of hair that were carefully laid across the dome of his head. Below that, a ring of hair cradled his skull like those neck pillows people wear on airplanes. He wore the hair unforgivably long, long enough to cover his ears and reach down to his shoulders. He looked like someone had taken a picture of one of the Bee Gees and photoshopped a Catholic monk's forehead onto it, one of the ones with the bald spot carved into the top of a full head of hair.

Despite the ridiculous appearance, Petterson was an imposing man. He had to have been at least six-foot-six-inches tall and maybe three hundred pounds. And it didn't look like it was all fat, either. He was a big guy, but he didn't have a beer gut. He was just an extra-large human. Ollie gulped at the thought of pissing him off.

The chair creaked and swayed under Petterson's massive bulk, but he didn't seem to notice. He reached down to the floor beside his chair and pulled up a land line, an old-style, cream-colored rotary phone like Ollie's parents had had at their house when Ollie was a kid. A long cord snaked down the side of the table and back toward the wall.

Petterson banged the phone onto the table and pulled a sheaf of papers and a ball-point pen from his inner coat pocket. He cast an irritated glance over his shoulder, back toward the kitchen.

As if the movement had summoned her, Teresa emerged from the back.

Ollie sat back in his chair with a start when he saw her face.

Where before there had been whispers of green and yellow bruising around her eyes, now those whispers were screams. A bloom of bright pinkish-red splotched one cheek and circled the eye above it. Ollie could see another red splotch forming a shadow beneath her jaw on the opposite side.

She hadn't even tried to conceal it with makeup.

How bad must things be if she didn't even bother to hide such obvious evidence of abuse?

Teresa crept up to Petterson's table, hunching her long, reedy body into a defensive crouch and stepping only as close to the table as she had to in order to hear whatever orders Petterson was muttering to her.

She nodded quickly and backed away, looking up briefly as she did so. Her eyes widened to saucers when she saw Ollie and Alli. She straightened immediately and dashed back into the kitchen with more quickness and agility than Ollie would have thought possible for her.

Watching the door swing shut behind her, Ollie's guts fell to the floor, and for a moment he was sure he would throw up right there on the carpet in the middle of the restaurant.

And not just from the food.

His heart broke for Teresa. She was like a ghost, a shell of a person. Beaten, cowed, utterly defeated. To the point of inhumanity, it seemed.

Ollie pulled his eyes down to Petterson. At his parents' wake, he had worn the face of a sympathetic friend of the family, one who grieved for Ollie's loss and his own. He'd shaken Ollie's hand warmly and offered condolences that sounded sincere, humane. Human.

But the man who sat at the table before him didn't seem remotely like the man he remembered from the wake.

The man in front of him seemed angry and petty. A small man in a huge body. A man who would stoop to harming innocent people. People who were weaker than him. For all Ollie knew, Petterson beat little children and kicked the homeless for fun. Now, looking at him in Petterson's own environment, he seemed the type.

Ollie had to do something. He had to help Teresa somehow, had to rid the world of this evil man. There were too many men like Petterson out there. Abusers. Bullies. If Ollie could take even just one such man off the streets, the world would be a better place.

He pulled his fury down into his gut, squeezed it down into a red-hot coal, forced his mind to cool and think rationally about how they could bring this asshole down. He closed his eyes and took a long, deep breath, calming his mind. Then he turned to Alli, ready to come up with a plan.

But Alli wasn't there.

"Mr. Petterson?"

Ollie heard Alli's voice.

"I'm Alli Thomas. I represent Ollie Wood Deli."

Alli stood at Petterson's table. Ollie saw Petterson lift his beady eyes up to Alli's face.

"Mr. Petterson, we need to talk."

Petterson's expression was not one of kindness and willingness to help.

He looked like he'd rather let his fists do the talking for him.

And Alli was his target.

**21**

PETTERSON LOOKED LIKE A SMALL-TOWN THUG. And it was clear that he had no compunctions about the use of violence.

Alli watched the dynamic between Petterson and the woman who had answered the front door earlier that day.

What was her name? Camilla? Trista?

She was a victim of domestic abuse. That much was obvious.

And Alli was surprised at how much her heart ached for the woman.

It was obvious that the woman was weak. Whether she was truly weak or had just allowed herself to fall into that role somehow, Alli didn't know, but the way she prostrated herself before Petterson, the way she kowtowed to him, was ridiculous and completely illogical.

Why didn't she just leave him? Alli truly couldn't understand why the victims of abuse would allow themselves to continue to be abused day after day when an entire world existed that did not include their abuser.

All they had to do was leave. Get into a car or a taxi, get on a bus or an airplane, or just walk away.

But invariably, they stayed.

They stayed out of fear.

How would they support themselves? they would cry. How would they feed themselves? They had no money, no job, no prospects. In many cases, they had a dependent minor under their care, as well. How would they support the child if they left?

These justifications never made sense to Alli. How would they survive if they *left*? How could they survive if they *stayed*? At least if they left, they would have a chance at building a life for themselves. If they stayed, their expected lifespan was surely much shorter, not to mention the misery that lifespan would contain.

And the dependent minor was equally vulnerable. In many cases, the minor was subject to physical abuse, as well. Even if the abuser never touched the minor, there was the emotional abuse to consider. For a minor to see their mother—or, more rarely, their father—abused day in and day out left emotional scars that were difficult to heal. Sometimes, they perpetuated the cycle of abuse, if the child never learned any other way of behaving. The child, if male, would grow up to be an abuser himself. If female, she would grow to allow herself to be abused, even seek it out on some subconscious level, because that's the only kind of relationship she ever knew.

It was fear that kept the abused person in the abusive relationship. Fear and, possibly, shame, if they had somehow come to believe that they deserved the abuse. Or they believed they were absorbing the abuse as a means to protect their dependent, that their suffering was a noble act.

Just another logical fallacy that led to suffering among humans.

Why the fear of potential economic difficulty was stronger than the pain of actual physical abuse, Alli did not know.

But clearly, this woman—Tamara? Teresa?—was suffering from these logical delusions in some way, allowing this cretin, Petterson, to beat her.

Alli sighed as she watched the woman skitter away into the kitchen.

Just one more misguided person in a sea of misguided people.

She stood and approached Petterson's table.

Alli wished the woman—Teresa, that was right. She wished Teresa luck, but there was little Alli could do to help her.

Instead, she focused on the business at hand.

"Mr. Petterson? I'm Alli Thomas. I represent Ollie Wood Deli."

Petterson lifted his head. His eyes looked sub-human, predatory. Like an alligator's eyes. Cunning, lazy, hungry.

"Mr. Petterson, we need to talk."

Alli's skin crawled as those reptilian eyes drifted over her body from top to bottom and back again. A flicker of primal interest passed over them, like the glint of a flashlight when it crosses over that same alligator, submerged save for two watching eyes, at night.

Then the eyes went dark and flat once more and Petterson looked away, back to the stack of creased and folded papers on the table in front of him. Names and phone numbers and other notes scrawled in a wild script that looked more like the scrapes of a rodent trying to escape a cage than human handwriting.

"You a lawyer?" Petterson growled without looking up.

"I'm an accountant."

"I'm busy."

"This is important."

Petterson looked up at Alli again and smiled, a patronizing leer that sent an involuntary shiver down Alli's spine.

"Contact my secretary for an appointment."

He turned back to his papers again.

"I'll only take a few minutes of your time." Alli pulled out a chair and sat down at the table.

The look Petterson gave her then was enough to carve the

muscles from her bones, if Alli were subject to the same kind of fanciful, overly emotional thinking that plagued most people.

Still, she had to remember that Petterson was dangerous, clearly capable of violence, if Teresa was any example. Logic was wonderful, but animal instinct had persisted for a reason through millennia of evolution.

Petterson opened his mouth to reply, then looked up over Alli's shoulder and squinted.

"Don't I know you?" he said.

"Ollie Wood," said Ollie, who had appeared standing beside Alli. He reached across the table to shake Petterson's hand. "It's good to see you again, Mr. Petterson."

Petterson glanced from Ollie to Alli. Alli could see connections being made, rusted gears turning on warped, second-hand shafts.

Petterson's mood changed in a flash. He set down his pen, stood, and shook Ollie's hand warmly, the hatred and violence on his face shifting immediately to pleasure, then to compassion.

"It's good to see you, too, son. It's been too long." He gestured for Ollie to sit and sat down again himself. "How've you been getting on since your parents passed?"

"Getting by," said Ollie, nodding. He gestured toward Alli, who had sat down beside him. "Alli's been a big help."

Petterson kept his eyes on Ollie for a long beat, deliberately refusing to acknowledge Alli's presence, let alone Ollie's comment.

"Horrible business, their accident," Petterson said at last, shaking his head sadly. "Your parents were good people. I didn't know them as well as I would have liked, but I like to think we were friends, all the same. Good friends."

"Thank you, Mr. Petterson."

Petterson smiled and nodded.

"What brings you here, son? Have you eaten yet?"

"Yes, we have. Thank you." Ollie swallowed hard. "It was delicious."

"It's on the house," said Petterson. He lifted his hand, looking over Alli and Ollie's heads. The maître d' appeared by Petterson's side. "Comp their meal, Jerry," said Petterson, swinging a meaty finger between Alli and Ollie. "It's on me."

"Yes, sir, Mr. Petterson," said the maître d' before scurrying away again.

"That's very kind of you, Mr. Petterson," said Ollie.

Petterson dismissed the comment with a wave of his hand. "It's the least I could do, son. And thank you for stopping in. Please, don't be such a stranger."

He smiled warmly, picked up his pen, and turned back to his paperwork as if Alli and Ollie had already left.

Alli sighed.

This was yet another one of those misogynistic assholes who was going to smile and do whatever the fuck he wanted to do, regardless of what she said or did.

He wasn't the first one Alli had ever met.

Unfortunately, she was pretty sure he wouldn't be the last one, either.

She shared a glance with Ollie, who furrowed his brow. *Be careful*, he mouthed.

"Mr. Petterson," Alli began, "I've found some... unusual arrangements between Ollie Wood Deli and several suppliers owned by your investment firm. I'd like to discuss them with you, if that's alright."

Petterson ignored her, running his pen down a column of names and numbers, occasionally making tiny check marks next to a name.

Before they'd arrived, Alli had hoped the arrangement had been an innocent mistake. Some kind of weird clerical error at the bank that had persisted for years due to simple negligence. It was highly unlikely, especially since it had occurred with three separate suppliers. But, it was a possibility, however remote.

When she saw Petterson walk in, her suspicion immediately changed from negligence to petty criminality, but she still hoped for a swift resolution.

Now, in the back of her mind, she started considering what evidence she would need in a court of law.

But it hadn't come to that quite yet.

"There's an unusual arrangement at present in which several of your wholly-owned subsidiaries have direct withdrawal access to the accounts of Ollie Wood Deli."

Petterson still did not look up.

Alli went on. "I'm sure you'll agree that this sort of arrangement between independent companies is highly irregular and extremely destabilizing to any business, especially one with finances as precarious as Mr. Wood's deli."

Still no response from Petterson.

Alli knew something that would get his attention.

"I'm sure you'll also agree that such an arrangement is likely to arouse suspicion with several governmental authorities. The Internal Revenue Service is the most obvious candidate."

Petterson didn't look up, but his pen stopped working its way down the column of names and numbers.

"But it's possible that other federal agencies would also show interest."

Petterson set down his pen and folded his hands on top of the papers.

"For example," Alli feigned musing, "the Federal Bureau of—"

"Ollie," Petterson interrupted. He ignored Alli, looked straight at Ollie, that unctuous smile on his face once more, "haven't you taught your girlfriend here better manners than that? To come into a man's place of business and start talking about unusual arrangements, government agencies, the IRS? That's no way to treat an old friend of your parents, is it?"

"Mr. Petterson," said Alli, not giving Ollie a chance to respond, "I'm not suggesting we involve those agencies. I'm sure we can find a resolution to this problem that works for all of us without escalating things further."

Petterson's eyes lost focus and he smiled as if lost in a reverie.

"You know, Ollie, your dad and I used to chat about business sometimes." His smile grew wider. "I'd come along with the delivery trucks, early in the morning. Your dad and I would chat out back in the alley, talk about all kinds of things. Business, family. The future."

His eyes focused again, staring hard at Ollie. The smile never left his face, but it abandoned his eyes entirely.

They were cold, hard, flat. The eyes of the submerged alligator eyeing its unsuspecting prey as it grazed unaware on the river bank.

"Mr. Petterson," Alli continued, "I'm going to the bank tomorrow to terminate these direct withdrawal arrangements. We're here simply as a courtesy to inform you of that impending change."

"He was a smart man, your father," said Petterson, his eyes still fixed on Ollie. "He knew how business worked. How the world worked."

"We will work with the individual businesses in your investment portfolio to shift to a standard net-ninety payment arrangement."

Petterson never took his eyes off of Ollie. Not even a glance at Alli as she spoke.

Ollie, for his part, returned Petterson's stare. There was no threat in his look, but no fear, either. His gaze was calm and steady.

"We worked together for a long time, me and your old man," said Petterson. "Set things up to run smoothly."

"If you or the business managers prefer net-sixty or even net-thirty terms," Alli continued, "we can discuss those on a case-by-case basis."

At this point, Alli felt like she was reading boilerplate legal text, like the disclaimers and interaction warnings that the announcer blasts through at super-speed at the end of a drug commercial.

Or like a cop reading a criminal his Miranda rights.

"You don't want to rock the boat, do you, son?" Petterson injected compassion back into his smile, softening it around the edges.

But his eyes maintained that feral hunger, that predatory threat.

"You don't want to undo everything your father and I worked for, right?"

He reached out, quick as an alligator strike, and grabbed Ollie's hand on the table. Alli could see Ollie's flesh turn white with the pressure of Petterson's grip.

"You don't want to undo everything your father sacrificed for, Ollie." His smile fell away like a guillotine. "Everything he suffered for." The smile returned, brittle and sharp. "Do you?"

Ollie smiled back at Petterson. His eyes were also cold and hard. Alli had never seen him this way before.

He lay his other hand on top of Petterson's, patted it softly, then gripped it, squeezed the muscle between Petterson's thumb and index finger.

From the way Petterson's flesh indented, it looked to Alli like he squeezed it quite hard.

Petterson's eyes pinched at the corners. His smile, his stare, didn't waver, but he released his grip.

Still holding Petterson's gaze, Ollie turned his hand under Petterson's, took the hand and shook it between his.

"It's good to see you again, Mr. Petterson," said Ollie.

He stood, still staring at Petterson.

Alli stood with him.

Ollie turned and put his arm around Alli's shoulder. As they walked away, Petterson called after them.

"I'll come round in the morning, Ollie," said Petterson, "with the delivery truck."

Ollie didn't turn back, didn't break stride. But Alli felt his hand stiffen on her shoulder.

"We'll talk about this some more," Petterson said.

Alli could hear Petterson's menacing rictus in his tone. She felt a chill in the air even before she stepped outside.

**22**

THE FRONT WINDOW of the deli was dark when they pulled up to the curb. It was after ten o'clock, and Ollie felt more tired than he'd felt in a long time.

And that was saying something.

He knew Alli was right. Ollie hadn't been aware of the arrangement between the deli and Petterson's businesses, but it was clear that the arrangement had to end. Even if Petterson were the sweetest, most trustworthy guy in the whole world, having an arrangement like that was just begging for confusion and mistakes down the road.

And Petterson was definitely not the sweetest, most trustworthy guy in the world.

Ollie had kept his hands in his pockets since they'd left Les Arômes. He could blame it on the cold, both in the air and inside Alli's car. But, in truth, his hands hadn't stopped shaking since they left the restaurant.

They were still shaking, even now.

"Do you want to come into the office with me?" said Alli. The car shuddered into silence as she turned it off. The parking brake made a tight creaking sound as she yanked it up.

The cold air and the dark night rushed in around Ollie like a shroud.

"No," he said, softly. "I'm gonna head home, get some sleep."

He nodded to Alli and got out of the car without waiting for her to reply.

Ollie drove the ten minutes to his house in a daze, that shroud covering his thoughts, weighing down his heart.

He knew Alli was right. The arrangement couldn't continue.

But he also knew that Petterson was dangerous.

And Petterson didn't like change.

Or dissent.

Despite what he'd told Alli in the car, Ollie didn't sleep much that night, and he didn't expect to. He lay in bed in the dark in the cold of his parents' house.

His home.

Echoes and ghosts of conversation and laughter surrounded him. They were joyful memories, for the most part. He'd loved his parents, and they'd loved him back. He'd never been one of those rebellious teenagers who claims to hate their parents, who runs from them at the first opportunity.

Ollie had left home at age seventeen, but he'd done so not because he was running away from his parents. He'd done so because he was running toward his dream. And his parents, as sad as they were to see him go, supported him one-hundred percent. They cheered him on from a distance, welcomed him home when he visited, listened eagerly to his stories about culinary school or working in the top restaurants in New York, working his way up all the way from commis chef to chef de partie to sous chef before their accident. They celebrated his successes and sympathized with his setbacks.

He welcomed the echoes and the ghosts in the house. They

made him miss his parents even more, but they comforted him, too. They helped keep his memories from fading.

But as he lay in the dark, other memories came back to him.

Memories he'd forgotten.

Or tried to forget.

Memories he hadn't understood as a kid.

His hands had finally stopped shaking about an hour after he got home. Something about Petterson crawled under his skin, sent an icy fear straight into his heart, into his blood, into the marrow of his bones.

The reaction was too strong for it to have come merely from their conversation at the restaurant. That conversation was tense, but hardly enough to shake Ollie that badly.

But as he lay in the dark in his home, the echoes and ghosts explained things to him.

His memories helped his mind remember what his heart had never forgotten.

That time in the deli, when was a teenager, when he'd followed his father to the back door.

He'd seen the Drayger's Meats truck, seen the large man pull the door shut, staring at Ollie with those cold eyes.

He'd remembered that much.

Now, his ghosts helped him remember more.

He remembered his father's face in the alley before the door had shut. His face had grown angry as he argued with someone in the back of the truck. Then, the anger drained when the two large men came on either side of Ollie's dad.

The anger drained, and was replaced by fear.

Ollie hadn't seen his father for the rest of the day. His mother had arrived at the restaurant, seen Ollie standing in the back hallway, and put him to work chopping vegetables.

He'd heard the back door open, heard his mother's footsteps as she turned the corner down the back hallway, carrying a hotel pan with a marinating brisket to the cooler.

He'd heard a little shriek, then a clatter, then rapid conversation that he couldn't make out.

Ollie had stopped chopping, unsure whether he should go into the hallway to see what was the matter.

Something within him had held him back.

He knew now it was fear.

"It's okay," his mother had called down the hallway after a moment.

Ollie returned to his chopping.

He'd heard his parents talking, murmuring, trying to keep their voices low. Occasionally, his mother's voice would rise in anger, and his father's soft, deep tones would soothe her to a lower volume again.

His mom had left, then come back half an hour later. It had just been Ollie and his mother in the deli the rest of that day. When they got home that night, his mother had fixed dinner and they'd eaten in front of the television, just Ollie and his mom.

"You're dad's not feeling well," she'd explained to Ollie.

The next day, he still wasn't feeling well.

The morning after that, Ollie's father was awake and moving about the house. He took Ollie to the deli, as usual. Back to their routine.

But there was nothing routine about his father that day.

There was a dark brown bruise under one of his eyes. Whenever he sat down or stood, he winced. He held on to table edges or walls when he walked. And he walked slowly, his steps mincing. Even smiling, which was his normal expression, seemed to cause him pain.

At the time, Ollie had pushed these inconsistencies to the back of his young mind. He didn't see the connections, didn't understand the world in that way. Aside from the petty drudgery of school, Ollie's world was one of happiness, of love, of curiosity and creativity. Violence was foreign to him.

Now, as the ghosts and echoes brought those memories back to him, he saw them more clearly.

His father wasn't sick.

And Ollie hadn't seen the person in the back of the delivery truck, but he knew who it was.

Petterson.

Petterson and his goons.

And their "chat" in the alley, their talk about "business", had been a beating. Petterson and his goons had beat his father into compliance with whatever arrangements Petterson demanded.

Direct withdrawal being one, apparently.

And now Petterson was coming in the morning to have the same kind of chat with Ollie.

But things were different now. Petterson was a lot older. And Ollie's father had had a wife and a young son to worry about.

Ollie didn't have anyone. Alli and Sarah and Tom wouldn't arrive until long after the delivery truck had left, so there wouldn't be any risk from opportunistic targets.

And Ollie knew what was coming.

Petterson could come for a chat, but he might find that Ollie wasn't quite as fun to talk to as his father.

Ollie lay in bed, staring at the ceiling, surrounded by his echoes and his ghosts, until the first rays of the sun lightened the darkness.

Then he got up and got ready.

## 23

ALLI HAD BEEN FUMING when she and Ollie left Petterson at the restaurant. She had never been treated with so much disrespect in her life.

Aside from her mother.

Her mother could get away with it.

But no one else.

Alli's mind had filled with acid, her anger and indignation getting the better of her. She struggled to push those emotions aside, to push them down before they overwhelmed her entirely.

Overwhelming emotions led to irrational thoughts which led to irrational actions.

This was the plague of modern humanity.

Alli refused to fall prey to it.

It took half the ride home, but she finally settled herself with deep breathing and a practiced, clinical detachment from the roiling sea of her emotions. When she did, she noticed that Ollie had been unusually quiet.

Though, to be fair, with the way Alli's emotions had been screaming in her head, she wasn't sure she would have noticed if he'd been talking.

But, she didn't think he had been.

He'd walked from the restaurant to the car in silence.

He'd sat in the car in silence.

Just sitting there, hands in his coat pockets, slumped in the seat, staring straight ahead through the windshield at the dark streets.

That was unusual for Ollie.

He was normally fairly loquacious. At least, by Alli's standards.

Not only was he quiet, he seemed to be brooding. There was a kind of mood emanating from him. A darkness. An intensity.

Is it possible for humans to emit resonances that correlate to their emotions? The new-agers and the hippies talked all the time about vibes or vibrations, about auras and such things. It had always seemed like nonsense to Alli.

But, our atoms resonate at certain frequencies. Those frequencies change as the atoms absorb energy. There was a certain amount of leeway, a certain amount of energy those atoms could gain or lose before they shifted into a different state. Before they lost or gained an electron and their qualities changed.

Is it possible that emotions could cause parts of our body to generate energy, to resonate in a way that was detectable on a subconscious level by other humans?

Alli could feel the brooding intensity coming from Ollie. In the tiny cabin of her little VW bug, with the anemic heater struggling to keep frost from forming on the windows, that intensity was impossible to ignore.

Were these perceptions what the hippies called vibes? Could there be a real, physical manifestation and communication of emotion?

It was an exciting idea.

Alli made a mental note of it, then pushed it aside as she turned the corner toward the deli.

The idea was exciting, but it wasn't important right then.

What was important right then was Ollie.

He was brooding.

He was unhappy.

This wasn't like him.

And Alli didn't like seeing him that way.

She had a lot of work to do in the office, poring through the bank records to document the withdrawals, checking against invoices and rate cards to see what exactly Petterson was up to. She had a hunch, enough to spice up a casual conversation with some vague threats of government involvement, but no hard data to support anything in court.

Maybe that kind of work would cheer Ollie up, would help get him out of his brooding funk.

Alli pulled to the curb in front of the deli and turned off the car. She ratcheted up the parking brake while the engine knocked and shook and finally settled into silence.

"Do you want to come into the office with me?" she said.

He just stared out the front window, silent for a long moment.

"No, I'm gonna head home, get some sleep."

He didn't even look at her. And his voice was unlike Alli had ever heard it before. It was low and quiet and distant.

And ominous.

Before that moment, Alli didn't think Oliver Wood had a dark bone in his body. But she'd only known him for a couple of weeks. Maybe he'd had this side to him all along. Maybe it was normal for him to slip into melancholy from time to time.

He nodded toward her and got out of the car, walked around the back of the building. Alli just sat in her car, the cold seeping millimeter by millimeter into her legs and her arms.

She was a bit stunned, if she was being honest with herself. Ollie hadn't been so dismissive with her since the first day or two she had been assigned to the deli, when she was still the assigned accountant intruding on his turf.

Thing is, that was still her role.

When had Ollie's feelings toward her changed?

And why?

Bright lights flashed through the windshield and blinded her. Ollie's car emerged from a narrow side street and turned right, his taillights receding in the distance, two angry red eyes burning in the night.

And then it was quiet.

And cold.

And Alli was alone.

Alli woke with a start.

Her head rested on the desk in the office.

On the keyboard, to be more precise.

Keyboards do not make for good pillows.

In the dark room, the shifting blue glow of the screensaver on the monitor made eerie patterns on the blank white wall in front of her. She lay still while her mind came online and oriented itself to her position in space and time.

She'd come in last night to research the transactions, to trace Petterson's activities.

And she'd found something.

A lot, actually. Enough to start an investigation.

Maybe even enough to put Petterson in jail.

But definitely enough for Alli to make credible threats to him.

And then she must have fallen asleep.

In her chair.

At her desk.

With her head on her keyboar—

Alli jerked her head up and immediately regretted it. The ache in her neck knifed down her back and across her shoulders.

She pushed that pain aside and entered her password on the keyboard, hoping, hoping that her work was still there, that she hadn't somehow deleted it when her head crashed down to the keyboard last night.

Alli breathed a long sigh of relief, letting the tension flow out of her body.

The work was still there.

She tilted and twisted her head from side to side, trying not to read anything into the alarming cracking noises she heard, like those tiny firework chains that foolish parents give to their children on the Fourth of July. As if it were fun and perfectly safe to let infants play with explosives.

She could feel the imprint of the keyboard on the skin of her cheek and her forehead, felt the impressions slowly releasing, the skin returning to form. She rubbed her cheeks as much to wake herself up as to hasten that return.

She would suffer all the late nights and stiff necks and facial indentations in the world if it meant she could get Ollie Wood Deli disentangled from Jack Petterson forever.

And now she thought she'd found the ammunition to do it.

She scooted up to the monitor again to organize her findings into a PDF document that would lay out her argument to anyone who read it. As she did so, she heard the buzz of a tiny bell.

Someone was at the back door.

She glanced at the time in the corner of her computer screen.

It was already morning. 7AM. Time for deliveries.

The office door was closed. Alli stood to check the back door and heard footsteps walk by outside, heard the back door open, heard men's voices in the alley.

Ollie was already here.

He'd arrived at the deli and hadn't said hello.

A cold sensation rushed over Alli's skin, raised the hairs on her arms and neck, crept over her scalp.

She didn't know what she'd done to upset Ollie, to offend him, but it had to have been something to do with Petterson. Until Petterson sat down, they'd been talking and laughing about the terrible dinner at the restaurant. Then Alli had confronted Petterson, Ollie had come over, and his mood had shifted completely.

Was Ollie angry at her for confronting Petterson? That was the whole purpose for their visit to the restaurant.

Was he angry at her for the way she confronted him? For the things she said?

Alli replayed the conversation in her mind. She felt she'd been professional. Direct, but even-tempered and cool. Even when she'd introduced the subtle threat of going to the authorities, she'd done so in a casual, oblique manner. Nothing heated or pointed in any way.

Could he be angry because Alli was the one who stood first? Because she, not Ollie, was the one who confronted Petterson?

Ollie didn't seem the type of man to be irked by such chauvinistic expectations.

But, Alli reminded herself, she'd only known him for two weeks, and she'd never seen him interact with someone like Petterson, someone in a position of authority. Maybe that was it.

Still, Alli didn't think so. It didn't seem right.

A shout and the clang of metal pulled her from her thinking.

It was coming from the alley, like something heavy had been dropped into a pile of metal trash cans, or had fallen against the side of a dumpster.

Alli pulled open the office door, willing to lend a hand.

And maybe extend an olive branch.

The back door was partially open, but opened inward, and its angle blocked Alli's view of the alley.

But she could hear everything that was happening.

"Your father was just as thick as you."

It was Petterson's voice.

That cold sensation rushed over Alli's skin again, a thousand-fold, like a thin layer of ice had swept over her entire body.

"I had to explain things to him over and over."

Alli heard a heavy thud, then a short scream of pain and that same clanging sound again.

She recognized the screaming voice.

It was Ollie's voice.

"It eventually sunk in," said Petterson. "It'll sink in with you, too."

Alli stepped back into the office and quietly closed the door. She pulled out her phone and dialed 9-1-1, told the police there was an assault happening outside. She gave the address.

She didn't know if Petterson was paying off the police department. She didn't know if he had that kind of power, if the local police were that corrupt, or if that kind of thing only happened in movies.

But she did know that the closest police department was only a few blocks away.

And she knew that, with the gentrification that was starting to happen in this neighborhood, the police presence had been increased. Not a day had gone by in the last two weeks that Alli hadn't seen at least one police car patrolling the area around the deli.

She hoped the police would be there in a matter of minutes.

But she couldn't count on it. She had to be prepared if they didn't arrive.

She looked around the office for something she could use as a weapon. All she saw were boxes of financial paperwork, her shoulder bag with her laptop inside, her desk chair. The keyboard, mouse, monitor, computer tower.

She could use these items, but the keyboard, mouse, and shoulder bag wouldn't inflict enough damage. And the other items would be too difficult for her to wield, especially in the close quarters coming out of the hallway into the narrow alley.

She could sneak into the kitchen to grab a knife, but she didn't want to engage at close quarters, if she could avoid it. And she wasn't sure she could get that far down the hallway without being seen.

She needed something long and heavy, something she could use to poke, to block, and, with enough room, to swing.

She got an idea.

Alli opened the office door slowly, quietly, wincing as it creaked slightly on its hinges.

She chided herself for her foolishness. She'd just come out this same door less than a minute earlier, and no one in the alley had noticed. Why would they notice now?

She stepped into the hallway, keeping her back flat against the wall, her eyes on the solid metal back door. Watching for movement. Watching for anything that would suggest she'd been seen.

She could hear the people in the alley, but she couldn't see them. If she couldn't see them, then they wouldn't be able to see her, either.

She slid along the wall to the next room, slipped inside and pulled the old mop from the cabinet, the same mop she'd used two weeks ago to clean the office. The long, heavy hardwood handle felt solid in her hand. She unscrewed and discarded the mop head and tested the weight of the long wooden pole, finding its center of gravity, its balance point.

Like one of those martial arts weapons.

Only Alli was not a fighter.

Not even close.

In fact, all violence was a failure, in her opinion. A breakdown in rationality, communication, compassion, and creativity.

The human propensity for violence and warfare was the biggest negative result of the failure of humanity to think clearly, to control their own emotions, to step outside of their own selfish interests and consider a bigger picture.

But, when faced with violence, in this situation, Alli felt she needed to at least have the ability to defend herself.

And Ollie.

She crept back into the hallway, keeping her back to the wall and the mop handle upright, close to her chest. She gripped it halfway up its length, using two hands to hold it, like a baseball bat held halfway up.

Or maybe it was more like a golf club. Or a tennis racket?

Alli didn't know much about sports, and she didn't care.

She heard coughing and retching sounds from the alley, followed by laughter.

"Didn't teach you how to take a punch in cooking school, did they?" said Petterson.

Alli heard several voices laughing.

Petterson had brought others with him.

His goons.

Made sense that Petterson wouldn't do the dirty work himself. He'd hire muscle to get their hands dirty for him.

Alli stood behind the door, gripping the mop handle, wringing it in her hands like she were squeezing water from the handle instead of the mop.

How would she do this? She'd have to pull the door open with one hand, run around it, though the doorway, and into the alley.

Odds were that there was a goon blocking the doorway,

preventing Ollie from escaping back inside. That meant that Alli would have to hit the man in order to get to Ollie.

She have to hit him hard enough to get him out of the way.

She had no doubt that the mop handle was heavy enough to inflict that kind of damage.

She had a lot of doubt that she'd be able to swing it hard enough to do so, especially as she was running out of the hallway in close quarters.

She could ram the man, like a knight jousting. Poke him in the sternum or the throat.

But he would likely be facing away from her. Poking him in the back wouldn't do much good.

Though she could go for the kidneys. Or she could swing the handle up between his legs and strike him in the testicles. That would undoubtedly bring him down.

As long as he was standing in such a way that Alli could slip the mop handle between his legs from behind.

And as long as he wasn't moving, which would block her blow, blunt its force, or cause it to strike his thigh or his knee instead of his testicles.

There were any number of ways this could go wrong, and every single one of them left Alli at a distinct disadvantage.

All of these thoughts raced through her mind as she stood in the hallway and wrung the mop handle.

The men outside were still chortling over Petterson's lame joke.

Alli needed more flexibility, more options to account for contingencies.

She needed that kitchen knife after all.

Standing close behind the door instead of in the office, Alli had a better view down the hallway toward the kitchen, a better angle on what the goons in the alley could see. She was better able to assess the risk of running that way. There was a risk of being seen, but it was slight, much less than she'd figured before.

And certainly less risky than jumping out into the alley brandishing a mop handle.

She slid along the wall as quickly as she could to the corner where the hallway opened up to the kitchen.

She pulled in a deep breath.

With a quick glance at the back door, she darted around the corner.

As she did so, she banged into a stack of hotel pans sitting on the counter just around the corner. They fell to the tile floor with a terrible racket, the sound of metal on ceramic ringing in Alli's ears like the clanging of a church bell.

Alli hesitated for half a second, holding her breath and crouching down below the counter just past the corner. Her pulse beat in her temples, in her chest, in her wrists. Her blood hissed in her hears, her nerve endings whining along with it.

She listened, every sense in her body heightened.

And she heard more laughter, fainter, from the alley.

Then she heard a voice, clearer and louder than before.

As if someone were sticking their head inside the back door.

Or they were standing in the hallway.

"You hear something, boss?"

"You got friends in there, Ollie?" said Petterson, his voice fainter.

Alli didn't wait for Ollie's response.

Her pulse screaming in her ears, thudding in her head, she raced down the aisle, crouching, standing only tall enough to grab a knife off the counter, then crouching down again and scurrying through the opening to the front of house and around the front counter.

She pushed her back against the front of the counter, laid the mop handle along the wall beside her.

She pulled her knees in tight against her chest, turned her

feet to the sides to make herself as small as possible, as invisible as possible.

She drew deep breaths in and out through her mouth, slowly, quietly, counting her racing heartbeats with each breath as the first rays of morning light speared through the front windows of the deli.

She waited.

Listening.

She heard nothing.

Nothing.

Then, a sound.

Metal scraping softly against tile.

As if a foot had moved one of the hotel pans just a bit.

"You see anything, Mikey?" Alli heard Petterson call from the alley.

Why were thug names always so juvenile?

The thought appeared unbidden in Alli's mind, then disappeared just as quickly.

Someone was nearby.

She felt them.

Even above the pounding of her heart, the electric thrum of her nerves firing, behind the random thoughts in her mind, she felt them.

Some kind of vibration.

As if her atoms were responding, adapting to the frequency of someone else's atoms.

Someone very close.

"Mikey?"

Alli held her breath, forced her muscles to relax so they wouldn't quiver from tension.

Without moving her head, she glanced to her right.

And saw the toe of a leather boot, poking just beyond the front edge of the counter.

"Come on, Mikey. Get back out here."

Could the goon feel Alli's atoms the way she could feel his?

There was dead silence for a long moment.

Then another.

Her atoms jangled and buzzed.

Her heartbeat stopped, waiting.

"Coming, boss," said a voice at last, loud and deep and directly above Alli's head.

She saw the toe of the leather boot retract, heard the man's feet scuff and shuffle as he walked away, the sound receding as he moved through the kitchen toward the back door.

Alli released the breath she'd been holding, let it out long and slow and quiet, just in case there was someone still there.

She gathered her nerve and peeked around the front counter.

The kitchen was empty.

The man had come all the way to the front. He'd stood inches from her.

If he'd stepped forward, he would have found her.

If he'd looked down, he would have found her.

And what would he have done then?

What would he have done to her?

What on earth had she gotten herself into?

Fear bloomed in Alli's chest, tightening it, pushing a flood of heat and tears toward her eyes.

Alli pulled in another deep breath, used it to push that flood, that fear, back down.

Now was not the time for emotion.

Ollie was still in trouble.

He needed Alli to act.

She knew now that violence—or even the threat of it—would be useless against Petterson and his goons.

Violence was their strength.

Even with the mop handle and the knife, Alli was essentially defenseless.

Her strength was her mind.

And she'd just had a new idea.

❧

Alli had only one advantage in this situation.

No one knew she was there.

She needed to use that advantage, maintain it as long as she could and hope that the police arrived quickly.

She unlocked the front door of the deli, propped it open with the rubber doorstopper Ollie kept on the ledge under the window, and raced around the corner.

She ran down the side alley, the mop handle in one hand, the kitchen knife in the other, hoping with everything she had that there were no other goons in the cab of the truck.

And that whichever goon had gone into the deli looking for her—Mikey—wasn't searching the back alley, too.

She came to the corner on the side of the building, where the side alley met the back alley. She pushed her back against the cold brick wall, felt the jagged edges of the brick poke into her back.

She was wearing only a button-down shirt. The sun had just come up and the temperature couldn't be more than forty degrees, but Alli didn't feel the cold.

If anything, she was sweating slightly.

Still, her breath plumed in the frigid air. She needed to calm down. She pulled in one deep breath, then another, willing her pulse to slow.

Until she realized it wasn't going to happen.

She peeked around the corner.

Dumpsters for the various tenants of the building stood against the wall of the alley, on the side to Alli's right.

Ollie Wood Deli had two dumpsters, one on each side of the back door.

Fortunately for Alli, the goons had thrown Ollie against the dumpster on the far side. She could see the head of one of them above the near dumpster. His back was turned to her.

Even if the goon looked behind him, if Alli stayed low, the near dumpster should keep her hidden.

Should.

But Alli had heard two voices, besides Petterson's. That meant there were two goons.

She'd located one of them.

Where was the other?

The large white delivery truck filled most of the remaining width of the narrow alley. It was one of those snub-nosed trucks, with no markings on the side, no company logo. Just plain white all around.

She didn't know why, but Alli had been expecting Petterson to have come in a real delivery truck, like a Drayger Meat truck or a Daisy Bread Company truck.

Alli crouched down low and peeked around the dumpster, trying to look for legs and feet beneath the truck. But the wide, tall tires blocked her view.

She had to get a better angle.

She needed to get in front of the truck anyway for her plan to work.

She'd have to risk being seen.

Where the hell were those police officers?

Alli took one more deep breath, then darted out from behind the dumpster and scurried in a crouch to the front of the truck.

Though the truck was no more than ten feet away, and though the empty space between the dumpster and the near side of the truck could be no more than three feet, Alli had never felt so exposed in her life.

Three feet of open space.

Three feet in which Alli could be seen.

Could be caught.

She crossed to the front of the truck, her steps measured in racing heartbeats.

She squatted down in front of the grill of the truck, careful not to let the mop handle clatter against the ground or knock against the metal of the truck.

She waited, listening for any sign that she had been spotted.

She heard only the crush of her own blood pulsing in her ears.

She heard another muffled thump, another clang of metal, another cry of pain.

And more laughter.

Petterson said something, but Alli couldn't make out the words. They were too muffled.

That meant Petterson was likely in the cargo area of the truck.

Observing his goons from on high, like a general surveying his battlefield.

One goon by the back door. Petterson in the cargo area.

Where was the second goon?

Alli dropped to her knees, bent her head down to look under the truck.

There.

Two legs, behind the truck, in the center.

And Ollie.

Laying on his side.

Curled on the cold, wet pavement beneath the dumpster.

Alli didn't see any blood on him, but he was clutching his stomach, his face screwed up in pain.

He opened his eyes.

Those gorgeous brown-and-orange eyes.

They were clouded and dull.

Alli watched him from under the truck.

His eyes found hers.

Everything seemed to fall away.

Petterson.

The goons.

The truck.

The alley.

Everything fell away, leaving just Alli and Ollie, locked in that gaze.

Ollie's eyes widened just a fraction.

Alli saw the second goon's foot swing into Ollie's abdomen.

Ollie's face contorted in pain once more.

And everything rushed back.

The alley. The truck. The goons. Petterson.

And Alli's resolve.

She left the kitchen knife on the pavement and stood with the mop handle. She balanced it carefully on the passenger-side wiper blade of the truck, balancing it just at the center of gravity of the handle. Half of the handle rested against the truck's windshield. The other half stuck out into the far side of the alley, away from the building.

Alli balanced the handle carefully, perfectly. If that balance were disturbed even just a little, the handle would fall.

And that's exactly what Alli wanted.

She picked up the knife, stepped around the far side of the truck. Gently, careful not to shake the truck and dislodge the mop handle, Alli drove the tip of the knife into the sidewall of the tire, twisted it to widen the slit into a hole, then slid the knife out again.

The air hissed as it escaped.

Alli watched with satisfaction as the passenger front tire began to soften.

Then she ran.

Back around the front of the truck, across the opening, behind the dumpster, down the side alley, around the front of the deli and inside the building. She kicked out the rubber doorstopper, locked the front door, and ran as quickly and as quietly as she could into the back hallway, again pressing herself against the wall so as not to be seen from the alley.

She willed her heartbeat to quiet, trained her hearing on the alley, closed her eyes, and focused all of her concentration on listening to what was happening on the other side of the half-open back door.

"You hear something?" said the goon, Mikey.

"Don't hear nothing," said the other goon.

In her mind, Alli watched it happen.

The air hissed out of the tire.

The truck slowly dipped in front as the tall tire flattened.

The carefully-balanced mop handle wavered, then tipped, then slid, the force of gravity finally overcoming the friction between the handle and the wiper blade.

And then it fell.

The heavy wooden mop handle falling five feet onto cold, hard pavement in the echo chamber of a narrow alley.

Alli heard the mop handle clatter, hard and loud, against the pavement of the alley.

Not in her mind. She heard it in her ears, in real life.

"I told you," said Mikey, his voice agitated.

She heard the sounds of bootsteps scrambling down the alley.

Alli peeked around the corner of the open back door, saw no one there except Ollie on the ground.

The goons were gone.

She didn't give herself time to think.

She darted out, grabbed Ollie under his arms, and pulled him backward.

Thankfully, he was awake and aware and capable of movement. Otherwise, he would have been too heavy for Alli to move him.

Instead, she helped him to his feet and they half-ran, half-dragged back into the deli.

Alli set Ollie down and spun back to the door.

The goons ran back just as she did so.

Rage contorted the closest goon's face as he saw Alli in the hallway and realized that she had tricked them. He ran toward her.

Alli didn't stop to think what he would do if he caught her.

She slammed the door and snapped the lock shut.

She leaned her back against the door, letting the tension drain from her body as the goons beat their meaty fists against the door.

The way her body bounced with each blow, it was almost like a massage.

That's when Alli heard the police sirens out front.

And the swearing from the goons out back.

The truck engine rumbled to life and pulled away.

And Alli's heartbeat finally began to slow.

She looked at Ollie on the floor in front of her. His face looked normal, but he was clutching his stomach and wincing with every breath.

His eyes fluttered open and met Alli's.

"Was this on your to-do list for today?"

"'Protect Ollie'? It will be from now on."

"Remind me," he wheezed, his voice thready and weak, "never to have a business meeting without you."

**24**

THE COPS DIDN'T STAY LONG, ONLY an hour or so. They took Ollie's statement, then Alli's. Ollie shook his head as Alli told her story. He couldn't believe what she'd done, how she'd risked her own safety, her own life, to help him.

The one thing he could believe was how smart she was. Rigging up a mop handle as a time-delayed distraction? Who the hell would think of something like that, especially in the heat of the moment with a gang of thugs outside?

Only Alli.

He answered all of the cops' questions, truthfully and completely. He didn't hold anything back. He didn't owe Petterson anything. He didn't feel any need to protect him. Petterson may have had something on his parents, but he didn't have anything on Ollie.

And what the hell did he have on his parents? Why would they ever do business with a goon like Petterson? His parents weren't like that. It just didn't make sense.

The cops checked out the hotel pans that had fallen in the kitchen. They poked around in the alley, stood over the mop handle and wrote things on notepads and typed them into tablets. They took Alli's and Ollie's descriptions of Petterson, the two thugs, the delivery truck.

The paramedics arrived a few minutes after the cops and checked Ollie out. They wanted to take him to the hospital for x-rays on his chest, figuring he probably had a broken rib or two.

The last thing Ollie wanted to do right then was sit in a hospital while doctors ran a bunch of tests on him. It wasn't until Alli promised to drag Ollie to the hospital herself within the next two hours that the paramedics agreed to leave Ollie alone.

Sarah and Tom arrived just as the cop cars and the ambulance were pulling away. Alli told the story all over again for their benefit as Ollie gratefully sipped the coffee Sarah had brought. Even though his side ached when he pulled in a deep breath of delicious coffee scent, Ollie didn't care. His morning coffee had never tasted so good.

"What the fuck?" said Sarah. "All this shit went down before nine in the morning? Couldn't you at least wait until I got here?"

Ollie laughed, then winced as a sharp pain tore into his side. "Next time we'll ask them to make an appointment."

Alli's face darkened when he said that.

"What?" he said to her.

She shook her head.

"Spill, Thomas," said Sarah.

She pressed her lips into thin lines. "I want to make sure there isn't a next time."

Two cracked ribs and a bruised lung. Not super fun, but nothing serious. No punctures, no signs of internal bleeding. Just a tight wrap around his ribs and advice not to laugh or cough for a few weeks.

Doctors.

Alli was on her cell phone when they wheeled Ollie back to the hospital waiting room. Her head was tilted to one side, spilling her long brown hair down over one half of her face.

Ollie's breath caught in his chest.

Alli was gorgeous.

He'd noticed her looks the first time he'd met her, of course, but he'd just registered her as "pretty" in his brain. He wasn't thinking about anything else.

But over the last couple of weeks, he'd spent a lot of time with Alli. He'd gotten to know her a lot better.

And now, he couldn't think about much other than how gorgeous she was.

He felt tongue-tied and awkward whenever he was around her, like he was back in seventh grade, trying to work up the courage to ask Colleen Spanger to the Spring Fling Formal.

As he rolled closer in the obligatory hospital discharge wheelchair, in the few moments he had before she looked up and saw him watching, he drank in the shine of her hair, the glow of her skin, the angles of her nose, the curve of her brow, her cheek, her lips.

His thoughts were lingering on those lips, moving as she spoke into the phone.

Then she looked up.

Her brow was creased and she didn't look happy.

"He just came out," she said, her voice clipped. "We'll be there in twenty minutes." She ended the call and stood.

Ollie folded his hands in his lap and smiled up at her. "We'll be where in twenty minutes?"

Alli's car pulled into the driveway of Ollie's aunt's house. Just a few minutes down the street from his parents' home, Ollie had spent almost as much time at his Aunt Jen's and Uncle Mort's house as a kid as he had at his own home.

Ollie opened the front door, knocking and calling out as he did so.

Aunt Jen and Uncle Mort were in the kitchen. Aunt Jen had laid out a spread of sandwiches and a large pot of herbal tea on the round wooden table in the breakfast nook.

They fussed over Ollie when he walked in. Aunt Jen squeezed his arms over and over while she surveyed his body, as if she would spot something broken that the x-ray machine had missed. Uncle Mort hovered behind her, looking like he wanted to give Ollie a hug but was afraid he'd hurt him if he did.

They both wore worried expressions that were far too deep, far too lasting for the relatively mild injuries Ollie had. He wondered how much Alli had told them.

He didn't have to wait long to find out.

"You said you know this Jack Petterson person?" said Alli.

"Alli," Uncle Mort sighed, "can we at least have lunch first? For cripes' sake, we haven't even sat down yet."

"This isn't a social visit," Alli retorted. "Petterson just attacked Ollie behind his place of business. We need information. Now. So this doesn't happen again."

"I'm sure the police will handle it," said Aunt Jen, her voice brittle. She stared hard at Alli, her face blank as stone.

Uncle Mort was a pushover. He blustered and bitched, but he had a soft heart and didn't like to see people suffer. He ran a successful accounting firm, but Ollie was fairly certain his main ambition in life was to sit in his easy chair, read his newspaper, and not have to worry about anything, ever.

Aunt Jen, on the other hand, was tough and smart and didn't take any shit from anyone. She was Ollie's mom's older sister. She shared his mother's intelligence and wit, but had the pragmatism of the eldest child. She didn't have any of his mother's sense of wonder or adventure.

That was probably why Aunt Jen had married Uncle Mort and Ollie's mother had married his dad.

"Why are you so sure?" said Alli. "They didn't seem terribly concerned when they were taking our statements, despite the fact that we'd given them names, accurate descriptions of all three men, even the license plate number of the delivery truck. And the perpetrators had left only a few minutes before they arrived."

"Petterson's still a powerful man," muttered Uncle Mort. "Not like he used to be, but he knows who to blackmail and when."

"So he's got the police in his pocket?" said Alli.

"I didn't say that," sighed Uncle Mort. "Can we please sit down? I'm starving."

"If he's paying off the authorities," Alli pressed, "we'll need to find another way to stop him."

"And what way would that be?" said Aunt Jen. "You gonna beat him up? Do you have a gang of bruisers with lead pipes? Huh? Or maybe the vigilante thing is more your style. Is there a Batman suit under your clothes?"

Alli squared her shoulders, her eyes blazing. "There are better ways than violence to fight back."

"Right," replied Aunt Jen, stepping right up to the challenge. "And you think you can defeat Petterson two weeks after learning about him? You think you're smarter than the rest of us? We've been dealing with Petterson for decades."

"I'm sitting down," muttered Uncle Mort.

Ollie realized he'd been holding his breath while Alli and Aunt Jean went back and forth. He took in a lungful of air and a stab of pain raked up his side.

"I think I'll join you," he croaked, wincing.

Alli and Aunt Jean immediately turned to him, reaching out to help him into a chair, all anger gone from their faces.

For the moment, anyway.

"Oh, Ollie," said Aunt Jen. "Do you need anything? Ibuprofen or coffee or anything? A pillow for your back?"

"I'm fine, Aunt Jen," smiled Ollie, "but thank you. I'm still doped up on the pain meds they gave me at the hospital." He gestured toward the empty chairs around the table. "Please, sit. I'm hungry, too, all of a sudden."

It was a lie, but only a small one. He hoped that if everyone sat and ate a bit, they could lower the tension level in the room. Food had that miraculous ability to bring people together, to help them find common ground. Everyone needed to eat. And when two enemies shared a delicious meal, they couldn't help but realize, even just a little bit, that they were more similar than they were different.

Aunt Jen passed the sandwiches around. Roast beef and cheddar, turkey and swiss, and caprese sandwiches, all on thick-cut slices of Aunt Jen's famous homemade wheat bread.

The four of them tore through the sandwiches, wiping the serving plate clean in a matter of minutes. The only conversation murmurs of pleasure or requests to pass the sandwich plate or refill mugs of tea. Ollie soon discovered that he really was hungry. He must have eaten three sandwiches himself.

Aunt Jen put the empty plates in the sink, rinsed out the tea pot, and refilled the tea kettle on the stove. They waited mostly in silence for it to heat, with Aunt Jen standing over the stove, tapping her long acrylic nails against the countertop, as if willing the water to boil with the heat from her intense stare.

When it finally did, Aunt Jen poured the steaming water over fresh tea leaves and set the teapot in the middle of the table to steep. She pulled from a cupboard a plate of cookies and chocolates for the table, as well.

Ollie was grateful that Alli waited for Aunt Jen to sit back down again before she started in with her questions.

"Why is Jack Petterson involved with the deli in the first place?" she asked, her voice quiet and slow. Respectful.

Uncle Mort creased his brow and darted a glance at Aunt Jen, but kept his mouth shut. Aunt Jen twirled her empty mug between her hands, staring at it in silence for a long moment. The ceramic scraped rhythmically against the wood of the table while Alli and Ollie waited for a response.

"Your parents ran into some trouble," she said at last, looking at Ollie. "Financial trouble. They ran up some debts and needed a loan."

"And they went to Petterson?" said Ollie. "Why didn't they go to a bank?"

Aunt Jen pursed her lips and shook her head, frowning down at her mug. "The banks wouldn't lend to them. Not as much as they needed."

"Was this before or after they sold the building the deli is in?" asked Alli.

Aunt Jen didn't lift her head, but her eyes shot up to Alli, glaring from under furrowed brows.

"What do you know about that?" asked Aunt Jen.

Aunt Jen had the ability—and she used it often—to dominate people just by her manner. She was blunt and direct and didn't shy away from letting you know when she wasn't happy.

But Alli wasn't the type to back down or be intimidated. She just stared back at Aunt Jen, eyes calm and cool, her expression neutral and relaxed.

"Not nearly enough," Alli replied.

Aunt Jen looked at Alli for a long time before responding. "It was after they sold the building."

"Who did they sell to?"

Aunt Jen stared hard at Alli, then dropped her gaze to her empty mug. She stood and picked up the tea pot, filled everyone else's mug before filling her own.

"Petterson," she said quietly, then returned to the stove, refilled the kettle, and set it on to boil once more.

"Petterson owns the building the deli is in?" said Ollie.

"No," said Uncle Mort, staring into his half-full tea mug. "We do."

"'We' as in you and Aunt Jen?"

"'We' as in me and Jen," he looked up from his tea, "and you, Ollie," replied Mort.

Ollie shook his head like a wet dog. He didn't know if it was the beating he'd taken that morning or the pain meds he'd been given or just the crazy day he'd been having, but his mind was struggling to absorb everything that was being said.

Uncle Mort explained. "We bought it back from Petterson—"

"At a very high markup," said Aunt Jen over her shoulder from the stove, her back turned toward the table.

"—and put it into your parent's trust." Uncle Mort held up a hand toward Alli, who already had her mouth open with a question. "Revocable, Ollie is sole trustee at age thirty-five. Jen and I are joint successor trustees until then."

Alli closed her mouth, leaned toward Ollie.

"How old are you now?" she asked.

"Thirty-four."

"When's your birthday?"

"August."

Alli nodded.

"When did you buy the building from Petterson," she asked, "and why?"

The kettle on the stove began to whistle, low and quiet at first, then rising quickly.

"The *when* was shortly after Ollie's parents died," replied Uncle Mort.

The whistle rose to a shriek, which calmed and faded when Aunt Jen pulled the kettle off the burner.

"The *why* should be obvious," she said, steam billowing around her as she poured the hot water into the teapot in the middle of the table. "We didn't want Petterson to have it."

"And where did you get the funds for the purchase? If banks

wouldn't loan against the business back when Ollie's parents wanted it, why would they have done so ten years ago?"

"We're good with our money," said Uncle Mort, drily.

"And my parents weren't?" asked Ollie.

He wasn't angry at the suggestion. He was just curious. But he heard defensiveness in his own voice, all the same, when he asked the question.

Uncle Mort and Aunt Jen shared a look. Like a warning to each other.

Or maybe an agreement. A joint decision.

"I know Dad was bad with the books, but that's why Mom did everything that had to do with money, right?"

Uncle Mort nodded. "Your father was very generous," he said, "but I wouldn't say he was bad with money. He just liked to help people."

"Liked it too much, if you ask me," said Aunt Jen.

"He would donate to charity, lend to friends in need, give money to the homeless."

"He would feed them, too," nodded Ollie. "Thanksgiving, Christmas." He smiled at the memory. "Even Valentine's Day."

Uncle Mort smiled, a tight, short-lived smile. "Any excuse to help." His eyes grew distant. "He really was a good man," he mumbled, then looked up at Aunt Jen.

She just sipped her tea, her eyes also distant, staring into her memories. She pressed her lips tight and nodded.

"Eventually," Uncle Mort continued, "he stopped looking for excuses and just fed the homeless. Period. First it was holidays, like you mentioned. After you left home, it was one day a month, then one day a week. By the end, it was understood that anyone in need could come into the deli and they would receive a hot meal."

"Good for the homeless," said Aunt Jen. "Not so good for business."

That explained why so many homeless people had been

hanging around the deli when Ollie first took over after his parents' death. He thought the neighborhood just had a lot of homeless. They never asked for anything, never came in for food. They just skulked around out front for a while, then eventually stopped coming.

"Is that why they needed a loan?" asked Alli. "To cover the cost of feeding the homeless? Are you saying that expense was so high that it was ruining the business?"

"That wasn't why they needed the loan," said Uncle Mort.

He looked toward Aunt Jen. She looked back, pursed her lips, and stood to refill everyone's tea mug from the teapot again. When she finally sat back down, she let out a long sigh.

"My sister was brilliant," she said, staring into the swirling, steaming liquid in her mug. "She was beautiful, too."

The tension in her face fell away, replaced by a blankness that made Ollie's heart break. It reached into her eyes, which were far away and filled with regret.

"I was jealous of her, if I'm being honest," she said, her mouth turning down. Her eyes flicked to Uncle Mort's. "I can admit that now. Out loud."

Uncle Mort smiled back, faintly, sadly.

"I was the oldest, the big sister. *I* was supposed to show *her* how to live." Aunt Jen shifted her mug, setting the stilled tea to swirling again. "But she already knew. Knew it better than I did."

Silence fell upon the room as Aunt Jen slid further into her thoughts.

"She was good at school, good at sports. The boys loved her." Aunt Jen laughed, a rueful cough. "So did the girls. Our parents." Slowly, bitterly, she said, "Everyone loved Mira."

She took a sip of her tea. Ollie knew from the heat of his own mug against his palm that it was still too hot to drink, but Aunt Jen drank, wincing and swallowing like she'd just had her tonsils removed.

It was clear that it hurt, but she took another too-hot sip, anyway.

"Maybe that's why I didn't do anything," she said to her tea mug.

"Jen," said Uncle Mort softly.

"No, Mort." Aunt Jen's eyes were suddenly wild, angry. "Don't help me rationalize it. Don't try to make me feel better this time."

Uncle Mort sighed and lifted up his hands in resignation.

Aunt Jen turned toward Ollie. He sat back hard in his chair, as if her intensity of her stare had thrown him back.

"Your mother was perfect." she said, "Perfect little Mirabel. Perfect except for one thing." Her stare softened, lost some of its edge, slid back toward the unfocused past. "She liked to gamble."

"You've got to be kidding me," said Alli, coming forward in her chair. "Gambling debts? That's why they—"

Uncle Mort grabbed her wrist. She darted a glance at him, and he shook his head slowly. She let out a long, slow breath and sank back in her chair, brow furrowed, arms folded across her chest.

"I know it probably seems silly to you," Aunt Jen said to Alli, her smile icy, "but that's because you don't know what you're talking about."

Alli scowled back at Aunt Jen, but said nothing.

"Mira didn't gamble on cards or horses. She was too smart for that. Too good at math. She knew the odds were terrible. And she was responsible for the business. For your future, Ollie."

She gave Ollie that hard stare again.

"Your future meant everything to her. You and your father were the only people she cared about. The two of you and that deli."

"So why did she gamble it all away?" asked Alli.

This time, even Ollie gave her a warning glance.

"Stocks," said Aunt Jen, boring a hole into Alli's head with her stare, her voice brittle once again. "She got into trouble in the stock market."

"She started investing when Ollie was born," said Uncle Mort. "Studied the market, made some money, then lost some of it in the dot com boom, but cashed out before she lost it all. She thought she'd learned her lessons. She put the money back in, and happened to catch the market bottom perfectly."

"She thought she'd figured out the stock market," said Aunt Jen bitterly. "Thought she'd outsmarted everyone." She stared hard at Alli again. "That's what did her in."

"She made some big gains in 2004, 2005," Uncle Mort continued. "Turns out, in retrospect, she was just riding the market up, but no one knew that at the time. She was confident."

"Overconfident," said Aunt Jen.

"She opened a margin account and started trading options," said Uncle Mort.

"And she over-leveraged herself," muttered Alli.

"And she over-leveraged herself," Uncle Mort nodded. "When the crash came in 2008, she ended up in real trouble."

"She put herself in trouble," said Aunt Jen. "She destroyed her family's future, its livelihood, because she was too arrogant to listen to the people around her." Her face was red, her eyes shining. Ollie had never seen her so livid.

"That's why she went to Petterson," said Alli, nodding, "because no banks would lend to cover a margin call."

"And Petterson knew it," said Uncle Mort.

"He raked her over the coals," said Aunt Jen, her face hardening. Ollie could feel the anger, the hatred for Petterson coming off of her in waves. "Took everything from her." She shook her head. "And she just gave it to him."

"She had to," whispered Uncle Mort. "If she didn't give it to him, she'd lose it all."

Ollie was keeping up, but barely. He didn't know what options were, didn't know what a margin call was, but they'd called it gambling earlier. He assumed his mom somehow ended up owning a ton of money to someone. But he didn't understand why she would lose everything if she didn't borrow from Petterson.

"The banks would seize her assets," explained Uncle Mort. "They'd take the business, sell off the building, the equipment, even your parents' house to cover the debt she owed."

Ollie sat forward. "How much did she owe?"

Uncle Mort shrugged. "She never gave us a solid number."

"At least two million dollars," said Aunt Jen. "Maybe more."

Ollie rocked back in his chair again. "And Petterson paid that for her?"

"He must have," said Aunt Jen, "but he's taken a hell of a lot more than that since then.

"How was she planning to get it back?" asked Alli.

"I'm sure she had some brilliant plan," laughed Aunt Jen bitterly. "Maybe even getting it back from the market."

"If she'd lived, she probably would have," said Uncle Mort softly.

Ollie thought back to those times. He was living in New York then, only coming home once in a while. He couldn't remember anything being different. His parents had seemed totally normal.

Then he remembered the goons in the back alley when he was a kid.

"Had they borrowed from Petterson before?" he asked.

Aunt Jen's face went to stone. "Once," she said. "When you were younger."

"When I was fourteen."

"Somewhere around that time," Aunt Jen nodded.

"Was it the same thing?" Alli asked. "Investments gone bad?"

Uncle Mort shrugged. "We didn't get the details that time."

"My dad covered for her, didn't he?" asked Ollie. "He dealt with Petterson himself."

"Petterson doesn't deal with women," said Aunt Jen.

"Okay," said Ollie, stepping back in his mind and trying to see the bigger picture, "so my mom needed money and they went to Petterson for it. But, that was a long time ago, and he's been taking money ever since. Hasn't the debt been paid by now?"

"That debt will never be paid," said Aunt Jen, her lip curling in a sneer. "That was what your mom never understood about Petterson."

"He let her pay off the first debt because he knew she'd be back for more," said Uncle Mort.

"And only he knows the terms of the deal now," said Aunt Jen. "Your parents are dead and Petterson has direct access to your business accounts. He can just say the loan amount was ten million dollars at one hundred percent interest and keep taking your money forever."

"It wouldn't hold up in court," said Alli.

"You think Petterson will let you take it to court?"

"How would he stop us?"

Ollie thought for a moment.

Then his blood ran cold.

"How…"

His voice quavered.

He swallowed hard.

"How did my parents die?" he said, his voice a whisper. "How did they really die?"

# 25

ALLI LEANED against the wall of the kitchen as Sarah and Tom absorbed what Ollie had just told them.

He'd told them everything they knew about Petterson and the deli, so that Sarah and Tom would be aware if Petterson or his goons ever came by when Ollie was gone.

On the way back from Mort's house, they'd picked up surveillance cameras to install inside the deli, in the alley, alone the front sidewalk, and on the paths to where they all parked. They would set those up that afternoon. Ollie would do the grunt work to hang them and wire them, and Alli would configure the computer in the back to feed the images to a couple inexpensive monitors they'd bought to set up in the kitchen and above the front counter.

But Alli knew that wouldn't be enough.

They knew now what Petterson was capable of.

They knew that if they pissed him off, he'd become truly dangerous. More than just a beating from a couple of goons behind the deli early in the morning.

And Alli intended to piss him off.

She was looking forward to it.

But they had to make sure everyone was aware of the risk.

Anyone and everyone who Petterson might target had to know what was going on.

Mort hadn't been happy about it, but he had agreed for both him and Jen.

Especially once Alli asked the question that had been nagging at her during that whole conversation over tea and sandwiches.

"If you had enough money to overpay Petterson and buy back the deli in 2013," she had said, staring right at Jen, "why didn't you just lend your sister the money to pay off the margin call?"

A hush had fallen over the room when she asked the question, like time had stopped dead.

Mort had been fiddling with his teacup, but his hands went still.

Jen's eyes had been hard and angry.

It was the first time Alli had ever met her, and she didn't seem like a very nice woman.

She was no idiot. She didn't fall prey to the usual bullshit other people did. But she had her own issues, different issues.

And the way her look shattered, just for a moment, when Alli asked the question, told Alli that she'd hit on one of those issues.

Dead center.

Jen said nothing in response.

"What makes you think we had the money?" asked Mort. "The markets were down—"

"You're good with your money," said Alli, keeping her eyes fixed on Jen. "You said it yourself. You would have reallocated your assets as soon as we hit a bear market. Before the crash."

"Well, I don't know—"

"She asked you, didn't she?" said Alli to Jen, ignoring Mort's weak, spluttering attempts at deflection. "Why didn't you help her?"

Jen still said nothing, but the hard pinch that had returned to the sides of her eyes softened, just a bit.

"You were her sister." She saw Jen wavering, her eyes watering. Alli pressed harder. "Her big sister. Her only family."

The wavering stopped immediately, the hard anger clanging shut like the door of a prison cell.

"She was a bad investment," said Jen. "You don't throw good money after bad."

She'd pushed back her chair then, the legs screeching against the wood floor. She set her cup in the sink, but it tipped with a clatter and rolled back and forth against the porcelain with a rhythmic, scraping whimper. Jen set her hands on the edge of the sink and stood with her shoulders hunched by her ears, her back to the table.

Mort looked utterly devastated.

"I'll walk you out," he said.

They walked to the curb in silence. Alli's thoughts were swirling. So much new information. So many moving parts, both in the past, as she rebuilt the timelines in her mind, and in the future, as she plotted all the possible paths forward.

But those thoughts suspended when she saw the wreckage on Mort's face, saw that same pain echoed in Ollie's.

"I'm sorry, Mort," she said. "I didn't mean to upset... everyone. I just needed to know the full story."

Mort shook his head, then smiled sadly at Alli.

"Alli, you're the smartest person I've ever met. I've said it a million times and I'm sure I'll say it a million more. You see things that never even occur to most people."

"And now you're going to fire me?" Alli said gently, a smile curling the sides of her mouth.

Mort laughed, a surprised sound that faded quickly in the chill air.

"You'll quit long before I ever fire you."

Silence fell between them.

For the first time, Alli felt something for Mort, something more than just an employee's appreciation for a kind and supportive employer. She could see his love and his humanity in the way he treated his wife. She could see his suffering right now at her pain.

And she felt compassion for him.

"I'm sorry, Mort—"

"It needed to come out," he said, nodding as much to himself as to Alli. "You needed to know it." He turned to Ollie, standing by the car, hands stuffed in his pockets. "You needed to hear it." He looked over his shoulder at the house. "And Jen needed to say it."

He turned back to Alli, his eyes still filled with sadness, but accompanied now with a quiet strength.

"Now maybe we can do something about it."

That was when Alli had started to formulate her plan.

Thanksgiving was in two days, and Alli wanted to get things in order before the holiday. Ollie had been attacked on Tuesday. They'd spent that evening setting up the surveillance equipment, making sure it was in place and recording if Petterson decided to make another early morning visit.

Thankfully, he didn't, but Alli knew it wouldn't be long before he returned. He wouldn't take kindly to being outwitted, or to being chased off by the police.

That's why she wanted to act quickly.

That's why she brought Ollie to meet the boys at JD Motorsports the next morning.

She introduced them, told them Ollie's story. All of them, seven enormous, burly mechanics, stood or sat in silence, listening intently, as she and Ollie spoke. By the end, Alli could have sworn she saw tears in more than one eye.

Then she told them what she had in mind.

Mug, the gentle giant, whistled softly, shaking his head. "You got some balls, kid."

"That's a bold plan, Alli," said JD, agreeing with Mug. "Dangerous, too."

"You don't have to participate," said Alli. "No hard feelings if you don't. I'll understand completely."

"Are you kidding?" said JD. "I won't speak for the boys, but I've been wanting to see Petterson get cut down to size ever since I made the mistake of taking his money in the first place."

Murmurs of assent came from the others. They were in.

"But, if you don't mind," said Carl, the computer-science hippopotamus, "I've got a few ideas for tweaks that might make things easier."

**To-do list:**

- End arrangement
- Stop Petterson

They didn't waste any time.

The next day was Thanksgiving, and the town was dead. Everyone was at home enjoying the holiday with their family. Most businesses were closed, including Les Arômes. Petterson would be there, they were sure of that. But there was less chance of any delivery trucks or kitchen workers coming that might get in the way.

Even so, they set to work early, pulling into the alley behind the restaurant just after seven in the morning, as the sun was starting to lighten the sky.

About the same time Petterson had visited Ollie just a few days earlier.

Alli and Ollie took Ollie's old minivan, figuring it was more reliable than Alli's VW bug, and backed it in at one end of the alley. JD and his crew pulled up in a huge pickup truck, parking at the other end. Both vehicles were facing out, ready to drive away in a hurry, if necessary.

Alli got out of the car, tucking two manila folders full of papers under her arm. She nodded to JD as they approached the back door to the restaurant from their different sides of the alley. JD and his crew pressed up flat against the concrete wall while she and Ollie stood before the back door.

Alli had run through the plan in her mind a thousand times since they'd worked out the details. Carl's additions had been brilliant, and his computer skills were above and beyond anything Alli had ever seen. With skills like that, he must have made a fortune in Silicon Valley.

Still, even with that preparation, her heart was pounding in her ears.

She chided herself in her mind. She was in no danger at the moment. Any fear she felt was purely anticipatory, as most fear was, and therefore completely foolish. It was merely an assumption about one possible future outcome. She could just as easily imagine a dozen positive outcomes.

But all the logic in the world wouldn't settle her heart rate in that moment, as she stood beside Ollie in the cold morning air and pressed the buzzer at the back door. All the logic in the world couldn't override the millennia of evolution that gave rise to emotions like fear, emotions that preserved life in times of potential danger.

Nine times out of ten, the emotion was illogical. But that one time was enough to make the other nine worthwhile.

She heard footsteps and glanced at Ollie. He looked nervous, his face pale and his lips thin. But he nodded to her firmly.

He may be nervous, but he was just as determined as Alli.

She felt a sudden, odd urge to hold his hand, but pushed that urge aside as the door handle turned.

As Alli had expected, Teresa answered the door.

And Alli's heart sank at the sight of her.

Dark rings draped below both eyes. Her left eye was swollen almost completely shut. The sclera of her right eye was shot through with blood. A large cut striped across the bridge of her nose, and curls of dried blood caked the sides of her nostrils where she'd missed wiping it clean.

One cheek was puffed and bruised, and, when she opened the door and stepped back, she moved gingerly, in mincing steps, wincing with each movement as if every muscle in her body ached.

It probably did.

This abuse was fresh. Petterson had to have done this to her last night, or even this morning.

"Come with us, Teresa," whispered Alli.

The words just popped out of her mouth. She didn't think about what she was saying, didn't consider the consequences or the logistics of how they would hide Teresa or stop Petterson from coming after her.

Alli just spoke, instinctively, in reaction to what she saw before her.

Teresa's head picked up at Alli's words, her unswollen eye widening slightly.

"You would... take me?"

"Of course we would," said Alli, her heart breaking at the hopeful incredulity in Teresa's cowed, shaking voice. "You can stay at my apartment with me."

"And I have plenty of room at my parents' house," nodded Ollie, keeping his voice low. "You can have a whole floor to your-self, if you want it."

Despite her pain, Teresa seemed to straighten, to stand a little taller at those words.

"Who the fuck is there?" growled Petterson from somewhere nearby.

At the sound of his voice, Teresa folded back in on herself again, into an instinctively defensive posture, protecting her vital organs, bending away from Petterson's voice, from the source of her pain. She opened the door wider and practically hid herself behind it.

"Mr. Petterson," called Alli, stepping inside the door. "We've come to give you your first and final warning."

The back door of the restaurant opened into a large square room used for storage and deliveries. The floor was concrete, textured for traction, sloping to a drain set in the center. On Alli's right were two wide metal doors that led, she assumed, to a walk-in freezer and a walk-in refrigerator, similar to what Ollie had at the deli.

Across the room in front of her was another door, this one with a clear window set into it. Through it, Alli could see shelves filled with dry goods. Unlike Ollie's dry storage room, which was neat and orderly, full to bursting with food and vibrant with the colors of fresh vegetables, this one was in disarray, the shelves sparsely populated with large commercial-sized cans with faded labels and opaque plastic tubs. Even from across the room and through the window, Alli could see the layer of dust on some of them.

To her left was a large doorway that led to the kitchen, which Alli could see was at least twice as large as the kitchen in Ollie's deli. Beyond that, on the far side, were the swinging double-doors that led to the dining room, to the table where she and Ollie had first confronted Petterson.

The kitchen was similar in makeup and appearance to the one in the deli. Tile floors, two rows of ovens and cooktops and workstations, all in stainless steel. However, unlike Ollie's spotless, well-organized kitchen, Petterson's kitchen looked like a hurricane had just passed through, with dirty pots and pans everywhere, bits of dried or charred food on the counters and floors and around the drains, and black stains on the walls above the grill.

Alli resolved then and there never to eat at Les Arômes again. There was no way that kitchen would pass a health inspection. Petterson must have been paying off the inspector.

Petterson stepped into the doorway to the storage room. His eyes drifted over Alli as if she weren't there and focused on Ollie, who had come in behind her.

"*You're* giving *me* a warning?" Petterson laughed, a low, scraping sound, like someone dragging a heavy safe down a gravel pathway. He shrugged. "I guess our little chat the other day got interrupted before I could make my point clear."

His eyes narrowed, turned predatory.

Alli felt a chill run down her spine.

An instinctive response to a dangerous threat.

This was the real purpose of fear, to signal a true threat and stimulate the fight-or-flight response.

Alli had no intention of flight.

She held up one of the folders full of papers.

Petterson's eyes flicked to the folder. "What's that?" he said to Ollie.

"Evidence," Alli replied.

Petterson scoffed.

"Evidence of what?"

Still talking to Ollie, ignoring Alli.

This time, it was Alli who shrugged. "Take your pick. Bribery. Extortion. Blackmail. Usury."

Petterson just smirked.

At Ollie.

"Assault and battery."

He rolled his eyes. Actually rolled his eyes.

"No?" said Alli. "How about money laundering."

His smirk wavered just a bit.

That one hit close to home.

"Consistent, widespread, and..." She clucked her tongue disapprovingly. "...very obvious, I must say. Amateur. Clumsy, even, don't you think, Ollie?"

Ollie didn't take his eyes from Petterson, their gazes locked.

The smirk returned to Petterson's face. "Why bother covering it up when you can just pay off the ones who would charge you?"

Alli nodded. "That would be the bribery, extortion, and blackmail I mentioned. But do the friends on your payroll know about the rest of it?"

She shook the folder in the air. Petterson's eyes slid sideways to it, his brow furrowed.

"No matter how much you're paying them, I can't imagine they'd be willing to overlook murder." Alli flipped casually through the papers in the folder. "You're a serial killer, Jack," she said. "You put Dahmer to shame. Wouldn't this just make some young attorney general's career, huh? To put you behind bars for life?"

They didn't have full evidence to support that claim. It was enough to give the authorities something to investigate, but everything they knew was anecdotal.

But the look on Petterson's face was all the confirmation Alli needed.

The smirk fell from his lips and his eyes met Alli's for the first time, fixed on her with an intensity that hitched her breath in her chest and sent a flush of prickly heat throughout her body.

That instinctive fight-or-flight response again.

She could almost feel the cortisol and adrenaline flooding from her adrenal glands.

"All that in that little folder?"

Petterson's sneer revealed the yellow gleam of his teeth. Alli could think of nothing but the incisors of a T-Rex, dripping with drool, fetid reek of rotting meat on its breath as it sized up its next meal.

Irrational.

But instinctive and uncontrollable.

She pulled in a long, slow breath through her nose, hoping it was imperceptible to Petterson, that he wouldn't sense her fear.

She didn't say a word, just returned Petterson's stare.

"Even if I did believe you," Petterson said, "what makes you think this..." He waved his hand toward the folder. "...evidence of yours would get to me? Huh?"

He whistled, a quick, shrill sound. Two goons materialized through the doors that led from the kitchen to the dining room.

It was the same two goons who had beat up Ollie in the alley behind the deli.

"These two think I kill people, boys. They think I'm a murderer. You believe that?"

The goons chuckled softly, their eyes fixed on Alli and Ollie, their stares filled with menace.

With eagerness.

"If you really think I'm out there in public killing people," said Petterson, shrugging, "what makes you think I won't kill you two, right here in my own place?"

Alli held up her phone, unlocked it, and showed the screen to Petterson. On it was an app with a countdown timer and a large green button.

"If I don't click this button in..." She checked the screen. "...four minutes and sixteen seconds, the information in this folder will automatically be sent to the police, the FBI, and the press—local and national—along with your picture, your website, and enough detail for them to find you pretty easily. And it will be posted online. The web, social media, everything."

This was part of Carl's contribution. Both the app and Alli's threat were real, though she wasn't sure the authorities would do anything about it once they got the information. They hadn't had time to prep that end of the plan.

"We'll click that button for you," said Petterson.

Alli clicked the button on the side of her phone.

"Sorry. Phone's locked. Need my face to open it."

"We'll make sure you still have a face."

Alli forced herself to make what she hoped was a nonchalant grin, ignoring the shiver in her spine. "Doesn't work if I'm dead."

Petterson stared hard at her.

"Takes a long time for someone to die," he said.

Alli fought the nearly overwhelming urge to turn and run. It took every ounce of courage she had to hold her ground, to maintain her gaze on Petterson.

"How about we save you the trouble," said JD, stepping through the doorway from the alley and into the room.

The rest of his crew filed in behind him, filling the delivery area with a literal ton of friendly muscle.

Alli's fear didn't dissipate, but it did ease just a bit. She felt the strength behind her, felt the resonance of all of that energy in every atom of her body.

Petterson's eyes widened, then closed to slits again.

Alli's fear surged once more.

"John Donner," said Petterson. "Didn't I already teach you to mind your own business?"

"I'm a very slow learner," said JD.

Petterson's eyes slid around the room. "You've made some friends since last time."

"And you've made some enemies."

Petterson looked from face to face for a full thirty seconds. His expression grew more and more sour, more and more menacing, with each passing second.

And then it changed. In an instant, it went from the face of a predator about to rip open its prey to that of a smiling, ingratiating host, looking to accommodate his guests in any way he could.

"What is it you want, Ollie?" he asked. "You've been so quiet. All this talk about this and that, but you haven't told me what you want from me."

He stepped forward, put his hand on Ollie's shoulder.

JD and Mug stepped to either side of Ollie, practically growling in warning at Petterson.

Petterson ignored them. His unctuous smile never wavered.

"All you have to do is ask, Ollie. I'll do anything in my power to help you. You know that. I was an old friend of your parents." He squeezed Ollie shoulder, his face bunching in sympathy. "May they rest in peace."

"You killed my parents," said Ollie, his teeth gritted.

Petterson's facade fell immediately. His grip on Ollie's shoulder tightened. Alli could see the white in Petterson's knuckles, could see his thumb indenting Ollie's jacket just under his clavicle.

It must have hurt like hell, but Ollie never flinched, just kept his cold, hard stare on Petterson.

Petterson released him, turned and swiped the folder from Alli's hand, gave it a perfunctory glance.

"What do you want?" Again, his voice had that low, scraping sound, like rocks being pulverized in a crusher.

"Sign this." Alli pulled a paper from the second folder, which she still had held under her arm. "It terminates your direct access to the accounts of Ollie Wood Deli and indicates payment in full of any and all debts between you and your holdings to the deli and its owners, past and present, in any capacity, business or personal."

Petterson swiped the paper from her hand and read it quickly.

Alli held out a pen.

The daggers in Petterson's eyes would have killed Alli in a heartbeat. He took the pen slowly, carefully.

Somehow, that movement was the most chilling of all.

He signed the paper.

"Two copies," said Alli. "One for your records."

Petterson's face was inscrutable as he stared at Alli, but she could feel the menace coming off of him.

Those atomic resonances, again.

He signed the second copy and held it out for Alli.

"You can keep the pen," she said.

Petterson looked at JD.

"And what do you want? You already paid back your debt. You don't owe me anything anymore."

JD folded his arms and smiled, a broad, bright grin that lit up the darkness that filled the room.

"I just want to watch you burn," he said.

26

Ollie felt like he was going to jump out of his own skin. His adrenaline was pumping so hard as they walked out the back door of Les Arômes that it was all he could do to keep himself from sprinting to the car and peeling out of the parking lot.

As it was, his heart rate didn't slow down, his hands didn't stop shaking, until hours later, long after they'd celebrated at JD Motorsports and long after they'd stopped to tell Aunt Jen and Uncle Mort what had happened with Petterson.

There were no illusions. Everyone knew that Petterson was more dangerous now than ever. They had the signed paper, but it was Thanksgiving Day. Alli couldn't lift Petterson's direct account access until the bank opened in the morning. Nothing was final until then.

And Petterson wasn't the type to give up after his hand had been forced. He would retaliate. There was no question about that.

The only question was when.

And how.

Ollie didn't know the answer, but he knew that it would involve a lot more than two thugs and a back-alley beating.

That was why the rest of Carl's computer work was so helpful.

He'd found a way to hack into the surveillance system at Les Arômes.

And he'd added recording capabilities to the security setup at the deli. As a result, in addition to recording the deli cameras, they were recording Petterson's cameras, as well.

Ollie and Alli were back in the office at the deli. The deli was officially closed on Thanksgiving, but every year Ollie would make a special meal for his delivery customers and bring it to them at dinner time. Turkey and stuffing, mashed potatoes and gravy, and pumpkin pie with homemade whipped cream for dessert.

Nothing too fancy, but a good, traditional meal that would hopefully brighten their holiday. Most of those customers had no family to feed them, no relatives to spend the day with. The least Ollie could do was bring them a hot meal and let them know that someone was thinking about them.

On the monitor in the office of the deli, Alli was flipping back and forth between the deli's cameras, to see what was happening outside their own building, and the cameras at Les Arômes, to see what Petterson was up to.

Right now, even hours after they'd left him, he was still breaking things in the kitchen and screaming at his two thugs.

Ollie's adrenaline spiked again when he thought about what Petterson would do if he turned that anger on Teresa. It was only a matter of time.

In securing their own freedom, they might have signed her death warrant.

They had to find a way to get Teresa out, and soon.

But, for now, the best they could do was keep an eye on the surveillance cameras and hope for the best. Teresa was a survivor. She'd made it this far. Ollie hoped she could survive a bit longer.

He turned his thoughts back to Thanksgiving dinner.

"Alli, I'll need your help tonight, if that's okay," he said.

"Of course. What do you need?"

Ollie grinned at her. "I need you to cook."

He walked Alli through the steps to making the mashed potatoes. Washing and chopping the potatoes, with the skins, boiling them in a large pot, putting them through a food mill, then mixing them with butter, cream, garlic, parmesan, and a handful of spices.

A simple recipe, but a delicious one.

And perfect for Alli, who struggled with every step. She didn't even know how to boil the water.

To be fair, she understood the concept, she just didn't know how to light the range or where to find the pots.

And her knife skills definitely needed work. When Ollie saw the way she was approaching the oblong potatoes, with the knife slipping off the side or the potato rolling under her blade, he was sure she would lose a finger before the night was over.

He stood side-by-side with her, showing her how to hold the knife, how to cut the potato in half to form a more stable base, then chop it down from there. How to always be conscious of her fingers, of safety first.

He tried not to think about how close she was. He could feel her next to him, like standing next to a huge magnet, feeling its pull even when you were five feet away.

He tried not to think about her scent, the rich paper scent mixed with flowers... and something else now, something earthier. Almost like sweat, if sweat smelled so good one whiff drove Ollie crazy. He tried not to think about how, when their arms or shoulders would touch, when he felt her heat through her shirt, he would feel lightning zing through his entire body.

He swallowed hard and pulled his mind back from the edge, where it stood ready and eager to dive straight into the gutter.

He tried not to think about that, either.

He focused on keeping her safe in the kitchen. I wouldn't do for Alli to survive a confrontation with a murderous felon, only to be killed by a santoku knife.

Ollie had met—and worked for—plenty of chefs who didn't care about safety. Who didn't care about their kitchen staff. They only cared about their next Michelin star and about the adulation of their acolytes and their customers. Those kitchens were cutthroat, stressful, and dangerous. Ollie's arms were scarred and pocked with knife gouges and oil burns to prove it. His tattoos were more than just decorative. They hid some hideous scars.

And some painful memories. The worst scars were on the inside.

He refused to run his own kitchen that way. Respect and kindness, above all.

And safety first.

Alli was green, to say the least, but she learned very, very quickly. Before long, she was prepping the potatoes like a professional.

Meanwhile, Ollie heated several turkey breasts in the oven, basting them with some stock from the walk-in cooler. He prepped the gravy and started on the stuffing.

Traditional Thanksgiving dinner was delicious, but it tended to be monochromatic. The turkey and gravy and potatoes and stuffing were all varying shades of brown. Ollie liked to mix things up, while also adding in a bit more in the way of vegetables and nutrients. It was a way to bring color and healthy food to his customers, many of whom were unable to leave their homes due to illness or disability. It was a small thing, but big things were built from a thousand small things.

Chives and spices added some visual panache to the mashed

potatoes. Some years, he would roast broccolini and heirloom carrots or other vegetables for their color and their nutritional value.

This year, he decided to present the stuffing dish via a panzanella salad. Panzanella is a traditional Italian salad made with old bread, soaked in water to soften it, then mixed with onions, tomatoes, cucumbers, and basil and dressed with oil and vinegar.

Ollie put a Thanksgiving twist on the dish by using stuffing instead of bread. He chopped the day-old bread into squares, baked it to dry it out, then added parsley, rosemary, thyme, turkey stock, and onions and celery sautéed in butter. Add some eggs, bake it and brown it, and out came a beautiful stuffing.

He pulled out the largest pieces and toasted those in the oven to make stuffing croutons. He added them to a mixture of radicchio, red endive, arugula, beets, and apples, dressed it with olive oil, red wine vinegar, a squeeze of lemon, and some honey for sweetness. He added pecans for crunch and mixed it all up for a lovely, colorful, healthy side dish for his customers.

Sarah and Tom had prepped the pies and whipped cream the day before. While the turkey rested, Ollie and Alli sliced three pieces of pie per customer onto a plate and packed them up into bags with the potatoes, gravy, and panzanella. Gravy and whipped cream in plastic tubs. Everything else in disposable aluminum trays, with foil-lined paper lids to keep the hot things hot and the cold things cold.

Ollie showed Alli how to slice a turkey breast properly, cutting across the grain of the meat using long smooth strokes with a very sharp knife. If you do it right, the meat should cut like butter.

He resisted the urge to do the rom-com thing, where he would reach around Alli's back, hold her knife hand, and guide her arm through the movements of the cutting stroke, all as an excuse to cop a subtle feel of her body. As if anyone in real life would ever do such a thing to another adult without an ulterior motive.

Much as his body craved that contact, that closeness—how it tightened just at the thought—Ollie remembered the look Alli had given him the last time he tried something like that. If she'd given Petterson the same look, he would have surrendered on the spot, packed up, and left town that night.

Ollie rolled up the last paper bag of food. He counted twelve sets, with two bags in each set, ready for delivery. One set per customer. Most of his customers lived alone, but each set would feed two people. Enough for dinner and leftovers.

"You ready?" he asked.

"Ready for what?"

"We made the food. Now we need to deliver it."

**27**

THEY LOADED the food into Ollie's minivan, since it wouldn't fit in Alli's VW bug. Alli knew Ollie would ask her to bring the food up to the doorsteps. Purely from a practical perspective, he couldn't carry the bulky, heavy bags without making two trips. It was simply more efficient for her to help.

And he probably had ulterior motives, as well. He'd been wanting her to meet these customers for weeks. Alli had no idea why, but she was less resistant that night than she'd been in the past. It had been a long, difficult, surprisingly emotional day, and she had little energy left for arguing.

Normally, after a draining day, Alli wanted nothing more than to be alone in her apartment working on her latest theory or tweaking her code or just reading a good book by Michio Kaku or the like. Surprisingly, tonight she was happy to be with Ollie, even if it meant delivering food and meeting a bunch of strangers.

Alli found Ollie's company to be at once both relaxing and invigorating. He approached the world in such a different way from Alli, but in a way that was generally free from the self-defeating misconceptions of most people. Alli felt no annoyance from his actions or his logic, just a curiosity about his patterns of thought. He focused more on people than ideas, and somehow extracted useful information and meaning from that approach.

Alli's experience with people had never yielded those results.

Plus, something about Ollie made Alli feel stronger. Maybe it was his endless optimism, his tendency to support the people around him. He seemed to sincerely want to see them for who they were, to find out what they wanted, and to help them achieve those goals.

He'd even done that with Alli. Never criticizing her, never mocking her. Even going so far as to encourage her to post her ideas and experiments on the web.

It was a refreshing change from the relationships Alli had previously experienced in her life. Most of the people Alli had known—her mother, in particular—merely wanted to extract value from Alli for their own use. There was no interest in discovering what Alli wanted, no attempt to help her meet her own goals. They just wanted Alli to behave a certain way, fill a certain expectation, act a certain role in the narrative in their minds. And don't do anything odd or unusual or interesting that might distract from what they wanted to be the real focus of everyone's attention: themselves.

But Alli neither needed nor wanted help from these people, nor did she need to be the center of anyone's attention. She preferred to be left alone.

And she refused to subject herself to the morass of meaninglessness that defined most people's lives. She would not be a futile sacrifice to another mindless, sightless drone, tethered by the snout to the stern of fashion, driven by the winds of advertising, forever buying into the myth of their own inadequacy, never seeking real value, real growth, real knowledge.

Never seeking reality at all.

But with Ollie—and Sarah and Tom—Alli had found a different kind of person, a different kind of relationship.

True, they weren't logicians or scientists. They weren't concerned with the kinds of problems that would scale in the way scientific discovery and technological innovation could scale.

But Ollie had opened Alli's eyes to another approach, a more grass-roots approach that worked at a cellular level within society. His approach worked the way evolution worked.

In evolution, one individual would experience a spontaneous genetic mutation that conferred some kind of advantage. That individual would use that advantage to breed more often, with heartier offspring, who would then breed more often. Their offspring would then do the same, and on and on until the mutation had become common in the overall population, and the species had become stronger.

That was the approach Ollie was taking. He worked individual by individual, spreading change through his kindness, his compassion.

And through his food.

It was a risky tactic. His efforts might fail. He was essentially acting as a mutagen, a change agent, seeking to create a favorable mutation in others.

But the mutation might not happen, or it might cause a slightly aberrant change, an unintended one, one that did not confer the same strength to the species.

Or it might not spread. Or the spread might be too slow to be observable.

But these were concerns of scale and span and scope. Not a concern with the system. Not a concern with the approach.

The approach itself was conceptually sound.

Just very different from the way Alli's mind naturally worked.

And she was grateful to Ollie for showing her another way. For teaching her something new.

They pulled up to the curb outside an old two-story home.

Even in the blue and fading light, Alli could see the paint peeling off the wooden siding, could see the warp in the steps, the bow in the porch. The house had seen better days.

"We've got ten customers to deliver to," said Ollie. "This first one is Mrs. Dunbarton." He looked past Alli through the window at the house. "Most of my customers are nice, but she's the nicest of all." He smiled to himself, then said, "Help me with these bags?"

Alli nodded and got out without fuss. Ollie carried the larger and heavier of the two bags, the one with the turkey, stuffing and gravy. Alli's bag contained the mashed potatoes and, on top of a piece of cardboard for separation, the pie and whipped cream.

As she climbed the stairs and stood on the porch, Alli could feel the warp in the steps and the bow in the porch through the soles of her feet. She felt tilted, askew, uneven.

Ollie pressed the button by the door handle. The doorbell stuttered and fizzed before it chimed, a choked song that died before its time.

Through the bottom of the paper bag, the heat of the potatoes in their aluminum tray stung Alli's palms. She shifted the bag to a more comfortable position in her arms.

Alli heard scuffling sounds behind the door, then heard the sounds of locks being opened and the door reluctantly unsticking from its jamb as it was pulled open.

Ollie stepped forward into the doorway, blocking Alli's view of the interior, and of the person who had opened the door. Alli heard Ollie's warm, sincere greeting, his low tones somehow reverberating in her own chest.

Ollie bent low, and Alli saw two gnarled, spotted hands work around to his back, giving him a soft hug.

"This is my... friend, Alli," said Ollie, turning aside. "Alli, this is Mrs. Dunbarton."

The proportions and features of the woman who stood before her had the same ratio to Alli as a raisin has to a grape. Mrs. Dunbarton was short and shrunken in her stature, wrinkled in her skin, and thin as a power cable. Gnarled fingers grew like brittle tree branches from bulbous knuckles. Her hair was grey and coarse. Above cheeks hollowed with age, her eyes sat deep in her head, clouded by milky cataracts.

The smile she had shared with Ollie melted from her face.

Alli suddenly felt the chill of the night air around her.

This was Ollie's kindest customer?

Mrs. Dunbarton beckoned Alli inside, like a witch in a decrepit cabin deep in a tangled forest would beckon a weary, rain-soaked traveler who appears at her doorstep.

With a glance at Ollie, who nodded in encouragement, Alli entered. Ollie followed, closing the door behind them.

Mrs. Dunbarton reached her crooked hands toward Alli, set them on her cheeks, ran them over her lips and nose and eyes, up to her hairline and down the sides of her head to her ears and her jaw.

Her hands, despite their disfigurement, were surprisingly strong. Her touch was firm and warm, her wrinkled skin soft and dry.

She screwed her face in concentration, but left her milky eyes open. Alli, the bag of food clutched to her chest, gazed into them. She could look at little else. The eyes could see nothing, but blazed with intelligence nonetheless as the woman probed and studied Alli's face.

At last, she slid her hands back to Alli's cheeks and patted them softly.

"Come sit with me, Alli," Mrs. Dunbarton said, shuffling toward a nearby recliner.

"We do have a lot of deliveries," muttered Alli with a glance back at Ollie. The last thing she wanted to do was to sit with this odd old woman. She had a quiet presence that Alli found unsettling.

Alli couldn't have said why, though. More atomic resonance, perhaps.

"I'll only take a few minutes of your time," said Mrs. Dunbarton, her voice kind, but suggesting she wouldn't take no for an answer. "I want to get to know you a little better."

"I'm not sure we have time for that."

"With most people, you might be right," Mrs. Dunbarton said with a sigh as she dropped the last few inches into her well-worn chair. Her voice grew sharp. "But you and I don't dick around like most people, do we?"

Alli froze halfway into her seat, stunned by the woman's unexpectedly coarse language and harsh tone. She looked again at Ollie. He stood, hands in his pockets, and just shrugged, a smile tugging at the corners of his mouth.

Alli lowered herself the rest of the way into her seat, but sat at the edge of the recliner, straight-backed.

Beyond all reason, Alli was nervous.

Mrs. Dunbarton regarded her quietly from her chair.

"What is it you want, Alli?" she said at last.

"I'm sorry?"

Mrs. Dunbarton turned toward Ollie. "I thought you said she was smart," she said with that sharp tone again.

Ollie just smiled at the floor, hands still in his pockets, rocking back and forth on his feet.

"I'll say it once more, Alli. As you said, and as you can see," she gestured up and down at herself, a sardonic smile on her lips, "we don't have a lot of time." She leaned forward in her chair, resting her elbows on her knees, and spoke very slowly, enunciating each word. "What do you want?"

A thousand answers flooded Alli's mind. All of them were deflections, polite ways to avoid the question. The kind of answers given when someone says, "Hey, how are you?" in a hallway in the office. Despite their words, they don't really care how you are. They don't really want to know.

After a lifetime of this kind of casual superficiality, even Alli found it hard to overcome the learned habit of responding in an equally superficial manner.

"I want freedom," she said at last.

The woman sat back and folded her hands together, forming a single twisted clump of fingers.

"Freedom from what?"

"Freedom from the expectations and demands of others."

Mrs. Dunbarton sat quietly for a moment. "Is that really what you want?"

As soon as the question formed on her lips, Alli knew the answer.

"No," she said, "it isn't."

"What then?"

"I want freedom to do what I want, when I want. Freedom to pursue my own ideas and follow them wherever they may lead."

The woman lifted her chin, appraising Alli, then nodded. "And what is holding you back from that freedom today?"

Alli shrugged. "Society. The demands of life. The need to feed myself, clothe myself, to work for a living."

"And if you were independently wealthy, the richest person in the world, with no need to work to meet those... demands of life, as you put it. Then you would be free?"

"Yes," said Alli, firmly and quickly, though in the back of her mind, she didn't feel nearly as confident in her answer as she sounded.

"And what would you do then, hm?" said Mrs. Dunbarton. "What would you do with all of this precious freedom?"

Alli let her imagination run with the scenario. Her chest expanded, her mind released as she thought about the boundless possibility. "I would study," said Alli. "I would conduct experiments and test my hypotheses."

"And then?"

"Then?"

Mrs. Dunbarton smiled patiently, as if she were teaching a young child how to do something trivial. Alli felt indignation rising at her condescension.

"What would you do once you'd conducted your experiments and tested your hypotheses?"

Alli shook her head and shrugged. "I would share them," she said slowly.

"With whom?"

"The scientific community. The medical community." Alli furrowed her brow. "Politicians, maybe, though that would probably be pointless." She shook her head. "It would depend on the idea, on the conclusion. I'd share it with whichever community was best positioned to act on the information."

"To act? Toward what end?"

"To implement the ideas. To improve life, increase longevity, advance technology. Whatever the idea was about."

"Those are the things that interest you? Those are your goals?"

"Yes."

Mrs. Dunbarton nodded, unfolded her fingers and set her hands on her knees. "And how would you disseminate this information?"

Alli shrugged. "Scholarly publications, talks at symposia, that kind of thing."

"Do you have the credentials to be taken seriously by scholarly publications or to be invited to speak at symposia?"

"The strength of the ideas would be credential enough."

"Perhaps," said Mrs. Dunbarton, "but how would they know how strong your ideas were if they never bothered to consider them at all?"

Alli thought about it. It was a good point. She glanced at Ollie. "I'd publish them on the web, send them to influencers in the field. Scientists I admire."

"How would you get their attention? They must get a dozen such inquiries every day."

"I'd just keep trying. I'd go to them in person, if I had to. Make an appointment or stop them on the street, even. Whatever it took to get my idea heard."

Mrs. Dunbarton nodded. "So, let me make sure I understand you. You want the freedom to pursue your ideas and follow them where they lead, but you feel that the mundane demands of your life deny you that freedom. If you could somehow obtain this freedom, you would study, experiment, and test various hypotheses you have. You would then disseminate your ideas by publishing them on the web and working to get the attention of key influencers, people you admire, as a means of broadcasting those ideas more widely and implementing them in the world at large to improve life for yourself and, presumably, all humankind. Is that about right?"

Alli suddenly felt wary. "Yes," she said, carefully.

Mrs. Dunbarton smiled kindly.

"Alli, you seem like a very smart young woman." Her smile dropped like a hammer. "But we don't have much time. If I know Ollie, you've got a trunk full of food getting colder by the second, so I'll make this short and simple for you."

Alli's indignation began to rise.

"Your thinking is utterly naive and foolish."

Alli's indignation spiked. She opened her mouth to protest, but Mrs. Dunbarton held up her hand to stop her, and went on.

"These demands of life you so desperately want to be free from?" Mrs. Dunbarton said. "They will never go away. No matter how much money you have, how many employees or assistants or servants, there will always be something that interrupts. Illness, hunger, even just having to use the restroom, something will always get in the way."

Alli shook her head. She didn't accept what the woman was saying. If Alli had all day to focus on her work, she would.

"You're young, so you don't believe any of this yet, but I'll spell it out for you, anyway." She leaned forward in her chair once more. "What's holding you back isn't your circumstances." She sat forward in her chair. "You're too smart not to know this already, on some level. That leads me to conclude that the only thing holding you back," she pointed her gnarled finger at Alli, stabbing at the air, "is you."

**28**

As they left Mrs. Dunbarton's house, Alli was unusually quiet.

That made Ollie nervous.

As night fell and the air grew colder, they delivered food to the next eight customers.

Alli's silence continued.

That made Ollie very nervous.

She was friendly with the customers, even sitting down for a quick chat with one or two of them. But Ollie could tell that her mind was somewhere else.

Still on her conversation with Mrs. Dunbarton.

And as soon as the customers' doors shut behind them, Alli's face fell into a furrowed, distant expression, and that same silence fell with it.

She didn't seem angry, really. Ollie had felt that before, and this was different.

But it still didn't feel good.

Ollie had called ahead and asked Mrs. Dunbarton to talk to Alli. He'd told her about Alli's intelligence, her ideas, and her reluctance to share them with the world.

He couldn't understand why someone as clearly brilliant as Alli would be nervous about sharing her ideas.

And she was nervous about it. Ollie didn't know why, and Alli probably would never admit it, but she was nervous to put her ideas out there.

Scared, maybe.

Maybe she was afraid people would laugh at her. Maybe she was afraid they would tear her ideas apart. Or worse, tear her apart.

And some people probably would. Some people were assholes, especially on the internet.

But most people weren't like that. If they didn't agree with Alli's ideas, most people probably wouldn't say anything at all. Or maybe they'd question one thing or another, but probably in a relatively decent, compassionate way.

It might feel harsh. It never feels good to have your ideas criticized. But Alli had never seemed to care about any of that stuff. She didn't seem to care what other people thought about anything, so Ollie couldn't understand why she would be so reluctant to share her ideas with the world.

And so he'd asked Mrs. Dunbarton to talk to her. As a scientist and a woman, he thought she might be able to give Alli some useful advice.

But that plan seemed to have backfired.

"You ok?" he said to Alli for the hundredth time.

She turned her head toward the window and didn't bother to respond.

"Who was that woman?" she said after a moment, facing the window. "Mrs. Dunbarton."

"What do you mean?"

Alli turned to look at Ollie. Her eyes were bright, angry.

Ollie had seen that look before.

He didn't like it.

"Who was she? Who is she? What did she do for a living?"

"She was a scientist. Some kind of brain researcher. She and her husband did it together."

"Brain research," said Alli, furrowing her brow. She looked out the window again, then snapped her head back toward Ollie, her eyes shot wide. "*Mary* Dunbarton? Like Edward and Mary Dunbarton, the neurochemists?"

"Maybe?" Ollie shrugged. "Her name is Mary Dunbarton, and she did some kind of brain research, so yeah, I guess that's her."

Alli's mouth dropped open and she stared straight out the front windshield.

"Why? Is she famous or something?" asked Ollie.

"She and her husband discovered the mechanisms for signal transduction." Alli glanced at Ollie, who probably looked as confused as he felt. "It's the way that signals are conducted through our nerves. We know all about synapses and neurotransmitters now, but she was one of the first to explain how it all works."

Ollie nodded. He still didn't know what any of that really meant, but he got the gist. They figured out how nerves talk to each other.

"She should have gotten the Nobel, but they gave it to Carlsson, Greengard, and Kandel instead," muttered Alli, staring out the window.

She went silent again after that, but it felt different. Before, she had been sulking, angry. Now, she seemed just as intense, but it felt more like she was thinking hard about something.

We pulled up to the curb outside a nondescript house packed close to its nondescript neighbors. Full night had fallen, and the thin haze from a lone porch light lit the path from their car to the door.

"Last customer," said Ollie. "Ms. Stonnard."

He glanced at Alli. She looked back at him, distracted, as if she'd just woken from a dream. Her eyes slowly came into focus. Back to reality.

"She's a little... salty," said Ollie.

Alli arched one eyebrow, but said nothing.

Before Ollie had even lowered his hand after knocking, Ms. Stonnard yanked open the door, like she'd been watching them through the window.

Which, with Ms. Stonnard, she probably had.

"Happy Thanksgiving, Ms. Stonnard," said Ollie in his most cheerful voice.

Ms. Stonnard just scowled at him and snatched the paper bag from his hands. She thrust some money toward Ollie, but he waved her off.

"My treat, Ms. Stonnard," he said, smiling as wide as he could, projecting as much happiness and holiday cheer as he could muster. "For the holiday."

Ms. Stonnard just grunted and shoved the money in her pocket. She tilted her head to the side to look behind Ollie.

"Who's that?" she growled.

"That's Alli," said Ollie, turning aside. "She's helping me out at the deli."

Alli stepped forward, holding out her bag of potatoes and pie.

"Nice to meet you, Ms. Stonnard," she said. "Happy Thanksgiving."

Her smile almost seemed sincere, but Ollie could see that it didn't quite reach her eyes. They still had that distant, distracted look in them.

Ms. Stonnard regarded Alli warily for a long moment, then glanced down at the bag Alli held out to her.

"Can't carry both," Ms. Stonnard grunted. "Bring it inside for me."

She turned without another word and stalked off toward the kitchen. Ollie shrugged at Alli's questioning look. Alli followed Ms. Stonnard in, and Ollie followed Alli, closing the door to keep out the chill night air.

Aside from Tom, Alli was the first person Ollie had ever seen

Ms. Stonnard invite inside. On other Thanksgivings, when Ollie had muscled both bags up to the door by himself, Ms. Stonnard had made him wait on the porch while she brought one bag to the kitchen and came back for the other.

They walked through the living room, which looked as it always did. There was a tall, glass-fronted armoire in the corner filled with old plates and covered sugar bowls and soup tureens, all with ornate, Italian-looking designs in vivid red and blue swirls. The carpet was low pile and grey. Clean, but worn. A sofa, a love seat, and an easy chair, were arranged in the center of the room, all with thin white squares over the armrests, like doilies without the lace. The furniture looked like it had been new in the seventies, which was probably when Ms. Stonnard had bought it.

Seemed like the easy chair was the only piece of furniture that had been used in decades, its cushions dented from long use. The chair faced a flat-screen TV that stood on a low, wooden, antique dresser. The TV was the one thing in the room that looked like it had been made this century. The sound was muted, but images flashed on the screen. A commercial showing a smiling older couple driving down a winding road by the sea, then, for some reason, sitting in a pair of bathtubs on a grassy cliff overlooking the ocean.

Ollie had expected the kind of old person smell a house can get when it isn't ventilated, when the inhabitants don't exercise or leave the house regularly, don't cook or move about much. A kind of musty staleness. Instead, he was surprised to find that Ms. Stonnard's house smelled of candles and potpourris. Strong and over-sweet, the kind of smell that gathers in the back of your throat, but better than he expected.

Framed photos lined the wall leading to the kitchen, a progression of family portraits of a man and a woman and two young boys over the years. The clothing fashions changed from photo to photo, leather blazers, feathered hair, and thick eyeglasses with tinted lenses giving way to matching blue denim shirts, frosted jeans, and the same thick, tinted eyeglasses.

In the faded colors of the photos, Ollie recognized a young Ms. Stonnard, surprisingly beautiful and happy. The two boys moved from their parents' laps to the center of the photos to the sides, growing taller in each subsequent photo. As the pictures progressed, teeth appeared in their grins, then gapped out, then filled in again. It was like a time-lapse video. As Ollie walked to the kitchen, he watched the boys grow from toddlers to school-age to tweens.

Then the photos stopped.

Not the wall. Just the photos.

"Put it there," said Ms. Stonnard to Alli, pointing to the counter. Alli set her bag down and removed the pie, the whipped cream, and the potatoes.

"Pie in the fridge," said Ms. Stonnard.

Alli did as she was told.

Even Tom didn't get this much conversation. Ms. Stonnard had let him put her lunch on the kitchen table, then had sent him back out before Ollie had even taken a step inside the front door. At least he'd made it to the kitchen this time.

"Sit down," said Ms. Stonnard gesturing to a simple, round wooden kitchen table with four wooden chairs.

Something made the table seem like it hadn't been used in a long, long time. There was nothing alive about it. No flowers or candles. No napkins or salt-and-pepper shakers. Just a bare wooden table and four wooden chairs pushed in all the way to their backrests.

Alli sat. Ollie moved into the kitchen to sit beside her.

"Not you," barked Ms. Stonnard. Ollie stopped mid-step, then backed up again, standing in the entryway. Ollie saw Alli suppress a smile.

They sat in silence while Ms. Stonnard took a plate and a glass from the cupboard. She filled the glass with water from the tap, then pulled the turkey, gravy, and panzanella from the bag Ollie had given her. Carefully, she folded that bag and Alli's now-empty bag and set them under the sink, where Ollie could see a small stack of brown paper.

He realized with a start that they were all bags from his deli, the bags he used to deliver her food each day.

Ms. Stonnard pulled a fork from a drawer and took the foil off the turkey. The rich scent of the roasted meat filled the kitchen. Ollie's stomach rumbled in response.

Ms. Stonnard stood at the counter, fork in one hand, empty plate beside her, staring at the turkey in its aluminum tray.

"I was young once," she said, distantly. She didn't look up from the turkey, and her voice was so faint Ollie leaned forward to hear her better.

She snapped her head over her shoulder toward Ollie.

"Don't you laugh at me," she said.

Ollie had no trouble hearing her then.

When she turned back toward her empty plate, something came over the room, something that seemed to stop time.

Something about that whisper, then the angry comment. Some truth had come out, a truth that stopped the world from moving. Ollie couldn't put it into words, but he could feel it, could feel an incredible sadness, like another person standing in the room.

He thought about the pictures in the hallway.

The stack of paper bags.

The snap of Ms. Stonnard's voice when she told him not to laugh.

When he hadn't even thought about laughing.

"When did your family pass away?" asked Alli.

Typical of Alli, she didn't ask the obvious question. Ollie would have said something like, "Is that you in those photos?" or something equally stupid. Alli skipped past all of that to the questions she didn't already have the answers to.

And she didn't soften her voice, like most people would have. Like Ollie would have. There was no pity in her question. No emotion at all. She asked it like she would ask for the phone number of the pizza place on the corner.

Ollie braced for Ms. Stonnard to explode, to kick them out of the house.

But she didn't.

"1986," she whispered instead. "Tommy was twelve. Would have been thirteen in two more weeks. Bill was nine."

Tommy.

Ollie's heart fell.

No wonder she took such a shine to Tom.

"They'd been pestering George to take them ice fishing with him for years. He finally gave in."

She skewered a slice of turkey and transferred it to her plate with a soft, wet slap. Her arm went slack.

"They begged me to go with them, but I don't like the cold."

Her eyes were unfocused, filled with memory and pain.

"I wish I had," she whispered.

She stood like that, caught between two times, for a long moment.

Then, another skewer. Another soft slap.

She covered the turkey and put the tray in the fridge, pulled out a spoon and dished out her potatoes, poured gravy over everything.

Ollie could see wisps of steam rising from the plate like the breath of ghosts in the air.

"What have you done since then?" asked Alli.

Again, straightforward. No pity. Just curiosity.

"Nothing," said Ms. Stonnard, setting the tub of gravy down hard enough for drops to jump out of the container onto the counter, onto the triangle of her hand between her thumb, her fingers, and her wrist. She stared down at the gravy on her skin like it had offended her, like she would track it to the ends of the earth to get her revenge.

"Nothing at all," she said. "I've sat here in this house, yelling at the idiots on the television, letting people," she gestured dismissively to Ollie, "bring me my goddamn food so I never have to walk out that door. Never have to face the world."

"Safer in here," said Alli.

"Goddamn right it is," said Ms. Stonnard. "People die out there."

She flung her arm out toward the front door. Tiny flecks of mashed potato flew from her spoon and landed on Ollie's chest. He brushed them to the floor.

Ms. Stonnard noticed what she'd done, glanced at Ollie almost apologetically, then shook her head quickly and packed up the potatoes and gravy and put them in the fridge, threw the dirty spoon in the sink with a clatter.

She dished out the panzanella in a fury, her fork scraping the aluminum tray, then clinking against the plate like a pick-axe hitting stone. The plate jumped and rocked with each forkful. Ollie was afraid it might come at him like the potatoes had done.

But it didn't. Ms. Stonnard packed up the panzanella and set it in the fridge, closed the door and stood there, her hand on the handle of the refrigerator door, staring into space.

"People die in here, too," she whispered.

She stared hard at Alli.

"I was smart like you," she said. "Once." She stalked from the fridge to the counter. "Not anymore."

Alli raised her eyebrows in question.

Ms. Stonnard nodded slowly. "Oh, yes," she said. "I killed that, too. Slowly. Thought by fucking thought. Hour by fucking hour. Thirty-six years alone in this house and it's well and truly dead."

She looked over her shoulder toward Ollie. He flinched

involuntarily, then realized she wasn't looking at him at all. She was looking past him, toward the wall behind him.

Toward the photos.

Ms. Stonnard turned back to the counter and picked up her fork, her plate, and her glass of water.

"Now get out of here," she said. "Jeopardy's on."

## 29

Alli could see why Ollie described Ms. Stonnard as salty. She didn't bother with the usual social niceties.

But Alli liked people like that. She had found Ms. Stonnard interesting. And, rare as they are, Alli enjoyed spending time with interesting people.

Her heart went out to Ms. Stonnard, though. It was clear that the death of her husband and two children had devastated her and she'd never recovered. Alli didn't know if they'd fallen through the ice and drowned or died in a car accident on slippery roads coming home or what.

Those were the kinds of salacious details many people would ask about. But the way they died didn't matter to Alli. What mattered was how Ms. Stonnard chose to react to it.

And Ms. Stonnard had chosen a path that had clearly made her miserable.

She'd chosen a path of fear.

A path of inaction.

Despite the heart-wrenching story, Alli came out of Ms. Stonnard's house filled with energy and optimism.

"You're a little early for a Dickens re-enactment," she said as she slid into the passenger seat of Ollie's car, "but I appreciate the effort, all the same."

"Dickens re-enactment?" said Ollie.

"It's supposed to happen at Christmas time, not Thanksgiving."

Ollie started the car.

"What are you talking about?"

"Mrs. Dunbarton as the Ghost of Christmas Present, warning me about holding myself back. Ms. Stonnard as the Ghost of Christmas Future, warning me about what may come to be. Did you plan this? Put them up to it?"

Ollie laughed and shook his head.

"I did tell Mrs. Dunbarton about you, and I asked her to talk to you, but I had no idea what she would say." He grinned as he pulled away from the curb. "And Ms. Stonnard was a total surprise. I've barely even heard her speak before tonight. That was the first time she's let me set one foot in her house."

"Well, thank you, all the same. I didn't think I would, but I actually enjoyed this. Talking to these people. Some of them were very interesting."

Ollie raised his eyebrows in surprise, then smiled and nodded his head.

Alli felt a flush of heat through her body at the way he smiled. Boyish and sweet. And it made Alli happy to know that she was the reason he smiled like that.

The smell of turkey and gravy wafted across Alli's nostrils. Her stomach groaned.

"Now," Alli said, "let's go eat. After driving around with all of this food, I'm starving. Back to the deli?"

Ollie's smile faded. He stared straight out the windshield.

"Actually, we've got one more stop to make."

"I thought you said there were ten customers. Ms. Stonnard was number ten."

Ollie nodded. Alli noticed him turning onto the freeway on-ramp.

Not the way back to the deli.

"Ten customers," said Ollie. "But there's one more person we have to deliver to."

He sped up, merging onto the wide freeway. This late on Thanksgiving eve, traffic was sparse. They had most of the road to themselves.

"One more ghost, I guess." His chuckle was weak, tentative. "Call it the Ghost of Christmas Past."

A light snow began to fall, tiny flakes dotting the night sky. They fell faster, forming a streaking veil against the yellow glow of the streetlamps, like a time-lapse video of the movement of stars in the night sky. A thin layer of white formed on the road ahead of them.

As the snowfall grew heavier, so did the feeling of dread in Alli's heart.

The feeling of dread turned out to be a premonition.

Alli looked out her window as they drove. They passed Les Arômes, a few blocks from the freeway as they sped through the center of town. Alli wondered how Petterson was spending his holiday. Did he have family nearby? If so, would anyone willingly spend their time with him?

And she wondered about Teresa, how she was faring. Left alone all day with Petterson in the state he was in after their encounter this morning. They'd seen him on the video feed they'd tapped into. Petterson was not happy.

Alli hoped Teresa was safe. She hoped Teresa had found a place to hide. Or, better yet, a place to go. Irrational decisions were one thing, but when a person found themselves in a dangerous situation, safety was the first priority. Safety was a biological imperative.

Alli made a note to herself to check the video feed again when they got back to the deli, to make sure Teresa was okay.

She had no idea how Teresa had wound up with Petterson in the first place. Petterson was a man not even a mother could love.

The skin on Alli's face felt suddenly tight. She felt the blood scurry to her core, felt her extremities grow cold.

They were on the freeway, headed east. Not the usual route Alli took, but then she usually took surface streets.

It took longer that way.

But this route would get them there.

She thought about the food in the back of the car. Two bags left, if she wasn't mistaken.

Enough for three people, with leftovers.

And Ollie had joked about one more ghost.

The Ghost of Christmas Past.

Alli closed her eyes and took a long deep breath.

Ollie pulled off the freeway, wound through empty streets, hushed and sleeping under the fresh blanket of snow. The tires of his car hissed over the wet pavement. They pulled up to a well-kept, well-lit home tucked in one corner of a cul-du-sac on a street lined with more cars than usual.

Families visiting. Gathering to enjoy the holiday together.

Alli ignored the furtive glances Ollie cast at her as they parked in the driveway, gathered the bags of food from the back of the car, and walked along the stone pathway to the front door. Each knock of Alli's shoes against the stone felt like a hammer blow in her heart.

Or like the ominous tolling of the midnight bells in the Dickens story.

As Ollie rang the doorbell, Alli stared straight ahead at the wreath that circled the door knocker. Bare twigs curled and bundled, forced into a circle, shot through with dying leaves in orange and yellow and red, with miniature pumpkins on tiny stalks scattered throughout.

A charming wreath.

A beautiful, festive, seasonal wreath.

Completely fake, naturally, and utterly useless.

The door swung open.

A tiny woman stood in the doorway. She was shorter than Alli by three inches, but made up for it with stiletto heels worn under dark slacks and an elegant cashmere sweater in autumnal yellow ochre. Overpriced and overdressed.

Her makeup was flawless, not a single hair out of place in a tasteful coiffure.

The mask of the modern woman.

This modern woman was sixty-one years old, but didn't look a day over fifty.

Her plastic surgeon made sure of that. The miracle of botulism toxin.

"Happy Thanksgiving," said Ollie cheerfully from Alli's side.

The woman didn't look at him, but smiled, revealing impeccable, gleaming white teeth. Movie star teeth.

Teeth that would rip your heart out and feast on it without even staining a veneer.

She looked straight at Alli. Her lips closed, stowing those deadly teeth for the next time they were needed, to dazzle and impress, to impale and to conquer.

The teeth were hidden, but her smile remained, a patient, expectant curve to her glossed and plumped and perfect lips.

She raised one eyebrow, waiting.

It was inevitable.

No point in delaying it.

Alli sighed.

"Hello, Mother," she said.

"Oliver tells me you've been learning to cook," said Alli's mother as they sat down at the table, their plates laden with Ollie's food.

The dining room was as Alli remembered it from her childhood. A large oak cabinet along one wall that held china and serving bowls. A matching oval table large enough to seat eight people comfortably. Caramel-colored wood polished to a shine. Carved chairs to match, with thick cushions on the bottom and firm, ornate, bare wood backs. In the center of the table, a tasteful centerpiece arranged from two kinds of flower Alli couldn't identify.

Didn't matter. They were fake.

"Alli made these potatoes," said Ollie, brightly, when Alli didn't bother to respond to the comment.

Alli could forgive Ollie these attempts to endear himself to her mother. Alli hadn't told him much about the woman, so he simply didn't know any better. And Alli couldn't fault him for his ignorance in this particular situation.

"Thank you again for inviting us over for dinner, Mrs. Thomas," said Ollie as he unfolded his napkin onto his lap.

"Call me Cecilia, Oliver," Alli's mother responded, "And thank you for contacting me." She unfolded her own napkin primly into her lap, flashing a brief, tight smile at Alli before unleashing its full brilliance on Ollie again. "I hear from Alli so rarely these days. It's lovely to know she's made a friend."

She paused just long enough on the phrase to let the jab land in a way that only Alli would feel.

*Friend, not boyfriend.*

"Especially one who values family so highly," her mother continued.

They dug into Ollie's food. For a few blissful minutes, the only sounds were the clink of cutlery against china and the soft knock of wine glasses being returned to the table.

As hungry as she was, Alli could barely taste her food. Her mind was spinning, working hard to map the myriad paths her mother could take to needle Alli, to demean her, to subjugate her once more to the almighty will of Cecilia Thomas.

So many people over the years had told Alli how smart she was. Nonetheless, she had never been able to outsmart her mother.

Perhaps it was an evolutionary trait. Perhaps daughters were hardwired to be ruled by their mothers. A way for them to stay safe in their youth, carried forward into adulthood. A rough edge yet to be smoothed by the slow turning of the evolutionary millstone.

No, that couldn't be true. This pattern was unique to Alli and her mother. She had a hold on Alli that Alli had never been able to shake.

Theirs was a battle of wills that would persist until the end of days.

That was why Alli stayed away. The battle was exhausting. And there were better ways for Alli to use that energy.

"When is the last time you two spent Thanksgiving together?" asked Ollie.

The innocent lamb, following the path of the fresh grass. Munching happily, unaware that the path had been carefully tended, clipped and pruned to lead him straight to the slaughter.

"My goodness," said Alli's mother.

As if she possessed any goodness at all.

"It must have been... what, Alli? Ten years ago?"

She reached out and placed one cold, bony hand on Alli's wrist.

Alli froze, as if her mother's touch had supercooled the blood in her arteries, like liquid nitrogen.

Her mother's skin was perfectly moisturized, yet dry as the grave.

Her touch was soft, yet it stabbed straight through Alli's soul.

Her mother was a walking contradiction, a master of disguise. The face she showed to the world was not her true face.

Her true face was reserved only for Alli.

"Once Alli left for college, I rarely heard from her," said Alli's mother. "Too busy to call her own mother, I suppose."

Ollie chuckled. "My mom used to say the same thing."

From what Alli knew of Ollie's relationship with his parents, she highly doubted that was the case. She suspected Ollie called his parents often and came home as much as he could.

But she appreciated his attempt to dull the thorns hidden in her mother's rosy conversational style.

It wouldn't work, but she appreciated it.

"And where are your parents tonight, Oliver? Won't they be missing you the way I miss Alli?"

The way a boxer misses his punching bag.

Ollie set down a forkful that had been halfway to his lips. "My parents passed away years ago. In a car accident," he said with a wan smile.

"I'm so sorry to hear that." Alli's mother put her hand on Ollie's, her eyebrows bunching as she donned her "concerned" mask.

Alli was surprised that Ollie didn't instinctively jerk away at her poisonous, super-cooling touch. Instead, he put his other hand on top of hers and smiled at her.

A real smile. Sincere. Grateful.

Her mother smiled back, of course, her usual impersonation of a living human being with a heart capable of compassion. And yet, Ollie fell for it, like so many others before him. Alli thought he had more insight than that.

"My husband, Brian, Alli's father, died nineteen years ago last week." Alli's mother spoke quietly, pulled her hand back into her lap. "Alli and I know what it's like to lose someone so important in your life."

"It's not easy," said Ollie, looking across the table at Alli.

Alli focused on her food, mechanically loading her fork and bringing it to her mouth. The food itself had lost its flavor, tasted like wet paper on her tongue. But it gave her something to do that didn't require eye contact.

She hadn't heard her mother speak about her father for a long time. Not since just after he died.

And never in front of a stranger.

"You were a single mother, then," said Ollie. "That must have been so hard. How did you manage it?"

Alli's mother let out a heavy sigh.

"Brian was a brilliant man. He taught physics at the college. *Quantum* physics."

She said it like she knew what it meant.

"His intelligence didn't end in the laboratory. He was very good with money, too. Made a number of investments that proved very wise in retrospect." She smiled faintly. "Very wise or very lucky."

She shifted her napkin on her lap, then shifted it again.

She was fidgeting.

Alli had never seen her mother fidget.

"We were fortunate that he left us with enough money that, with careful management, I didn't have to work and could focus on raising Alli."

Alli brought another forkful of food to her mouth, if only to stifle the urge to shout at her mother. She hadn't focused on raising Alli. She'd only focused on herself. Constantly nagging Alli to look better, to act more appropriate, all so she didn't reflect badly on her mother's image.

That was what passed for mothering in Alli's home growing up.

"That couldn't have been easy," said Ollie.

What was that supposed to mean? Alli threw a withering glance at him, but he was looking at her mother, his full attention on her, worry and what looked like genuine empathy on his face.

Another person fallen victim to the wiles of Cecilia Thomas.

"Actually," her mother laughed, "I think Alli saved my life."

Alli's head jerked up, mouth still open to receive the forkful of food she held in front of her.

That was a new line of deception. Alli hadn't heard that one before.

"What do you mean?" asked Ollie. He looked at Alli and raised his eyebrows. There was a hope in his eyes, an optimism that Alli didn't understand.

One that made her mildly irritated.

She breathed slowly through her nose and continued eating like nothing was wrong.

Alli could feel her mother's stare burning into the side of her skull. Over the years living with her mother, Alli had developed the sixth sense of a war prisoner, one who always knows when her captors are watching. She kept her eyes fixed on her plate, chewing slowly, slicing another bite of turkey in slow-motion.

Her mother's gaze moved on, enough for Alli to sneak a glance.

"Alli is so like her father," her mother said, her eyes cast ahead, down the length of the table, unfocused. "Brilliant. Even more than her father. But just as headstrong."

A spontaneous, girlish laugh escaped her lips, surprising both Alli and her mother. Her mother's hand came up, hiding her mouth. Had she not known better, Alli would have sworn she saw a flush of color in her mother's cheeks. The gesture was shy, vulnerable, almost embarrassed.

Words that had never entered Alli's mind in relation to her mother.

If that laugh was an affectation, her mother's acting skills had improved dramatically.

Her mother dropped her hand, gave a quick, apologetic glance toward Ollie before letting her eyes lose focus once more, slipping back into her memories. She smiled again as she caught up to the loose thread of the thought that had made her laugh, the smile lighting the memory in her eyes. "They're both horribly messy, Alli and her father. Unkempt. In everything but their work. And they're terrible eaters." She looked up at Alli, eyes glistening. She gestured toward Alli's plate. "Or they were, anyway."

She made a sound that was half laugh, half sob.

Alli had never seen her mother cry. Maybe the surprise of that first laugh had thrown Alli off-balance, but seeing the tears gathering in her mother's eyes brought a stinging flush to her own cheeks and sent a warm prickle up her neck.

"They're so similar that all the things I used to do for Alli's father," her mother said to Ollie, "I started to do for Alli. Just transferred them from one to the other." She sighed. "The way I would check his tie and his collar before he left the house each morning. I did the same for Alli, fussing over her clothes all the time. The way I would nag Brian to eat lunch, to eat something healthy instead of just grabbing a snack from the vending machines down the hall. Same for Alli, pestering her to eat healthy. The way I would clean up his office at home for him each day after he'd leave it a disaster the night before. Same for Alli."

Alli's head filled with her mother's voice.

*Comb your hair.*

*Stop dressing like a street person.*

*It wouldn't kill you to put on lipstick once in a while.*

*How can you eat that junk all the time and still stay so skinny?*

*Your apartment looks like a garbage truck crashed and tipped over inside.*

Her mother grinned at Ollie. "I don't think Alli appreciated it very much." She laughed again, this time a sad, soft chuckle as she fussed with the napkin in her lap. "What teenager would?" She folded and re-folded her napkin before pressing it down against her legs. "But it let me pretend, at least a little bit, that Brian was still with me." She smiled again toward Ollie, her lips quivering. "I'm not sure I'd still be here if it weren't for that. For Alli."

Alli felt her mother's soft, dry hand on her wrist once more. She looked up and found both Ollie and her mother staring at her, expectantly.

As if they were waiting for a response.

But Alli didn't know how to respond.

Her mother had never said these things to Alli before.

Had never said these things in front of Alli before.

These things had never even occurred to Alli before.

In Alli's mind, her mother was a selfish, image-obsessed nag.

The woman her mother had just described was a grieving widow who poured all of her focus onto her sole surviving family member, transferring her love for her deceased husband onto her daughter.

Foolishly.

Clumsily.

Unskillfully.

But understandably.

Alli could not reconcile the woman in the story with the woman who had lived inside Alli's memories for the last nineteen years.

*Sometimes you learn stuff that can surprise you.*

Ollie's voice echoed in her head.

When had he told her that? Had he actually said it or was Alli just imagining it? It certainly seemed like something Ollie would say.

What would Ollie do in this situation, if he were in Alli's shoes?

He would never be in Alli's shoes. He wouldn't have such a toxic relationship with his own mother. He would have spent time with her, gotten to know her. He would have shared his thoughts and feelings with her, and she would have shared her own with him. They would have been close.

But that's how he was with his own mother. Would he have been the same with Alli's mother? Would he have been the same if his own father had died when he was ten years old?

Alli felt a sudden emptiness open up inside her, a dropping away deep within her gut that brought a wave of nausea over her, once so strong she brought her hand to her mouth, afraid she might vomit right there on the table.

The silence in the room persisted. It aged from expectant pause to stale delay.

Alli knew she was supposed to say something, but she couldn't form words. What words could possibly convey the upheaval inside her? All of the defenses and justifications she'd formed over nineteen years had just been shown to her to be stage props, cardboard cutouts cleverly painted to seem like iron-clad, airtight protections.

And now she saw that she was just as much an idiot as the people she dismissed in her mind all day, every day.

The silence in the room moved from stale delay to sour omission. Alli could feel the disappointment, from both her mother and from Ollie.

But she simply could not bring herself to respond.

She was paralyzed by her emotions.

Ollie cleared his throat and stood. "I'll get dessert ready. Would anyone like coffee or tea?"

He gathered the empty plates and disappeared into the kitchen, leaving Alli alone with her mother.

Normally, alone in her mother's presence, Alli's throat

would fill with bile, her mind would fill with acerbic thoughts, and her mouth would fill with the iron taste of blood from biting her tongue so hard to keep those thoughts from spilling out.

But this time, she didn't hear those thoughts, didn't taste that bile or that blood.

The tempest of emotion finally calmed, like a storm-tossed sea when the clouds have moved on.

What remained was a small voice, quiet in the back of her mind. A voice that Alli recognized the way one recognizes a relative in an old photograph. By intuition more than by intellect.

"Do you really think I'm as smart as Dad?" Alli said, her voice hoarse.

Alli's mother's eyes grew wide with surprise. "Your father and I both knew you were brilliant when you were young," said her mother. "You taught yourself to read when you were three, just by watching the words while we read to you. You could multiply in your head before you started kindergarten."

She smiled, an endearing, crooked, multi-layered smile that Alli had never seen before.

Or had never noticed.

"Your father came home from the university one afternoon and found you in his office. He had a broken clock radio that he hadn't gotten around to replacing. And there you were, parts scattered around you, screwdriver ten sizes too big for your hand."

Alli felt warm, like a blanket had been pulled over her shoulders. "I remember," she whispered.

"At first, Brian was afraid you would electrocute yourself. But you just looked at him, he said. Looked at him like he was an idiot. 'It's not plugged in, Dad,' you said to him. 'It's perfectly safe.'"

"That sounds like Alli," said Ollie, standing in the doorway to the kitchen.

"Brian just got down on the floor with you and watched you put everything back together again, plug it into the wall."

"And it worked," said Alli.

"It worked," nodded her mother. Her nod became a slow, incredulous shake of the head. "You were seven years old."

Alli remembered that day. She hadn't thought about it in years, but the memory flooded back into her mind. The smell of her father's office, a mix of pipe smoke, oak, and leather. The way the tiny screws from the radio would disappear into the deep pile of the beige carpet, until Alli finally retrieved a clean ashtray to put them in. The way the inner workings of the clock radio seemed to hover in midair like a hologram, assembling themselves in her mind.

"Brian came back to me that day and said you would upend the whole world one day with your mind."

Ollie set three cups of coffee on the table and went back to the kitchen collect the pie.

"When you chose Physics for your major in college," Alli's mother continued, "I thought you'd be off to the races then. Thought you might be a professor like your father, or maybe go into tech. Quantum computing in Silicon Valley or something like that. Follow in your father's footsteps."

"I'm sorry to disappoint you," said Alli.

It was the usual cutting comment she would make toward her mother, but this time it lacked venom, lacked bite. And Alli didn't feel the usual self-righteous indignation when she said it.

Instead, it felt sincere.

Her mother stared at her lap for a long moment, gave a heavy sigh.

"You've never disappointed me, Alli," she said softly. "Not once." She fussed with her napkin again. "I know you don't believe that. I wish I had done better at showing it to you over the years."

Alli opened her mouth to offer another knee-jerk retort, but she closed it again before she made a sound.

Did she believe it?

If she'd been wrong about the nagging over the years, if that was a way for her mother both to grieve and to show her love, could Alli have been wrong about her mother's disappointment?

In her mind, as a thought experiment, Alli assumed her mother was not disappointed in her.

Alli still felt disappointment coming from somewhere.

But if not from her mother, then from whom?

"Do you think Dad would be disappointed in me?" she said in a whisper.

"Never," her mother replied without a moment of hesitation, without a hint of doubt. "You're finding your way, Alli," she said. "Your unique path in life. For someone like you, or like your father, people who think differently, that takes time. Neither one of you followed a well-worn path. It takes time to discover your place in the world. It took your father years to find his footing."

Alli stared at her mother's eyes, searching to see if she was lying or not.

Her mother's eyes were clear and blue.

And beautiful.

Alli had forgotten how beautiful her mother's eyes were.

And, in that moment, they were guileless. Completely sincere.

Her mother was telling the truth.

And Alli believed her.

But if her mother wasn't disappointed and her father wouldn't be disappointed, what was the source of the disappointment Alli felt inside?

Ollie returned with three plates of pumpkin pie, piled with whipped cream.

"My goodness, Oliver," said her mother. "This looks positively decadent."

Ollie and Alli's mother dug into the pie, their forks clinking against their plates. Her mother nodded in appreciation at the first bite.

Alli held her fork and stared down at her dessert. Her mind was whirling. Her entire world, her entire belief system had been turned upside down. Like she was a character in a snow globe diorama that had just been shaken. Her thoughts whirled around her like snowflakes.

"You ok, Alli?" asked Ollie.

She looked up at him, looked across the table at those orange-flecked brown eyes, those incredible, gorgeous eyes that had become so familiar to her so quickly. They felt like a hot bath, safe, secure. She'd only known Ollie for a few weeks, but already he'd become a fixture in her life.

Did he know that? Had she ever shown Ollie how she really felt about him?

In an instant, like a supersaturated solution when a seed crystal is dropped in, Alli's thoughts came together and formed a clear, focused picture in her mind.

She knew what she wanted to do.

She knew who she wanted to become.

And she could see clearly her path to get there.

And she owed it all to the man seated across the table, staring at her with concern in those beautiful, warm eyes.

"Never better," she said, cutting a forkful of pie and bringing it to her lips.

Nothing had ever tasted sweeter.

**30**

Ollie had been nervous about bringing Alli to speak with Mrs. Dunbarton.

He'd been absolutely terrified to bring her to her mom's house for Thanksgiving dinner.

He knew Alli didn't care for her mother, but there was something in the way Alli talked about her that made him feel like something was off. Some unresolved business.

And, for some crazy reason, he took it upon himself to resolve it.

Or at least to bring them together to resolve it.

And then when he'd found Alli's mother's number and spoken to her, had found her to be a kind, intelligent, compassionate woman, he knew that something had gone horribly wrong somewhere along the line between Alli and her mom.

He followed his gut and set up the dinner, knowing that it would either work out or he would lose Alli forever.

It was a big risk, but he felt like he had to take it.

Ollie would give anything to be able to have one more dinner with his parents. He couldn't sit by and let Alli squander what time she had left with her mom, all because of some misunderstanding, if that's what it was.

All through dinner, Ollie was certain he'd failed, that he'd lost Alli forever.

Not just romantically. He was fairly sure she'd never want to even talk to him again after that night.

She wouldn't even look at him during dinner, and she certainly wasn't engaging with her mother. She was just shoveling food into her mouth like a robot, eyes down on her plate.

And then, they'd started talking about Alli's father.

And everything changed.

It was like a painful, festering wound had finally been opened, cleaned, and dressed.

Alli had become animated, talking to her mother. Ollie had excused himself to give them privacy, but he could still hear them from the kitchen. Alli sounded not just interested, but emotional. When Ollie had come back with coffee, she'd been smiling. And it even looked like she might have had a tear or two in her eye.

Alli had even hugged her mother on the way out the door, a long, sincere hug.

Her mother had looked as surprised as Ollie had been. The way the tears had jumped into her mom's eyes, Ollie had the feeling that was the first hug they'd shared in a very, very long time.

Alli had been quiet in the car since they'd left, but that silence didn't feel like the angry silences Ollie had already experienced too many times for his taste. It felt more thoughtful, emotional. Like she was processing everything that had just happened.

So Ollie kept his own mouth shut and left Alli to her thoughts. As much as he wanted to ask her how she was feeling, he knew that she would have to work through that on her own before she could talk about it with him.

If she even did want to talk about it with him.

In just a few weeks, Ollie had come to think about Alli like she'd been in his life forever. Every morning, he looked forward to seeing her. Every night, he thought about her as he fell asleep.

But to Alli, Ollie was just a job assignment. A client that Uncle Mort had assigned to her.

And she'd be leaving soon. Uncle Mort had told Ollie about the ultimatum he'd given Alli. Fix the deli by Thanksgiving or she'd be fired.

And somehow, miraculously, Alli had succeeded. She'd modernized the accounting system and the cash register and shown Sarah and Tom how to use it. She'd identified the cash flow problems and adjusted things accordingly.

And, most importantly, she'd figured out what was going on with Petterson.

Ollie shook his head as he drove through the night, light snow streaking by, the lines on the road like strobes under his headlights.

That morning felt like a lifetime ago, but he still couldn't believe that Alli, in just a few weeks, had brought the great and fearsome Jack Petterson to his knees.

She really was brilliant.

And once the business with Petterson was finalized at the bank tomorrow, that brilliant woman would be off to another assignment. Another hopeless business case for her to rescue.

Ollie gripped the steering wheel tight, set his jaw. He wouldn't let Alli go without telling her how he felt. He couldn't live with himself otherwise.

But what good would that do? She'd already shown, several times, that she wasn't interested in him that way. Baring his soul to her, professing his feelings like a lovesick grade-school kid would only make her uncomfortable. And it would probably ruin any chance he had of being friends with her in the future. He'd lucked out that the dinner had ended well. He didn't want to push his good fortune any further.

As they sped down the freeway, now driving through the heart of the city, Ollie glanced over at Alli.

She was staring out the side window. Her hair was thrown back over her shoulder. In the glow of the streetlamps that bathed this section of the freeway, Ollie let his eyes trace the sweep of Alli's long, graceful neck, the soft curve of her jaw, the velvet expanse of her cheek. He wanted to press his lips against that neck, that jaw, that cheek. He wanted to whisper his love into her ear, track kisses down to her full lips.

He pulled his mind back from his fantasies, stared out the windshield. He was going to get them both killed on the freeway if he didn't stop gawking at Alli.

But he couldn't help himself. He glanced back at her again, again swept his eyes over her neck, her cheek, up to her ear. Bathed blue in the light from the streetlamps, her small silver earring dangled just below her earlobe, her delicate earlobe that Ollie wanted nothing more in that moment than to nibble gently. The silver earring glowed, a hint of red in the flickering light.

Ollie frowned.

Why was it red?

That's when Ollie heard the sirens.

A police car raced by on his left, sirens blaring, lights flashing red and blue.

Then another police car right behind it.

Glowing up from the surface streets, Ollie saw the flash of emergency vehicles, heard the wail and honk of fire trucks.

He turned his head toward them as they sped along on the freeway, keeping pace with the fire trucks for a moment. A few blocks away, Ollie saw an orange glow beneath a thick cloud of grey smoke, a darkness within the night.

A building was on fire. In the center of town.

A thought came to Ollie, a chilling thought.

He turned to Alli, who was looking across the car, out Ollie's window.

"Is that...?" he said.

Alli nodded.

"Les Arômes," she confirmed.

They got off at the next exit and crept along the surface streets, needing to see for themselves.

The snow was deeper and fresher there, the only tracks those left by the fire trucks, police cars, and ambulances.

Ollie could still see the glow of the fire above the tops of the buildings as they wound through town. At the final corner with the street Les Arômes was on, the flashing lights from the emergency vehicles lit the brick sides of the buildings, forming flickering shadows from the streetlamps and mailboxes, dark forms there, then gone, there, then gone again, framed in blue and red halos.

Ollie drove close, slowed the car to a crawl as they pulled up across the street in the front of the restaurant. The police were still setting up their perimeter. Firefighters were working in teams, laying out their long hoses, working open a fire hydrant, darting to and from the fire trucks, the burning structure, the neighboring buildings.

The flames were brightest in the back, where the kitchen was. But it was clear that the entire building would be lost. The building was old, poorly maintained. Ollie would have bet money that the fire suppression systems hadn't even been inspected, let alone serviced or upgraded, in the twenty-plus years since Oncle Jean had died.

And now the flames engulfed everything. The fire chief

barked orders and pointed directions, but he wasn't even looking at the restaurant. His focus was on the buildings around it. He must have known the restaurant was a lost cause.

A police officer, bundled in his thick canvas winter uniform jacket and looking extremely annoyed, tapped on Ollie's window, shouted at him through the glass.

"Get outta here," he said, his voice muffled. "Keep moving. Let's go. Not safe here." He pointed one gloved hand down the road and waved his other in a tight circle. The universal signal to move along.

Ollie nodded and raised his hand in apology. He eased the car forward as the snow fell more furiously around them.

As they pulled away, two firefighters ran from the side alley, huddled around a third figure carried between them. One of the firefighters shouted toward a waiting ambulance, calling the paramedics over for assistance.

The figure between them was a tall, thin woman. She was barefoot in the falling snow and wore only a thin nightgown. Her face was streaked with smoke and soot. She coughed again and again, a rough, hacking cough that Ollie could hear through the closed window, even at this distance.

The paramedics ran to her, holding thick blankets open to throw around the woman's frail shoulders. As they bundled her tight and took her from the firefighters, led her toward the ambulance, toward Ollie, she glanced up.

Looked right at Ollie as he rolled slowly by.

Eyes dark as cinders against pure white skin.

Teresa.

Ollie could see the recognition in her soot-streaked face as she looked back at him, the light from the flames casting a golden glow in her dark eyes.

And he was sure he saw the hint of a smile on Teresa's face.

## 31

ALLI BARELY WAITED for the car to come to a full stop before jumping out and racing through the front door of the deli to the office in the back.

She pulled up the app that they used to track the video footage from Les Arômes. The live feed was offline, of course, but the app was set to record everything and keep the recordings for thirty days, batched into one file for each hour of the day.

She opened the most recent file and scrolled to the end. The last timestamp was from twenty-five minutes earlier, about when she and Ollie were leaving her mother's house.

Alli still couldn't believe what had happened at that dinner. Twenty years of misconceptions. Twenty years of self-sabotage, self-torture, had shattered around her, revealing themselves for the deceptions they were.

Self-deceptions and lost opportunities.

She felt that gnawing emptiness deep inside once again, but forced herself to push those thoughts and feelings to the side.

For the moment. Only for the moment.

She needed to focus, to figure out what had happened that night at Les Arômes.

Ollie came into the office, pulled over a cardboard box of

files, and sat down beside her. Alli could feel his warmth. It seeped into her cold bones, bringing her to life, warming her fingers, stiff on the keyboard.

She scrubbed in reverse through the footage from the kitchen, where they had confronted Petterson that morning.

It seemed like a lifetime ago.

The feed was black-and-white, the resolution grainy. It seemed Petterson wouldn't even spend money on his own surveillance system.

But, it was good enough for Alli to see what had happened.

As she scrubbed through the footage, rolling back in time, the feed started full black.

Offline.

Destroyed by the fire.

She scrubbed back further. The image flashed bright white, the entire screen a white blur, then flickered.

These were the flames licking up the walls, filling the room, covering the front of the camera.

Alli scrubbed back further.

Slowly, the flickering subsided, the flames died down. Through a dark haze of smoke clouding the image, Alli watched the kitchen re-order itself, plastic bowls and utensils unmelting and reforming, fallen items leaping back onto the walls or the shelves.

The smoke slowly dissipated, then disappeared entirely as Alli scrubbed backward. The image was crystal clear.

"Pause it there for a sec," said Ollie.

He leaned in close to the monitor, across Alli's body. She could smell him, his earthy, masculine scent, cedar and cherry. She closed her eyes and pulled in a long, slow, deep breath.

When she opened them again, Ollie was watching her, his head turned over his shoulder, a queer half-smile on his face.

Alli felt her cheeks instantly flush hot.

Thankfully, Ollie didn't say anything.

"Look there," he said, pointing to the screen.

Alli peered more closely, bringing her face close to the monitor.

Close to Ollie.

Almost cheek-to-cheek.

She pushed that thought from her mind, along with the tingling sensations she felt much deeper inside her body.

"What am I looking at?" she asked, distracted.

"The burner." Ollie tapped the screen with his finger. "Back in the corner. It's on fire."

In the upper-right corner of the screen, Alli could see a white spot, irregular and shifting in shape.

The stove was on fire.

A dark spot sat in the center of the shifting flames. A pot of some kind.

And there seemed to be an unusual amount of stuff stacked in that corner, too. Boxes stacked on a shelf beside the burner. Oven mitts and aprons hanging on the wall beside it.

"Can an oven mitt catch on fire?" she asked.

"Definitely," said Ollie. "Those suckers will go up in a heartbeat if you put them next to an open flame."

Oh, the irony.

Alli rolled the video back further.

That's when she saw Teresa leaving the frame.

After the fire had already started.

Okay, so she was cooking something, it caught fire, got out of hand, and she left to get help?

Alli rolled the video back further, scrubbing very slowly backwards in time.

She saw Teresa standing at the stove, watching the flames grow higher.

Back in time.

Teresa lighting the burner, twisting the dial up to high.

Putting something into the pot, something that immediately started to smoke.

Back in time.

Teresa entering the kitchen.

Walking backwards.

Hunched over, arms stretched out in front of her.

Like she was dragging something heavy along the floor.

"What is she doing?" asked Ollie.

Alli scrubbed further back in time, but the angle of the camera gave them no way to see what Teresa was dragging.

The restaurant surveillance system had several cameras, arrayed mostly in the dining room, with one in the kitchen and another in the storage area. Alli closed the video file and scanned through the other folders, each one corresponding to a different camera within the restaurant.

From the video they'd just watched, it seemed like Teresa had entered the kitchen from the dining room. After a moment, Alli located the folder for the best camera angle, pulled up the most recent file, and skipped backward to the timestamp just before they'd seen Teresa in the footage from the kitchen.

The camera angle here was from across the dining room, looking back toward the kitchen door.

They saw Teresa bend down to the floor behind a table.

Petterson's table, the same one where they'd met him just a few days ago.

When she stood up, she was holding something in each hand, something long and straight, like the handles of a wheelbarrow. Teresa leaned her weight back, slowly inching backwards toward the kitchen door in jerks and shuffles.

As she backed into the swinging saloon-style doors, in the light spilling from the kitchen, Alli could finally see what she was dragging.

A body.

Petterson's body.

She heard a sharp intake of breath from Ollie and knew he had seen it, too.

Alli scrubbed further backward on the video, setting the video to play slowly in reverse. They watched Petterson rise up from the floor like a marionette, loose-limbed and flopping, and rearrange himself at the table. A plate and a tall beer glass came up with him, the tablecloth straightening.

Back in time to Petterson draining his glass in one long swallow, then calling out over his shoulder to Teresa, who appeared, her head visible in the window of one of the doors to the kitchen, watching as Petterson bunched the tablecloth in his fists and dragged it down with him as he collapsed onto the floor.

Back in time to Teresa serving Petterson, bringing the plate and the glass out from the kitchen.

"Can we go back to see her preparing the food?" asked Ollie.

Alli pulled up the kitchen footage again, scrubbed back to the last timestamp they'd seen from the dining room, then back a little further. She set the dining room feed to the same timestamp in another window, side-by-side with the kitchen feed.

Now they could watch the video from both rooms, playing back synchronized with each other.

Teresa was plainly visible in the kitchen, facing the camera. She was wearing an apron and standing at the counter preparing a dish. She arranged the food on the plate, wiped it carefully with a napkin. She pulled a tall beer glass and a bottle of beer from a cooler, opened the bottle and poured it into the tall glass.

"Wait, what's she doing now?"

Teresa pulled something from the pocket of her apron. Something tiny, a small bottle or a vial of some kind, completely obscured by even her small hands. She twisted off the top, then dumped the contents into the beer glass and swirled it gently.

Then she looked at the camera.

She looked straight at the camera.

And smiled.

Alli saw none of the fear that had previously lined Teresa's face, the permanent mask it seemed she wore. None of the insecurity or indecision.

Alli saw only pure, calculated confidence.

And glee.

"What the hell was that?" asked Ollie as they watched Teresa take off her apron, hang it in the corner by the burner that would soon catch fire, and bring Petterson's meal to him. "What did she put in his drink?"

"I don't know," said Alli, "but I hope it won't show up in an autopsy."

She and Ollie shared a long look, the realization sinking in to both of them at the same time.

Teresa had killed Petterson.

They watched the scene play out, side-by-side from the two video feeds.

Teresa had drugged Petterson's beer. Petterson had wolfed down his food, downed his beer. A moment later, he stiffened, called out to Teresa, clutched the tablecloth, and collapsed. Teresa dragged his body into the kitchen, lay it on the floor by the stove. She lit the burner, threw something very flammable in the pot, cranked up the gas, and waited, watching, while first the pot, then the aprons and oven mitts above it, then the entire building caught fire.

No movement to put the fire out.

No effort to rescue Petterson.

Nothing at all but what Alli imagined to be a quiet satisfaction in a plan well executed.

Teresa had committed arson and murder.

And Alli and Ollie had the evidence that would convict her for it.

Alli and Ollie stared at the monitor as the two video feeds flickered white, then went completely white from the increasing flames, then went black, one by one, as the fire melted the cables powering the cameras.

They sat in silence for a long moment, staring at the black screen in front of them.

"What do we do?" whispered Ollie. "If we don't turn this in, we'll be accessories to murder or something. Isn't that what they say on TV all the time?"

Alli said nothing, her mind spinning, cold logic working through all the possibilities and permutations of their options.

"But if we turn this in," Ollie continued, thinking out loud, "Teresa will go to prison. For life. She doesn't deserve that. Not after what Petterson put her through."

Alli's mind kept spinning. She knew the right thing to do. She just needed to play it out in her mind, make sure she wasn't missing something, a key detail that might affect her calculations.

Ollie took a deep breath beside her.

"We should turn it in," he said, then groaned as if in pain. "I don't want to. It's not right." He sighed. "But it's what we should do. It's the legal thing to do."

He shook his head in frustration, smacked one fist into the other palm. "But Teresa doesn't deserve that. What she did was self-defense, really. Self-preservation."

He sighed again. "But there's no way to prove that in court."

He growled in frustration. "What do we do?"

He pulled his hands through his hair, bunching his fingers in his long, soft locks. Alli looked at him, at his face, twisted with indecision, with conflicting emotions.

He was a kind man. A compassionate man.

A gorgeous man.

A good man.

He was caught between what logic told him was the right thing to do, and what his heart told him was the right thing to do.

He was struggling to reconcile those two opposing forces.

But Alli had already reconciled them in her own mind.

She knew the right thing to do.

She closed the windows with the now-black video feeds. She pulled up the folders with all of the video files.

And with a few quick keystrokes, she deleted them.

Permanently.

A wave of contentment came over Alli as the files disappeared from the screen, a peaceful stillness she hadn't felt before.

She turned to Ollie. Hands still bunched in his hair, eyes wide with amazement, he stared back at her.

"Not the logical thing," said Alli softly, a smile teasing her lips, "but the right thing."

**32**

OLLIE WENT through his day in a daze, still having trouble processing everything that had happened the day before.

It was definitely the most eventful Thanksgiving he'd ever had.

Strong-arming a crime boss, helping an estranged family reconnect, then destroying evidence of a murder.

It had been a busy day.

And through it all, Alli had taken everything in stride. She never lost her cool, never seemed to waver or doubt herself. Even when she hit the delete button on the video footage, which Ollie couldn't even bring himself to suggest, let alone do, she just turned to him and smiled, cool as a snow cone.

She was not only the smartest person Ollie had ever met, she was the strongest, too.

And Teresa would be second on that list for strength. After what she'd been through, after the way she'd been bullied and beaten and demeaned for God knows how long, Ollie couldn't even imagine how much courage it took for her to stand up for herself and do what she'd done.

There was bound to be an investigation. By the insurance company, if no one else, assuming Petterson had insurance.

Ollie didn't know what would come of that, didn't know how well Teresa had hid her tracks.

But there would be no evidence coming from Ollie or Alli to convict her. He could guarantee that much.

As far as Ollie was concerned, justice—divine justice—had been served.

And suddenly everything was in the clear.

No more Petterson.

No more direct access to the deli's accounts. Alli would make it official at the bank that morning.

No more accounting problems. The new system was up and running. Sarah and Tom had it figured out, and Ollie was learning how to use it himself. Slowly, painfully, but he was learning.

And he owed it all to the woman walking toward him from the office, her beautiful brown eyes staring down at her phone, her brow furrowed in thought.

She was so gorgeous, so incredible.

Ollie felt lucky just to have had the chance to meet her, to get to know her. If she left him behind and he never saw her again, he'd remember the last three weeks for the rest of his life.

For the first time in his life, Ollie Wood was in love.

He knew Alli didn't feel the same way, and that was okay. She deserved someone better than him, anyway.

But Ollie couldn't let her leave without telling her how much she meant to him. He owed it to her.

He owed it to himself. He couldn't bear the thought of living the rest of his life wondering what might have happened if he'd taken the risk and bared his soul to Alli.

He knew she'd probably just thank him and walk away, probably just think he was an idiot for getting so emotional about what was, for her, just another job assignment. Ollie would probably be just one more in a long line of guys throwing themselves at Alli.

And that was okay.

He still had to take the shot.

He just didn't know when to do it.

Or how.

As Alli came into the kitchen and stood beside him, still staring at her phone, Ollie screwed up his courage.

No time like the present.

"Morning, guys," called Sarah as she banged through the front door. "How bad did you miss me?"

Ollie turned to her. Sarah cracked into a huge grin when she saw his face, her eyes darting between Ollie and Alli, who was still staring down at her phone.

"You missed me bad," she said. She set down a cardboard carrier holding three cups of coffee, removed two cups, and held them out for Ollie and Alli.

Ollie took his, looking down at the floor. His emotions were stumbling over each other. Just as he was about to say something to Alli, Sarah had walked in the door, like a palm slap to the face. His feelings were smushed and jumbled like one of scenes in the movies where a line of people race through a door only to find it leads to a closet.

Alli tapped something on her screen and finally looked up, slipping the phone into her pocket and accepting the coffee gratefully.

She took a long sip, then said, "Got a signed form from Petterson relinquishing access to Ollie Wood Deli's accounts."

Sarah held up a hand for a high-five.

Alli just stared at it.

Sarah turned toward Ollie. He pressed his hand softly against hers like they were on opposite sides of a prison visitation window.

"Damn, what's wrong with you two?" said Sarah. "We got out from under Petterson. That's high-five worthy, if anything is."

Ollie slid past the two women to get to the stove on the far side where he'd prepped breakfast, a twist on Eggs Benedict using a croissant instead of an English muffin and thin-sliced salmon instead of ham, topped with roasted asparagus, Hollandaise sauce, and grated Asiago cheese.

"Petterson's dead," said Alli flatly as Ollie set two plates of food in front of her and Sarah.

Sarah coughed and spluttered her sip of coffee, looking at Alli and Ollie with wide eyes. "Shit," she whispered to Alli. "Remind me not to get on your bad side."

Sarah bit into a forkful of breakfast and closed her eyes, chewing slowly, savoring the meal as Ollie had taught her, letting the flavors touch all of her tongue so that it could pick up every subtle aspect of the dish.

She rattled off the ingredients flawlessly, even spotting the Meyer lemon in the Hollandaise. Then she cocked an eyebrow at Ollie.

"What?" he said. "You got them all."

"I didn't miss one?" she said.

Ollie frowned at her. What the hell was she getting at? She knew she hadn't missed one.

Alli pulled her phone from her back pocket again, typed on it for a moment.

"Who's texting you so early?" said Sarah.

"My... mother," Alli replied.

Sarah again choked on the sip of coffee she'd been taking. She hacked and coughed for a moment, then slapped both hands on the counter.

"What the fuck happened yesterday? Did I step into an alternate dimension? You and Ollie are vigilantes now and your mother is your best fucking friend?"

Alli looked up at her. "She's not my best friend."

Something about her stare made Sarah blush.

Sarah.

Blushing.

That was something Ollie had never seen before.

A thought niggled at the back of his mind.

Could there be something between Sarah and Alli?

Sarah was as cool as they come. Smart, talented, good-looking, funny. If Alli were into women, Sarah would be a catch.

Hell, if Sarah were into guys, Ollie might have gone for her.

In an earlier life. If she hadn't been his employee and he hadn't been losing his mind trying to run a deli without his parents.

"But, we're working things out," said Alli. "It seems I may have misjudged her all these years."

Olli lifted his eyebrows at the shocked expression Sarah gave to him.

"*May* have," Alli emphasized to them both, a flash in her eyes. "I need more data to be sure. So, we're arranging some time to spend together."

Her phone rang in her hand.

"Sorry, that's her. My mother, apparently, does not enjoy texting."

She walked back to the office to take the call.

"What the fuck, Ollie," said Sarah. "Did you tell her how you feel about her?"

Ollie felt the blood drain from his face. "What do you mean?" he said, cringing at the way his voice shook as he spoke.

"Don't bullshit me, Oliver," said Sarah. "I know you. And I have eyes. You haven't taken your eyes off of her since she parked her car across the street that first morning. You need to tell her how you feel."

Ollie threw his hands up. "I was about to," he said through clenched teeth. "But then you stormed in."

"Well, excuse me for being punctual. When are you going to tell her?"

Ollie sighed and shook his head.

"What's the point? She doesn't feel that way about me.

Maybe I shouldn't say anything at all. I don't want to ruin a chance at a friendship."

Sarah leaned across the counter, leaned over her empty plate, and smacked Ollie on the side of his head.

Hard.

She wore a bunch of heavy metal rings on her fingers when she wasn't working. One of them smacked against Ollie's skull hard enough to make a dull thunking sound.

It hurt.

"Stop being such a numbnuts," Sarah said. "Be brave. Put yourself out there and let life do its thing."

"'Let life do its thing'? What are you, a fucking guru now, Oprah?"

"I know an idiot when I see him about to give up on an amazing girl without even trying."

Ollie looked back over his shoulder toward the office and sighed. "She is an amazing girl, isn't she?"

"Believe me, if she were on my team, I'd be all over that."

"Yeah?"

"Like flies on shit."

"Nice."

"Like white trash on Black Friday."

"I don't even know what that means."

"Like a priest on a little—"

"Okay, I think I got it."

Alli came out from the back.

"All set?" smiled Sarah.

"Yes," said Alli. "We're meeting for coffee at 10am. I'll stop by the bank first to finalize the Petterson arrangement, then head over to meet my mom."

"Perfect," said Sarah. "I'm sure Ollie will be happy to drive you."

Alli frowned to herself while Ollie glared hard at Sarah. He quickly smiled and nodded when Alli looked up at him.

Sarah grinned at them both as she took the empty plates back to the kitchen.

~

For the next three hours, Ollie had busied himself with prepping for the day, doing his best to avoid Alli and Sarah and to push from his mind all thoughts of confessing his feelings for Alli.

He failed on every single account.

The deli was just too small to avoid Sarah, and Alli was bustling around a lot that day, checking on the register and the security cameras and the Wi-Fi.

And Ollie's mind could think of nothing but what he would say to Alli when they got in the car together.

Every scenario he imagined was worse than the last. More embarrassing, more cringe-worthy, more likely to make Alli never want to speak to him again.

He was no good at this. He had never felt anything like this for anyone before. Ever. He'd always just thrown himself into his work. He really didn't think about women, other than the occasional—very occasional—tumble with a co-worker after a long shift and a few drinks. And that was usually when they came on to him. He'd never had to put himself out there before.

He'd never wanted to put himself out there before.

And he wasn't sure he could do it.

~

Alli stood in front of Ollie, ready to leave.

Ollie swallowed hard.

Behind Alli's back, Sarah flashed him a big, comic grin and two thumbs up. Ollie rolled his eyes at her and grabbed his keys from the counter.

They went straight to the bank, just a short drive away. Over the next couple of hours, Alli worked with the bank manager to make all of the necessary arrangements to officially revoke Petterson's access to the deli's accounts. As the deli owner, Ollie signed where they told him to sign, nodded his agreement and gave his approval where they told him it was needed.

But his mind was still spinning through scenarios, each one more disastrous than the last.

Why was he struggling so much with this? Ollie may not have experience with these kinds of feelings, but he was good with people. He loved talking to people, and he loved sharing his thoughts and feelings with them and listening to them share with him. This wasn't really any different, was it?

Only it was completely different, obviously.

Ollie had decided that the drive from the bank to the coffee shop was his best chance to talk to Alli. If he was going to do it, that was the time.

As they left the bank, his mind was racing, trying to come up with a smooth, un-embarrassing way to ease into the conversation.

*So, Alli, there's something I've been meaning to tell you.*

*Alli, can I tell you something?*

*Alli, have you ever felt a certain way about someone...*

*Alli, it's funny how life works sometimes...*

*AlliIloveyouandIcan'tlivewithoutyouIneverwantyoutoleavemeev-ereverever.*

He was leaning toward the last one.

"You just passed it," said Alli, pointing out the window as Ollie drove past the coffee shop.

They were already there.

And Ollie had wasted the entire drive in tortured silence.

He flipped a U-turn and parked on the curb in front of the coffee shop. Alli opened the door to get out, but he stopped her with a hand on her arm.

"Wait, Alli," he said. "Can I talk to you for a second?"

She pulled the door shut again, folded her hands on her lap, and looked at him, those calm, brown eyes waiting, watching.

Thinking.

Processing.

Thinking what an idiot he was.

Processing how much of her time he was wasting.

Ollie closed his eyes and shook those thoughts from his head. He couldn't let himself get distracted now.

He just had to go for it.

But those thoughts kept coming back, grabbing at him like vines pulling him down as he tried to scale a wall, tearing at his arms and legs. With each movement, jerking him tighter, pulling him off balance.

"Alli, I think I'm in love with you," he blurted, the words stumbling over themselves as they came off his tongue in a torrent.

Immediately, the wall fell away, the vines fell away.

Leaving Ollie in free fall.

His heart rate tripled in the blink of an eye. His skin burned. His chest felt like a thousand Dutch ovens were stacked on it. His stomach leapt out of his mouth and into the distance, leaving an empty pit as Ollie fell into oblivion.

It wasn't quite the word vomit of the last scenario he'd imagined, but it was embarrassingly close.

Ollie opened his eyes wide, in shock, and stared straight out the windshield, gripping the steering wheel until his knuckles were white.

Alli didn't say anything.

For a long time.

Ollie slid his eyes to the side and turned his head just enough to catch a peek at her face.

She was watching him.

Calm.

Composed.

When he turned to face her fully, she spoke.

"You... *think* you're in love with me?"

She didn't whisper. Her voice wasn't hoarse or shaky or touched by any emotion whatsoever. Her voice was as calm and as clear as if she had simply asked him if he wanted anything from the coffee shop.

Ollie gulped and nodded.

She watched him for a few more unbearable moments, then furrowed her brow.

She did that a lot.

And something about it drove Ollie wild.

But at the moment, that wildness was secondary to his soul-crushing embarrassment.

"Isn't that something one normally would feel?" said Alli. "Not think?"

That definitely wasn't what Ollie had expected her to say.

He wasn't sure how to respond to the question. He opened his mouth, then closed it again, opened it once more and closed it once more.

Then he felt a new flush of heat across his entire body at the realization that he was flopping his mouth like a goddamn fish.

"Well, I—"

A sharp rap on Alli's window snapped both of their heads around.

Alli's mother was standing on the curb. She waved at them both, smiling broadly.

Alli turned to Ollie. Her face was passive, collected.

She looked exactly like she'd looked while she was waiting for the bank manager to process their paperwork that morning. Patient and calm.

And dispassionate.

"Thank you for the ride," she said. "I'm sure my mother will drive me back."

And then she got out of the car, shut the door, and didn't even look back as Ollie watched her walk into the coffee shop with her mother.

Into the coffee shop, and probably out of his life.

Probably forever.

## 33

**To-do list:**

- ???

Alli usually did not have trouble focusing.

Actually, Alli *never* had trouble focusing.

Mental focus was a muscle that needed to be built up over time and exercised to keep it strong. Alli had been building that muscle since she was a small child, and she exercised all day, every day. It was a part of who she was.

Strong mental focus was critical to the kind of work Alli enjoyed doing. Not the accounting work, though it was important for that, too. But the kind of speculative, theoretical, scientific work she liked to do in her free time.

When you're dreaming of new nanotechnologies for medical use, there was nothing to watch. No screen to keep your focus or tools to manipulate. All of the work was in the mind.

Same with quantum physics or imagining the world of the future. All of these pursuits involved theoretical questions that only existed inside the mind. Focus was essential to making progress in any of them.

In order to focus, one needed to push away distractions. External pressures had to be ignored. If you had a big presentation or a looming deadline or an uncomfortable dinner date, it had to be pushed from your mind.

Similarly, intrusive emotions needed to be ignored. If you were unsure of your hypothesis, insecure about your abilities, or afraid of how your colleagues might react, those emotions had to be sequestered, at least for a while, so you could focus on the task at hand, on the theoretical question being considered.

Sharp mental focus was key to Alli's work.

To her entire being.

And Alli could focus her mind as well as anyone on the planet.

Just not right then.

And not right there, in the coffee shop, seated across from her mother.

Alli barely even noticed when the server set two steaming mugs of coffee on the table. She looked down at the drink, something with foam heaped on top, dusted with some kind of brown powder.

Alli hated foamy coffee drinks almost as much as she hated the powder that inevitably came on top of them. She preferred espresso with a tiny bit of sugar and a bare breath of milk.

She had no idea how she'd ended up with the monstrous concoction in front of her.

And she had no idea what her mother had been saying since Alli had gotten out of the car.

Since she'd left Ollie.

Since he'd professed his love for her.

He'd professed his love for her.

Alli still could barely believe she had heard him correctly.

And what had she said in reply?

*You* think *you're in love with me?*

That was her response? To quibble with his diction?

If Ollie had loved her in that moment, he probably didn't anymore.

The irony was that diction was the last thing on Alli's mind when Ollie had uttered those words.

But she couldn't recall what was on her mind, because that was the exact moment when Alli lost her mental focus.

And she had yet to regain it.

*You* think *you're in love with me?*

She remembered hearing her voice say those words, but she didn't recall consciously uttering them. Didn't recall even thinking them. The phrase seemed to have sprung up and escaped her mouth without her awareness.

All while her brain, her body, was occupied with a flood of emotions and physical responses that Alli had never felt before.

Ollie, with the beautiful orange-flecked eyes, the pipe-smoke scent, the smile that could charm the most hardened shrew. Ollie, with the easy way with people, was in love with awkward, nerdy, anti-social Alli? The woman who had punished her own mother for twenty years for a crime she didn't commit, when all the while a simple conversation could have cleared things up?

It didn't make sense.

Alli's mind had been swirling, darting in a thousand directions at once, like a flock of startled birds.

Her body had been frozen, as if she'd lost control of her limbs, her mouth, her tongue.

Inside, she'd felt like a nuclear reactor melting down. Heart rate spiking, core temperature overheating, alarm klaxons blaring, nuclear scientists racing every which way in a headless panic.

She'd felt nauseous, vertiginous. She felt like she would puke or pass out. Or pass out in her own puke.

And then she'd asked that ridiculous question.

And then, before she could recover, could take it back, her mother had knocked on the window.

And Alli's body had removed her from the car. It had followed her mother inside, agreed to whatever her mother had suggested to Alli at the cash register, and dutifully sat Alli down at the table.

Only now, some unknown duration later, was Alli starting to regain control of her physical form.

Only now was she able to focus once more.

It was like returning to your apartment after a long vacation only to find that it had been broken into while you were gone. Your window left open, your curtains blowing wild in the wind, your bedding disheveled, mattress upended, possessions smashed and strewn across the floor.

"Alli?" said her mother. "Alli, dear, are you alright?"

Alli looked up.

The coffee shop was crowded, filled with people getting sandwiches and coffee for lunch, or sweets and coffee for an after-lunch dessert. The sounds of their talking, the clatter of glasses and silverware filled Alli's ears.

She looked across the table at her mother, who was staring back at Alli with concern in her eyes.

Real, sincere concern.

This was another anomaly, another thing out of place in Alli's mind.

But this particular discontinuity was, surprisingly, welcome.

"I..." Alli began, but didn't know how to continue.

She'd never thought about men before, let alone spoken about them with anyone. Certainly not her mother.

Alli was attracted to them, physically, but in a very distant way. Her attraction to men was almost theoretical. Unlike other women, who would go to great lengths to attract a man—garish makeup, uncomfortably tight clothing cut far too short along the midriff and thigh, shoes in torturous designs that would have made Torquemada drool with envy—Alli had other things, more important things on her mind.

But in that moment, seated in the coffee shop across from her concerned mother, men were all she could think about.

One man, in particular.

"Ollie just told me he loved me," she said, her voice wooden, stunned.

Her mother's eyes popped wide. "That's wonderful, Alli." She squeezed Alli's wrist and smiled, a broad, warm smile. "Oliver seems like such a good man. Kind and generous and talented." She cocked one eyebrow at Alli. "And handsome."

Alli laughed at the youthful leer on her mother's face.

The sound of her laughter seemed like it came from somewhere behind her, from another table, another person.

Her mother grinned back at her, then tilted her head, frowning. "This is good news, isn't it? Why do you seem so upset?"

Alli looked down at her lap, shaking her head.

"Don't you care for Oliver?"

"No, I do," said Alli quickly.

Surprisingly quickly.

Her response had been instinctive.

Emotional.

Emotions precede thought. It's an evolutionary advantage, one that has saved humans in countless situations of physical danger over millennia. Our brains perceive a dangerous stimulus, we feel fear, and our bodies act instinctively, pre-cognitively, to fight or flee. Only then does rational thought kick in to evaluate the situation.

Too many people were all too happy to rely on these instinctive reactions. It was what made their lives so ridiculously messy. A life driven by emotion was a life of chaos.

Alli liked to think that she had trained herself to override that foolish vestige of evolution. There were very few life-threatening situations in modern society, so there was little need for this short-circuit path to action. Alli prided herself on her ability to maintain calm and focus, even in the face of emotion and instinct. To override or wait out the instinctive pathway so she could make a rational choice, and could act accordingly.

But, for some reason, when it came to Ollie, she'd lost that ability.

"I do care for him," she whispered.

"Then what is the problem?" asked her mother. Alli looked up at the sharp words, but found only kindness in her mother's face.

Kindness and...

Alli looked more closely.

Her mind fought against the idea.

But in her heart, she knew it was right.

Yes.

In her mother's face, she saw kindness...

...and love.

Something crumbled in Alli then. Some edifice, a towering wall she'd been building for decades, first of wattle, then of stone, then of steel. Ever harder, ever taller, ever stronger over the years, she'd walled herself off from the world, bit by bit, piece by piece.

And now it fell around her with a thundering crash.

Alli couldn't remember the last time she cried.

She wanted to cry right then.

Right there in the coffee shop, she wanted to crawl into her mother's arms and cry until she fell asleep listening to the sound of her mother's heartbeat, wrapped in the warmth of her mother's body.

But tears would not come.

Just wide, burning eyes. And the feeling of the worldview she'd built up her entire adult life, falling apart inside her.

She felt ungrounded, disoriented in her own mind, the one place she'd always felt sure.

She felt empty, felt the gnawing hunger of loss, the clawing, hopeless wish to get back to what once was.

And, above all else, she felt exposed. Vulnerable. Shivering naked in a cold wind, covering herself with her arms.

Amid all of the emotion raging within her, she knew, some observing part of her mind knew she was at a crossroads.

She could choose to rebuild the wall, retreat once more inside herself, hide from the cold wind, fill the emptiness within herself once again.

Or she could step forward and see what the world could offer.

And what she could offer the world.

"Come on, dear," said her mother, standing from the table, smiling gently, holding her hand out for Alli to grasp. "I think it's time for you to get back to work."

~

~

Alli burst through the front door of the deli and nearly bowled Sarah over as she sprinted around the front counter and down the aisle in the kitchen.

"Fucking hell, Alli," said Sarah, spinning away deftly and setting a hotel pan full of marinated brisket on the counter before it spilled all over the floor. "What's your problem?"

"Is Ollie here?" said Alli, breathless from her sprint.

Sarah stood straight and grinned at her, all irritation gone in an instant.

"You love him, don't you?" she said.

"Sarah, is he here?" Alli wanted to scream at her, but managed to keep her voice even.

"You got him pretty good," Sarah said. "'You *think* you love me?'" She cackled. "Classic."

Alli growled in exasperation and tried to push past Sarah to check for Ollie in the back of the deli. Sarah grabbed her arm and spun Alli to face her.

Her face was no longer smiling. It was hard, serious.

"I love you, Alli," she said, then grinned. "Not like he does, but I do love you."

Her face grew hard and serious again.

"But Ollie is my family," she said.

Her grip on Alli's arm tightened.

"*Do not* fuck with my family, Alli."

Alli took a deep breath and let it out. She straightened her back, stood tall, looked Sarah square in the eyes.

Sarah examined her, her eyes boring deep into Alli's soul for a long moment. She nodded and released Alli's arm.

"He just went out to his car." She jerked a thumb toward the back. "He's heading out to make the lunch deliveries."

Alli was halfway down the hall before Sarah finished speaking.

"Don't fuck it up," Sarah called as Alli threw open the door to the back alley and careened around the corner toward where Ollie normally parked his car.

She caught up to him as he was slamming shut the rear hatch.

He turned, his eyes first widening, then narrowing when he saw her.

Alli's heart dropped at the change.

Ollie was hurting, and it was her fault.

Then Ollie looked away. Anywhere, everywhere but at Alli's face. His expression downcast and crestfallen.

At the look on Ollie's face, something dropped away deep within the pit of Alli's stomach. She knew she was the reason he looked that way.

And now she had to make it right.

A jumble of words crowded her brain. A thousand apologies,

professions, displays, grand gestures. But every scenario that played in her mind felt like the last scene in a bad romance movie.

And that was not how Alli wanted this to go.

Ollie meant too much to her for that.

He'd welcomed her, even when he didn't want her there.

He'd supported her, even when he didn't believe in what she was doing.

He'd followed her, even when it meant endangering himself.

He'd helped her, even when she didn't think she needed help.

He'd loved her, even when she didn't think she was worth loving.

She couldn't say all that to him in a parking lot in a side alley behind a deli.

She had to do this right.

When Alli didn't say anything for a few seconds, Ollie shoved his hands in his pockets and blew an angry breath out his nose. It plumed in the cold air. He shook his head, muttering something to himself, staring at the icy pavement.

"Can I help you with those deliveries?" said Alli.

Ollie looked up at her, confused.

Confused and angry.

Alli lifted her eyebrows and shrugged at him.

Ollie let out a long sigh. The anger softened in his face. He rolled his eyes and waved for Alli to get in the car.

34

"Wʜᴀᴛ's ᴏɴ ᴛʜᴇ ᴍᴇɴᴜ ᴛᴏᴅᴀʏ?" said Alli brightly.

Ollie frowned and cast a sidelong glance at her as he drove.

She was sitting in the passenger seat wearing a sorority smile. An expression he'd never seen anywhere near Alli's face before.

She was trying to make small talk.

Ollie snorted a laugh.

Small talk suited Alli Thomas about as well as flippers suited a Ford Fiesta.

She pulled in a long breath through her nose and put on a thoughtful expression. "I'm guessing brisket sandwiches with coleslaw and cornbread," she said.

Ollie cocked an eyebrow at her.

She smiled back at him. "I'm not as expert as Sarah yet, but I'm learning."

*Yet.*

She'd said *yet*, which implied more to come.

Ollie tamped down the flash of hope that surged through his body.

He could only handle one crushing rejection per day.

They pulled up to their first stop, Mrs. Dunbarton's house.

Alli jumped out before Ollie, raced around to the back of the car, and had grabbed a bag and was knocking on the door before Ollie even made it to the bottom of Mrs. Dunbarton's stairs.

Alli was certainly trying hard.

She must feel pretty bad about hurting Ollie's feelings.

Not the emotion he was hoping she would show him, but he was grateful that she at least liked him enough to feel bad about not loving him.

"Hello, Mrs. Dunbarton," said Alli brightly when the door swung open. "Do you mind if we come in for a moment?" She tilted her head and smiled conspiratorially. "We'll only take a few minutes of your time."

Mrs. Dunbarton looked as shocked as Ollie felt.

Alli was inviting herself in? That was new.

Mrs. Dunbarton opened the door wider and led them to the sitting area. She and Alli sat across from each other in the exact same positions they'd been in the night before. Ollie sat opposite them on the couch.

Alli set the bag of food on the coffee table in the center.

"I just wanted to take this opportunity to thank you, Mrs. Dunbarton," said Alli.

Mrs. Dunbarton raised her eyebrows and darted a glance at Ollie. Ollie shrugged, as surprised as she was.

"I want to thank you for helping me to move past something that I see now has been holding me back for a very long time."

"Oh?" said Mrs. Dunbarton, a smile touching the corner of her lips. "And what is that, Alli?"

"My own pain," said Alli without melodrama. "My own grief. My own insecurities. My own fear." She shrugged. "You can call it whatever you like."

"Or maybe it's all of those things intermingled." Mrs. Dunbarton sat back in her chair, steepled her fingers. She glanced again at Ollie, then considered Alli for a long moment. "You're a very quick study, Alli."

"I've had help from some very good teachers," Alli replied, flashing that bright smile at Ollie again.

He'd never seen that smile on her face before, but now that he'd seen it a few times in a row, he never wanted to stop seeing it. Something about that smile lit Alli's eyes. It brought a fire into their depths, a warmth and an aliveness that quickened Ollie's heart.

True to her word, they left Mrs. Dunbarton's house only a few minutes later and delivered the rest of the meals. Alli practically bounced as she greeted each customer with a cheerful voice and that same glowing smile.

Until they found themselves at the last stop, Ms. Stonnard's house.

The television blared in the background as Ms. Stonnard opened the door. Someone was trying desperately to guess the final puzzle as Pat Sajak stood smugly beside them. The gruff old woman greeted Alli and Ollie with her usual pleasantries.

"You again?" Ms. Stonnard grunted when she saw Alli. But she turned and sat down in her recliner, leaving the front door open.

Ms. Stonnard's equivalent of welcoming them with open arms.

She muted the television as Alli and Ollie filed in and sat down with her.

"I'll be quick, Ms. Stonnard," Alli began, "since I know Jeopardy is almost on."

Ms. Stonnard grunted again in reply, her eyes fixed on the silent television.

"I want to thank you," said Alli.

"For what?"

"For your warning last night."

"What warning? I didn't give you any warning."

"And for your advice."

"I sure as hell didn't give any advice."

Alli leaned forward in her chair and grasped Ms. Stonnard on the arm.

Ollie sucked in a quick breath. He'd never touched Ms. Stonnard before. Not even a handshake or a pat on the shoulder.

She didn't seem like the type who liked physical contact.

Ms. Stonnard's head snapped down, staring at Alli's hand on her arm like she was trying to burn it off with the fury of her gaze.

The feeling in the room shifted in an instant. It felt to Ollie like he was standing on a hill of gunpowder with someone trying to light a cigarette.

But Alli didn't pull back. And she didn't waver. She just stared firmly at Ms. Stonnard.

The bright smile was gone, but that intense fire still burned within her eyes.

"Yes, you did," said Alli.

Ms. Stonnard raised her eyes to Alli's.

Alli tilted her head down slightly, still holding Ms. Stonnard's gaze.

"You did," she said softly, "and I want to thank you for it."

They stared at each other like two heavyweight prizefighters at the start of a bout. That powder keg feeling grew thicker, the air heavy with the weight of it.

And then Ollie saw a shimmer in Ms. Stonnard's eyes.

He had to blink to make sure he wasn't imagining it, to make sure it wasn't just some trick of the light.

But it was real.

Tears.

In Ms. Stonnard's eyes.

As quickly as they formed, they were gone again.

Ms. Stonnard thrust her chin out stubbornly.

"What are you gonna do about it?" she said.

Alli shook Ms. Stonnard's arm where it rested on the arm of the recliner. A firm shake.

A promise.

"I'm going to take it," Alli whispered. "I'm going to walk out that door, and I'm going to face the world."

Ms. Stonnard's eyes widened just a bit, just for a moment. She swung her eyes to Ollie, like a steel beam slamming him in the head. Involuntarily, he sat up straighter in his seat.

"I suppose he had something to do with it," she said.

"If it weren't for him..." said Alli, looking at Ollie.

Her voice trailed off.

Ollie saw something in her face in that moment that he'd never seen before. A kind of shift, like the way he imagined the earth would shift in an earthquake. Whole sections quivering and moving in odd ways.

In Alli's face, in her eyes, he could see those shifts. Movement where there had always been stability. Softness where there had always been strength.

Ms. Stonnard's gaze shifted back to Alli, her brow furrowing.

"Thought by fucking thought," Ms. Stonnard said.

Alli locked eyes with the woman.

"Hour by fucking hour," Alli nodded.

Like a pact.

Like they had just made a promise to each other, one of those deep, soul-binding, life-long promises that children make.

Ms. Stonnard stared hard at Alli for a long minute, then coughed gruffly and cleared her throat. She shifted in her chair and leaned forward to grab the bag of food off the table where Alli had set it.

"Jeopardy's on," she said.

Alli smiled and stood. Ollie stood with her.

As they opened the door to leave, Ms. Stonnard called out to them.

"Alli," she said.

Alli and Ollie both stopped and turned toward her.

"Don't..." Ms. Stonnard said, her voice choking off into silence.

Her eyes flicked toward the photographs hanging on the wall, then back to Alli.

"I won't," said Alli softly.

## 35

Alli still hadn't told Ollie how she felt about him.

All through the deliveries, all through the drive back to the deli, she'd made nothing but small talk.

She'd done her best impression of a perky, vacuous schoolgirl and talked about nothing of any importance whatsoever.

Oddly, interestingly, people had responded well toward her.

They looked at her strangely. They didn't really engage with her inane patter, thankfully.

But they responded to her body language. They returned her smile, and the warmth that she naturally projected along with it.

And—oddly, interestingly—Alli responded to it, as well.

The simple act of smiling that broad smile lifted her mood. It generated feelings of warmth and optimism that then compounded the sincerity of the smile, which led to more feelings of warmth and optimism, and so on in a self-reinforcing cycle of happiness.

It was very strange.

But it worked.

And when Alli did drop the meaningless chatter and spoke of real things, important things, as she did with Mrs. Dunbarton and Ms. Stonnard, they were received more readily, more openly.

Alli wished she could have done an A/B test. In both test variants, she would say the same things in the same way to Mrs. Dunbarton and Ms. Stonnard. But in one variant she'd keep the smiling, warm mood and in the other variant she'd fall back to her normal self, serious and neutral, just to see if the results would be materially different.

But the real world was not a well-controlled experimental environment. There were no clean A/B tests, and Alli couldn't control all the environmental variables.

All she could do was put herself out there and hope for the best.

And all the way back to the deli, she'd been working up the courage to do just that.

Then the car came to a stop, the parking brake creaked up, and they were at the deli, exiting the car.

All that time, wasted.

As they walked down the alley to the back door, Alli finally settled on a plan and screwed up her courage. She wouldn't initiate the conversation in the back alley, but she would steer Ollie into the office as soon as they entered the building.

She took a deep breath.

"Ollie—" she began as Ollie pulled the back door open.

"There you are," shouted Sarah, stomping down the hallway toward them. "Your uncle is spewing bullshit, Ollie."

All the way down the hallway, Alli could see Mort standing in the kitchen behind Sarah, sighing his usual world-weary sigh.

"He's saying some shit about Alli leaving," Sarah continued. "Tell him to fuck off." She glared at Ollie.

Ollie just walked past her.

Sarah's eyes fell to Alli, widening. Her mouth fell open.

"You're not fucking leaving, are you?" she said to Alli.

Alli didn't know what was going on, but she felt something

hard form in the pit of her stomach. She followed Ollie into the kitchen.

"Alli," said Mort, nodding to her.

Alli nodded back.

Ollie had his hands on his hips, staring down at the ground.

"I didn't think you could do it," Mort said. "I don't know why I doubted you. I guess I didn't think anyone could teach this fool how to run a business."

Ollie glanced up at him, a weak smile flashing over his face before he fell back into a pensive investigation of the floor tiles.

"You're goddamn right she did it," said Sarah. "Alli's a fucking genius. She saved this place, and she's a part of it now. Which is why she isn't going anywhere. Right, Alli?"

Alli didn't look at Sarah. She stared hard at Mort, who stared back.

His eyes looked sad, his face tired and lined with worry. He looked like a man who had spent too many years doing things he didn't want to do, carrying burdens he didn't want to carry.

A few weeks ago, Alli had thought he was just a typical man who had made foolish choices.

Now she knew differently.

Mort didn't carry those burdens because he'd brought them on himself.

He carried them because he didn't want the people he loved to have to carry them alone.

"Ollie," Sarah continued, "tell Mort he's full of shit. Tell him Alli isn't going anywhere."

Ollie folded his arms over his chest, but didn't look up.

And didn't say anything.

"Your client has requested another accountant, Alli," said Mort gently.

Alli had heard those words a hundred times.

She'd heard them at the end of every assignment Mort had ever given her.

And she'd accepted them. Every time.

Because she'd never cared one way or the other.

"Mark Neese will be here tomorrow," said Mort to Ollie. "He's no Alli, but he's a competent accountant and he's been with the firm for a long time. He can run whatever system Alli has set up here."

Alli had never cared whether she stayed with a client or left them for another. They were all the same to her. Just idiots who didn't want to learn, didn't want to grow, didn't want to challenge their own misguided assumptions about business and life.

"Alli can show him the ropes," Mort continued.

But this client was different.

"Should only take them about an hour."

Ollie was different.

"And then Mark will be your assigned accountant from then on."

And Alli was different.

"No," she said quietly.

Mort turned to her.

And Alli could see something in his eyes.

A little less sadness.

A little flash of hope.

Ollie looked up.

"Alli, I think this is for the best," Ollie said, his voice strained and weary.

Sarah opened her mouth to say something, but Alli silenced her with a sharp look.

"I know you do," said Alli.

She stepped to Ollie, looked up into those magical eyes of his.

She wanted to fall into them, to let go and fall deep into them forever.

But she had something she had to say first.

"I know you do," she repeated, "but that's only because you don't have all the data you need."

Ollie shook his head, confused.

"You don't know how *I* feel," she said, "about *you*."

Ollie huffed. "I think you made that pretty clear this morning."

"No," said Alli, shaking her head. "No, I didn't."

She took Ollie hands in hers. In his gaze, she could see the pain she'd caused him. She could see him guarding himself, protecting himself.

But she could also see hope there, and a flash of warmth and light that she now knew was love.

Love for her.

"I am not in the habit of dating my clients," said Alli. "In fact, I am not in the habit of interacting with my clients in any way whatsoever, beyond what is required by my employer."

"And even sometimes then," muttered Mort.

"But something about you, Ollie, was different from the start. You came to me, pulled me out of my shell." Alli laughed. "Literally tapped on the window of my VW bug and tried to drag me out of it."

Ollie laughed in return. The sound lightened Alli's heart, send a bolt of joy through her.

"Your accounting system was... not a system. At all. It was a total nightmare."

"I'm not a numbers guy," laughed Ollie.

"Or a computer guy," said Sarah.

"But you are a people guy," Alli said. "Something I have never been."

"I don't know about that, Alli," said Ollie. "You have your own way with people, too."

"Away, away, away with people," Mort quipped. "All people."

Everyone laughed at that, including Alli.

And when she drew in a breath afterward, she sniffed.

Her nose was running.

She held her hand up to one cheek and found it wet and hot.

She looked up at Ollie. His eyes were wide and shimmering, looking back at her.

No matter what, Ollie always found the good in any situation. He always saw the best in people.

In Alli.

"You opened me up, Ollie," she said. "I solved your business problem. You solved my people problem."

Ollie shook his head. "I just held the door for you. You're the one who walked through it."

"I wouldn't have even noticed the door if it weren't for you."

They stared at each other, holding hands, for a long moment. Alli's vision blurred and cleared with each blink.

She'd never felt the way she felt in that moment.

Frightened.

Exposed.

Naked and vulnerable.

But also strong.

Powerful.

Warm and compassionate.

Filled with a fierce need to love.

And to be loved.

By the man whose kind and loving eyes she could finally let herself fall into.

"Is that it?" said Sarah. "Thanks for holding the fucking door? That's the big message you had to say?"

"*You* definitely do *not* have a way with people," said Mort. He put his arm around Sarah and led her back toward the office. "Why don't you and I go in here and discuss it for a moment?"

"Fuck off, Mort," said Sarah, her voice fading as they walked down the hall. "I want to hear what they're—"

The office door closed and cut off Sarah's words, leaving Alli and Ollie alone together.

"Is that the message you wanted to tell me?" whispered Ollie. "Is that the... uh... data I needed?"

"No, Ollie," smiled Alli. "That's only part of it."

Her eyes were dry now, her voice steady and sure. She looked up into his limpid brown eyes, the orange flecks swimming like koi fish inside. She hoped she never stopped staring at those eyes.

"What's the rest of it?" asked Ollie, his voice soft and distant, like he were speaking from a trance. His eyes were locked on Alli's.

She reached up one hand, stroked it along his cheek. She felt the sweep of his skin, the soft stubble, the firm line of his jaw.

"Just this," she said, her voice low and husky.

She slid her hand around the back of his neck and pulled his head down to hers, pulled his lips to hers. Feathery-soft at first, then she pulled him down harder, pressed his lips against hers.

He slid his arm around her waist, pulled her hard against him.

She parted her lips and pulled his tongue inside her mouth, feeling it hot and slick inside her, he exploring her just as she explored him.

The world around them vanished. Nothing existed but that moment, their hands, their lips, their tongues. Nothing existed but the feeling of Alli and Ollie.

Together.

## 36

SIX MONTHS LATER

The lunch crowd was even heavier than usual that day. The POS system had rung up four hundred thirty-two customers over two hours, with a few more still straggling through.

Alli tapped a few buttons on her tablet computer, summing the totals for the week.

Another record.

Every week, another record. Both for lunch service and for dinner service.

The community was loving the new design of the deli, even though it was still partially under construction. They'd knocked down the wall to the vacant space next door, creating room to expand the kitchen and add a seating area for guests, as well as a coffee station with a very expensive espresso machine from Italy.

Personally, that was Alli's favorite part.

Once the deli's bank account had been freed from Petterson,

cash flow increased immediately, and to a significant degree. As it should have been all along with a business growing as quickly in customer traffic and word-of-mouth acclaim as Ollie Wood Deli.

With the extra cash, they'd quickly been able to move forward with the big ideas that Ollie had been dreaming of.

In the expanded kitchen, Ollie finally had space to install the bread ovens he'd been wanting for years. He now made his own bread every morning.

*Early* every morning.

*Very early* every morning.

He was out of bed by 4am just about every day of the week now.

Alli's only request to him was that he keep the lights off so he didn't wake her. As a result, Ollie had taken to creeping around their bedroom in the morning wearing a dim headlamp.

It wasn't enough to let Alli sleep, but she loved watching him sneak around, bumping into furniture and trying to figure out if his clothes matched. More often than not, she would sit up in the darkness, laughing, and turn on the light to find Ollie, one leg up in the air, trying to pull on his pants backwards.

And then she'd just get up with him.

Or pull him back into bed.

"Need more rye, chef," called Sarah from her workstation near the front of the kitchen.

"Three in the oven, chef," replied Ollie from the office.

The bread Ollie made was incredible. A hundred times better than the stuff Daisy Bread Company had been providing, and it was always fresh and hot for the customers.

Ollie claimed not to have known much about making bread beyond what they'd taught him in culinary school. But he had learned quickly, so quickly that he was now making breads that couldn't be found anywhere else between New York City and

Chicago, maybe even San Francisco. Breads from Italy and France, but also Australia and China and Israel and Palestine. Some were used on sandwiches, some were sold to customers whole.

And now Ollie was talking about starting a breakfast service.

Ollie was more excited every day than Alli had ever seen him.

And that made Alli excited, too.

Ollie walked out from the office, holding a piece of paper and a pencil, a pair of reading glasses perched on the end of his nose. He stood beside Alli and Sarah at the front of the kitchen.

"Tom," he cried, "why does the supply ledger show an order for a hundred pounds of wheat flour when the delivery log only shows fifty?"

"Snafu with the wheat farm, they said," Tom replied as he walked out of the cooler with a hotel pan of smoked turkey. "Said they'd bring the fifty they owe with the next delivery."

Ollie clucked his tongue.

"All right," he said, shaking his head, "I'll make a note in the software so that the reports reconcile, but tell Bill Barker he owes me the recipe to his wife's mincemeat pie."

Tom laughed. "Good luck with that," he said.

Ollie turned back toward the office, scribbling something on his paper.

Alli smiled at Sarah.

"Never thought I'd see him learn how to turn a computer on, let alone how to reconcile reports," said Sarah. "You're a magician, Alli."

The front door swung open, ringing a small bell they'd installed above it. Teresa strode through, a long roll of paper under one arm.

"Ollie," Teresa called. Ollie stopped mid-way to the office. "Hang on a sec. I need to show you some buildout plans."

Ollie and Alli came to the front, where Teresa spread the roll of paper on the counter. They were blueprints, plans for the rebuild of Les Arômes.

After the fire, Teresa had been under suspicion for a little while. But with no evidence to pin against her, the police were unable even to detain her for questioning. And once the news outlets and the public got wind of the woman who had survived a building fire and years of abuse at the hands of a tyrannical mob boss, public opinion was fully on her side.

And it turned out that Petterson had had insurance after all. Lots of it. Especially fire insurance. Seems he might have been planning an accidental fire of his own one day to cash out.

Once that detail leaked out, the case was closed.

With no will and no next of kin, ownership of all of Petterson's possessions and holdings had fallen to Teresa under the state's common-law marriage statute.

Wealth and freedom agreed with Teresa. She was no longer the lanky, sunken-cheeked specter shrinking into every shadow out of fear. In just a few months, she'd gained weight and muscle. Her hair had grown longer and taken on a silky shine. She walked straight and tall, with a grace Alli hadn't previously noticed.

She still had her moments. Still darted a glance around the room whenever a burly stranger came in. Those wounds would take a long time to heal.

But she had someone to help with that now.

"Hey, babe," said Sarah, coming around the front counter, wiping her hands on her apron, and giving Teresa a quick peck on the lips. "This the new vision for the dining area?"

"Two stories," Teresa said, widening her stance and holding her hands up in the air like an impresario painting a picture. "Rooftop seating, with a glass canopy that can be opened in the summer. Views of the downtown skyline every night."

Petterson's holdings had included the property under what was left of Les Arômes. And Teresa was eager to rebuild.

"That's a big idea," said Ollie. "I love it." He leaned in to look more closely at the designs.

A notification popped up on Alli's tablet. She smiled to herself and slipped away, leaving Teresa, Sarah, and Ollie to argue and iterate on the blueprints.

Ollie and Alli had partnered with Teresa on the new restaurant, bringing Mort and Jen in as silent partners. By all indications, the new establishment would be a game changer for fine dining in the city. She knew the designs were well in hand with that crew working on them.

Alli sat in front of the computer in her office and first pulled up her website. She scrolled quickly through the comments on her last post. There were over two hundred now. She didn't know how, but at some point about two months ago, her blog had moved beyond the small community of scientists she'd initially targeted and was now attracting the attention of advanced hobbyists, laypeople with day jobs who were interested in theoretical physics, nanomedical technology, food insecurity, and space exploration.

It was an eclectic bunch, but Alli had finally found her people.

And the views on her blog had exploded.

"Professor Kaku?" said Ollie, leaning around the doorjamb.

Alli flipped to her email to check the notification she'd received.

She nodded. "He says he'll be in town on Friday. Wants to meet for dinner."

Ollie smiled. "We'll have him to the house."

"I'll invite Mom," Alli smiled. "She'll love to meet him. She thinks he's sooo handsome."

They both laughed.

"Perfect," said Ollie. "I'll make venison."

"He's vegan."

"I'll make quinoa with beetroot & romanesco," said Ollie

without missing a beat. He stepped back into the hall. "Tom," Alli heard him call, "how much eggplant do we have?"

Ollie swung back into the room and gave Alli a long, soft kiss on the lips that set something tingling deep within her. She trailed after Ollie's lips and pulled him back for more.

She would never have enough of those lips.

"Eggplant?" yelled Tom from the kitchen. "We don't have any eggplant."

Ollie stepped back into the hall. "We'd better get some then." He pulled his phone from his pocket. "I'll add it to my list," he said, tapping on the screen, his voice fading as the door closed behind him.

The taste of Ollie still lingered on Alli's lips. She closed her eyes and took a long moment just to savor it. She loved that taste.

She loved that man.

She loved her life.

She let out a long, contented sigh, then opened her eyes.

What had she been doing? She checked her list.


**To-do list:**

- End of month deli reports
- Les Arômes budget review
- Reply to website comments
- New post: LLMs, AI, and creativity
- New post: Thoughts on fusion
- New post: CRISPR and personalized cancer treatments
- Dinner with Prof. Kaku

Right.

Email.

Alli wrote a quick reply to Professor Kaku. No matter how many times he asked her, no matter how many emails they sent back and forth, she still couldn't bring herself to call him Michio.

Maybe once they'd finally met in person, she would.

# ACKNOWLEDGMENTS

Great thanks to Kim for her help in editing this novel. The collective groans of a thousand readers have been averted by your keen eyes.

As always, my love and thanks to Holly. Without your support, my love, none of this would be possible.

# ABOUT THE AUTHOR

Kevin Robert Aldrich lives in California and is the author of several romance novels:

If you love heart-pounding romantic suspense, you'll love Bare Trap and Flames of Freedom.

If you like vampires, witches, and forbidden love, get a copy of Spellbound now.

And if you love powerful contemporary romance, try Racing Hearts and Ollie & Alli today.

# MORE FROM THE AUTHOR

To learn more about Kevin Robert Aldrich and stay up-to-date with all of his stories and novels, please visit his website:

www.kevinrobertaldrich.com

To be automatically notified of every new release, join the Kevin Robert Aldrich mailing list at the website above.